Traitor's Knot

Cryssa Bazos

First published by Endeavour Press Ltd in 2017.

For Angelo-my-Angelo

TABLE OF CONTENTS

Acknowledgements

In the words of a 17th century poet, no man is an island. This is especially true for a writer. It is only through the support and encouragement of family and friends that this journey has been possible.

First and foremost, I owe everything to my husband, Angelo, for always believing in me, and to my sons who never fail to inspire me. Their support has kept me going.

Thank you to everyone who has read my story and generously offered their assistance: Denice Morris, my earliest reader and oldest friend; Pat Ward who kindly answered my horsey questions (any errors are solely mine); Lora Avgeris who was there from the beginning; Sally Moore whose love of the era matches my own; Sharon Overend for providing plenty of flip charts and weekend Skype sessions; beta readers G.L Morgan, Yvonne Hess, and Lisa Marinakis; and Barbara Kyle for her encouragement and manuscript review.

I owe a huge debt of gratitude to the past and current members of my critique group for their unrelenting determination to hold my feet to the fire, particularly Connie DiPietro, Fred Ford, Angie Littlefield, Jay Stewart, Tom Taylor, Gwen Tuinman, and Andrew Varga, Thank you to the Writers' Community of Durham Region and Mark Cullen for awarding me the Len Cullen Scholarship in 2016. Writing need not be a solitary act, and I have been grateful for the WCDR's support.

Last but not least, a special thank you to Jenny Quinlan of Historical Editorial whose editorial expertise and enthusiasm helped me bring this story home.

Chapter One

Naseby, 14 June 1645

The Roundheads were closing in.

Cut off from his men, Captain James Hart galloped along Broad Moor, dodging dragoon fire and enemy cavalry. From the hedgerows, musket shot screeched past his head, and he flattened against the neck of his bay mare. Fog obscured the moor as acrid smoke choked his throat and sweat stung his eyes. His lathered horse nearly stumbled on the muddy turf.

James pulled hard to the left to avoid a company of pikemen. The field grew hazier; he advanced another hundred yards before he realised that a fallen soldier blocked his path.

Digging his heels into his horse's flanks, he leant forward to take the jump. The bay arched in the air, and before they could clear the body, a volley of wild musket fire hit the horse. The mare screamed and lurched sideways. James kicked his feet from the stirrups and launched himself off. He slammed against the ground and rolled several teeth-shattering feet.

Spots fired across his eyes. James pushed himself upright, past the barrier of screaming muscles and ringing ears. The ground rumbled from the pounding of a thousand horses. His own wounded beast thrashed in the mud.

James staggered towards his horse. Her liquid brown eye rolled, and white foam trickled from her mouth. Her screams cut through him.

"Christ's teeth." He swallowed the lump in his throat and crouched beside her. "Damn."

James drew his carbine, took a steadying breath and aimed at the horse's forehead. In the last second before firing, he turned his head. The shot resounded in his ears—her pain was silenced.

He had to get out of here. By now, the rebels were swarming the field, closing the net on the king's infantry. On the northern ridge, King Charles's colours snapped in retreat. Odds were against an unhorsed Royalist.

James searched for an escape, and his attention lit on a Roundhead dragoon lying dead several feet away. He scrambled through the mud to reach the fallen rebel. When an enemy trooper drew closer, James flattened to the ground, face down. Willing himself to lie still, James's heart hammered in his throat. The muscles between his shoulder blades twitched as he anticipated a shot in the back.

The trooper passed without slowing. James lifted his head and crawled the last foot to reach the dead man. He pulled off his own montero hat and exchanged it for the dragoon's distinctive pot helmet.

"I scorn to take quarter," James muttered under his breath as he worked to cut away the dead man's cartridge bag, "from base rogues and rebels." Next he pried the musket from the man's claw grip.

James grimaced when he realised that he still wore his regiment's blue ribbon tied around his sleeve. He ripped it off and prayed his ploy would work. If he could blend in with the bloody rebels long enough to skirt past their lines, he might rejoin his commander, the Earl of Northampton, and what was left of their regiment.

But first he needed to get past those hedgerows.

As he ran across the moor, James slammed into a maelstrom, dodging past an enemy determined to kill as many Royalists as they could. In pockets, the fighting continued—men fought with bloodied swords or swung the butt-end of their muskets as clubs.

Hundreds of soldiers littered the moor, a carpet of buff, blue and red coats. James tried to focus on getting off the field until a familiar blue ribbon stopped him.

Stokes—his cornet.

Face up, the man looked as though he slept until James neared and saw that half his face had been torn away by shot. A corner of their troop flag peeked from under his body. Even in death, the cornet had protected their colours.

James stuffed the flag inside his coat.

Another troop of enemy cavalry headed towards him. This was useless. He'd never make it off this godforsaken field. There had to be another way.

A trio of riderless horses balked several yards away. Two trotted off, leaving the last one, a black, penned by the currents of cavalry crisscrossing the field. A young, disorientated animal—James only had a moment before it bolted. The black saw him coming and reared, forelegs testing the wind. James approached him warily, murmuring in a soothing tone until he managed to get close enough to seize the bridle.

Hoisting himself into the saddle, James took command of the beast. "Hope you still have a good run left in you." The moment he touched his spurs to the horse's flanks, the animal flew across the field, churning up the turf. James fought to adjust his seat.

They galloped along the hedgerows, frantically searching for a break. Ahead, the line ended, revealing a rolling meadow beyond. This was his chance. James raced through the gap and gave the black his head. He stole a glance over his shoulder—he couldn't believe his fortune. No one was in pursuit.

The field sloped towards a wooded gully. James found a narrow path leading into a shallow creek. They splashed their way northward, hugging the tree line. The sounds of battle dropped off behind them. He had made it—for now.

James slowed to let his horse catch his wind. Rubbing his stubbled beard, he grimaced. What the hell had happened? How had this engagement unravelled? At the outset, the King's cavalry had managed to smash through the enemy horse—how had the other lines failed?

He thought of Stokes, and his conscience gnawed at him for leaving his man behind. The cornet had been a good Warwickshire man, full of fire and loyalty to the crown. He deserved better than being left for carrion. After three years of fighting, it never got easier.

James couldn't stay here—he had to keep moving and find the rest of his unit. Where? He glanced over his shoulder towards the battlefield, and his mouth went dry. Nay. He had to believe they escaped. It was up to him to find them. He visualised the area from memory. The King had set up temporary headquarters in Market Harborough to the northeast. His best chance was to continue north several miles, then cut east to reach the Leicester road.

James urged his horse upriver. He followed the gully a couple of miles until he reached a stand of trees and followed a trail into the forest proper. The path narrowed, becoming more treacherous, with tangled roots heaved up across the track. He picked his way carefully, heading deeper into the woods.

After advancing a quarter of a mile, the black's ears flicked a warning. James reined in and strained to listen. Wild whoops and laughter grew more distinct.

More bloody Roundheads.

James knew he should search for another way past them, yet something inexplicable pulled him forward. He advanced cautiously.

Through the trees, James spied the King's baggage train. Rebels swarmed the site, crowing over the richness of their prize. He couldn't see any of the baggage guards—didn't know whether they had escaped or had been taken prisoner. Most of the carts and wagons were still there, pulled up in a defensive line. A few had been overturned, their contents raked across the ground. Casks and boxes were being smashed open as the looters seized the King's effects—coin and private documents.

Back away—nothing you can do about it.

Shrill whistles and shouts farther down transformed the swarming men into a semblance of order. They jumped into the wagons, gathered the reins and set the horses in motion. The wagons creaked and rocked down the road, one by one disappearing from view.

All except the last one.

Two men pushed against the wooden panels, rocking the wagon back and forth to free the wheels from the mud while another tried to use the horses as leverage.

James studied the road. Here was a chance to salvage something of this day and save at least some of the King's effects. One against three—and none with their muskets within easy reach.

He alighted from his horse and tied the animal to a sapling. After priming his carbine, he checked the charge on the stolen musket. The irony of using the enemy's weapon against them brought a grim smile.

James crept towards the Roundhead soldiers, careful where he stepped lest a snapped twig alert his quarry. Oblivious, they continued at their labours, swearing and cursing.

When he reached as close as he dared, James lifted his carbine and aimed at the nearest man. Releasing a slow breath, he squeezed the trigger. A bark of an explosion—the man crumbled to the ground. The other two scrambled to take cover.

James dropped the carbine and settled the musket in his grip. He lined the sights on another who nearly disappeared behind the wagon. *Fire.* The Roundhead grunted and flew to the ground.

James sprang through the trees after the last man. By the time he reached the lead team of horses, the rebel soldier was already halfway down the footpath and barrelling back to camp—he'd never catch him in time. James whistled for his horse, then winced, remembering. He ran back towards the forest and trailed to a halt when he finally saw the road.

At first, he only registered the clothes strewn on the ground—cloaks, skirts and aprons trampled into the mud—and he wondered at the rebels for scattering them. Then with a slow, creeping horror, the truth set in. These weren't just clothes—these were women—at least a hundred. Their camp followers—all massacred.

The shock drove a fist into his gut.

Broken bodies littered the ground. Their faces were slashed; fistfuls of tangled hair torn in clumps. Shredded skirts hiked up over smeared limbs—twisted, mangled limbs. So much blood—pooled in a scum over soaked ground. They had tried to defend themselves with whatever weapon they had on hand—kitchen knives and iron skillets. But they were no match against broadswords, muskets and an enemy fuelled by bloodlust.

James choked back the bile that rose hot in his throat. He bent over his knees, fighting for control.

He had never seen anything like this—even through three brutal years of war—*nothing* like this.

Three years of mourning men lying dead on the field, their bodies ravaged by shot, was nothing compared to seeing these women torn apart like corn dolls. At least the soldiers had a fighting chance. What ground had these rebels tried to take? Nothing strategic like a bridge or a pass. Just a group of wagons defended by women with kitchen knives.

Cowards—depraved, rabid dogs. Roundheads.

James recalled the ribald laughter as they drove away and now understood its darker meaning. And they had thought nothing of it—those damned, holier than thou, godly Puritans—preaching out of both sides of their mouths. Haranguing the King for not being godly enough, then tearing apart the country while they played the downtrodden and ill-used.

13

Damn them.

James began to search for faces he knew and squatted beside one woman—glassy eyes stared up at the sky, her legs set at an unnatural angle. *Long Meg.* She had been a matronly woman who scolded the lot of them with the authority of a hen-mother. A blade had sliced her from ear to jaw and finished across her throat. Her bodice was stained red, as though she had been dipped in a vat of dye. James reached across and gently closed her eyes. He bowed his head. Burning fury squeezed his chest like an iron band.

A scurrying from the direction of the forest alerted him. James straightened and drew his sword, advancing slowly towards the sound.

Let it be one of those whoresons.

As he drew closer, he heard a crack of snapped twigs and a muffled sob. He parted a low-hanging bough and found a cowering woman backed under a blackthorn shrub. Her white face was stark against smears of blood and mud. Her clothes were torn, and she clutched her shredded bodice with shaky hands.

"Keep away," she whispered. "In God's name, mercy."

James smothered his surprise and lowered his sword. Extending his hand, he said, "You're safe with me, lass. Come out."

She shook her head and wedged herself even tighter. "I've seen the devil, and he is you."

James frowned, puzzled, then it occurred to him. He yanked off his helmet and tossed it away. "I'm not one of them," he tried to assure her, but her expression remained terrified. "I'm a king's man, of that you may have faith." He pulled out his troop's flag from his buff coat and showed it to her.

A guarded relief replaced the panic. James squatted down so he could meet her at eye level. "You'll not be harmed," he softened his tone, "but we have to leave now—they'll be upon us any moment."

Tentatively, she accepted his hand and allowed him to help her to her feet. He led her to his tethered horse. By now, she was shaking uncontrollably. He had to get her out of here while he still could.

A blare of trumpets sounded in the distance. Their time had run out.

*

Over the next fortnight, James came to the realization that the King would not win the war. This bleak thought twisted in his gut and made

14

him silent in dread. It hadn't taken root because of the thousands of men they lost at Naseby, or the vital munitions they had also lost, but from the King's crippling inaction. When one of the generals, Lord Goring, sent a formal reply about why he hadn't marched three thousand of his men to Naseby when it had been requested of him—three thousand would have assured them victory—the King mildly accepted Goring's excuses for keeping his troops in the West Country.

Still worse, the King had not acknowledged the massacre of the baggage women. He expressed more concern about his lost papers.

Reports had spread quickly after the battle, and the bloody Roundheads tried to play down the carnage. They claimed that the women had been naught but Irish prostitutes and filthy papists. Before long, people had begun to believe the propaganda. What would it take for them to open their eyes to the hypocrisy of these traitors? Most of the women who had served the King's men their supper and mended their clothes had *not* been prostitutes, papist or Irish. They were good, solid Welsh women who had accompanied their men to answer the King's muster—many of those same men were buried on the moor or herded to London like branded cattle. The damned rebels shouldn't be allowed to walk away from this.

Neither could he. Long Meg's glassy eyes and slit throat haunted James. He had been in the saddle constantly since Naseby, more his choice than need—except for their initial flight north. Any request for a scout and James took the assignment himself, hoping to catch one of those bastards. James itched to get one of those New Model Army whoresons within pistol range.

His men had begun to comment on his withdrawal. Before, he'd join them for an evening of Irish—backgammon to the novice—but he'd lost the taste for the game. James hadn't missed the looks exchanged between his men whenever he snapped over the state of their supplies.

During a stalled meeting in Hereford where finger-pointing became a new sport, James lost all patience and stalked out. His commander took him aside, and James braced himself for a dressing down. Instead, the earl laid a hand on his shoulder and said, "I have an assignment for you, James. I can trust no other."

Glad for the reprieve from the soul-grinding politics, and honoured to have been handpicked by the earl, James headed south to Bristol on the black horse he had found at Naseby. In his saddlebag, he carried the dispatches for the young Prince of Wales along with a coveted introduction.

A dirty wind, full of biting rain, kicked up just as he reached the Bristol road. The air carried a taste of salt, and he gauged that he was close to the port town. Rather than turning up his cloak against the elements, he tipped his head to the streaming rain and let it scour away his tension.

In the late afternoon, Bristol Castle came into view just as the rain trickled to naught. James crossed a stone bridge that spanned a fathomless river. Wheeling seagulls flew overhead, screeching their discontent, an endless whirl of white and grey wings casting shadows on the wet cobbles.

A company of musketeers manned the city gates with a pair of matched cannon lined up to the approach.

"What news, Captain Hart?" the lieutenant asked, inspecting James's pass.

"The rebels are pillaging Dorset, Christ rot their soul," James said.

"As long as they stay clear of here."

"Wish for something else, friend," James muttered.

"Have you heard aught?" The man leaned in closer.

James looked past him to the crowded streets. "Where can I find His Highness, the Prince of Wales?"

The guard's eyes narrowed, then he nodded. "Report to Richard Fanshawe, the prince's secretary. You'll find him in the town hall. He'll make sure your messages get to the prince, God save him."

James touched the brim of his hat in agreement. "God save us all."

Bristol was clogged with Rupert's men. Following Naseby, Prince Rupert, the King's nephew, had hurried back to see to the town's fortifications. They couldn't afford to lose this port town.

When James reached the town hall, a clerk directed him to the library to wait while he fetched Richard Fanshawe.

James idly leafed through a book placed on a stand. The scent of bindings and leather encircled him. For a moment, he was back in Oxford, forced to study numbers by his father, who had hoped to make more of his son than a farmer. Books made everything deceptively simpler. Every problem lined up neatly in meticulous order on the shelf.

His father had always been rigid in his misguided view of the world. James slammed the book shut.

"Captain Hart?" A man in the dawn of his middle years approached. "I am Richard Fanshawe." He had an intelligent face and the thoughtful expression of a man who guarded his words with care.

James pushed aside all traces of irritation and tried to smile. "Well met, sir. I carry dispatches for His Highness."

"Your timing is impeccable. The prince is with his advisors at this very moment. Come with me."

He followed the secretary down a warren of corridors and staircases until they reached a large room filled with noblemen of every cut and cloth. And in the centre of their universe revolved a single figure clothed in blue silk breeches and coat.

James had only seen Prince Charles a couple of times, and only from a distance. He looked nothing like his father—neither his olive complexion, which favoured his French mother, nor his height, for even at fifteen, he towered over the others and was already as tall as James.

"Dispatches from the King, Your Highness." James stepped forward and bowed respectfully. A page appeared at his side and relieved him of the letters.

"How fares my father?" the prince asked.

"As well as can be expected," James said.

"And your name, sir?" the prince asked while he cracked the seal.

"Captain James Hart, Your Highness. I have the privilege of serving under my lord, the Earl of Northampton."

"You're from Warwickshire?"

"Aye, Your Highness."

"And your family? Who is your father?"

James hesitated a moment. "Edward Hart, a yeoman."

"You've risen in Northampton's ranks. He must value your family's support during these difficult times."

James's jaw tightened. He forced himself to meet the prince's questioning gaze. "My father counts himself with the rebels." He paused a moment. "Though not to the extent that he'd ever take to the field. I earned my commission on my own merits."

The prince's brow lifted slightly. "I see." He studied James for a few moments, his expression unfathomable. Finally, the prince turned his

17

attention to his letter, frowning as he read it. When he finished, he handed it to Fanshawe. "Captain, I would know your thoughts on these rebels. How is the war progressing?"

The enquiry surprised James. His commander had often asked his opinion, but as they were both of the same age and had served the late earl before his death, they had developed an unusual camaraderie.

James glanced around the room. These men, dancing in attendance, were no different than the ones who surrounded the King.

What to tell him? James had heard enough nobles stroke the King's ego with flattering optimism, truth be damned. And yet was this not what the King and his generals wanted to hear?

The prince waited for his answer. James studied Charles's expression. There was a keen intelligence in those dark eyes, and he didn't look like he'd be satisfied with platitudes.

"Not well," James replied. "The loss at Naseby was significant. We lost too many men and munitions to recover with ease. If your cousin, Prince Rupert, can't hold Bristol, all may be lost."

A number of the nobles in the room snorted their disbelief that the rebels could ever have the upper hand. Naseby was a setback, they insisted—naught but a minor one.

James pressed his clenched fists against his thighs and held his tongue. He anticipated the prince's outrage, but Charles only nodded.

"As I thought, Captain. I appreciate your honesty. I better understand the urgency of this dispatch." Charles faced his puzzled advisors. "My father desires my withdrawal to Cornwall posthaste, where I'll be further removed from these rebels."

A fresh wave of murmured conversation rippled through the room. James listened in growing alarm as they started tallying up the logistics of moving the prince's household. He saw the royal convoy growing until it became a small army—and ripe for Parliament to pluck.

"Your Highness," he raised his voice to be heard. "I've been entrusted by my lord to ensure you reach Cornwall *safely*. Such a large . . . party . . . would attract unwanted attention."

"It hardly matters—Parliament wouldn't dare accost the prince," a grey-haired courtier said with a dismissive wave of his hand.

"You are mistaken, my lord, if you believe these rebels are strangers to atrocity," James replied curtly.

"And what do you recommend, Captain, that our sovereign's son should slink away like a guilty thief in the night?"

Fools. Vacant fools. Must be the layers of brocade that had addled their brains. They might as well hand the prince over to the New Model Army. And whose fault would it be if the prince's household was caught on the road? James Hart, scapegoat.

He counted slowly to three before responding. "The prince will have a better chance of reaching Cornwall safely if he travelled lightly with one or two trusted retainers. I see no reason to announce his departure."

"And expose himself to highwaymen and brigands? Captain, you haven't thought this through," the courtier said, condescension dripping off his tongue. "Is this the best that Northampton could send? A man whose own people are amongst the traitors? The late earl would have shown greater judgment."

"With all due respect," James said, "I will not condone any disrespect to my lord." Of his own father, he would spare no words for his defence.

"Peace, Captain, neither will I hear a word spoken against the earl," Charles said. "Your *loyalty* commends you, as does his letter of introduction. He mentions that you were crafty enough to elude the enemy at Naseby. Courage and loyalty are a prized and rare combination."

James bowed to the compliment.

"But I must mind my advisors," the prince continued. "My household is dependent upon me as I am on them. It's impossible to leave them behind. We'll leave at the end of the week. Fanshawe will make the necessary arrangements."

James took a deep breath and exhaled slowly. He shouldn't have been surprised—in fact, he rather had expected something of this, though a small part of him had hoped that the prince would see reason. The King had never been able to fathom that his life was ever in danger; why would the son, at the indestructible age of fifteen, believe otherwise? "I am at your service, Your Highness."

"In the meantime, you'll find accommodations at the Nag's Head with my compliments. Get some rest, Captain. The next several days will be busy."

James bowed to the prince and nodded curtly to Fanshawe. Without another glance at the advisors, he strode out of the hall. He spent the next couple of hours walking off his aggravation before returning to collect his horse and seek out the Nag's Head. The city was bursting with soldiers, and rooms were dear. Without the prince's recommendation, he'd have been hard-pressed to find a corner in the stable, though in his present mood, being forced to share a room with two others made him reconsider this as the better option.

He found a seat in a quiet corner of the Nag's common room and had worked his way through the greater part of his tankard when a servant boy ran up to him.

"Are you Captain Hart, sir?"

"Aye, what is it?"

"You're needed in the stables, sir. Right now."

James rose to his feet. "Is aught wrong with my horse?"

"Nay—nothing like that," the boy said quickly. "A gentleman wants a private word."

"Who is it?"

"That I can't say."

Before James could question him further, the lad whirled around and darted out the door. James tossed back the last of his ale before following him.

The clouds had lifted, leaving the moonless sky riddled with stars. James made his way around the empty courtyard and found the stable doors wide open. Instead of finding the ostler, the prince's secretary waited for him.

"Master Fanshawe?"

"A moment of your time as well as your discretion."

James frowned, his curiosity instantly piqued. "I am at your service."

"I thank you, but there is another who needs it more." Fanshawe glanced over at the stalls to the rear of the building, drawing James's attention there. Even in the dim lantern light, James recognised the prince. His confusion deepened.

As James approached, he noticed that the prince stood by James's horse. The black preened over the attention.

"What a magnificent animal," Charles said, running a hand over the horse's sleek neck. "He has some Friesian in him."

"He's an undisciplined beast," James replied.

"Ah, he's yours," Charles said, clearly impressed.

"One of the spoils of war, you could say." James looked around, expecting to see a guard, but instead there were only shadows. "How may I serve you?"

"Prepare to escort me to Cornwall before daybreak."

James had not expected this. "Has your household managed to do the impossible and finish their packing in a few hours' time?"

As soon as he said it, he immediately regretted the flippancy. But to his surprise, the prince grinned.

"Hardly. They're still debating about how many silver candlesticks to bring. The argument will last for days."

James smiled wryly. The prince had a sense of humour. Another difference from his father.

"Now tell me truthfully. Has the earl exaggerated your talents?" Charles asked.

"My lord does not throw words away."

Charles smiled again. "As I had hoped to hear. Your suggestion to travel light has merit, and I'm willing to entrust my life to your plan, Captain."

James frowned, wondering if he had heard aright. "If I may ask, what changed your mind?"

"Nothing—my mind was set on this course from the beginning," Charles said. "I understood the need for discretion. Though my cousin holds Bristol for the King, I'm not naive enough to believe that all her citizens share the same loyalty. Let everyone think we're leaving at week's end. Fanshawe will perpetuate the fiction—by the time anyone has realised, we'll be halfway to Truro."

James's smile deepened. "Well done." He nodded appreciatively. This was a refreshing change. "We'll need to get you a change of clothes. Something a young apprentice might be able to afford."

"Fanshawe has already sorted that out, Captain."

"He's a good man."

"The very best. I like to believe that I'm a good judge of character," Charles said. "I like to weigh a man by his actions. Give me your word that you will see me to the west safely. I will not be the means to give victory to my father's enemies."

James took a deep breath. "You have my word on it, but you'll have to trust my methods, no matter how unconventional they are. We've underestimated these bastards long enough."

The horse decided at this moment that he had had enough of being ignored and nudged the prince. Charles looked up and laughed. "Brazen fellow. What's his name?"

"I don't know—I haven't yet given him a new one."

"He's a kingly brute," the prince said. "Call him Sovereign."

For the first time in weeks, James cracked a genuine smile. The horse's former master would be rolling in his shallow grave. "Very well. Sovereign he'll be—just as you will one day when you succeed your father."

James drew his sword from its scabbard with a soft hiss of metal against metal and presented it to the prince. "You have my pledge to defend and keep you safe. Upon my honour."

Chapter Two

Weymouth, Dorset 1650

Elizabeth Seton couldn't understand the greed of seagulls. The two birds beat their wings and fought over a scrap of offal while ignoring the endless sea. She had a desire to pick up her skirts and, so running, scatter them to the sky. But from behind her, a rock was thrown at the birds. It bounced off the cobbles a foot away from them. Gulls took flight, and Elizabeth whirled around, equally startled. A soot-faced urchin winked and scampered off.

Elizabeth smiled in the direction of the retreating boy and continued down the quayside towards the market. The wind off the bay freshened, whipping her dark hair and skirts. She tucked an errant lock back into her coif and snuggled deeper into her blue woollen cloak. No time to tarry. She had business to attend.

When she neared the market, her stomach gave a nervous flutter. *Positive thoughts breed true.* She adjusted the basket that rode in the crook of her arm and pressed on.

Elizabeth wended her way through the market stalls, not stopping at the rows of long whitefish laid out silvery across wooden boards. Their fresh scent of the sea beckoned for a closer inspection, but her business was with the oystercatcher's wife. If it went well, she'd return for one of the smaller ones.

Elizabeth's boots tapped against the stone cobbles, and she practised under her breath, "I hear, Fishwife Midden, that Margery has left your employ." Annoyed with herself, she shook her head. The woman would think she was a gossip, and no one trusted a loose tongue. Elizabeth needed to impress her. The Middens preferred their help young enough to be trained to their ways, but at twenty-two, Elizabeth found herself at a disadvantage.

There was a time when Elizabeth didn't need to worry about finding employment. Before the war, her father, Thomas Seton, had once been a respected shipwright, his trade crucial in a seaside town, while her mother, Mary, was a healer and the first to be fetched for matters regarding childbirth and sickness. Elizabeth had expected to follow her mother's calling.

She passed a row of empty stalls and for a moment considered selling their ointments, but she knew better. A gift for a gift, never coin—her grandmother's mantra. No matter how reduced their circumstances, Mary Seton would never accept payment for physic. It didn't matter. None would purchase in public what they now avoided in private.

When Elizabeth spied a knot of women at the cheesemonger's, she slowed down. Here was the elite of Weymouth—officers' wives and those closely connected to the Parliamentary governor. They were particular friends of her older sister, Kate Hallet, though none of hers. Elizabeth considered skirting their position, but instead she lifted her chin, held her breath and stayed true. As she passed, one said, "There's Seton's girl. Shame about that business."

Elizabeth flinched, but she forced herself to ignore them.

Though the war had ended a year earlier with the King's execution, the divisions had never been repaired. Even Kate, who had married a Parliament garrison soldier, kept a resolute distance from Elizabeth and their mother. Only a handful of Royalist families still concerned themselves with her family's welfare.

Up ahead, the oystercatcher's stall thronged with customers. Elizabeth took heart and made her way to the front.

"There you are, mistress." Fishwife Midden greeted her with a smile. Her nose was tipped pink, and her hands were gnarled from working in the cold seawater. "You've picked a good day. The oysters are plump and juicy. Six or eight?"

Elizabeth hesitated. "Four, if you please."

"Only that?" The woman's brow's puckered. She bent over a barrel and scooped out the oysters, placing them in Elizabeth's basket. "How's your mother doing? I heard she ain't well."

"Better, thank you," Elizabeth replied, handing over two of her remaining coins. "I'm certain she's taken a good turn."

"God save her," the fishwife said. "We've missed her these past few months."

Elizabeth watched the old woman edge away, her eyes darting to the next customer. This was her chance. "I was wondering . . ."

"Aye, deary?"

"I ran into Margery the other day—"

"Did you now? Stopped to chat, did she?" Fishwife Midden rested her hands on her round hips.

"I had a thought—since my mother is doing better, she'll need less of my attention," Elizabeth said. "You'll need help now that Margery is gone. I can attend behind the counter or sort out the catch."

Fishwife Midden's expression softened. "I'm afraid not, deary." She started to turn away, and Elizabeth laid her hand on the woman's arm.

"You can pay me half of what you paid Margery. I'll still bless you for it."

"You're worth more than that, sweetling," she replied, "but I can't take you on."

"Please." Elizabeth hated to beg but swallowed her pride. "For the regard you and your husband once bore my father, for all the repairs he made on your fishing boats without a shilling . . ."

"Mistress Seton," she said with the slightest emphasis on her last name, "it's impossible." She glanced past her shoulder and nodded to someone. Elizabeth turned and found the officers' wives flanked behind her.

"Are you done, Fishwife?" their leader asked. "If I'm delayed in this manner, I'll press on to another stall."

"Apologies, mistress," Fishwife Midden said. "Did you want your usual quarter barrel?"

The flow of the market passed over Elizabeth, rendering her invisible. It always came down to that. Not many in Weymouth dared doff their caps to the memory of those, like her father, who had taken a stand for the King.

The rest of the town still called them traitors.

*

Elizabeth hurried past Chapel Fort, a garrison still manned by Parliament. Over the last five years, she couldn't walk past it without averting her gaze. Ghosts, she had once quipped. Her mother had not laughed. If there were ghosts anywhere, it would be at Chapel Fort.

The fight for Chapel Fort had started with one word: *Crabchurch*. A byword for loyalty, and a secret call to action.

The first time Elizabeth heard the word was the night the Royalists enlisted her father for the uprising. She had listened from the stairs, hugging her knees to her chest, as they made their plans to seize Weymouth and the ports for the King.

The town constable had arrived with a stranger, a hard-edged man named Hodder.

"You're loyal to the King, Seton. Join us and take a stand against Parliament," the constable said. Elizabeth drew her cold feet beneath the hem of her gown and tried not to make a sound. "On the appointed hour, we'll move against the garrisons at Chapel Fort and the Nothe and take back Weymouth and Melcombe for the King. The ports will be ours."

"Our chances are grim," her father said. "None of us are soldiers. Loyalty alone cannot be our sword."

"Master Hodder has already secured the support of the King's commander in Dorset, who marches this way. We will not fail."

"Five pounds to every man with us," Hodder said. His words caused a shiver to snake down Elizabeth's spine. "On the word *Crabchurch*, we strike."

"How many have you bought?"

"Sixty so far."

There was a pause. "I'll give you my answer in the morning."

After they left, Elizabeth's mother pleaded with him to reject their offer. Their words became heated, forcing Elizabeth to press her hands against her ears.

"This is not your fight, Thomas. They will use you as cannon fodder."

"The time is past for sitting on the shale. My silence will not give them approval any longer."

"Think of your eldest—her husband is for the governor, for God's sake." Mary was close to tears. "Think of Kate; I beg you. Please—don't do this."

Her father gathered a reluctant Mary in his arms. He looked over his wife's shoulder and spied Elizabeth on the stairs. He held her gaze for a long moment. "I *am* considering my family. We've kept our head down long enough. I mean for it to end now."

The next night, Thomas Seton left to join the conspirators. Sixteen days later, he returned lying on a bier, covered with a bloody sheet. Her mother had never been the same—neither had she.

Elizabeth shut her mind to the ghosts and locked away the familiar pain in a rarely opened corner of her heart. She trudged across the newly ploughed fields and took stock of her situation.

Matters were dire. They had gone through the last of their winter stores, and their garden beds had only been recently sown with spinach and leeks. Fishermen friends often dropped off a fish or two when they could—an extra bit of catch, Elizabeth would assure her mother to save Mary the embarrassment of charity. But no one had recently visited them—not even her sister, Kate, though that wasn't new.

There had to be a better way, Elizabeth thought as she gazed across the grey waters of the bay. At least she still had her father's fishing boat—she'd just have to gather her own oysters.

By the time Elizabeth reached her lane, the sun had disappeared behind a bank of sullen clouds. The wind snatched the gate out of her hand and slammed it against the post. She climbed the steps and paused on the doorstep. Her father had often complained that the concave threshold, hallowed by the passage of many feet, would need to be replaced. A bittersweet smile hovered on her lips.

Elizabeth's mother hadn't stirred from her makeshift cot in the kitchen since she left, and the blanket was still tucked under her chin. Careful not to disturb her, Elizabeth settled her basket on the worktable. Half-empty glass jars, dimmed by dust, clustered together. No ointments or tinctures waited for collection. No orders to be filled.

A draught whistled through the cracks of the windowpanes. In the months following her father's death, her mother had sold what she could to survive—fine linens passed down from her grandmother, Holland cloth and laces, and a carpet given to her by an uncle. It had been galling at first, but her mother, ever pragmatic, shut her eyes to the sentiment. Only a few small treasures remained. The silver brush set, a wedding gift from her mother's widowed sister, Isabel, who lived in Warwick, still had a place on her plain dresser.

Elizabeth stared at the brush set. It could fetch enough to fill their bellies into the next year. She'd have to sell it—there was no choice. But then her mother would realise just how desperate they were, and Elizabeth couldn't do that to her. She had managed to hide their circumstances for the past several months. Mary's health was poor, and she had lost enough—she didn't need this extra burden. When her mother fully recovered, matters would improve. In the meantime, Elizabeth would have to find a way.

The chill had suddenly deepened. Elizabeth looked over at her mother in the cot and frowned. The first stirrings of disquiet crept into her, and she hugged herself. A hollow silence pressed upon the room.

Her mother hadn't stirred.

*

Elizabeth prepared her mother's body for burial in a fog of disbelief. Working alone, she gathered their best linens, then crushed sprigs of rosemary and lavender into a jar of oil, letting them steep while she washed her mother's face. Gently, she closed her mother's blue eyes, so like her own, and smoothed her mother's hair. After Elizabeth finished, she folded her hands in her lap and held a numb vigil. An emptiness filled her, a gaping hole. The candlelight played across her mother's still features, giving the illusion of life—but it was only that, an illusion and therefore no comfort.

The next morning, three old friends of her father's, brothers in spirit who had never forsaken them, arrived to take Mary to church. A painful lump formed in Elizabeth's throat when she saw them at her doorstep, wearing their best navy coats and most sombre expressions.

The leader of the trio, Old Nick, patted her on the shoulder and said, "God keep her soul."

Elizabeth nearly broke down, but she gathered the edges of her tears and tucked them away. "I have no gloves or ribbons to hand out at the church," she said with a catch in her voice. This bothered her more than she expected. Anyone who came to show their respect should be given even the meanest of gloves as a token, even if they hadn't given Mary a hand in five years.

"Your mother, bless her, never stood on ceremony, lass," Old Nick said. "Rest easy. Maybe your sister will bring them."

Elizabeth allowed that to pass. She hadn't any assurances where Kate was concerned.

The men lifted Mary onto the bier and carried her to the wagon they used as a hearse. Elizabeth climbed in the rear to stay with her mother. All along the bumpy way, Elizabeth fixed her attention on the unravelling road. She couldn't look at her mother's shrouded body lying under the pall.

They reached the little whitewashed church, and the minister waited for them at the churchyard stile. Only a handful of people were gathered, but Elizabeth's focus centred only on her sister. Draped in her blacks, Kate leaned against her husband, Cornet Hallet of the Parliamentary garrison.

Elizabeth searched her sister's face, hoping for an acknowledgment, some hint of the warmth they once shared before the troubles of the war, but aside from a quick nod, Kate hid behind her linen handkerchief. Elizabeth glanced at her brother-in-law, her old contempt once again stirring. She knew who was to blame for keeping Kate away from them. The only reason he was here was to signal Kate's claim on their mother's cottage.

The minister stepped up to Elizabeth and murmured vague words of condolence. She barely paid attention to what he said and only gave him the most perfunctory of responses. Each moment became less bearable than the last.

Before Old Nick and his companions could bring out the bier, two Hallet servants stepped forward to take over.

"That won't be necessary—" Elizabeth tried to stop them from interfering.

"Surely, you aren't expecting to do this yourself?" Hallet asked.

"My mother will not be carried by strangers."

Hallet looked at the old sailors and lifted his brow a fraction. He didn't even try to hide his disdain. "The minister is waiting," he said and nodded for his servants to carry the bier.

Kate touched Elizabeth's elbow. For a brief moment, Elizabeth thought she would open her arms and gather her to her chest like she used to, and Elizabeth felt the tears starting to gather. But Kate held herself distantly. "Don't make a fuss; my husband will be insulted."

Hallet guided Kate away, leaving Elizabeth to stand alone by the stile. She had to go on—for her mother. This ordeal would be over soon. The thought brought its own sharp pain.

The minister waited for them before a fresh-turned grave. The slashed earth finally brought home to Elizabeth the depth of her loss. She dug her fingernails into the palms of her hands to will away the tears. After several deep breaths, she fastened her gaze on the greening hills beyond the grave. No one would see weakness.

Elizabeth didn't follow the minister's prayer. Instead, she recalled an old blessing her mother sang when she worked in the garden or at her worktable—words passed down from mother to daughter. Elizabeth's grandmother was a legend in Dorset. They said she could heal a bird just by whistling at it. Her mother and Aunt Isabel were blessed with the same gift. This was Elizabeth's legacy as it had once been Kate's.

You will not walk alone.

But her mother had. How had Elizabeth missed the signs? Mary had shown a little more colour in her cheeks and a renewed brightness in her eyes. Elizabeth had been certain, with the false confidence of an apprentice, that her mother's improvement was like the first warm day heralding spring.

She died alone. Elizabeth couldn't escape the truth—she hadn't been there to hold her mother's hand as she crossed the sea.

Old Nick touched Elizabeth's arm. The sudden contact startled her from her thoughts. "Time for your farewells, lass."

Elizabeth's feet had taken root, and she couldn't move.

"Lass?"

Elizabeth forced herself to take that first step. She passed Kate and reached the bier. *I can do this.* She would show these faithless people the true meaning of resilience.

Elizabeth placed her hand on her mother's unyielding body. A bleak coldness seeped through the pall, and she nearly pulled back. She squeezed her eyes shut and gathered her strength. Elizabeth bent over her mother to press a kiss on her shrouded forehead.

When had she ever turned to her mother and not been met with an answering reaction—a hug, a gentle squeeze, the smallest reminder that she was not alone? It had just been the two of them for so long, each relying on the other, and now Elizabeth had no one.

When she tried to step away, her knees buckled, the strength sapped from her limbs. She clutched the sides of the bier to keep from falling, struggling to keep from going under.

Then Old Nick lifted her and helped her from the grave.

*

Elizabeth's mother had been buried only a day when Kate and her husband paid her a visit. She braced herself for a battle, for as eldest, the cottage went to Kate. Elizabeth only hoped that since it was a modest dwelling, it wasn't worth her brother-in-law's trouble.

Hallet surveyed the bare kitchen as though tallying each candlestick. When he met her hard stare, he didn't even have the courtesy to flush.

Elizabeth turned to Kate. "You've found the path home. I thought you might have forgotten."

Kate gathered her shawl closer around her shoulders. "Pack your things; you're coming home with us."

Elizabeth's eyes widened. "You want me to live with you?" Her sister's expression grew shuttered. "I see. It's expedient."

"A single woman can't live alone. Your reputation will be irreparably ruined," Hallet said.

A bitter laugh escaped Elizabeth. "Worse than now?"

His mouth curled. "I will not allow you to tarnish my wife's good name."

"*Your* good name, you mean."

"Come, Elizabeth, be reasonable," Kate said. "We're offering you a bed and place under our roof."

"This is my home."

"No longer," Hallet said. "The cottage now belongs to my wife, and so to me. I see no reason to keep it open."

A horrible, sinking feeling gripped Elizabeth. Hallet regarded her with the implacable manner of a mind long made up. "You have no need of it. You already have enough."

"There is nothing to discuss," Hallet said.

This couldn't be happening. He couldn't really force her from her home. Elizabeth had to do something—appeal to her sister's reason if not to the affection they once shared. She drew Kate aside. "Please. This is all I have. Surely, you cannot begrudge me this."

Kate averted her gaze. "I would that there was another option. We'll find you an acceptable husband, and you'll have your own household soon enough."

"A Crabchurch orphan is hardly fit for a *respectable* man—is this not what people say?" Elizabeth said. "Difficult to invite the governor to share a meal with such a wife carving up the Twelfth Night goose."

"I have a position here in Weymouth. You could have the same."

Something deep inside Elizabeth welled up in protest. "I'll not be a disadvantaged wife who owes her bread to her husband's sufferance."

"A salve for your pride does not earn you a hearth of your own," Kate finally snapped. "You've deluded yourself into believing that your prospects are better than they are and that one day the town will come to their senses and embrace the daughter of a traitor. Even more incredibly, do you truly believe that they will ever trust you with the well-being of their children by accepting any physic you brew? They will never give you the respect that once was ours," Kate's voice trembled. "The sooner you understand your place in this world, and its limitations, the better off you will be."

Elizabeth drew back, reeling from the sting of Kate's words. "Is this my sister? Who are you, and when did you become a small, bitter woman? Mother would never have recognised this in any of her daughters. You were raised with a greater sense of your worth." Elizabeth's frustration nearly crushed her. Kate so little valued her gifts while she, Elizabeth, who wanted nothing more than to follow in her mother's and grandmother's footsteps, was forced to see these same talents shrivel from disuse. "When was the last time you prepared a tincture or a simple syrup—you, who could continue to practise our art with honour and not suspicion or doubt? If I thought for a moment this was possible—"

"And you think that will make it all right?" Kate said. "Mix a decoction of senna with chicory and all the venomous humours will be purged—is that what you think? You prattle on with the sensibility of a child. Our family has no standing in this community, shunned by all respectable folk who will never forget that 'twas our father and the other criminals who betrayed the town and allowed the Royalists to seize the garrisons."

"Don't speak of him like that to me," Elizabeth said. "Our father was true to his beliefs. 'Tis you who have proven false to his memory."

"It's time to look towards the future, Elizabeth," Kate said wearily. "Surely, you can't be satisfied here."

Elizabeth shook her head. "What you're offering is worse." Servant in her brother-in-law's home, she could not stand to be suffered by a man who had distanced himself and his rising career from his wife's infamous relations. "How do you think I'll feel brushing your husband's garrison coat, wondering if his musket shot father?" She choked and turned from Kate. When her gaze lit on Hallet, she found him examining her mother's silver brush.

Elizabeth darted over and snatched it from him. Hugging the brush to her chest, she pointed to the door. "Leave. Just go."

Kate looked as though she would continue to argue, but Hallet drew her away. "By week's end, I'll send a wagon for you, mistress. Collect what you will."

Elizabeth remained in the centre of the kitchen long after they left, clutching her mother's silver brush. How had things sunk this low? When had she become a piece of flotsam churning in the surf?

All she had ever wanted was to live in peace without the need to constantly defend her family's name. Look to the future, Kate had said. Elizabeth swiped at the sudden tears that pooled in her eyes. She wanted nothing more than to knock the dirt of the past from her boots and embrace the future, but she couldn't, not without denying those whom she loved beyond herself.

The flat of the brush reflected the candlelight and captured Elizabeth's attention. A voice whispered in her brain, *Aunt Isabel*. Her aunt had no one left either. Husband and son had died in the war, and Isabel's remaining daughter no longer lived with her. An idea began to germinate, twining around Elizabeth with equal measures of daring and audacity.

Elizabeth dug out her writing box and took out a pot of ink, a gull's quill and one last sheet of paper. She smoothed out the paper and began to write. "As your niece, I beseech you for a place in your household."

Chapter Three

Elizabeth received a response a fortnight later. The letter arrived with a knot device pressed into the red wax. Isabel Stanborowe wrote, "I will do my duty for my poor sister's daughter and invite you to Ellendale."

The surge of anticipation became tempered with the bittersweet sense of loss. This was the only way.

It didn't take long for Elizabeth to close up the cottage, and to pay for her trip, she finally sold the silver brush set.

The day of her departure dawned grey and brooding. Her bags were ready at the door as Elizabeth waited for her ride. She was wrapped in her blue cloak, and the tips of her black boots peeked from beneath the hem of her skirt.

"Old Nick is late." He had promised to arrive before dawn to drive her to Dorchester. Elizabeth crossed the floor to peer through the window.

The rising sun had topped the cedars when she spied a wagon pulled by a pair of cobs jogging down the lane. Behind them sat Old Nick, puffing on a pipe set between his teeth. He pulled up to the cottage and called, "Heigh-ho."

"One moment." Elizabeth paused at the threshold. Her gaze lingered on the empty cot in the corner where her mother had spent the last few months of her life. Elizabeth didn't want to remember the invalid, only the woman, vibrant and alive, working over her mortar, head upturned in laughter. A tightness squeezed Elizabeth's chest. Her blood was here. In trying to defy Kate and Hallet, was she making a mistake?

"Lass, are you coming?"

Old Nick waited for her by the wagon, looking more like himself than he had at the funeral. He was a large man with stooping shoulders. Deep lines gouged his clean-shaven face like the driftwood tossed upon the shale. He wore a knitted Monmouth cap and fishing coat, its sleeves speckled with dried fish scales. Though everyone along the harbour called him Old Nick, he had always been Captain to her father. As the master of a seaworthy vessel, he deserved that minimum of respect.

"Is this all?" he asked her.

"Aye, and you're welcome to the rest." She forced a smile, thinking of the bare floorboards and dusty shelves. "Only the best jewels and carpets inside. You can give up your Channel runs."

"And who says I want to, eh?" He tossed her bags into the back of the wagon. "My customers have a taste for French brandy. I'm not about to disappoint them."

Elizabeth accepted his help to climb atop the perch. The cottage, with its shutters slightly askew, stared back at her.

The wagon dipped when he joined her. Heaving a sigh, he settled in his seat. "It's unnatural, you leaving like this."

Elizabeth nodded. She couldn't trust herself to speak.

"I'll take you as far as Dorchester, to my brother's inn. He'll arrange passage north for you." Old Nick gathered the reins but held them slack. "Do you have enough coin? Board will be dear."

"Aye, enough to get to Warwick."

Old Nick pulled out a small leather pouch and pressed it in her hand. "A little more to get you settled."

"I can't—" Elizabeth blinked back the sudden tears.

"When I says a thing is to be done, best start hauling. Your pa was a good mate. One of the best shipwrights along the Dorset coast. The craft he built me skims like silk over the water. 'Tis the least I could do for his girl." Old Nick flicked the reins and set the cobs on their way.

They drove along the shore road, normally one of Elizabeth's favourites for its view of the bay. Today, the mist clung to the beach, and overhead sky smudged into sea. Seagulls rode the fickle currents of air and screeched over the pounding surf. The salt spray tasted bitter on her lips.

The white beating wings blurred, and she remembered her father hoisting her in the air. Between shrieks of laughter, with arms outstretched, she'd cry, "I'm flying." For that moment, she had been one with the surging tide.

They reached the town and turned onto High Street. One house drew Elizabeth's attention. Freshly painted shutters framed the windows, and even the doorstep had been swept clean. No salt-scrubbed facade for Kate's home. Hallet wouldn't hear of it.

A seagull alighted on the house's hitching post in smug defiance of order. From beyond the reaches of fog and mist, a bell clanged as it did whenever a ship left port.

Elizabeth leaned over and touched Old Nick's arm. He adjusted his grip on the reins, and the cobs slowed. This was her last chance to reconsider. Over time, her relationship with her sister might improve if she stayed.

Old Nick waited for her answer.

It didn't matter. To Kate's husband, she would always be a Crabchurch orphan. He might suffer her a roof and a meal, but never a home.

"Drive on," she said. "Warwick awaits."

*

"Just as far as Warwick. My horse has fallen lame, else I would not seek your services," the gentleman announced to the coachman.

Elizabeth craned her head out the window and rested her arm against the panels of the coach. After five days of weary travel, getting up before dawn and stumbling into the next inn well after dark, she was eager for the change a new passenger would bring. The couple that rode with her from Oxford, the Pritchetts, had driven her desperate with boredom. She couldn't face another reading from Leviticus and missed Old Nick's company. Elizabeth studied this new arrival with interest. His name, she learned, was Sir Richard Crawford-Bowes.

"A common carriage? Have you nothing with more privacy? I am inconvenienced as it is."

Sir Richard was of middling height and wore a black travel coat with matching felt hat. Although his clothes were trimmed with simple lace, there was no mistaking the fineness of the broadcloth. The gentleman held himself aloof, and while he gave no outward sign that the deference pleased him, he preened while the lackeys scurried around.

A liveried servant unhitched the team of chestnut bays from their traces. Halter in hand, the groom led the pair to the stables, casting a hasty glance as he passed. Elizabeth could not tell which horse had fallen lame.

"Mind the roads, my good man," Sir Richard said. "There has been much talk of black villainy along Moot Hill."

"Aye, my lord," the driver bowed. "Naught to worry. A proper villain wouldn't dare raise a hand against a justice of the peace."

Sir Richard climbed inside and selected the empty seat across from Elizabeth. He looked at the appointments as he adjusted his sleeves and collar. When he appeared to be satisfied, he nodded to the Pritchetts. The carriage started, and Sir Richard turned to stare out the window, thumping his fingers on his thigh.

The couple took keen interest in the new passenger. Master Pritchett appeared to be on the verge of striking up a conversation and prepared himself by smoothing the wisps of hair curling on his balding pate. He opened his mouth several times only to lose heart and worry it shut.

"My lord, I wonder how the quarter sessions went," he finally said. "I imagine there were many rough characters to sort through."

"Not yet, my good man. I'm on my way to Warwick to open the Easter sessions now." Then muttering under his breath, he added, "And late."

"My lord?" Master Pritchett asked.

Elizabeth wondered at the sudden twitching of Sir Richard's right eye.

"Tardiness is an intolerable failing, but in this case, 'tis the fault of a wretch with no respect for the laws of the Commonwealth or God's natural order. The ungodly must be taught to obey. The lesson took longer than expected."

"Pray, was he a murderer, or worse, a shaver of coins?"

"Neither," Sir Richard said. "The villain had the effrontery to pasture his sheep on church grounds."

"Why would he do such a thing?" Mistress Pritchett asked.

"Hush, woman," her husband said. "Such is beyond your understanding."

Mistress Pritchett lowered her head, her expression worn. Suddenly, Elizabeth was reminded of Kate. Unable to help herself, Elizabeth said, "Perhaps the sheep needed divine inspiration." The others fell silent. Three pairs of eyes stared at her, unblinking.

"Who can say what was in his head?" Sir Richard addressed Master Pritchett. "He claimed that his fields flooded and he had no other pasture."

"Hardly an excuse," Pritchett said.

"The rains were unusually heavy this spring," Elizabeth persisted. "If they were as flooded as we were in the south country, 'twas no small hardship."

"God's punishment on the wicked," Sir Richard replied. "The court's justice is equally unswerving. The man had to pay a fine of ten pounds or forfeit the sheep to the county."

Elizabeth was shocked by the crippling fine and more so by Sir Richard's insensitivity. The poor farmer had likely done what he could to provide for his family. "How will he manage?"

"It would seem that you would treat these wretches with pity and save them from righteous judgment," Sir Richard said.

"I should think that a man's worth ought to be considered and his actions weighed against his intent, my lord."

"They are a lawless, greedy element, I assure you, and not deserving of your pity."

Elizabeth's eyes dipped to a slim book of Psalms in the judge's lap. "Have you a reading, my lord, that you might share with us on God's benevolent mercy?"

Pritchett held up his Bible. "I know the very passage."

With a pained smile, Elizabeth turned her attention to the window and contented herself with the passing countryside, dull like a cloak of dun and grey. Warwickshire was a world apart from Dorset. In Weymouth, the shoreline had been mercurial, the tides a stirring, breathing force, sullen one moment, beguiling the next. But here, she was struck with a sense of permanence, of lives bound to unchanging hills. Though grasses bent under the wind, their roots remained fixed to the soil. She felt not a little daunted by it.

From nowhere, a racing black horse flashed past her window, the rider passing close to the carriage. Startled, Elizabeth craned her head, wondering at his reckless pace. Without warning, the coach veered off the road and pulled up, throwing her onto the floor. The others shrieked and braced themselves. They heard panicked shouts from the driver and the deep, jarring voice from another.

"Stand and deliver!"

Elizabeth heard the measured clopping of a single horse drawing close and the nervous shifting of their team. She crept to regain her seat. Mistress Pritchett shook with terror, and Elizabeth reached out her hand to reassure her.

"One inch more and your brains will lie in a pool at your feet." They heard the click of a cocked pistol.

Elizabeth froze, fearful that he spoke to her. But with his next words, she knew that he still dealt with their driver.

"Toss your musket over the side."

"You'll have no trouble." The driver's voice cracked, and the carriage swayed and creaked as he scrambled down from the top seat.

"Everyone out!"

Elizabeth followed the Pritchetts, nearly stumbling on her skirts. Her foot found the first step and froze. A pair of pistols trained upon her, unwavering and baleful. Slate-grey eyes burned with equal intensity above a black scarf. Although every instinct screamed retreat, Elizabeth descended the coach.

The highwayman rode a large black horse with a white blaze on its forehead. He commanded the powerful animal by his slightest touch, moving like one, rider and horse, fluid and instinctive. The highwayman wore all black from his heavy cloak to his mud-splattered boots.

"Richard Crawford-Bowes." The highwayman's voice cut through the stunned silence. "Step forward. I would fain make your acquaintance."

Sir Richard did not twitch.

Provoked by the absence of a response, he pointed his pistol at Sir Richard's stubborn head. "Mark this well—I never repeat myself."

"I am he," he said and stepped forward.

The highwayman circled Sir Richard with the imposing horse. "This is a unique pleasure, my lord. Are you beating the countryside looking for desperate souls to fill your court, or have you reached your quota?"

"Now listen here," Sir Richard sputtered. "If you persist in this venture, I vow to bring you before the assizes and see you hang!"

The highwayman shrugged. "You deserve nothing more than to share the same fate as the honest men you rob in the name of your Commonwealth. Strange idea that—common wealth. As though the wealth stolen from the King would ever be given to the common man. Deliver your coin or die."

Sir Richard's brow darkened. From his pocket, he withdrew a handful of shillings.

A shot fired. Elizabeth jumped and smothered a scream, pressing her hand to her mouth. Shouts and shrieks erupted from the people around her. The highwayman lowered his smoking pistol. Sir Richard remained standing, a foot back from where he had been and pale as chalk.

"My patience is nearing an end," the brigand said, levelling his other pistol. He tucked the spent one in his belt and replaced it with a primed carbine. "A few pieces of silver. I'm sure you have more than thirty."

Colour returned to Sir Richard, and his thin mouth pressed into a resentful line. "You will regret this." He drew a larger pouch from his cloak and took a step forward, but the rogue's next words stopped him.

"Take one more step and it will be your last. I care little for the honour of judges and trust their intent even less. Hand the purse to someone else." His flinty gaze passed over the huddled couple and singled out Elizabeth. "Come forward, mistress. You're neither fainting nor quivering."

Startled, she considered pleading to be left alone but smothered the impulse. She would not show fear to this villain. Taking a deep breath, Elizabeth walked towards Sir Richard. A sheen of sweat beaded his forehead, and his Adam's apple bobbed in this throat. She held out her hand and tried to keep it from trembling. Her nape prickled as if the pistol pressed against her skin. Sir Richard clutched the purse, glaring at her as though she was the villain.

"Your purse, my lord," she whispered. "Please."

Sir Richard hesitated for another moment before shoving it into her hands.

Greedy wretch. Elizabeth's annoyance with Sir Richard gave her the courage to walk up to the brigand. With every step, her determination grew. She would be quite happy to hand over Sir Richard's money.

The rogue motioned her to give him the pouch, and when she dropped it into his outstretched hand, she met his direct gaze. Elizabeth expected to see the cold eyes of a ruthless madman, but to her surprise, she did not. There was a hardness in those grey depths, but also a keen, calculating intelligence that heightened her curiosity. He stared back at her boldly, and she could not look away.

"My thanks." His tone was an unmistakable dismissal.

Elizabeth stood puzzled. Old Nick's small purse rested under her cloak, the sum of everything she owned. She would have been sick over parting with it but wondered why the highwayman had made no demands on her or the others.

"Was there anything more, mistress?"

She was about to shake her head and back away, but the muffled weeping behind her ended thoughts of retreat. Having reached the end of her endurance, Mistress Pritchett began to cry, soft at first and then with more violence. She would have collapsed to the ground had her husband not supported her. Elizabeth grew outraged for the hysterical woman. The audacity of the scoundrel, with all that he dared, awakened her. "Pray, what is your name, sir, so that we may know the *coward* who threatens us behind a scarf?"

The highwayman's eyes narrowed. The silence unnerved Elizabeth. Beneath him, the great black shifted. "Who are you?"

"Elizabeth Seton, late of Weymouth."

"So, Mistress Seton from Weymouth dares where others fear to tread."

"Your words suggest you were once a King's man," she said, ignoring her better judgment.

"Aye, proudly so."

"Your manner disclaims it. The Royalist soldiers I knew did not hide behind scarfs."

His expression darkened. "Times have changed," he said in a rough voice. Instead of firing his pistol, he urged his horse closer. Its shadow cast over her. "Your people fought against these rebels?"

Elizabeth's stomach gave a sick lurch as she realised her blunder. She prayed that Sir Richard didn't mark the significance of her words. Being caught between a highwayman and a Roundhead justice, she should have had the wits to mind her tongue. Elizabeth's eyes darted to Sir Richard— his entire attention seemed to be focused on the purse in the brigand's hand.

The highwayman waited for her response, and when none came, it seemed to Elizabeth that he smiled behind his scarf. He leant forward as though they were the only two on the road. "'Tis a shame that we had not more with your bravery. We may have yet won the war."

With a curt nod, he spurred his horse and disappeared down the road.

Elizabeth released her breath in a rush, and her limbs dissolved into unset jelly.

*

The quarter moon had not yet topped the hedgerows when James Hart rode up to an isolated cottage south of Warwick. Squat, fat chimneys hugged a slate roof, built to accommodate a fire hot enough to roast a boar. Times were otherwise, and the thin curling tendril of smoke seemed solitary. The green was soft and spongy, and the damp ground muffled Sovereign's hooves. This suited James, for he didn't want to alert those within.

Five years ago, he had ridden up to this leasehold, a scant four months after Naseby. James had owed it to his officer, Stokes, to return the man's effects to his father, especially after he had died protecting their colours. The only reward for loyalty was loyalty.

This night, at least, his errand would bring relief instead of grief.

James reined in Sovereign and dismounted. From inside his coat, he drew a hefty purse and dropped it on the doorstep. He grasped the saddle pommel and prepared to mount his horse when the door of the cottage opened. A man appeared on the threshold with a poker held aloft in his hand. James turned away from the doorway's meagre light and raised his scarf to hide his face.

"Who are you?" the man demanded. "What are you doing in my yard?" His gaze strayed to the leather pouch on his stoop.

"I regret disturbing you, Goodman Stokes. I came to return your purse." James lowered his voice.

The man's wife peered over her husband's shoulder. She opened her mouth to speak, but her husband stopped her. "'Tis not ours," he said. The bag was squat and full. "There must be a mistake."

"Indeed, I don't believe so," James said while he swung himself atop Sovereign. "I found it on the road outside your lane."

The farmer took the purse in hand. Weighing it, he raised his eyes, and for the first time, a smile tugged his sunken cheeks. "'Tis a goodly sum."

"Aye," James agreed. "More than enough to recoup your losses. My advice to you is to find another pasture for your sheep. The church only suffers Christian animals to graze their turf."

*

James finally returned to Warwick's Chequer and Crowne Inn just before midnight. He avoided the front of the building, with its waning lights and fading laughter, and proceeded to the stables. The courtyard was silent. They didn't expect another coach until the morning.

Inside, the familiar smell of horses greeted him. Tin buckets hung from the posts, and a pitchfork rested prongs down in a reduced bale of hay. Halters in various sizes draped over iron pegs.

As the Chequer's ostler, this was James's domain. No one, including the landlord, Henry Grant, dared suggest otherwise, for James had a talent that every innkeeper prized. Master and craftsman, his art was horses.

James had slipped into this living shortly after the fighting had ended as he had nowhere else to go. Returning home was impossible—he refused to grovel to his father, nor did he have a living to return to as his employer had also favoured Parliament. Before the war, James had been clerk to a prominent Coventry gentleman. Now he was little more than a farrier.

As he dismounted, he looked around for his stable boys. "Lads?" No answer. James absently stroked his horse's dark neck. He examined the animal's forehead and rubbed away the last of the white chalk. "Aye, you'll get a proper brushing in the morn." Sovereign nudged him in response, and James smiled faintly. He rubbed a hand across his stubbled beard.

Stretching, he eased the knots between his shoulder blades. Working quickly, he unsaddled Sovereign and saw him bedded down in his stall before taking care of his own business. James went into the tack room and dropped his saddlebag on the workbench beside a stack of ledgers and a dog-eared book.

Bracing his arms on the bench, he faced the government poster pinned to the wall—the Oath of Allegiance to the Commonwealth. To the victors, the oath represented the might to dissolve the allegiance owed to the King, but to James it was a daily reminder that the dogs had seized control of the kennel. He would not allow himself to slip into apathy and forget that they were still the enemy or what they were capable of.

These bastards had them all by the stick. Swearing the oath was a requirement for a business licence and all rights of a freeman of the city. Without it, he couldn't take up his former living. Damn them all, his allegiance would not be held hostage—he'd rather muck stables. Having "Oath of Allegiance" marked beside his name was no better than reneging on his pledge to the crown, and there was at least one Hart who wouldn't do that.

James opened his saddlebag, and rooting past the scarf and tin of chalk, he removed his doglock pistols. He traced a finger along a groove on the wall just beneath the poster and was rewarded by a click. Beneath his touch, a hidden compartment sprang open.

He tucked his pistols inside and took stock of his growing hoard of stolen coin. James had been accumulating them for over a year, starting the day after the late King's execution. Every last shilling belonged to Charles against the day he'd return to claim his father's throne. Men needed to be outfitted with horses, arms and gear, and this required coin. But the Roundheads had sequestered Royalist lands and rents—most, like the Earl of Northampton, were exiled and bankrupt from the crippling fines.

There was only one solution—let the enemy pay.

The hour grew late, and James locked the compartment. A letter fell flat on the table. Someone must have propped it against the jar of saddle grease. When James examined it, he drew a sharp breath. The crest of the twin stags. The seal was as familiar as his own signature—used on hundreds of letters in the service of his former master, Sir Piers Rotherham.

The first time James had seen the seal was when his lordship invited him to Bideford Hall. His father, Edward Hart, had been proud that Sir Piers, a gentleman and Member of Parliament, had taken an interest in his son's future. Two years of faithfully serving Sir Piers had led to the man sponsoring James's education at Oxford.

However, the last time James had seen this seal—in fact, the last time he had used it in his master's employ—was to convey to General Fairfax, commander of the Parliamentary army, the news that Sir Piers would join his division within a month. But when James left Bideford, it had not been under the Rotherham colours. Instead, he had joined the Earl of Northampton's cavalry as a lieutenant. His father had been infuriated.

James turned the letter over. He noted a slight hesitation in the flow of the script. The stags watched and waited. During the five years he had been in the man's employ, Piers Rotherham never acted lightly or without purpose. James cracked the seal.

Bideford Manor
My dear boy,

We have much to atone for, you and I. The severed link between Master and Servant spawns regret and misery. It is my heartfelt desire to forge a new connection, stronger for having been tested by unnatural war.

I am resolved to rebuild my house and look to the future. If you are of like mind, I invite you to return to Bideford.

Yours in sympathy,
Sir Piers Rotherham

James rubbed the back of his neck. There was something odd about the choice of words, as though each was weighed and assessed against an invisible yardstick. The man he had known preferred direct speech over subtle nuance.

Too much had changed; he was past doing any Roundhead's bidding. James left the letter on the bench and walked away.

Chapter Four

Elizabeth caught her first glimpse of Ellendale when the hired wagon passed the last row of poplars. Buttressed between golden meadowland and a ridge of charcoal clouds, a two-story country house stood with a steeply gabled roof. Its mullioned windows reflected the early morning light.

She turned to the gangly youth who drove the wagon to offer a comment but reconsidered. Daniel Ledbrook was the son of her aunt's tenant and barely spoke a word throughout the drive. At times, he snuck curious glances from under his cap and displayed a tendency to colour in response to her enquires.

It had been Henry Grant, the innkeeper of Warwick's Chequer and Crowne, who had made the arrangements after he managed to settle the distraught passengers. Elizabeth had felt sorry for the innkeeper, dashing around in his shirtsleeves while reassuring the Pritchetts. Sir Richard, however, remained implacable, scorning all manner of solicitation. Nothing except rousing the garrison to hunt for the highwayman satisfied him.

Only the currency of her aunt's name served to cut through the innkeeper's distraction, replacing his frown with a beaming grin. "Well now, I have all the time in the world for Mistress Stanborowe."

Elizabeth had forgotten a time when the mention of her family's name would generate a willingness to please. She wondered at which precise moment she had become Isabel Stanborowe's niece and no longer Thomas Seton's daughter.

"Your aunt asked me to keep an eye out for you, though she didn't expect you for another fortnight." His smile faded. "You've come a long way to be troubled by a brigand—though you likely have your share of troubles in the south. Hampshire isn't it?"

Elizabeth tried to correct him, but he dashed off before she could.

Daniel turned into the Ellendale lane. The gravel crunched beneath the wheels as the wagon pulled up before the gate. Not waiting for assistance, Elizabeth scrambled down and started up the walkway. The forecourt was paved with wide, flat stones, and lavender beds ran along the flags. In the centre of a weathered door hung a knotted wreath.

Elizabeth hung back, suddenly nervous. The wind freshened, carrying a splatter of rain and the scent of rain-soaked earth. She laid a hand to her coif to prevent the wind from snatching it away.

Daniel passed her with the bags, but before he reached the entrance, a servant opened the door. She was a plump woman with rounded cheeks and silver-threaded hair.

"Daniel? What are you about?" The woman craned her head to look past his shoulder and finally saw Elizabeth. "Oh!"

"She's early," Daniel said.

Flustered, the maid sidestepped him. "Jennet Lynde, at your service."

"Elizabeth Seton, at yours."

Jennet drew Elizabeth inside and patted her arm. "Come in before the chill claims you." As she crossed the threshold, her shoulder knocked the wreath off its hook. "I'll get that later," she muttered. "Put the bags down in the hall," she said to Daniel. "I trust your trip wasn't too trying, mistress."

"Well, actually—"

Daniel dropped the bags with a thump. "There's been trouble in the town."

"Trouble? What trouble?"

"Another robbery along Moot Hill."

Jennet clicked her tongue as she took Elizabeth's cloak, then stalled mid-stride. "Surely, not your carriage?"

"Aye, the very one."

"Goodness, you weren't harmed, were you?"

"Nay, rest assured," Elizabeth said quickly. "The brigand was fearsome enough, but he only took the purse of the justice. I'm afraid that gentleman smarted over its loss."

Sir Richard had been quick to blame Elizabeth for his misfortune. When he had heard her tell Henry Grant that no one had been harmed, Sir Richard had rounded on her in a fury. "I am poorer by fifty pounds! The least you could have done was argued for my purse."

Elizabeth nearly called him a Mad Tom.

"The justice—Sir Richard was there?" Jennet choked.

"Aye, but 'twas Mistress Seton who told the highwayman off," Daniel said and flushed when Elizabeth looked at him.

Jennet's eyes widened, and she pursed her lips. "Did you now? Some might say that took courage, though others would warn against such rash action. Best to keep your head down."

"I'm not one to cover my eyes," Elizabeth said. She caught sight of Jennet's troubled frown before the maid turned to the youth.

"Daniel, you're welcome to visit the buttery and help yourself to a cup of small beer."

"I can't stay . . . best be getting home."

"Well then, give our regards to your father." Jennet walked him to the door. Daniel gave Elizabeth a bashful smile before he left.

"Come, take your rest in the parlour, mistress. I'll let your aunt know you've arrived." Jennet stoked the small fire into a cheery blaze before she excused herself.

Elizabeth looked around the grand parlour, eyes wide. The floor was tiled in a black-and-white chequerboard pattern, and dark wainscoting clothed the walls. The haunting scent of marjoram and sage perfumed the air. At the far end of the room, a trio of well-stuffed chairs faced each other. Elizabeth selected one and sat on the edge of the seat. To still her hands, she clasped them on her lap.

Her heart fluttered in anticipation as she watched the entrance. Any moment, her aunt would rush in and welcome her. Elizabeth could almost feel the warmth of her aunt's embrace.

She continued to wait.

A ringing chime from a chamber clock mounted on the wall startled her. The ninth bell faded, and still no one came.

Elizabeth's gaze strayed to the carvings on the fireplace mantel, and she rose to take a closer look. A series of Celtic scrolls twisted and flowed upon themselves like a never-ending journey. She ran her fingers along the whorls. Having lived around woodworkers all her life, she found the skill in the carvings a marvel.

A throat cleared. "Jennet didn't warn me that you were so curious."

Elizabeth whirled around, cheeks blazing.

Isabel Stanborowe leaned on a cane, her fingers coiled around the handle. She wore a mint-green skirt with linen bodice. A silver knot brooch secured her muslin partlet. Isabel looked older than Elizabeth had expected, certainly older than the eight years that separated her from Elizabeth's mother. White hair framed her face like a cloud, but this seemed the extent of her softness. Vivid blue eyes gave the impression that nothing escaped their attention.

Elizabeth clasped her hands tightly. "I couldn't help myself. It's quite lovely."

Isabel's expression didn't betray her thoughts. "My husband carved that—late husband. Robert's been gone these past two years."

Elizabeth searched for a response. Her mother had never stopped grieving for her father. "You must miss him."

Isabel's mouth softened into a hint of a smile. "'Twould seem that we've both lost those we hold most dear. Alas, your loss is more recent." She stopped a couple feet away. "So you are my niece. Mary named you for our mother, Elsa—a truly formidable woman." Isabel held Elizabeth's gaze as if she would fathom the depths of her character.

Elizabeth returned the frank appraisal, not once lowering her eyes or bowing her head as perhaps she should have. She was too keen to find the similarity between this woman and her mother in the shape of her face or her expression. But she found nothing.

"You look like Mary," Isabel said. "I wonder what part of you runs to your father."

Elizabeth frowned, not sure how to answer. "I'm grateful you've taken me into your home." Searching for common ground, she added, "I hope to be of assistance. My mother taught me about herbs and physic."

Isabel didn't reply. Instead, she selected the chair closest to the fire and motioned for Elizabeth to join her. "I believe you have a sister. Is she not married and living in Weymouth?"

"Aye." Elizabeth stared at the floor. She clenched her fists in her lap. "Kate and I have been estranged since her marriage. Her husband is one of the governor's men. It wasn't an ideal arrangement."

Isabel looked at her sharply. "An unfortunate affair." Another pause. "I don't recall hearing that your father was ever in one of the fighting bands."

Elizabeth tried to swallow the lump that rose to her throat. "He was not—he acted under his own initiative."

"I see."

Elizabeth forced herself to remain pliant under her aunt's scrutiny. "My father followed his conscience."

"Indeed," Isabel said. "Jennet mentioned your ordeal with the highwayman. Are you in the habit of risking your safety, or is this how they treat with brigands in Weymouth?"

Elizabeth stiffened. "Nay, 'tis not a sport there yet."

Isabel lowered her head. Elizabeth couldn't be sure, but she thought she saw the corners of her aunt's mouth twitch. But when her aunt faced her again, her expression remained grim. "I didn't think that much had changed. What, then, were you thinking drawing attention to yourself in that fashion?"

"All I could hear was the poor woman's cries and so reacted."

"Had she been beaten?"

"Nay."

"Did the brigand threaten her with his pistols?"

"He did not."

"I see." Isabel sniffed. "I have yet to hear of a single case where tears threatened a woman's health."

Stung, Elizabeth lifted her chin. "It was the right thing to do."

Isabel leaned back in her chair, and her hand strayed to the knot brooch at her throat. "Right and wrong are terms of perspective and depend greatly on what section of the ship you happen to be standing on. I have my answer as to which part of you comes from your father." Isabel tapped her cane against the floor. "While you are in Warwick, do not mention your father's disgrace to anyone. Warwick is not Weymouth. You'll find that most people do not share your sense of right or wrong. They are decidedly on a different part of the ship."

Her aunt's tone wounded Elizabeth. She searched for a reply, but anything that came to mind only showed her in a worse light. "Aye, I won't forget."

A sterile ground of silence lay between them. Relief came in the form of Jennet's arrival. The maid bustled in, carrying a tray of cakes and a jug of mulled cider that she placed on a sideboard.

"I assumed you wanted your refreshments here instead of the dining parlour," Jennet said.

"Quite so. Did you remember to bring the cherry preserves?" Isabel's sharp edge melted. There, finally, a hint of Mary Seton in the cadence of her tone. Elizabeth blinked away the sudden tears.

"As though I would forget your fondness for them after all these years. But we're down to the dregs." Jennet handed Isabel a generous slice of cake and rested a hand on her hips, appearing less like a servant and more like a hen. She then handed Elizabeth a piece with a healthy dollop of the preserves. "We have not had a young person in the house for years." The maid smiled her encouragement.

Though the food looked better than anything she had seen in years, Elizabeth couldn't find her appetite.

"Jennet likes to fuss." Isabel shook her head at the cider. "Our needs have diminished. The household was once larger, but Jennet has only me to mind."

"Enough to keep me busy," the maid quipped. A look passed between the two women.

"As you can see, she's close to being kin without the bother of blood."

Elizabeth's plate nearly slipped. *The bother of blood.* The plate rattled as she set it down on the table. "I won't be a burden to you. You won't have cause to regret taking me in." This meeting had not gone as well as she had hoped. *I have to make this work.* Return to Weymouth was impossible.

"You are my sister's child," Isabel said. Deliberately, she settled her plate on the tray and brushed the crumbs from her skirt. "When you're finished, Jennet will show you to your new quarters. Although it is rather set apart, it offers a view of the brook. I trust you won't mind its isolation."

Elizabeth rose to her feet when her aunt stood, and one thought plagued her. *Have I made a mistake?*

*

James entered the inn's common room with his ledgers tucked under his arm. Henry Grant balanced a tray of foaming tankards with his shirtsleeves rolled to the elbows and an apron tied around his broad middle. James reached over and plucked one as he passed. Henry scowled but didn't break stride. By the time James settled in his usual place in the corner, Henry joined him.

James nudged the ledgers towards the landlord. "The price of barley is ruining us. We'll have to cut back somewhere. Charge more for each cup of sack and bragget."

"I have a better idea." Henry slapped a placard on the table—*Wanted*! *Highwayman of Moot Hill*. "Ten bloody pounds for your head."

"Or we can find cheaper barley."

Henry's glare turned into a reluctant grin. "Cunning shaver." He slipped into the next chair and scanned the taproom. The only patrons were a small group of journeymen. "Od's blood, I could use that money."

James leaned back and stretched his legs. He sampled his ale, enjoying its bite. Not caring to admit it to Henry, the furore over his last robbery had surprised him. After a year on the highway, he was used to dragoons shaking their fists and spinning excuses for why they had been bested. This had been the first time anyone offered a reward. But he had never robbed a justice of the peace before. "Aye, 'tis a goodly sum."

Henry rubbed his forehead. "It's got the Roundheads swarming Warwick like maggots over spoiled mutton."

"They'll lose interest."

"With a ten-pound reward, your own father would turn you in."

James snorted. Raising his cup, he tossed back his ale. "You wouldn't be thinking of chasing that reward, would you?"

"I'm waiting for them to raise the stakes. Ten pounds are hardly worth the bother." Henry's ruddy face split into a wide grin, and he tapped James on the arm. "Now twenty pounds would suit me well. At twenty pounds, watch your back, Hart."

James smothered a smile. "Warning accepted."

Henry leaned his elbow against the table. "Sir Richard stepped up the patrols along Moot Hill."

"Double shifts, aye, I know," James said. "We're getting all the lame horses—at least there's profit in that. I should have considered this sooner." He lifted his empty cup to Lillian, Henry's serving girl, and she nodded.

"Remind me why I put up with you?"

James patted the ledgers. "You can't afford a licenced clerk. That and the pride of knowing the Chequer keeps the best stables in Warwickshire."

"Pride will not save me if they find a highwayman under my roof."

The landlord's brusque manner didn't worry James. Henry never allowed his conscience to get in the way of common sense. "You've naught to worry," James said. "I'm always careful."

"Is that what you call it, stealing from Sir Richard?"

"After a fortnight, Henry, I would have thought you'd have finished chewing that piece of gristle."

"Not yet—I thought I'd wash it down with a draught of Isabel Stanborowe's niece."

James winced. Henry had spit glass over that affair. How was James to have known that the niece would have been in the bleeding coach? At least she had a backbone; he had to give her that. But it still chafed that she had called him coward. He rubbed his stubbled chin. What did she expect him to do, pull down his scarf and declare himself to the world? He wouldn't be a coward, he'd be dead.

Lillian arrived with a fresh tankard.

"Thanks, lass," James said.

"Good job, Lil," Henry said.

She murmured an indistinct reply and sidled away. Five years at the Chequer—five years since James had rescued her at Naseby—and the girl still kept to her own. Some considered her odd; James understood better than most.

Across the room, the journeymen agitated for more ale. Before Henry left to attend them, he faced James, all humour gone. "The war's over, lad. Put it behind you, and look to the future before it's too late."

James studied his chipped tankard. "You have tables to clean."

Henry merely snorted and left.

Put it behind him? He'd have to accept defeat first. James traced his thumb along the hairline cracks in his cup, then rotated it until he found a smooth, unblemished curve. If he only saw this section, would he fool himself into believing the tankard was undamaged? Frowning, he took another swig of ale. The brew failed to wash the bitterness away.

The inn's front door rattled as a newcomer walked in. Dressed in sable black, he wore a jaunty feather in his cap. Tow-coloured hair stuck out like a messy pile of straw, spoiling the elegance of his costume. Wide-set eyes darted around the room until they finally settled on James. Instead of joining him at the table, the man took a seat near the kegs. James met him there.

"Hart."

"Rand," James said. "I expected you over a week ago." He glanced down at the badge emblazoned on the man's cloak. "Have you time for an ale, or is your master waiting outside in the comfort of his coach?"

"A cup would do me fine." Rand's grin revealed a broken row of teeth. "I've come from Coventry. The road was dry and my lord overly loud."

James smiled. "Sir Richard's known for that." Not waiting for Henry, James filled a tankard. As he slid the Chequer's best to the groom, he placed a small pouch between them. "Five coach wheels, with my thanks."

Rand glanced over his shoulder before tucking the purse inside his cloak. "My pleasure." He drew a long pull from his tankard and smacked his lips. "I thought Sir Richard would burst a gut. Don't know what threw him off more—the loss of his purse or his bruised vanity."

"How did you explain it when he realised his horse wasn't lame?"

"'Twas a nasty stone in her hoof. Shame I missed it, but sometimes only a proper blacksmith catches these things. Got a solid cuff to the head and a sound whack with his cane, but it was still worth seeing him put out." Rand smacked his lips. "This is good ale."

"What news from Coventry?"

"Naught of any interest to you. Only the usual trouble with recusants— same argument over compounded estates. This time a fine of ten thousand for having followed the King." Rand smirked in his cup.

James's curiosity fired. He had been born in Coventry and once expected to end his days there. His thoughts turned unbidden to his letter from Piers Rotherham. "Who was it?"

"Old Lloyd—his estate is a few leagues south of Coventry. Well-stocked ponds and forest, fine grazing land. Aye, Sir Richard has been slavering over the seizure, but the arrest warrant was plum in the pudding. They tried to nab him two days ago, but except for a few knocked heads, they were left with nothing. The old man has more fight in him than the buggers expected."

James hid his surprise. Barton Lloyd had been a lieutenant major in Northampton's Regiment of Foot and captured after the siege of Banbury. For his release, he had to give his word never to raise arms against Parliament. Clearly, they hadn't been satisfied with the man's honour, golden though it was—they needed to take his life blood as well. Greedy bastards.

"Anything wrong, Hart?"

James shrugged and scratched his chin. "Do you think I care for sheep and pastures?" He moderated his tone with an edge of boredom laced with impatience. Rand didn't need to know everything. In fact, it was better that he didn't. "Why should the cod's heads in Whitehall be the only ones to line their pockets? You're an enterprising fellow. Find me another prize and there's five more coach wheels for you. Sir Richard has worthy friends, does he not?"

"Doing what I can. I've got me ears to the keyhole, but most of it is fiddle-faddle," Rand said. "They mewl like old maids, fearing the Prince of Wales will break his exile and return with a foreign army. It's nauseating, that is." Rand held out his empty cup for James to refill. "If I were you, Hart, I'd not ride out at the moment. Sir Richard is in a proper froth and has appointed a new constable to track you down. Aye, he begged his friend, Colonel Harrison of Parliament, to send someone of quality."

James snorted. Typical Sir Richard, ingratiating himself. Not only was Colonel Harrison one of the regicides who had signed the King's death warrant, but his star had continued to rise with Oliver Cromwell's. Sir Richard probably wanted to hitch a ride. "Of course, who else would you petition for a law man if not a regicide?"

"A tad surly the day, aren't we?"

James snorted. "Who is this constable?"

"Lieutenant Ezekiel Hammond—shit deep in New Model Army. Already started sniffing around."

"What does a London man know about Warwickshire?"

Rand waggled his finger at James. "I can tell you're ready to piss on this one, but I'd think twice if I were you. Have you heard about the foiled plot to assassinate Cromwell?"

"Nay, but if it worked, I would have had something to celebrate."

Rand grinned above the rim of his cup. "This Hammond discovered it. He also sent a dozen Royalists to the Tower for conspiring with the Prince of Wales in The Hague."

James stared at the stacked kegs. "The King."

"What?"

"Simple rules of succession, Rand. When the old King died, his son became the new King."

"Don't let anyone hear you. They have a law against declaring that."

"They have a law against everything."

Rand grinned. "You can still scratch your balls and fornicate."

"Give them time."

"That's the truth," Rand said. He emptied his tankard and wiped his sleeve across his mouth. "Pleasure doing business with you, Hart." He tipped his hat and left the inn.

Henry returned with an empty tray of tankards. "What news?"

James leaned forward on the table. "Another recusant is on the way. Busy time for the Knot."

*

Isabel's healing skills drew a regular procession to Ellendale. Elizabeth watched new visitors arrive daily, wishing she could do more than accept their baskets of eggs or jars of preserves while Jennet fetched their physic. Like Elizabeth's mother, Isabel accepted gifts but never coin.

On Monday mornings, precisely at eleven, the haberdasher's wife, Mistress Rathbone, came for the ointment to soothe her chapped hands. Elizabeth timed the woman's next visit and waited for her at the door. She wasn't disappointed.

Fridays started when the Chiswells' boy arrived for his master's valerian root syrup. Elizabeth mused that if the syrup remained uncollected by the time the sun reached its zenith, a constable should be fetched to investigate.

When Isabel heard her, she replied in a crisp tone, "Careful, you're bound to summon one. We've done quite well these past years without a constable to meddle in our affairs."

Perhaps Jennet had intervened on her behalf or Isabel had finally decided that Elizabeth needed occupation, but one morning she handed Elizabeth an apron. "About time I see how skilled you are."

Elizabeth hurried behind her aunt to the stillroom, knotting the apron around her waist. A large ring of keys dangled from Isabel's belt, and she selected one with an elaborate scroll forming the bow. The other keys tinkled while she unlocked the door.

Elizabeth's mouth parted when she stepped inside. Along one wall, rows of glass jars filled sturdy wooden shelves while bunches of drying lavender and meadowsweet hung in an airy corner. In the centre of the room stood an oak worktable, upon which all the tools they required were at hand: sieves, mortar, pestle and a pewter still. Elizabeth picked up the worn pestle. The wood was stained from years of use and balanced well in her hand.

Without speaking, she continued to the shelves. Each jar had been carefully labelled with the name and date of preparation. She found her aunt appraising her. "I've never seen such a place."

"Where did your mother work?"

"She had a space set aside in her kitchen." Elizabeth's fingertips brushed over the labels: monkshood, foxglove and sweet woodruff. *I could lose myself in this place.* A thrill rippled through her. "Where do I start?"

Isabel approached the shelf and handed her a book. "Do you read?"

"Aye, my father taught me."

"This book is everything you need to know."

Elizabeth looked at the slim volume of herbal recipes. She flipped the pages, careful not to crease them. *Ointment of nightshade, syrup of maidenhair, gentian water.* Remedies for coughs, wounds and purges. To her delight, hand-painted plants and flowers were sprinkled throughout the pages. "This is beautiful." She tipped the book to show Isabel a spray of dainty heartsease. "Who drew these?"

Isabel turned away to adjust the cuffs of her sleeves. "Mind the instructions, not the drawings. Those won't soothe an aching stomach. Look up the instructions for preparing snakeweed. The root is on the second row, centre shelf. I'll need two drams."

Elizabeth settled on the stool and started grinding the snakeweed. Black and knobby on the outside, its inner core was as deep a russet as the New Model Army dragoon uniforms. "Jennet mentioned that there's a ten-pound reward posted for the highwayman's capture. They've nailed placards up at the market."

Since the robbery, a compulsion had gripped her to picture the scoundrel beneath the scarf, imagining his soul twisted and warped. She conjured a leering face, teeth surely rotted and breath smelling of stale ale, but oddly the image did not take hold. Instead, the memory of piercing grey eyes could not be purged while his scathing voice repeated in her head like snatches from a childhood refrain. "'Tis an outrageous sum. It's only a matter of time before he's caught," she continued.

Isabel looked over her shoulder. "What's this about? You weren't planning on capturing the rogue, were you?"

Elizabeth's cheeks warmed, and she bent over her bowl. "Nay."

"Good. You've gained enough attention over that business as it is. How's the snakeweed coming along?"

For the next hour, Elizabeth kept her mind on her work as a growing mass of powder accumulated in the mortar. Every so often, she paused in her task, dipped her fingers into the bowl and tested the consistency. The dust tickled Elizabeth's nose, and she rubbed the sneeze away with the back of her hand. "That should be enough." She wiped her hands on a stained towel. Her arm and shoulder ached.

"Is it ground fine enough?" Isabel appeared at her elbow.

"I believe so." Elizabeth tapped the sides of the mortar to loosen the rusty powder.

Isabel placed her hands on her hips. "Do you think, or do you know?" She scooped up a pinch of the ground snakeweed, rubbed it in the palm of her hand, and then brushed it back into the mortar. "More grinding. The snakeweed should be like silk."

Elizabeth stifled a groan and rubbed her right shoulder. Her palm burned from the friction of the wood.

"If it's too much, Niece, you're welcome to take your leave for the day."

Although Isabel's tone was solicitous, Elizabeth wasn't fooled. It had taken her a fortnight to be invited into the stillroom. Were she to leave now, she might not see this place for another month, if at all. "No need." She smiled and picked up the pestle. Her tender palm protested. "The finest silk it shall be."

Another half hour passed, repetitive and gruelling. Her arms felt like jelly, and her hands burned from the repeated turning and grinding of the pestle. One more turn, she promised herself, until finally she could do no more.

"Is it done?"

"Aye," Elizabeth replied with finality.

"Very well." Isabel lifted a small pot from the fireplace. Halfway to the table, she faltered.

Elizabeth rushed to give her a hand. "Here, let me take that." When she took it from her aunt, she realised Isabel's hands shook.

"Set it down on the table." Her voice sounded breathless.

"Are you all right?" She noted how her aunt's pulse quivered in her throat.

"Are you testing your skills on me? You needn't bother." The sharpness returned to Isabel's voice, along with the colour in her cheeks. "Instead, tell me what's in the pot."

Elizabeth chose not to press the matter. She bent over the pot and wafted her fingers over the steam. The aroma that rose up with the stream reminded her of sweet grasses. "Tormentil?"

"Very good," Isabel nodded. "On the shelf, you'll find a bottle of Venetian treacle. It has the apothecary's mark. We'll need that, too."

Elizabeth considered the two compounds in her head. Her mother often mixed them for advanced ague, but she recalled that Mary would also add a pinch of snakeweed. *Just a pinch*. "I'll bring the snakeweed."

"Whatever for?"

"Don't you need it for the physic?"

"What does my book say?"

Elizabeth bent over the pages and frowned. "It's not mentioned."

"Then we don't use it."

Elizabeth held her tongue, not wanting to be considered impudent. It was not her place to question her aunt. Besides, if she spoke up, she'd give her aunt a reason to banish her from the stillroom. But as she watched Isabel distil the tormentil and add the few drops of treacle to it, the snakeweed kept bothering her. "Tormentil is governed by Jupiter, is it not?"

"Of course." Isabel continued to stir the solution.

"Snakeweed is its opposite—ruled by Saturn?"

Isabel stopped her stirring. "What are you saying?"

Elizabeth bit her lip. "A pinch of snakeweed with the tormentil balances the humours. Each is effective in purging the fever, but used together, the dosage can be increased."

"Where did you learn that?"

"From my mother."

Isabel rested her hands on her hips. "You must be mistaken. We have never added snakeweed to tormentil."

Elizabeth smoothed the folds of her apron. This was the moment when she should nod, smile contritely and apologise. Then there was the truth. "She did use it."

Isabel's gaze pinned her. "Physic is a complex art. If we stray from the standard wisdom of those who have practised this science for generations, we risk our reputation and the life of the patient. We can't afford mistakes. Remember that, Elizabeth Seton."

"I will." Elizabeth drew the bowl of snakeweed towards her, almost protectively. "What shall I do with this?"

"Seal it and we'll use it tomorrow." Isabel paused. "Be certain to hide the jar in a dark corner. Some things do not take kindly to the light."

Chapter Five

James entered the common room and came upon a sea of red—the worst shade—New Model Army russet red. James's gut tightened. A dozen dragoons clustered in the inn, standing to attention with their muskets at their side. Henry's voice rang over their heads.

"I told you, Lieutenant, I already swore the Oath of Allegiance."

James pushed his way through the dragoons. At the other end of the room, he found Henry, his round face livid. A soldier stood with his back to James, rigid and unyielding. Close-cropped light brown hair brushed the top of his collar. The folds of his russet coat were crisp, and his black leather belt gleamed.

Henry didn't wait for a reply. "Tell me where it's written that an oath once sworn must be renewed every year."

"All right, Henry?" James called as he approached the innkeeper.

"Aye, lad," Henry grumbled. "We're having a discussion over the finer points of law. This is Lieutenant Ezekiel Hammond from the garrison. Our new constable."

The stranger turned around, and his ice-blue eyes flicked to James. He didn't try to hide his disdain. "Who's this?"

"James Hart, my ostler."

Hammond waited, no doubt for James to show obeisance, but James remained with hat firmly on head. He outranked a lieutenant, no matter that the rebels won.

"Captain Hart, at your service." With a measure of satisfaction, he noted the man's annoyance.

"Captain is it? Which commander did you serve under?" Hammond asked.

"Earl of Northampton's Regiment of Horse."

The man's thin mouth curled into distaste, accenting the sharp cleft in his chin. "Cavalier."

"I overheard something about renewing the oath?" Even the word soured in his mouth.

"I am now accountable for the lawfulness of the county, and I will be satisfied that everything is in order."

"Did Henry Grant give you any reason to doubt him?"

"I prefer to hear the oaths myself."

"You're from London?" James lifted a questioning brow, then nodded. "I know not how things are done there, but in Warwickshire, we do not besmirch a man's honour without cause."

The lieutenant's expression hardened. "I'm not accustomed to being lectured by an ostler."

"And our Henry isn't accustomed to having his word doubted."

"Be that as it may, every business in the county must swear before me. No exceptions. I will see this matter to my satisfaction."

The smile did not reach James's eyes. "I wish you joy of your commission, Lieutenant."

"There's no shortage of work," Hammond said, straightening his coat. "I will root out disobedience and ensure Warwick is fully compliant with the laws of the new Commonwealth." He grabbed his horse switch and gloves from the counter and turned to Henry. "There's also the matter of past-due ale quarterages. Be at the garrison tomorrow by ten to settle both matters." He gave Henry a crisp nod and James a cold shoulder before leaving the inn. The other dragoons followed in his wake, backwash after brackish water.

When the last one left, Henry slammed his fist on the counter. "Od's blood, lad! What's in your head? You did everything but challenge the man to pistols."

"He's a cod's head." James glanced out the window to see the last of the dragoons ride away.

"I hate this," Henry said. "Bad enough to swear the damned thing once." He continued swearing. "At least he didn't ask about the highwayman."

"Who said he didn't?" James said. "Our Lieutenant Hammond plans to deliver up the Highwayman of Moot Hill."

"'Twas a good run while you had it."

"Good run?" James lifted his brow. "I've yet to spring the partridge."

*

The garrison men swarmed Warwick market. James watched as they examined every horse in the pens.

The meal-man appeared at his elbow. "Another robbery, they say."

"Aye."

"Horses this time. Made the buggers walk eight miles back to the garrison with their saddles on their heads."

"So I heard," James said. He had wanted to keep the saddles, but the stitching gave them away as New Model Army. He pointed to the bags of barley stacked in the stall. "Give me three, mate."

"Only three?"

"Lean times," James replied. He tossed the man a sixpence, then brought the inn's wagon close to the stall to load the grain.

James hoisted the first bag over his shoulders and threw it in the wagon. A fine dust exhaled from the rough burlap. As he lifted the second sack, he caught sight of a slim woman in a faded blue skirt wending her way through the market stalls. Her dark hair gleamed against the whiteness of her coif. Unmindful of the grain slung over his shoulder, James admired her lithe grace. When she finally turned, he straightened in surprise. Elizabeth Seton.

A smile curled over his lips. Giving little mind to where the bag landed, he tossed it in the back. Leaning against the wagon, he watched her progress through the merchant stalls. When the grain merchant thumped him on the shoulder, he realised the man had been speaking to him.

"Forget not the last one. I won't have Henry claiming I cheated him."

"I won't." James kept the maid in view. Why not make her acquaintance? She wouldn't recognise him since he had worn a scarf. *Step to it, man.*

James scooped up the last sack and then latched the wagon gate. Dusting off his hands, he turned around to find his view blocked by Lieutenant Hammond and a pair of dragoons. He smothered a groan, barely hiding his irritation. "Lieutenant. If you've come to lend me a hand, I fear 'tis too late, but thank you for your courtesy." He tried to step around them, but Hammond moved to block his way.

"Are you in a hurry, ostler?"

James looked past Hammond but had lost sight of Elizabeth Seton. She couldn't have gone far. "If you'll excuse me, I have business to attend."

"A few moments," Hammond said. "I'm sure you can muck the stables another time."

James clenched his jaw and considered the dragoons at Hammond's side. The lieutenant would like nothing better than an opportunity to crow before his men. "What can I do for you?"

"How goes it at the inn?"

James shrugged. "Busy enough for a living. Come by for an ale later. The landlord brews Warwickshire's best."

Again he tried to move past, but this time Hammond halted him with his horse switch. "I haven't come to discuss the merits of your innkeeper's ale."

James glanced down at the switch and wanted to twist it around the Roundhead's neck. Though it galled him, James forced an even tone. "Pity."

"The garrison is investigating another robbery," Hammond said. "'Twas the work of the highwayman. Have you heard aught of it?"

James leaned against the wagon. "Aye, all of Warwick has. A patrol losing their horses, or did I hear an ill account?"

"You heard right."

"How embarrassing," James said. "I wish you joy of finding the villain. If the garrison is looking for new mounts, I may be able to help since the horse fair is not for another month. There are a couple of spritely cobs I can recommend."

Hammond's mouth curled down. "Did any strange horses pass through the stables this week?"

"Lieutenant, we run an inn. Strange horses arrive every week. Just the other day, we stood courtesy to a rather shady piebald gelding."

Hammond slapped his switch against his thigh. "I don't appreciate cheek, ostler."

James smothered a grin and assumed a contrite expression. "Forgive me. What kind of horse are you searching for?"

"A dark horse, likely a black, with white markings."

"Aye?" James allowed a trace of scepticism to creep into his tone. He scratched his head as though in doubt.

"Have you heard aught else?"

Over the past year, James had taken care to spread differing stories every chance he could. Henry's inn proved the best place to ferment rumours. Few, when threatened, could recall the exact details of the encounter, and men believed anything they heard in a public house.

"Naught but stories, though most agree that he rides a mahogany bay. Mind, I've also heard he favours a liver chestnut. 'Tis easy to mistake one for the other." James shrugged. "Not sure that will help though. They say he steals the mounts he uses and discards them at will." He paused for a fraction. *Devil take my soul.* "Perhaps, Lieutenant, you should be searching for garrison horses."

An angry flush stained Hammond's neck. The other dragoons averted their eyes and examined the cobbles. "You find this amusing, ostler?"

This constant reminder of his profession grated on him. "Do they not steal horses in London, Lieutenant? Question those who keep a straight face. You'll have a better chance of finding them. Now if you don't mind, I've pressing business elsewhere. But I'll keep a sharp eye at the inn. With a ten-pound reward, I'm eager to collect."

Hammond's knuckles whitened. "You do that, ostler." Straightening his coat, he glowered. "As will I."

James watched them leave. What made him do that? He knew he played a dangerous game, but the man set his teeth on edge.

A pox on him. He had better ways to occupy his time.

James looked around the market for the maid. Such a comely woman would attract the attention of many. He should have no trouble finding her. Convincing the meal-man to mind his wagon, James settled his hat on his head and went off in search of the elusive Elizabeth Seton.

*

People clogged the market, moving as slow as a herd of sheep and with as much purpose. Shrill cries of, "Wool, thirty-six shillings to the pound!" cut through the crowd. James scanned the square, looking for a dark-haired woman in a blue skirt. It was as though he searched for a chaff of barley in a stack of wheat.

James manoeuvred against the tide of people. Soot-faced urchins ran between the channels that opened in the crowd, jostling as they darted past. In an effort to avoid further collision, he nearly bumped into a matron, her basket loaded with packages.

She beamed a bright smile. "God save you, Master Hart." Her free hand fluttered over her lace collar like a butterfly.

"And you, Mistress Boddington." James tipped his hat to her. "I trust the family has fared the winter well." The moment she lowered her eyes,

James tried to steal a glance over her shoulder. At of the edge of his vision, he caught a flash of blue.

The woman bobbed her head. "With God's grace. My daughter, Sibyl, has been a blessing. She has become such an adept housekeeper."

James ignored the expectation in her tone. Sibyl Boddington was too timid for his taste. "Please give my compliments to your daughter. If you'll excuse me."

The matron opened her mouth to continue the conversation, but James managed to extricate himself into the safety of the crowd.

He quickened his pace. Where could she have gone? Taller than most, James commanded a better view of the market, but still he could not find her. How difficult could this be? He rolled his eyes at the irony. He, James Hart, once the best scoutmaster of the King's army and famed for his ability to track a field mouse, could not find a slip of a maid in a Warwick market.

James made his way down Jury Street through the livestock market and pens of bleating lambs. Someone had forgotten to latch a crate properly, and a pair of fluttering chickens escaped from their coop. The butcher tossed a scrap of offal over his shoulder, and stray dogs darted in before they were beaten away.

Turning on Market Square, James paused to survey the haberdashers. Surely he would find her here, amongst the stalls of linens, laces and ribbons. Hats and coifs intermingled, and for a moment all he could see was a blur of white and grey. About to turn away, his eyes at last fell upon the one he sought.

Elizabeth Seton browsed the household stalls, strolling at her leisure. James walked towards her, his eyes fixed firmly on the prize. She hovered over a collection of linens, and her fingers brushed over the cloths, but she did not linger beyond a curious moment. James kept a discreet distance, ever narrowing the gap. One slim hand held her skirts, raising them slightly to avoid a muddy puddle before she continued on her way.

He halted his progress when she became rooted at the bookseller's. While fancy ribbons and laces had not attracted her interest, a stack of pamphlets and chapbooks made the difference. She struck up a conversation with the bookseller, laughing at something he said. James rubbed his chin, engrossed. An unusual maid, he thought, and drew closer.

Leaning over the small collection, her head tilted to peer at the titles. Hair secured in a sedate knot, a wayward tendril escaped its constraint. The wind lifted and teased the stray lock, contrasting to the paleness of her nape. James fought the urge to reach out and twist the strand in his fingers.

He bent forward and addressed her in a low tone, "Are you looking to improve your mind, or to seek instruction?"

Elizabeth started in surprise. Her eyes widened, and for the first time, he realised how blue they were. Almost immediately they narrowed, as though she wasn't sure how to respond to his boldness. He knew he was being forward, but he had never won a thing without pressing his advantage.

"I am looking for a book on good manners, sir. I would not expect you to recommend one."

James grinned. Without looking away, he addressed the bookseller, who watched them. "Master Ward, would you be so kind as to introduce us?"

"I would," the man said. "Only I haven't made the maid's acquaintance myself."

Amusement flitted across her lips. "Elizabeth Seton," she announced.

"Mistress Seton, may I present James Hart, ostler at the Chequer and Crowne," the bookseller said, fulfilling his duty.

James swept his hat from his head. "Pleased to make your acquaintance, Mistress Seton." He rather liked saying her name.

"Master Hart." Elizabeth canted her head and hesitated for a fraction. She looked at him openly and did not avert her eyes in modesty when he returned her gaze.

"You're new to Warwick," he said.

"How would you know this?"

"I know everyone here."

"Not so," she said. One brow arched ever so slightly. "You did not know me until this moment."

James found her bewitching. "I stand corrected, Mistress Seton. Still, you are new to Warwick."

Elizabeth's head dipped.

"If I were to guess, I'd say you were Mistress Stanborowe's niece. I've heard that Ellendale has a new resident."

"Indeed, your information is correct."

"Pray, allow me the privilege of calling on you." James leaned against the stall and nearly sent a stack of books tumbling.

"My aunt values courtesy, and you, sir, are quite forward. I can only assume she would object."

"I assure you, mistress, I am not an objectionable fellow," he said. "Is that not right, Master Ward?"

"Quite true." The man's voice shook with laughter.

"There you have it," James said. "If you can't trust the word of a bookseller, all is lost."

A small smile flitted at the corner of her mouth. James found the resulting dimple intriguing. "I must be leaving." She picked up her purchase and prepared to depart. "God save you, sir, and good day." She reached over to pay the bookseller, but Master Ward caught James's warning frown and casually turned away.

"Are women from the south always so aloof?" James blurted, then cringed. *Lagging wit—you can do better.*

She halted in surprise. "How did you know I came from the south?"

"Far south, I would guess," he said, grasping the first thing that came to mind.

"How do you suppose?" Her eyes narrowed.

"Naturally, by your speech."

"Indeed? I could be from London," Elizabeth replied.

"You are as likely from London as I from Scotland."

Elizabeth gave up trying to attract the bookseller's attention and laid her coin atop a pile of chapbooks. She clutched her purchase to her chest in preparation for her escape.

"I will make you a wager," he said. "If I can guess where you came from, you'll allow me to call on you."

"And if you're wrong?"

"I'll wish you good day and trouble you no more." James offered his hand, but she ignored it. "Do we have an agreement?"

Elizabeth held his gaze for a moment. She pursed her lips, and a hint of a dimple lurked at the corners. "Agreed."

James smiled. He hadn't forgotten what she had told the highwayman. "Let's see—I'll need one word from you."

"Which one?" Elizabeth asked.

"Owl."

"Owl?"

"Aye, the very one. Say it again." He crossed his arms and waited. When she repeated it, he nodded. "'Tis perfectly clear. Your speech has a Dorset flavour." For truth, she did have a lovely, soft way of speaking.

Elizabeth's brow arched slightly. "Are you certain I am not from Hampshire?"

"Aye. Admit it, I'm correct."

"Fine, then, but Dorset is quite large, and that does not prove your wit."

"An exacting maid. No doubt you'll want me to do better," he said with a slow smile. "I'll need another word from you, then. Two, if you please."

"Truly? Which ones?" The breeze strengthened, and she brushed a tangled strand from her face. James caught the haunting scent of lavender.

"Welcome home."

With a smile, she repeated the words. The rosy bow of her mouth fascinated him.

"Unmistakable." He grinned.

"The verdict?"

"I would lay my life upon it. 'Tis a Weymouth cast."

"Truly impressive." Elizabeth's blue eyes narrowed. "Such a clever fellow to know this only by my speech. Would you not agree, Master Ward?"

This time the bookseller laughed out loud. "Quite so, Mistress Seton."

"Thank you for your stimulating instruction, Master Hart. I find my time has grown short. Good day." She nodded farewell to the bookseller and started to walk away.

"What of our wager?" James called out to her.

Elizabeth stopped to face him. "I'll honour our wager at the time of my choosing. You didn't stipulate otherwise."

James chuckled. *Damned captivating woman.* He crossed his arms across his chest and watched as she walked away. With a last swish of her blue skirts, she melted into the crowd.

"Aren't you going after her, James?" Master Ward leaned forward.

"Nay, not yet," he smiled, savouring the anticipation. He dearly loved a challenge.

*

Years ago, Elizabeth's grandmother gave both her and Kate a pair of diaries. Beautifully bound in soft brown leather with thick blank pages, it was a rich gift and one meant to be cherished. Practical Kate recorded household recipes while Elizabeth drew childish drawings of the flowers she collected: sweet violet, willow herb and her favourite, sea lavender. Kate scolded her for wasting valuable paper, but their grandmother smiled her encouragement.

After the initial splurge, Elizabeth became torn between a desire to express herself and to preserve the remaining pages. By the time the war started, the writing had trailed off to a rare trickle.

When Elizabeth returned from Warwick market, she excused herself and went straight to her room. She knelt before the leather-bound trunk, feet tucked in the hem of her gown. Lifting the lid, she set aside the few articles she had brought with her from Weymouth: a pair of gloves, a pine box with a half-full bottle of ink, and a gull's quill. At the bottom nestled the diary, its leather shiny with the patina of age, and still smelling of musty calf's hide. She eased open the book and started to write.

"I met a highwayman today in Warwick market. A curious affair."

Chapter Six

Elizabeth returned from the barn, having helped Jennet with the milking, and was surprised to hear a man's voice coming from the drawing room. Isabel's amused response followed. She stepped into the doorway to greet her aunt and halted when she saw Isabel's visitor.

Sir Richard Crawford-Bowes.

The justice was ensconced in a well-stuffed arm chair with his left foot propped on a stool. He still wore the severe black coat as when Elizabeth had last seen him, but his manner was more at ease. This evaporated the moment he noticed her in the doorway.

"This is your niece?"

Isabel glanced over her shoulder. "Sir Richard, here is my sister's daughter, Elizabeth Seton."

"I've already made her acquaintance," Sir Richard said, his tone decidedly sour.

"Such an unfortunate affair," Isabel said with a pained smile. She motioned for Elizabeth to take a seat beside her. "The poor girl has been a nervous wreck over it. She's had trouble sleeping and wakes up in the middle of the night plagued by nightmares. Don't you, dear?"

This was news to Elizabeth, but she followed her aunt's lead. "It's been dreadful."

"It was such a comfort to her that you were there, Richard," Isabel continued. "You stood between her and certain death."

Sir Richard's hardened expression softened, and he rewarded Isabel with an indulgent smile. "He was an uncouth knave who hadn't realised whom he had caught in his rough net. He backed down easily enough once he found out. Nay, mistress, you were in no immediate danger while I was on hand."

Elizabeth listened in amazement. The highwayman had specifically targeted Sir Richard; any fool who had been there would have realised this. Surely, Sir Richard didn't truly think she was a vacuous twit. But her aunt smiled and nodded and encouraged Elizabeth's response.

"Of course you acted in our best interests, without thought to your own inconvenience or personal safety. I had not thought that Midlanders were so chivalrous," Elizabeth said.

When Sir Richard frowned, Elizabeth turned to Isabel, wreathed in an innocent smile. "Aunt, you didn't tell me you were acquainted with the gentleman," and indeed she wondered why. Had she known, she would have better understood her aunt's annoyance over her disagreement with Sir Richard following the robbery.

"Did I not?" Isabel lifted a brow. "The Crawford-Bowes and the Stanborowes are both old families in the county. Sir Richard's wife was distantly related to my Robert. Third cousins, if I'm not mistaken?"

"Indeed." Sir Richard nodded gravely. "The families are sterling, with nary a base metal." He glared at Elizabeth, as though accusing her of being a cuckold in a swan's nest. He gave a dismissive sniff before turning to Isabel. "That reminds me, I am well pleased with the constable I've appointed to bring this highwayman to justice. Ezekiel Hammond is a man of quality—a decorated officer in the New Model Army." He positively glowed.

Elizabeth straightened in her chair, her interest suddenly piqued. She hadn't said a word over her suspicions about James Hart, and had indeed struggled over it. In Dorset, a bit of skirting the law amongst picaroons was a nearly respectable enterprise. Half the sailors ran the Channel for luxury goods, even Old Nick, and no one got hurt except the Exchequer. But the game that James Hart played was considerably more dangerous, and yet, she couldn't bring herself to sound the alarm. She found herself sympathetic to his harassment of the Roundheads.

"Where did you find Lieutenant Hammond?" Isabel asked.

"He was recommended by my particular friend, Colonel Harrison of Parliament," Sir Richard said, beaming.

Elizabeth knew *that* name. Colonel Harrison had been one of the regicides who had signed the king's death warrant last year. Sir Richard had high friends indeed. And somehow her aunt was included in this odd little circle, at least indirectly.

"Has Lieutenant Hammond made any progress with finding the highwayman yet?" Elizabeth asked. She toyed with the folds on her skirt.

Sir Richard sniffed. "He is, no doubt, carefully laying out his traps."

"How fortunate that he's joined our little community," Isabel said.

"Aye, when approached for this position, the man said he could think of no greater honour that to serve me here in Warwick," Sir Richard said. He looked like a cat lapping up a vat of cream. "I have hopes that he'll choose to settle permanently in Warwick—strengthen ties to Whitehall and draw more attention to the county as a cornerstone for the new Commonwealth. He'll no doubt need a wife—a helpmate." Sir Richard's gaze strayed to Elizabeth and then, no doubt realising what he was saying and in whose company, he frowned and cleared his throat. "A godly woman, I would say. Indeed, he should find a godly woman." The corners of his mouth curled down.

For the rest of the conversation, Sir Richard did not once look at Elizabeth, treating her as though she was a spirit in the room. Isabel, meanwhile, continued to flatter him.

Elizabeth held her tongue throughout their exchange. She felt uncomfortable, with an odd growing alarm that she couldn't name. Was this the polite society that she had aspired to? Kate would have been delighted, and not a little envious, but her mother wouldn't have given this braggart a cup of water on a hot day. Elizabeth somehow thought less of her aunt for catering to Sir Richard's vanity.

"Is aught the matter, dear?" Isabel asked.

"Not at all," she replied quickly. She looked down at her lap. Somehow she had to find the middle ground if she wanted to live here in peace.

"I understand, Richard, that there has been some controversy in Coventry?" Isabel asked. "Jennet says the market is abuzz with it."

Sir Richard shifted in his chair. "An unfortunate business. I shan't trouble you with it. The county is thick with recusants—bloody-minded papists and Cavaliers. But we are relentless against them, and they will be dealt with by the fullest extent of the law."

"My dear," Isabel squeezed Elizabeth's arm, "will you kindly fetch Sir Richard's gout powder? You can't miss it—it's in the stillroom."

"Of course," Elizabeth said. The relief to leave this company overwhelmed her, and she fought the urge to bolt. And yet, just as she left the room, Sir Richard said something to her aunt which made Elizabeth pause on the other side of the door.

"Isabel, is it really prudent of you to take in this girl?"

"She is my niece, Richard."

"Admirable of you to concern yourself with her welfare, but she doesn't quite fit into our little community," Sir Richard pressed on. He didn't even attempt to lower his voice. "She's entirely too outspoken. Even when she's quiet as a mouse, I can tell her manner hides an impudent nature. I don't mean this in any way to disparage you—I've always had the highest respect for you, Isabel. And your health is troubling—nay, don't deny it. You're not as sprightly as you once were. I should hate this girl to be a burden to you, and worse, for our little community to think less of you should this hoyden—yes, I dare call her that; I'm only speaking my mind—*when* this hoyden shows her true nature."

Elizabeth's face burned, and she trembled in fury. Her fists were balled, and she wanted to march in there and fling this arrogant man's words in his face. Instead, she waited to hear her aunt's rebuttal. Had it been her mother, Sir Richard would have been shown the door. She held her breath, waiting for her aunt's response.

After a moment's hesitation, Isabel said, "I will think about this, Richard."

The placid words made Elizabeth squeeze her eyes shut and turn her head. She felt the sting of her aunt's unwillingness to defend her.

*

Since Elizabeth's arrival in Warwick, her aunt had never missed Sunday worship, but this morning Isabel had been unable to lift her head. She appeared shrivelled within the bedding, and her condition alarmed Elizabeth.

"I feel the ague coming on," Isabel said.

"I'll stay and boil a cup of masterwort root." Elizabeth had long suspected that her aunt's heart was a concern. She had noticed Jennet adding a pinch of May lily to Isabel's broth. But the ague was inconsistent with heart palpitations.

"No need—Jennet will attend me," Isabel assured her. "I rely on you to represent the family."

When Elizabeth arrived at church, heads turned and bemused expressions followed her to the Stanborowe pew. The place was crowded and stifling. Elizabeth turned away from the curious glances and focused on her Common Prayer book. A dried sprig of rowan still marked her place. She saw none of the words on the page, but it served as a shield until people lost interest.

The vicar droned on in a monotone voice that continued unchecked above the sounds of coughing and creaking wood. Elizabeth scanned the room, her interest captured by the forced starkness of the interior. After the war, the last vestiges of the Anglican Church had been stripped away and exchanged for Puritan severity. Where altar rails would have been affixed to the wall, patched-up plaster stood out like a scar. No icons or stained glass remained with the exception of one colourful window high above the altar, likely too much of a bother to have been replaced. The churches in Dorset had suffered a similar fate during this past year, and yet Elizabeth still felt the tugging sadness over their loss.

Her gaze drifted to a garrison officer standing near the pulpit. While others fidgeted, the man held his Bible with precision and care. But when it was time to sing a hymn, instead of joining the chorus, he shut his prayer book and set his jaw in a rigid line.

Elizabeth looked away. She could never understand Puritan objection to music.

A strange feeling penetrated her distraction, as physical as a touch. When Elizabeth glanced up, she met the pale blue eyes of the garrison officer. Instead of starting in embarrassment for having been caught, he held her gaze as though he had the right.

For the remainder of the service, Elizabeth was aware of his unflagging interest.

*

Following service, half the congregation gathered on the green. As Elizabeth paused on the steps, she wondered how she should manoeuvre through this daunting sea of strangers. Neighbours greeted one another as they postured and preened. Isabel had not made any social calls since Elizabeth's arrival to Ellendale, so the only people she knew were those who came for physic. She'd not be warmly greeted if she walked boldly up to the glover's wife to ask how her liver was faring.

Elizabeth looked foolish standing alone. She clutched her prayer book and skirted through the crowd, heading towards the road.

"Mistress Seton," a feminine voice called out. "Oh, Mistress Seton!"

Elizabeth searched for the source of the strident tone. One of her aunt's neighbours, Mistress Rathbone, rushed to greet her.

"Your aunt is not well? She takes on those spells now and again. Come, allow me to introduce you to a few people." Mistress Rathbone guided Elizabeth to a cluster of people. The company parted and welcomed her with flattering smiles. But the one Mistress Rathbone most wanted to present was the garrison officer.

"May I introduce Lieutenant Ezekiel Hammond." She turned to the man with a pleased smile. "Our new constable."

Up close, Elizabeth noticed his square jaw and the pronounced divot in his chin. He was somewhat handsome, and he appeared to have won the esteem of these influential townspeople. Elizabeth imagined Kate nudging her forward with a whispered word, "You could do worse." Her sister would have approved of the man's neat appearance. Elizabeth wasn't a fool to have held all this against him. "Pleased to make your acquaintance, sir," she said with a smile.

Hammond tipped his hat to her. "We have something in common, mistress. We are both new to Warwick. You've come to us from Hampshire?"

Only one man in Warwick had the right of it, but then he had had the advantage. Elizabeth found herself scanning the crowd for James Hart but couldn't see him. "Nay, Lieutenant, farther west—from Dorset. And yourself?"

"London. Near Charing Cross," he said. "My position demanded that I maintain lodgings close to Whitehall. No rest in God's work."

"I'm sure you were indispensable, Lieutenant," Mistress Rathbone said.

"I'm unfamiliar with London," Elizabeth said. "But how disappointing it must be for you, being so far removed from Whitehall."

"I've not been exiled, I assure you, mistress. My appointment came with the highest recommendations from my mentor, Colonel Harrison."

The constant reminder of Hammond's association with the powerful regicide began to irritate Elizabeth, but then she reminded herself to be charitable. He couldn't possibly have known that this was all that anyone heard. "As long as you are content," she replied with a smile.

"I am," he beamed. "There is important work needed across this divided land. We have been sent forth, like disciples bearing witness to the Truth."

Her smile faded. She had never been comfortable with the Puritan fire-and-brimstone view of man's salvation. The truth was composed of multiple shades of grey laced with honest compassion.

"I understand that you are orphaned?" Hammond's question cut into her meandering thoughts. Its bluntness startled her.

"Recently, aye."

"Ah, I had the sense that your father was killed during the Revolution."

Revolution or rebellion? As her aunt had said, that depended on which part of the ship you were standing on. Elizabeth had enough of it either way.

"Five years ago. My mother, Mistress Stanborowe's sister, only recently joined him in the afterlife."

"If they are both of the Elect," Hammond lifted his brow as if instructing a child on their catechism.

Elizabeth stiffened at his rudeness. "I'm sure they are together." She kept her tone even, not desiring to be baited into a theological argument.

Hammond nodded. "Of course."

To Elizabeth's relief, he did not pursue this discourse. She nearly relaxed until his next question.

"Did you say you were from Dorset?" Hammond said. "Dorset mostly stood for Parliament. Your father, which side did he fight on?"

Elizabeth's mouth went dry. She felt the stares of everyone in the circle as they waited for her response. Even if her aunt hadn't warned her to be discreet, she knew enough not to admit her father's role in a Royalist conspiracy. She had come too far to be haunted by it again. The Stanborowes had managed to remain neutral, a rarity in these times. If she were fortunate, they would believe that the Setons had remained so as well. "My father was no soldier, sir. He was a master shipwright and died during a Royalist uprising in the town of Weymouth." Though true, her words felt like chalk in her throat, and guilt stabbed her. She glanced down, hoping he would interpret her expression as modesty.

"Weymouth?" Hammond tipped his head to the sky and appeared to be mulling on a memory. "I seem to recall something of this. Was it in '45?"

Elizabeth's heart pounded in her throat. "It pains me to speak of it, sir." *Change the subject.*

"Aye, I do remember it well. The governor at the time was Colonel William Sydenham. His brother lost his life in that same engagement. Tragedy."

Elizabeth held her breath. Hoping to hide her alarm, she forced a smile. "I'm impressed, Lieutenant, that you would know so much of our small town."

Hammond chuckled at the compliment. "I admit, only a little. Colonel Harrison held Sydenham high in his esteem, and we followed his travails with concern. We were pleased that he so ably put down the traitorous action."

A wave of melancholy washed over Elizabeth. "Indeed." All eyes were fastened on her. "My brother-in-law was assigned to my lord Sydenham's guards." *There, I've sunk to the dregs.* How galling to use Kate's husband as a shield.

Hammond's face brightened. Clearly, any doubts or questions regarding her family's loyalties had been wiped away.

I am no better than Judas.

"I must be leaving," she said, desperate to get away. "My aunt will be expecting me."

Hammond looked as though he wanted to say something more, but when he met the curious glances cast between them, he nodded. "God save you, mistress."

Amen.

*

Elizabeth rode through Warwick, paying no mind to where she directed the mare. Her mood was low, the lowest it had been since leaving Weymouth.

Turning down Market Street, she finally looked around. Instead of reaching the East Gate, she had ended up in the square. Several people lingered in this short time between church and the contemplation of the Sabbath at their hearth.

Two young boys stood before a post in the centre of the square, and she thought to ask them for directions. Surely, they wouldn't demand to know where she came from, which side her family fought on or anything else she'd be forced to lie about. She dismounted and tied her reins to the hitching post.

The boys exchanged glances and scuffed their boots into the dirt. "We were just leaving, mistress."

"Aye," the other said. "Our prayers await."

Their darting eyes and guilty expressions spoke of their reluctance. Every moment to tarry, to enjoy the fresh air before the cage was shut. When had the Sabbath become so strict? Dragoons approached, and she knew the answer.

They boys edged away, and she called out to them, "Which way to the East Gate?"

"Down Swann Lane and across High Street to Jury, mistress," one boy said, tugging his cap. The pair scampered away.

A gust of wind snapped the edges of a nailed placard and drew her attention. *Wanted*! *Highwayman of Moot Hill.*

Someone had drawn a crude picture of the thief with a broad, sweeping hat and a scarf around his chin. An ugly leer and a hooked nose completed the caricature. It looked nothing like the highwayman and even less like James Hart.

Elizabeth stared at the placard. She had denounced him for hiding behind a scarf. But what of her—hiding behind her brother-in-law's colours? Who was the greater coward?

"Warwick is not known for its artists."

Startled, Elizabeth turned around to find James standing behind her, his hat tucked in the crook of his arm. His buff coat was unfastened, revealing a plain linen shirt beneath. Thick brown hair fell to his shoulders, and a smile lit his grey eyes. A strange wave of gladness lightened her sullen mood, and her heart thrummed in her chest. "Are you an expert on the matter, Master Hart?"

"I have an eye for details and an appreciation for beauty, Mistress Seton." His smile deepened.

Elizabeth looked away so he wouldn't see her warm cheeks. She should make her excuses and leave. No good would come from this conversation. Yet the impudent drawing of the highwayman stared back at her with a challenge. "The picture is dismal. I've not seen its match."

James chuckled. "Indeed. Were I the highwayman, I'd take offence."

Elizabeth marvelled at his unruffled tone, with the red-breasted dragoons in shouting distance. *Absolutely brazen.* She tilted her head and contemplated him, wondering why he was troubling himself with her.

Surely, he must know who she was. A man like this courted danger and flirted with discovery. Here was a Midlander who thought he could fool a true Dorset born. Let him learn his folly. "It looks nothing like him."

"I should hope not." He narrowed his eyes speculatively. "Such a face would frighten small children."

"The rascal was more hideous."

"Indeed?"

"Aye, they missed a mole or two."

"Did they?"

"On the nose." Elizabeth reached out and jabbed the centre of the drawing. "Right there."

"I see."

"And those eyes." She tapped her finger to her mouth. "The eyes are all wrong."

"They do seem rather insipid. Blazed in anger, did they?"

"Not at all. Indeed, they were sly and crafty." Elizabeth wiggled her finger over the drawing. "They should be smaller, no larger than a pair of beetles."

James frowned and peered closer at the picture. Elizabeth nearly laughed and covered her mouth with her hand. When he glanced back, she coughed.

"Of course, you should know. Did you not have an encounter with the rogue, Mistress Seton?" There it was again, the way his tone lingered on her name, same as during the robbery.

"I had that unfortunate distinction."

"What are your thoughts on the villain?"

"Baseborn scum."

"I see." James rubbed his chin. "I understand you called him coward."

Elizabeth winced. "What are your thoughts of this reward? Will it stop him, do you think?"

James shrugged. "Not unless Parliament prostrates before the rightful king."

Elizabeth nibbled on her fingernail and noted the tightening around his mouth. "I've heard they say he only steals from Roundheads."

"Aye, all others are safe."

His casual manner annoyed her. Although she wouldn't turn him in, that didn't mean he should escape so easily. "That depends on your definition of safe. Mine doesn't include facing a pair of loaded pistols."

"And yet you weren't harmed."

"The villain threatened violence, and at any moment I expected to be shot. A woman in our party had a hysterical fit and may yet be a nervous wreck to this day. Aye, my coin and virtue were not taken, and for that I am most grateful, but I have earned the ire of Sir Richard, whose purse I was forced to turn over. So when you say I wasn't harmed, what precisely do you mean?"

James rubbed the back of his neck. "I'm sorry for your distress."

"Thank you, but 'tis the rogue who has much to account for." Elizabeth smiled when James's jaw twitched. "There's also the matter of my reputation."

"The devil," he said. "You weren't accosted."

"Aye, but I was foolish enough to have challenged the villain. People now consider me a forward chit."

James snorted. "What care you for their good opinion?" He stared down a pair of matrons who slowed as they walked past. He nodded crisply to them. "They are a severe, godly lot."

"Warwick is now my home. I will not make it difficult for my aunt."

"Isabel Stanborowe has a sensible head on her shoulders," he said. "Speaking of Ellendale, when would be a good time for that visit?"

Elizabeth ignored the sudden fluttering in her stomach. This was an ill-advised acquaintance. "Alas, such a thing is impossible."

"What do you find objectionable?" He bent closer.

Nothing. Elizabeth swallowed. *Everything.*

"My profession?" he pressed.

Elizabeth nearly choked and struggled to find her voice. She glanced over her shoulder at the dragoons who hovered near.

"Admit it. You object because I'm an ostler?"

Elizabeth had an urge to laugh in relief and irony. Instead, she met his gaze without wavering. "I have no objections to an honest living."

"I see," he said. His mouth turned into a wry smile. "Well then, what is it?"

"'Tis the fault of that dastardly highwayman."

"Pardon?"

"My aunt is most distressed over the affair, in particular its effect upon my reputation. So recently in Warwick and at the heart of controversy, she frowns on callers of any sort." Elizabeth grew more confident as inspiration seized her by the throat. Time to thicken the stew. "I'm sure you understand. I regret that this has arisen out of my impetuous actions and through no fault of your own. This is why I cannot receive you at this time. Perhaps when they resolve this matter and capture the rogue. Be assured, I have not forgotten our wager." She bit her lip so that she wouldn't laugh at his stunned expression. "Good day, Master Hart. God keep you well."

With a slight curtsy, she turned and walked back to her horse and untied the reins. When she chanced a glance back, she found him staring after her, his hands on hips. He looked as though he had been smacked by a six-foot wave.

That should be the end of that intrigue, she thought, leading her horse down the street.

Chapter Seven

James stared at the board and considered his next move. A small crowd had gathered around him and his opponent, Isaiah, a sharp-faced man who did occasional masonry at Warwick Castle. James didn't consider Isaiah good company, but the man had challenged him to a game of Irish, and being a point of pride, James couldn't walk away.

"Planning to move the draughts anytime soon, Hart, or are you courtin' them?" Isaiah snickered and folded his arms across his thin chest.

James ignored the jibe. Isaiah had been blocking his running game, but the contest was far from over. You kept at it, no matter how deep in the hole you were. The words had been drilled into his head by his father. James rubbed his hand across his mouth.

Edward Hart had been unbeatable at Irish—backgammon, as they now called it, but he never called it that. He was from a generation that considered this more than a way to pass the dark winter hours. You had to earn a lesson with him—not a right, but a rite of passage to be negotiated.

"Keep at it, boy." His father's words came to him as clear as though they were still in their kitchen with the board stretched between them. "Skill over fortune, discipline over rashness. Your enemy will make a mistake, grow too cocky and turn their eye from the prize." This was true on the battlefield as well.

James reached across, scooped up a pair of draughts and slapped them down on the board. An aggressive strike for home field and not without its risks. All Isaiah needed was one lucky roll of five and six. His father would have scolded him for dismissing a steady holding game—always rash, never thinking—this had also been drilled into James as well.

"Over to you," James said before sampling his ale.

Isaiah grinned and snatched the dice eagerly. "You've left yourself wide open, Hart." He rattled them in his cupped hands and tossed them against the side of the board. The dice dashed over each other, churning until they landed—four and five. James's supporters cheered while Isaiah spewed a curse and slapped his leg. "Damn you."

James smiled and scooped up the dice, waiting for Isaiah to make his move.

Several garrison men had wandered into the inn at the end of their Saturday night shift, and the cheering attracted their attention. One rose from the table, hitched his breeches and sauntered over. The spectators melted away.

"Wagering, are we?" the Roundhead said. "It's against the laws of the Commonwealth."

"This is an honest game," James said, leaning back so the dragoon could clearly see the board. "There are no coins at stake—only our reputations. Is that against the law?"

The dragoon sniffed. "Nay, but cheek will do you in."

James rolled the dice in his hands and let the comment pass.

"I'll be watching you both. If I see even a pence cross the board, I'll haul you both to the pillory."

"Warning accepted," James said. Turning his attention back to Isaiah, he said, "Your turn."

The game continued, and with every roll Isaiah grew more morose as his advantage began to slip. Henry pushed through the growing crowd to reach James. A few called out a greeting and his answer was friendly enough, but James sensed his distraction. Finally, Henry bent down and whispered to James, "Meet me in the buttery." With that, Henry left the circle and headed to the kitchen.

James's curiosity was piqued. After waiting a few moments, he pushed his chair back and rose. He hated to hand Isaiah the win, but something was afoot. "I yield."

"Really?" Isaiah said, mouth hanging open. He recovered and started collecting the draughts before James could change his mind. "Had you running scared, Hart."

"Another time, Isaiah."

James cut through the kitchen, past the loaves of bread piled on the table and the mutton simmering over the fire. The rough-planked door to the buttery was unlatched. When James entered, he found Henry and a man who sat before a row of stacked kegs. Only a single tallow candle lit the room, but it was enough for James to recognise Barton Lloyd.

"I found him in the laneway," Henry said grimly.

"Major?"

"James Hart?" Barton squinted, then looked relieved. His shoulders slumped slightly. He looked fragile, and dried blood covered one side of his thinning pate. "No one's called me that in years," he said with a weak smile.

James squatted on his haunches to get a better look at him. The man's face was covered in abrasions and bruises. "Where have you been? How did you get here?"

"I had heard you were here—dragoons after me. Hoped to persuade you to give me a night's shelter."

"No persuasion required."

"I need but a few hours' rest—I'll leave before first light," Barton said.

"Purge the thought," Henry said. "You'll not be turned out of doors on my watch. We'll sort something out."

"We have a bloody inn full of garrison men," James said, rising to his feet. "His face is too well known. I'll take him to Samuel Ledbrook's. He'll keep him at least until we can arrange another safe house."

"He needs better care than Ledbrook can manage," Henry said, indicating Barton's cuts.

"Our options are limited," James replied. "I'll get the horses."

James hurried to the stables. The lads were too busy with newcomers to question why he was saddling Sovereign and the inn's dray horse. James tarried long enough to retrieve his pistols from the hidden compartment. Leading both horses by their bridles, he returned to the back laneway that opened up to the inn's kitchens. He had finished hitching the horses when Henry and Barton emerged from the back doorway. Barton leaned heavily on Henry and lurched slightly on his feet. James hurried over to support Barton's free side.

"Our luck, a Puritan bugger from the garrison comes out for a piss in the laneway," James muttered. "They'd think he's drunk and arrest us all for licentious behaviour."

"Don't even jest," Henry grunted.

Together they helped Barton mount the horse, and after he settled himself in the saddle, James handed him the reins.

"If there is any reason to separate," he told Barton, "head east towards the woods. Follow the river road, and I'll catch up."

Barton turned to Henry. "I am in your debt," he said. His voice was weak and raspy. "If there is any service I can do for you, it would be my honour."

They left Henry and threaded through the back lanes of Warwick. James took the lead, tracing a circuitous route to the East Gate. The church spire, sitting above the gate, rose like a sword in the black sky. The gate was otherwise unmanned.

Once through Warwick, they continued at a steady trot down the river road until they reached a fork. James took the northern branch, and after another mile, they reached a timbered cottage skirted by ripening fields. At the front gate, James dismounted and hitched both horses to the post. A knotted rope was nailed to the top of the post.

All was silent except for the ghostly hoot of a barn owl. The cottage was dark and shuttered.

"What is this place?" Barton asked as he dismounted.

"Refuge." James rapped on the door. A few moments later, a flickering light shone between the slats of the shutters. The door opened half a fraction, then fully. A man filled the doorway, his nightshirt hanging to his knees. The light of the candle revealed a ruddy face weathered by the elements.

"James? What's wrong?" He lifted the candle higher to see Barton.

"We need your help, Sam," James replied, offering his hand. "The Roundheads are after this man. It's not safe for him at the Chequer."

"Of course."

"Thanks, mate."

Samuel stepped aside to allow Barton to enter. "The Knot welcomes you, traveller." He called over his shoulder, "Daniel, come down here, boy."

Samuel's son didn't need to be called twice. Daniel appeared behind him. "Aye, Father?"

"Help this man upstairs. Give him my room. There's a good lad." Samuel's expression softened as he squeezed his son's shoulder.

A wave of melancholy washed over James, but he forced it down. "Samuel will see to your needs," he said to Barton.

"Thank you." Before Barton allowed Daniel to lead him upstairs, he asked, "What is this Knot?"

James considered his reply. "Proof that we haven't rolled over in the gutter and died."

*

Elizabeth couldn't sleep. A restless edginess charged her limbs. At first, she tried to focus on the soothing sound of the leaves rustling outside her window, but the midnight creaking of an old house tapped through her head. Pushing the quilt aside, she rose and slipped out of her room.

Downstairs, she padded through the dining parlour. This room bore the ravages of the war, more than any other. Elizabeth had always felt a sense of loss in it. Forlorn and empty, the china cabinet stood sentinel along one corner. Once its shelves had displayed the pride of the Stanborowe plate; now only a single jelly dish remained. Heirlooms had at one time been sold as a means to eat. The only remaining valuable was her aunt's Venetian mirror, reflecting the moon.

In the hall, the chamber clock struck three haunting chimes. A draught rushed across Elizabeth's bare feet, then a door clicked shut. The hairs on her nape lifted.

She crept down the passageway, ears straining. Voices hushed to a faint whisper led her towards the kitchen. As she drew closer, she recognised her aunt's voice and heard Jennet respond. Then a third voice— low pitched, a man's voice. Callers at this early hour never boded well.

Elizabeth entered the kitchen, and Jennet spun around. Isabel started and pressed a hand to her throat. Her braided hair hung down her back like a white rope.

"I've startled you—sorry." Elizabeth expected her aunt to relax, but Isabel's shoulders were drawn tight. Jennet stood beside her mistress with her apron twisted in her hands. "Should you be up, Aunt? Jennet said you needed rest." For the past week, her aunt had kept to her bed.

"God praise, I'm better."

Elizabeth's gaze fell on the man. He snatched off his cap, revealing thinning hair peppered with grey. Leathery skin hinted at hours spent working under the sun. He stared at Elizabeth as though *she* were an apparition.

"Is aught amiss?" Elizabeth asked no one in particular.

Isabel's eyes darted between her niece and the man. Elizabeth hadn't seen her aunt at a loss for words, and she found her manner alarming. Isabel gave Elizabeth a tight smile. "We didn't want to disturb you, child. What are you doing up at this hour?"

"I couldn't sleep."

Jennet hurried to Elizabeth. "Shall I get you a warm posset? Just the thing to help you sleep."

Elizabeth shook her head. The tension was palpable, like a gathering of storm clouds. She stepped around Jennet, and the man shifted his position. The shadows behind him expanded.

"Samuel, this is my sister's daughter, Elizabeth," Isabel said in a rush. "She comes to us from Weymouth."

The man's manner eased, and he turned to Elizabeth with a nod. "Samuel Ledbrook, mistress." He stood poised as though on the edge of his toes.

"You're my aunt's tenant, then. I met your son when he drove me up here," Elizabeth said. "Daniel, isn't it? He's been a help to my aunt. Is anything the matter? Daniel, he's not ill?"

Isabel's expression eased. "Nay, the lad is well enough. Samuel has a guest in need of attention."

"Aye, my... cousin," Samuel said. "I've done what I could for him," he said to Isabel, "but we'd be grateful if you might have a look."

"He must be ill indeed if it couldn't wait until the morn," Elizabeth said. "What's the matter with him?"

Isabel shot her a stern glance. "Elizabeth, there's no need to fuss. I've got this matter in hand. Return to bed, and I'll see you in the morning."

Once again Elizabeth felt herself being shunted off to the side, but this time she was determined to put aside hurt feelings and resist. Her aunt had to accept that she was here to stay. "Aunt, I really couldn't sleep a jot. You've been lying abed for the greater part of a week. At the very least, I should come with you to make sure you don't become a patient yourself."

Isabel's mouth pursed, and her attention darted to Jennet. A silent communication seemed to flow between both women.

"The lass is right," Jennet said. "Let her go with you."

"Very well," Isabel said. "Get dressed and then gather the necessary herbs to make a strong poultice and something for the pain. Samuel has his wagon ready in the front."

Elizabeth dashed off, and in less than a quarter hour, she rushed down the steps with her cloak billowing behind her and a satchel swaying against her skirts. Her aunt was already seated on the wagon's perch beside Samuel, and Elizabeth scrambled up to sit beside her. She had barely settled before Samuel set the horse down the lane.

After a half-hour ride, they finally came into sight of the Ledbrook cottage. Before they could fully stop, Daniel opened the shutters from the second story window. Elizabeth alighted from the wagon and helped her aunt down. Samuel ushered them inside the cottage.

"This way," he said, and led them upstairs to the first of two rooms.

A man lay in the bed, with the light of a tallow candle spilling over him. When he heard them enter, he struggled to get up, but Daniel urged him in a low voice to keep still. To Elizabeth, it sounded as though the lad had called him "my lord".

"Who have you brought Goodma—Samuel?" the man asked.

When Elizabeth drew closer, she saw his blood-smeared forehead, a swollen nose and half-closed left eye.

"This is Bart, my cousin," Samuel said. A strange look passed between the two men.

"Let's have a look. Niece, shine the light on our patient."

Elizabeth held the candle high to get a better look of the injured man. He tilted his head and winced when Isabel probed his wound.

"It looks putrid," Isabel said.

"What happened?" Elizabeth asked. "Someone attacked you. We must alert the constable."

"Constable?" Bart jerked up and pulled away, his eyes now lucid and wild with fear. "Nay, that won't be necessary."

"There's no need to trouble the constable," Samuel said. "'Twas an accident. In our barn. A board—a board crashed upon his head."

Elizabeth lifted a brow. Though the gash and broken nose may have happened from a falling board, the eye clearly hadn't.

Samuel cleared his throat. "Our new constable—he's an ambitious man who tries to justify his position by any means. Won't bode well to drag him into this."

"Niece, since you insisted to help, what physic would you recommend?"

"A poultice to draw out the poisons," Elizabeth said, touching the man lightly on the cheek. He winced at the slightest pressure. "And mullein powder to ease the pain."

Isabel nodded. "Very good."

For the next couple of hours, Elizabeth attended the patient on her own, rationing the questions she directed to her aunt. She fell back on everything she had been taught. After she gave him the last of the mullein, she stepped back to survey his progress. Bart's eyes fluttered shut, and he soon fell asleep. She smoothed out the folds of his soft linen shirt and lifted the quilt to his chin.

"He just needs his rest," Elizabeth told Samuel in a hushed tone.

Isabel touched her shoulder and gave her a smile. "You did well. Dawn is breaking, and I need my rest. Samuel, can you ask Daniel to drive us home?"

"I'll drive you myself," Samuel said.

Elizabeth enjoyed the ride back, though she had to fight from being lulled to sleep by the steady clip-clop of Samuel's plough horse. Isabel had lost that battle, and her head nodded in slumber.

The sun had crested the hills when Samuel pulled up to Ellendale's front gate. As Samuel helped her down, Elizabeth stared at the sleeve of his homespun shirt. The cloth was rough and unbleached, and it suddenly occurred to her that Bart's linen shirt was made of fine cambric. The two men had a very different social standing. She somehow doubted they were kin.

*

On the next market day, James hurried across the courtyard to grab his list of provisions. He had overslept and didn't have time to stop inside the inn to break his fast. He entered the stables and halted. A half-filled bucket lay abandoned by the cistern, and a stream of water trailed down to the ditch. He expected to find the lads at work, but instead of the familiar sounds of a ringing hammer and good-natured bantering, all was silent.

"Joshua? Kit? Diggory?"

He heard running footsteps in the courtyard and turned around in time to see one nearly run past.

"Ho! Joshua!"

The boy skidded to a halt. Flame-red hair shielded brown eyes, and an abashed smile passed over his freckled face.

"Where is everyone?"

"Did you not hear?" Joshua said. "They're putting Samuel Ledbrook in the pillory for not keeping the Lord's Day! Everyone's down in the square. Kit swears they're going to pummel him."

James grimaced. Parliament had recently passed a new law for keeping the Sabbath that included a ban on travel except for church. Samuel had run afoul of that nonsense after dropping Barton Lloyd off at the next safe house a week later. Hammond had no idea how close he had come to nabbing a Royalist fugitive. "Did you say the pillory?" he frowned, recalling Joshua's words. "Samuel already paid the fine. He shouldn't be in the pillory."

"Lieutenant Hammond is having both."

James swore under his breath. "Show me."

As it was market day, the main square was crowded. Many of Warwick's leading citizens looked on, clutching their Bibles, their shoulders squared and faces animated.

Set apart like an invisible dividing line, another group coalesced around the vicar. Angry mutters spoken in low undertones rippled through them. The vicar's face was longer than usual. James respected the man, and he could see how he struggled with this debacle.

Near the platform, Henry stood with Daniel.

When Hammond marched into the square, the crowd hushed. The lieutenant paused until all eyes were upon him. He wore the triumph of a man who, having long fasted, gorged himself on the feast before him. James burned to smash that self-satisfied smirk from his face.

Hammond climbed the platform, followed by the two guards who hauled up the prisoner. Upon seeing the pillory, Samuel's half-dazed state lifted. He thrashed against his captors, fighting to pull free. Startled shouts turned to anger, and the heavy fists of the guards hammered back. Samuel abandoned his attempts to flee, raising his arms to protect his head. He crouched low over the boards as they continued to pummel him.

James balled his fists, and his hand strayed to his empty belt. A pistol wouldn't have helped—at least not here. Forced to watch, his rage burned hotter each time a fist connected with Samuel.

Daniel tried to rush to his father's aid, and Henry held him back with a firm grip. The innkeeper bent closer, muttering something in the boy's ear, and the young man straightened to his full height.

The soldiers hoisted a subdued Samuel to his feet, lifting the long wooden bar of the pillory. They forced Samuel's head into the rounded openings and splayed his arms to an obtuse angle. The bar slammed shut, and with a quick snap of the iron padlock, Samuel froze in a humiliating and painful position.

Hammond planted himself to the side, giving everyone a clear view of the prisoner. In his hand, he clutched a rolled parchment and lifted it over his head as though it were a mighty staff.

"Awake, awake. Put on thy strength, O Zion, for henceforth no more shall come to thee uncircumcised and unclean." His usually monotone voice now carried across the square with ringing fervour. "By the blessed laws of the Commonwealth, let those who do not respect the Lord's Day tremble in fear."

Every hypocritical word dredged up the past, bringing to mind crumpled clothes strewn across a forest road. James fought down the bile in his throat, and his bridled hatred nearly choked him.

A movement in the crowd caught his eye. Elizabeth pushed her way to the platform with Jennet Lynde scrambling to catch her. Twin spots of colour flamed her cheeks.

"Lieutenant," Elizabeth called out.

Hammond turned around, and his expression bore a mixture of incredulity and surprise. Then his expression softened.

James straightened. *Overreaching bastard.*

"Did you wish to speak against this man, mistress?" Hammond asked.

"Against him? Not in the least." Her reply caused the crowd to murmur.

"Well, what is it, then?" Hammond gave her an indulgent smile.

Back off, Roundhead.

"This man is my aunt's tenant," Elizabeth said. "Someone should speak on his behalf. I will vouch for his character."

Hammond frowned. "His crimes are grievous. A pretty plea will not change that."

"Sir, my aunt regards him highly for his industry and integrity."

"He profaned the Lord's Day."

"If he doesn't have the fine to forgo this punishment, I will bespeak it for him." She reached for the purse at her belt. "Five shillings, I believe?"

"The fine has already been paid—"

"Then you must release him," Elizabeth said. "To Caesar, Caesar's due. The rest is between him and his maker."

Sharp lass. But then, James had already discovered that.

"The fine does not eliminate the need for punishment," Hammond said, no longer indulgent. "One cannot erase the debt to one's soul."

"So you won't be fining him, then?"

Hammond flushed. "Godly men would not dare to break God's laws. Therefore, let him pay what is dear to him. One debt to the Commonwealth, the other to the Lord." He looked around at the gathered crowd, his expression stern. "The laws of our new Commonwealth are not to be trifled with." He snapped his fingers to the guards.

James drew Joshua closer. "Help Jennet Lynde take her mistress away from here." The lad darted through the crowd and reached Elizabeth's side. After a few moments of arguing, Joshua and Jennet ushered her past the gawking crowd.

Hammond's eyes followed the retreating maid as he continued his sermon.

"Learn to live with disappointment, Roundhead," James muttered under his breath. He scanned the crowd. From experience, he knew there was always one who threw the first salvo, the initial push launching the crowd into mindless depravity. Isaiah was positioned dead centre in the square with a sack of mouldy potatoes and sufficient space cleared for him.

While the lieutenant preached on his crude pulpit, James walked up to Isaiah and slapped a hand on his shoulder. "Are you sure you want to cast that stone?" He shook his head, a barely perceptible movement. "Put that away. You've broken the Sabbath often enough."

Isaiah smirked and wiped his sleeve across his bulbous nose. "I know nothing 'bout that, Hart. You must be thinking of old Ledbrook."

James tightened his grip, and the man squirmed. "Throw anything towards that platform and I'll swear I caught you drinking at the Swann last Sunday past."

"You'd be lying." Isaiah gaped in horror. "You'd swear a clanker for Ledbrook?"

James smiled grimly.

"Damn it, Hart," Isaiah muttered. "You're a mean cove. Aye, have it your way." He dropped the potato.

James crossed his arms, his stance wide, and stared at the prisoner in the stockade. The crowd seemed to catch his sullen mood, and little by little the eagerness for the sport faded.

Hammond finished reading his sermon and stepped aside to avoid the first volley. When none came, he scanned the faces of the crowd, puzzled. Most avoided his gaze—except one.

James tipped his hat to Hammond.

*

James waited, hidden in a forested hillock while he surveyed the road leading into Moot Hill. A goshawk broke the stillness and swooped in to snatch its prey from the forest floor. Speckled wings beat against the crisp air, followed by a triumphant shriek. The hawk had gotten his meal; James still waited for his.

He had strategically chosen this spot to ambush Hammond. The road sharply twisted through the forest, and there were many side tracks he could use to disappear, then reappear to surprise his enemy. And on this afternoon, rain clouds threatened, leaving the pass darker and more brooding than usual. It matched his mood entirely.

For the past two days, James had been nursing his rage over Samuel's beating, distilling it down to a single driven purpose. Every fist and every boot kick would be avenged, and rather than going after the mindless sheep who had carried out this travesty, James cast his eyes on the shepherd.

The trap had been set with Rand's help. The carrot was a reported highwayman sighting along Moot Hill. Rand had timed it for when the regular patrols set out from the garrison, leaving Hammond behind with a couple of dragoons.

Hammond seized the bait.

James had been tracking his quarry's progress since Hammond and another dragoon crossed into Moot Hill. James had lost sight of them when he circled around to take up this position, but they should have been here by now. A cold thought drenched him. What if Hammond outfoxed him and went another way?

There—a movement. Where the woods swallowed the twisting road, two russet smudges approached, their garrison coats a beacon in the dim light.

James checked the priming of his doglock pistols and loosened his sword in its scabbard. To disguise his voice, he put a few pebbles in his mouth before lifting a scarf over his begrimed face. He pressed his knees into Sovereign's flanks and rode along the higher trail. A tangled shield of yew, blackthorn and gnarled elder separated him from his quarry. He headed towards a junction where the hillock met the road and the advantage of higher ground was his.

Voices carried over the trotting horses. One of the men burst into raucous laughter. His laughter echoed in the narrow hollow before Hammond cut him off. James twisted the leather straps around his fisted glove.

Hammond drew closer. Blood pounded in James's temples. Sovereign tensed beneath him. *Wait for it . . . now*!

James squeezed his knees and pushed forward. They gathered speed and rushed down the slope. Sovereign's muscles bunched beneath him. As they burst onto the road, James bore down upon the hindmost rider.

The dragoon twisted in the saddle and scrambled to draw a pistol from its holster. James rose in his stirrups, and Sovereign charged into the other mount, crowding it with his broad chest. The black leaned in and pushed the other horse off the road. Wild-eyed, the animal stumbled and threw the dragoon into the ditch.

James rounded on Hammond.

Horse and rider were fleeing pell-mell down the road. Hammond whipped his horse to get every ounce of speed from it.

Sovereign raced after them, devouring the distance between them. James focused on snatching his opponent's reins. He leaned forward, but before he could seize them, Hammond veered sharply to the left and pulled away.

James dug his boot heels in his stirrups, reined in Sovereign and circled around. He levelled his pistols just as Hammond raised his carbine.

The two men squared twenty feet apart, flintlocks aimed upon the other.

James called out, his voice deep and gravelly, "What now, Roundhead?" The double click of his fully cocked hammer echoed like a shot. He kept his pistol fixed on his target.

Hammond breathed heavily, but he held his carbine steady. His pale blue eyes didn't waver. "I've captured the Highwayman of Moot Hill."

"Is this how you see the game ending?" James withdrew his other pistol from its holster.

"I see you with a noose around your neck," Hammond spat. "Drop your weapons."

"I can think of no reason to oblige." James kept his attention focused on Hammond's face. He could always tell seconds before a man attacked by the wildness in his eyes.

"I am a duly appointed officer of Parliament—it's treason to raise arms against me."

"Now I'm even more inclined to shoot you."

"You're outnumbered, highwayman. You won't get far." Hammond lifted his chin sharply towards his companion. Fifty feet and closing, the other man approached with a primed musket.

James cursed himself for losing track of the other one. He dug his knees into his horse's flanks, and the beast backed up slightly, just enough to train his pistols on each dragoon. "Even odds. We're equally matched in shot." His attention darted between the two men.

Sweat beaded on Hammond's forehead. His worried horse sidestepped and pulled on its bit. Hammond's eyes narrowed, and his carbine rose a fraction. A second before he fired, James kneed Sovereign to the side.

An explosion shattered the air, and a sharp whistle grazed past James's ear. He ducked, and a tree splintered into a shower of wood behind him. On the ground, the other dragoon struggled to light his musket. This was his chance.

James spurred Sovereign and charged straight for Hammond, who still held his smoking pistol. The other horse panicked and reared, threw Hammond from the saddle, then bolted down the road. Sovereign wheeled around and James fired his pistol at the feet of the dragoon with the musket. The man scrambled back, feet over arse. James once more levelled his pistol on Hammond.

"Let's try this again, Roundhead," James said through clenched teeth. "I've saved a shot for your head. Don't think I won't use it." He motioned to the other dragoon. "Drop your musket and join the constable."

"Don't disarm, soldier," Hammond barked. "We have the Lord on our side, and He will see us triumphant."

"He'll see you dead." James toyed with his trigger. "Gather up your purses and put them in this bag." He tossed a leather satchel to the dragoon. The man's gaze darted between James and Hammond. "Now!" The dragoon abandoned the musket and scurried forward.

Hammond looked apoplectic. "I'll see your head severed and impaled on a pike." He nearly struck the dragoon, who held out his hand for his purse, but he gritted his teeth and slapped the purse in his hand.

James caught the satchel and hefted it in his hand to gauge its weight. He shook his head in mock sympathy. "Sir Richard isn't paying you well." He looped the straps around the pommel. "Cheap bastard."

"I serve my conscience and a higher God."

James's anger flared, and it took all of his self-control to not pull the trigger. After what they did to Samuel, and to others besides, that bastard had the gall to prattle about conscience and God. "You're a damned hypocrite, Roundhead." He lifted his pistol and aimed it at Hammond's head. "I should put you down like the rabid beast you are. Then you can meet your maker and tell him all about it."

Hammond swallowed hard and kept his mouth shut.

"Start walking. A hundred paces, no less," James said.

Hammond and the dragoon backed away. When they were far enough to satisfy him, James called out, "Count yourself lucky that I let you live. Very lucky." He wheeled Sovereign around and set off down the road.

James smiled grimly as he left Hammond behind. It was possible to bleed a man without firing a shot into him. Hammond prized his reputation as did a miser his gold, and James had just stolen it from him.

Chapter Eight

Isabel slammed the kitchen door behind her. She marched to the table that separated her from Elizabeth. "What were you thinking?"

Elizabeth stepped back, disoriented. "Is this about Samuel Ledbrook?"

Isabel's eyes went nearly black. "I should hope that you haven't made a fool of yourself more than once. I heard all about this from Mistress Rathbone. She dodged past wagons and horses to reach me. I can't *believe* you challenged the constable in that manner!"

Elizabeth tried to collect her scattered thoughts. "Samuel paid the fine, yet they still put him in the stocks."

"Lieutenant Hammond was appointed by Sir Richard to root out disobedience in Warwick," Isabel ground out, speaking as though to a small child. "He's looking for an excuse to pry into everyone's affairs. You may as well have carried a banner that declared yourself insolent and malignant."

Jennet left the hearth and edged closer to Elizabeth. "Mistress." Her brown eyes darted between Isabel and Elizabeth. "You didn't see him— Samuel was in a bad way." She gave Elizabeth's arm a reassuring squeeze.

Touched by Jennet's action, Elizabeth's resolve strengthened. "The guards beat him soundly. You couldn't have stood there and done nothing. "

Isabel grimaced. "Your heart serves you well; now use your head."

"The man spent three hours locked in the stocks in the cold rain and now can barely lift his head from the fever. Are you saying he deserved it?"

"I am not, Niece," Isabel's voice lost the edge of sharp glass. She paused as though to compose herself. "This is Warwick. Matters are more complicated here. We do not charge in half-cocked. There are no uprisings here, not like Weymouth. We prefer survival."

"This is about my father, isn't it?" The blood drained from her face.

"I see shades of him in you."

"I should hope so," Elizabeth said. "My father was true to what he believed."

"Is that why you've cast him with Parliament?" Isabel said with the harshness of a slap.

"How did you find out?"

"This is Warwick," Isabel said. "Never mind, that was probably the most sensible thing you've done."

Her aunt's grim acceptance of the deception made it worse. Isabel should be outraged, and the fact that she wasn't diminished her in Elizabeth's mind. "Sensible? Though I spoke no falsehood, I am still ashamed of it." A painful band tightened around Elizabeth's chest. "I've spent the last five years of my life defending my father, even to my sister—hearing him called traitor when once he had everyone's respect. How do you think I feel knowing I've turned my back on him so that none would think ill of me—so whispers of *traitor's daughter* do not follow me from Weymouth? You call it sensibility—I call it betrayal." Elizabeth started shaking, her thoughts tumbling in her head. "I didn't think I needed to defend him here. If you loved my mother, you would not criticise the man who had been her life. My father did what he had to do."

Elizabeth saw the fury in her aunt's eyes and braced herself, expecting a slap for her impertinence. But Isabel didn't move. Instead, her tone was clipped and measured and lashed like a whip.

"He did what he had to do? What was that—provide for his family or keep them safe?" Isabel raised her finger to halt Elizabeth's response. "Did the Roundheads throw you out of your home? Did they burn you out or leave you to starve? Nay, I warrant they did not. You had the sea to provide and a softer clime for shelter. Weymouth did not experience nearly as many of the deprivations as we faced. None of you knew what it meant to have every scrap of food you've gathered taken away to feed an enemy's belly." Isabel straightened her slight frame and held her ground like iron and rock. "Nothing so dire as to risk everything to prove a point. My sister lost a husband and you"—she locked eyes with Elizabeth—"you lost a father and the security of his protection."

Isabel held Elizabeth's gaze for a few moments. "There is a time for bravery and a time for self-preservation. Rashness disguised as bravery is a luxury we can't afford. You punish yourself for not keeping his standard, but had you waved those colours in their faces, I would have sent you back to Weymouth. Now is not the time for fruitless stands of bravery."

Elizabeth blinked away the tears. A painful lump lodged in her throat. "He was my father, whatever his faults."

"Ours is an uneasy peace. Open rebellion is not an option. Better a pragmatist and survivor than an idealist. You're clever enough to know the difference."

Elizabeth fought to keep the tears from falling. She whirled around, and dashed out the door.

*

Elizabeth threw a stone in the river. *Plop, splash.* It shattered the flow of the water before sinking into the muddy depths. She grabbed a larger rock and aimed for the middle of the river. It arched across and dove straight into the centre.

Elizabeth swiped away a stray tear and searched the ground for something to make a spectacular splash and drown out the memory of her aunt's words. She seized the very one and aimed for the heart of the swirling current. The rock sailed over and landed in the neck of the eddy.

"Excellent throw."

Elizabeth whirled around. James Hart stood under a willow tree with his horse tethered several paces behind. How did he always manage to sneak up on her? "What are you doing here?"

"Watching a maid feed a river." He left the shelter of the tree and stopped beside her. His hands rested on his hips while he surveyed the river. "People from the south have strange customs. I'd not have thought it. Tell me, does its diet require steady attention, or is it content to be fed once a day?"

Elizabeth flicked a lock of hair away from her face. Likely, he'd expect a demure protest, but she wasn't in the mood to humour anyone. "As long as it has a balance of sand and loose shale, it suffers infrequent care."

He flashed a smile. "I'm encouraged to hear it." Somehow she didn't think he meant the river. He bent down and selected a flat stone, half the size of a robin's egg. He hefted it in his hand, aimed and released. It skipped seven times before finally dropping into the water.

"You are an expert, I see," she said.

"I've had practise. I may yet hold the Coventry record for stone skips."

"You're from Coventry?"

"I'm not from anywhere." James dropped on his haunches and selected another stone, a flat one with rounded edges. "The angle prior to release makes all the difference." He tossed the rock, and this time it skipped nine times before dropping into the river.

Elizabeth crossed her arms. "'Tis a good thing for Samuel Ledbrook you weren't in the square the other day."

"What makes you think I wasn't?" James walked a few paces along the shore. "The show was spectacular. I particularly enjoyed watching our constable choke on your censure."

"You were there?" Then the implication hit her. "You didn't speak up for Samuel."

"What would that have served?"

She had enough of this. "What is the matter with you people? You're prepared to be bold behind a mask but won't stand for common decency. I suppose there is no profit in that." Elizabeth clapped a hand over her mouth. Good Lord, what had she blurted? She stared at him, painfully aware they were alone.

James shrugged and looked upward to examine the sky through a patchwork of leaves. "There isn't. Nor in decorating a gibbet either."

His indifference took her aback. There it was out in the open, and he had brushed it aside, giving it no more mind than an inconvenient fly. She suddenly found herself wishing that she had been wrong, or that he would have made an attempt to deny it. No remorse, no shame. "There's a simple solution to avoiding the gibbet. Stop before someone gets hurt."

James picked up a stick and pointed to the river. "Your water looks hungry. It's begging for more rocks."

An overwhelming urge to scream her frustration undercut her like a wave. Hurt and anger over the argument with her aunt boiled over, and she wanted to prove that she was of some account. Whirling around, she searched the ground for a large rock and seized a cumbersome thing. Anger fuelled her strength, and cradling it in her arms, she waded into the river, unmindful of the cool water soaking the bottom of her skirts. With a heave, she threw it in as far as she could, but not far enough to her satisfaction. A deep, gurgling splash sprayed her. She wiped away the droplets and turned around to glare at him, hands on her hips. "Done!"

James threw back his head and started laughing, a low chuckle that escalated to a hearty guffaw. Elizabeth turned away, annoyed at first until the ridiculousness of her situation seized her. Verbally sparring with a highwayman while standing in a river was mad. James's mirth finally breached her defences, and the humour of it began to tickle her.

"You'll catch your death if you stand there long enough. Your river will not be satisfied with that. Here, let me help you," James said and offered his hand.

Elizabeth waved him away. "I'm fine, sir. I can manage perfectly." She began to wade into shore, but the river claimed its ownership of her. Her left foot mired into the muck, and she nearly pitched forward.

"No need to be stubborn about it," he said, coming after her. "Unless I alarm you?"

She looked at him askance, holding her sodden skirts. "You know nothing of the matter. I'll have you know that people from Dorset are afraid of naught."

"Dorset? I thought you were from Hampshire." James smiled. "My undoing." Again he held out his hand to her, a challenge she couldn't decline.

Elizabeth accepted his assistance, and his strong, lean fingers curled around hers. His warmth seeped through her chilled skin. James helped her from the river and didn't release her even when she once more stood on the bank. The earthy scent of river, green leaves and dusty rocks filled Elizabeth's head.

He looked down at her hand, turning it over in his own. "I have heard, Mistress Seton," the texture of his voice coursed through her, "that women from Weymouth have rough, chapped hands from the seawater." His touch was warm and stirring, the contact intimate. His fingers explored her palm, following the gentle curves to its hollow, then lingering on the tips of her fingers. The way his fingers brushed over her skin felt as she imagined a kiss to be.

James's smile deepened, his grey eyes mesmerising. "Untrue. Your hands are quite soft after all."

Elizabeth looked at him in confusion, her mouth suddenly parched. Then she snatched her hand away. "You've mistaken us again for Hampshire, Master Hart."

"It's James."

"Pardon?"

"You have my leave to call me by my given name. Indeed, I would prefer it."

"Should I be surprised that a highwayman disregards convention?"

James chuckled. "Disregarding rules is prime on the highway. Any rum-padder found in direct violation faces ridicule and must exchange his spurs for coddled milk. I hate coddled milk."

"We mustn't have that." Elizabeth smiled back.

"There, I've won a smile. Now you'll need to forgive me the rest."

She had done so long before now.

"I didn't know you knew Samuel well. Has he been over to Ellendale often?" James asked with an odd inflection in his voice.

"Not really," Elizabeth said, nudging a rock with the toe of her boot. "Does it matter that our acquaintance is not long? Being true to what is right has no restrictions. Would it make more difference had he been an old friend?" Now she thought of Old Nick. Her father would never have left Nick in the stocks—nor betrayed him. The pain in her chest grew.

"It's more than Samuel, isn't it?"

Elizabeth felt exposed under his unwavering gaze, as though he beheld her raw soul. She hugged herself and could not answer.

"The other day, I stood a drink to the haberdasher, Rathbone, and he told me an odd tale," James continued slowly, as though testing his words. "I questioned the man, but he was certain of his facts. I was surprised to hear that your people were Roundheads."

Elizabeth winced. Somehow it was worse to admit her betrayal to James Hart. "My father was a Royalist. He died for the King's cause, and aye, I allowed them to think otherwise." She searched for an excuse to show him that she wasn't as shallow a creature as she must appear, but then a part of her thought, *Aye, you are worse than that.* "You're welcome to scrape me over the shoals. I deserve it."

"Me? I'm the man hiding behind the scarf. I don't get that privilege." His tone held no contempt. "But neither do they. The usurpers have no honour. Pay them no further mind."

Elizabeth read kindness in his gaze and—could it be—understanding? She studied him, curious about the contradiction she found in the man. Even though her father had sheltered her from the worst elements, she had seen enough rough men around the ports—ruthless men, lacking in morals and decency, who drank or gambled away every farthing they made. She did not recognise any of this in James Hart.

"Why do you steal from them?" she asked. "You have a decent living, a roof over your head. You don't appear extravagant in your lifestyle. A wife to support? Children to feed?"

James's brow lifted slightly. "I wouldn't have asked to call on you if I did. I do have some standards."

Elizabeth felt her cheeks flush, but she would not allow her head to be turned. "Then why risk the gibbet?"

He didn't answer at first. Instead, he tossed another rock into the water and appeared to weigh something in his mind. Finally, he said, "I have never forsworn my oath to the crown. I'm still pledged to our rightful sovereign. Every purse I steal is added to his account. When he returns to claim his birthright, every farthing will have gone to his cause."

Whatever she expected to hear, this wasn't it. Finally, something she recognised; his was the same cause that had driven the Crabchurch men to have risked—and lost—everything. Only this time she knew how it would end. "The war is over."

James whipped his last stone in the river. He brushed the grit from his hands and faced her. "Not while our sovereign lives, it isn't. Far from it."

"The world has changed, whether you admit it or no," Elizabeth said.

"With all due respect, you don't understand."

Elizabeth's eyes widened. "You don't think so? I lost a beloved father to the Rebellion, and while it hurts that the cause for which he bled failed, I am determined to look to the future. Who have you lost that you cannot do the same?"

James shook his head with a wry curl of his lips and glanced to the sky. "Is this why you've come to Warwick, Elizabeth Seton? To look to the future, even if it means accepting the enemy as a friend?"

"And why not? I see nothing wrong with desiring the security of a home or to live in peace with my neighbours."

When he turned to her, his eyes had darkened to slate. "Don't be fooled by them. They will try to win you over with their soft words and promises for a golden age, but under that rock lay only woodlice. You don't know what they're capable of."

"And what have you accomplished by following this course? One day, they will track you down and give you no quarter. They'll shoot you and laugh as your life's blood soaks the ground." Elizabeth took a steadying breath. "They're not worth it. You just told me this."

A smile flitted at the corners of his mouth. "You're concerned for me."

"I am not," she said, crossing her arms. "You are a festering canker."

"So you mean to heal me, then?" James asked.

"No poultice will draw out that poison."

James smiled wryly. "I'll give you that."

After a few moments of awkward silence, Elizabeth said, "I should leave. They'll be wondering where I've gotten to." As she headed towards the towpath, she heard the crunch of his boots following behind her.

"I'll walk you home." James paused to untie his horse, but Elizabeth had already reached the trail.

"No." Elizabeth stopped and faced him, the sun slanting in her eyes. "It's best that we part ways here," she said with genuine regret. "We are, after all, headed in opposite directions." When she rushed up the trail, she didn't dare look back.

*

Elizabeth slipped into the house and continued down the hallway, glad to see the stillroom door shut. She dashed up the stairs to her room. The click of the latch triggered relief. So much had happened this day, and she needed to sort out her churning thoughts.

A hesitant rap sounded on her door. "Elizabeth?" Isabel called. "Can I speak with you?"

Elizabeth started. "One moment." She wasn't sure she was ready to speak to her aunt just yet, but she could hardly turn her away. After taking a deep breath, she opened the door.

Isabel hesitated before entering. "Thank you." She wandered to Elizabeth's night table and idly picked up a ribbon curled on top. A strange smile passed her lips. Finally, she turned again to Elizabeth. "I owe you an apology for my harsh words. Your heart spoke true, and I should never have belittled you for it."

Elizabeth twisted her fingers and looked to the ground. A flood of warmth washed over her. "I should know my place better. I had no authority to speak on your behalf."

A ghost of a smile played over Isabel's mouth. "I don't stand on ceremony, child. Surely, you have discovered this for yourself?" She moved closer and searched Elizabeth's face. "'Twas fear and worry, nothing more. This was all my fault—Samuel should never have been placed in that position. There is much astir here in Warwick. I want you to remain clear of it. I'm afraid that it does not serve to draw attention to ungodly practises, however righteous they are."

Elizabeth swallowed the lump in her throat and nodded. Odd how her aunt's words mirrored James's. "I'll take care in the future."

Isabel smiled and reached up to touch Elizabeth's hair. "*Dark as the woods, maiden faire*," she quoted. "'Twas a line in a song that your grandmother sang when she dressed ribbons in your mother's braids." Isabel sighed. "Such an unusual shade. Nearly black, but not quite. Dark as the woods." She tipped Elizabeth's chin up so she could have a better look at her. "But your eyes are the same dark blue as your grandmother's. You remind me of her, mostly." Isabel smiled. "You're of my blood, child. I do not wish to see you come to harm."

Elizabeth closed her eyes, not realising how much she craved her aunt's kindness. "Thank you."

Isabel nodded and stepped away. "Jennet has supper waiting. Will you come?"

Elizabeth laughed, blinking away her tears. "Aye, I'd hate to come against Jennet. I'd run most afoul here in Ellendale." She studied her aunt. Isabel's colour was a touch sallow. Should she take the opportunity to ask her if all was well, whether there was anything she could do for her?

"What's the matter?"

Elizabeth shook her head. She'd only get defensive. No need to spoil this moment. "'Tis nothing."

"Very well," Isabel said as she crossed to the door. "Don't take long, then."

The door closed. Elizabeth looked down at her hands and traced the path where James's fingers had followed. A liaison with him would have ended poorly. She did well to have ended it.

James returned to the Chequer just as dusk set in. As he unsaddled Sovereign, Henry strode into the stables. James gave him a brief nod before putting away his gear.

"Where have you been?" Henry asked.

"Went for a ride." James reached for a brush and started running it through Sovereign's coat with brisk strokes. He made several passes before the horse tossed his head and took a step back. "Easy," James said, and grasped him by the halter. When the horse continued to agitate, James grimaced and eased the pressure.

"You were gone for a while," Henry said, his tone testy.

James turned his head slightly and noted Joshua hovering close. "Nothing to worry about."

Henry's attention flicked to the boy. "Give us a moment, lad." His jaw was set in a stubborn angle, and a muscle under his right eye twitched.

James waited until Joshua crossed the courtyard. "What's the matter?"

"Rand came."

"Sorry I missed him." *Not really.* He didn't need Rand rounding out his day. "What news?"

"Sir Richard increased the ale quarterages."

James stopped mid-stroke. "What?"

"He *doubled* them."

"Christ's teeth—that greedy bastard."

"Try smart bastard—*canny* bastard—and you'll be closer to the mark," Henry ground out. "He's squeezing the public houses, figuring that one or more of us receives the highwayman's custom."

"Can't be—not because of the robberies. That's too subtle even for Sir Richard. It's just another way to increase taxes, greedy bastards."

"Betwixt themselves, they're calling it the highwayman tax. Rand's words," Henry said tersely. "They expect that one of the innkeepers knows who he is and will spit him out if choked."

"Christ's teeth!" Even in his anger, James felt a grudging respect. "How did Sir Richard think of that?"

"He didn't. Hammond's idea, and Sir Richard signed the order quick enough." The twitch under Henry's eye increased. "In fact, he liked it so well that he made Hammond first lieutenant."

"Not captain? That must sting."

Henry slammed his fist into the post. "He's saving that honour for when he brings you in," he barked. "Damn me!" He began to pace back and forth like an agitated beast. "My inn is barely hanging on. No ale quarterages, no ale. How the hell will I afford this?"

"Will you just take some of the gold, Henry? It's all yours," James said. Who was he fooling? Charles was in exile, and nothing James did on the highway would alter that. "I'm sitting on a bleeding fortune, and what I want isn't for sale."

Henry faced James, nostrils flaring. "I will not take it. That's your play, not mine."

"Cut my pay, then."

"Damn right, and I don't need your blessing either," Henry said. "Give it up. The war is over, and nothing you do will change the fact that these Roundheads control our lives, from that horse brush you're holding to the ale that flows through my kegs."

"I will not accept that," James snapped and whipped the brush into the bucket. The tin rattled and nearly tipped. "If I could, I'd have gone back to Coventry, belly exposed, to take my kicks there. I am not a beaten dog. I will not stand by while long-faced hypocrites prattle about religion and godliness one moment and destroy a man the next. I will not accept that they can betray and still be rewarded in this life. I cannot believe that loyalty means nothing under this goddamned sky." With a growl, he kicked the bucket and sent it clattering across the straw. Sovereign whinnied and backed away.

Henry splayed his fingers through his grizzled hair. His rage dissipated, and he suddenly looked older than his forty years. "I hear you, lad, but the sooner you make your peace, the sooner you can get your life sorted. That matters more in the end. You're still young. Find yourself a good woman and sire a few sons." He laid his hand on James's shoulder. "I'll give you a tip—Mistress Stanborowe's niece is a fine lass. Pay a visit to Ellendale."

"Thanks," James muttered. Was he supposed to laugh or yell? He had already travelled many leagues along this road. He couldn't rein in now.

Chapter Nine

James's mood plunged even farther the next day when, upon returning from Kenilworth with the post, he found the courtyard clogged with dragoons and a backlog of incoming travellers. Angry shouting erupted from the stables, followed by slamming and the whinny of nervous horses. Had they found him out? A part of him urged flight, but he smothered it. He owed Henry more than that. *This Hart is no coward.*

James left Sovereign at the hitching post and hurried to the stables, clamping down on his rising alarm as he pushed his way through the garrison troops. When he reached the entrance, he halted in shock. Tools had been pulled from their hooks and scattered across the workbench and floor. Near the cistern, tipped bags of oats were soaking in a pool of spilled water.

Kit had planted himself in the centre and argued with one of the dragoons. "Master Hart will be spitting mad—leave those bridles alone." The lad tried to block them with the length of his shovel. "There, you've done it—a right tangle now. Drop those harnesses!"

"What's going on here?" James barked. "What madness is this?"

The dragoon whipped around and faced him. "We have orders to search every public house in Warwick for signs of the highwayman."

"You're looking in the wrong place. Moot Hill is to the south."

Hammond stepped out of the back room. A chill snaked down James's spine. What was he doing in there?

"We tried that, ostler," Hammond said. "I decided a change of tactics would serve our needs better." He tapped a horse switch against his thigh. A cold smile played over his dour features.

"Trust you to be behind this nonsense," James said. "There are two carriages full of thirsty and weary travellers waiting to pull into the Chequer while your men justify their pay. Unless they are allowed through, another inn will receive their custom. Tell me, Lieutenant, do you lie awake devising ways to ruin the livelihood of honest men, or is this a natural talent?"

Hammond's chin quivered, and when he responded, his tone was bleak. "If you have a care for your landlord, you'll watch your mouth, ostler."

James gritted his teeth. "Do what you must and get out."

"I'm not waiting for your permission."

James watched while the soldiers tore out drawers and pounded on the walls. They wreaked as much damage as crosswinds in a thunderstorm.

Kit sidled to James's side. "What are they doing?"

"Testing for hidden compartments," James said in a tight voice. There was only one compartment, and his life and possibly Henry's depended on Hammond not finding it. He prayed they wouldn't look behind the poster. James itched to join the dragoons into the tack room and distract them if they got too close to the stolen gold, but he forced himself to remain where he was. Hounds always sniff where the bone is buried.

Hammond came up beside James and surveyed the carnage like a general. With every crash and rip, his amusement deepened.

"How is our friend Ledbrook doing?" Hammond asked.

James narrowed his eyes. Now he understood. "Behind in his farm work, as I understand, thanks to ill health."

"There is a consequence for everything."

"It must be difficult for you," James said.

"How so?"

"Determined to convert everyone," James said. "Alas, the sweet women of Warwick are not so easily moved. Not even those from the south."

Hammond's jaw clenched. "I understand you've been away?"

"Aye, running the post to Kenilworth and back. The Chequer carries a licence."

"Kenilworth? Coventry lies in the same direction."

What was he on about now?

Hammond examined the end of his switch. "I understand you're from Coventry."

James shrugged. The soldiers were still in the back room. What was taking them so long? "Not these past eight years. Why your interest in Coventry? Sir Richard hasn't appointed you her constable has he? We'll be sorry to see you leave Warwick."

Hammond smiled. "You'll have the pleasure of my company for some time." He didn't speak for a few moments, as though he savoured the persistent rapping of his men. One shouted and James's blood froze. He braced himself, but no one came charging out of the back room.

"There's been a rash of malignancy coming from Coventry," Hammond continued. "We've been hearing rumours of a Royalist plot. Know anything about it?"

James laughed. "You're scraping the barrel. The good people of Coventry are more for Parliament than ever Cromwell was. Someone has sold you a spoiled haunch of mutton."

"So you haven't been there recently?"

"I have nothing there," James said, his annoyance increasing.

The dragoons finally left the back room and shook their heads. James released a slow breath of relief. There was something to be said for that blasted Oath of Allegiance.

Hammond turned to Kit. "Boy, fetch what the ostler has in his saddle bag." He turned to James. "Let's see what post the Chequer carries."

"If it will speed you on your way."

The boy returned shortly with the packet, but when he tried to pass the bundle to James, Hammond seized it. As he flipped through the stack of letters, his expression soured.

"Kenilworth, as I've told you. Are we finished, Lieutenant?"

Hammond threw the letters into the mud. He shoved past James and bellowed over his shoulder for his men.

"Saddle up, dragoons. Next public house." Before he left, he turned to James and tipped his hat to him.

*

James knew that the key to survival was to listen to his instincts. He had gone years without hearing any mention of Coventry, and now it repeated like an echo. Something was afoot, and he had waited long enough to answer Sir Piers's letter.

For the first time in eight years, James stood on the doorstep of Bideford Manor, home of Sir Piers Rotherham, Member of Parliament and former major of the rebel Foot. An iron-studded portal had guarded the rear entrance for three generations. Though the pale moon hung above the slate roof, the threshold remained in shadow.

What was he doing here, and how could he remain civil towards a man who had betrayed the crown?

Before he could change his mind, he knocked.

A middle-aged servant answered and held aloft a candle. Its flame illuminated a gaunt face and steadfast brown eyes. The servant's reaction changed from annoyance to surprise. "James Hart?"

"God save you, Emery."

"We did not think to see you, not after all this time."

"Nor I."

"Come in."

James stepped into the stone-tiled vestibule. The familiar scent of lye hit him right away. Two young maids stepped into the hallway and craned to see past Emery's shoulder. One held a fireplace shovel, her apron dusty with the ashes of banked fires.

"Perhaps I should return in the morning," James said. He hadn't given any thought to the hour and now wished he had waited. Sir Piers had often worked late into the evening, but it occurred to him this might have changed.

"That won't be necessary. My lord is in his private chambers. He sleeps even more poorly since he returned from war," Emery replied. The servant had always attended his duties without comment, but James sensed that something weighed on the man's mind. "Wait here. I'll let him know you've arrived."

James took a seat in the hallway and stared at the tiled floors. This was the same bench he had warmed when he first came to Bideford, a young man of sixteen wearing his best coat with his father's admonitions rattling in his head. The third plaque from the left still had a crack running diagonally. Above him, flush against the whitewashed wall, brass sconces reflected the golden tallow light. No smoky rush-lights for Bideford even now.

Nothing had changed.

James thought of Piers's letter. *I am resolved to rebuild my house and look to the future.* Perhaps he had read too much between those few vague lines. No matter what happened, he refused to beg the man's forgiveness for not following him down the path of treason.

Emery returned and motioned James to follow down the corridor. "I had not thought to see you again, given the circumstances. Our master was furious when he heard that you joined Northampton."

"The war divided us all."

"You can imagine my surprise when Sir Piers had me post that letter to you."

James stopped. "Out with it, Emery, what does he want with me and why now?"

Emery didn't break stride. He had always been tight-lipped on matters touching his master.

They reached the study and found the door slightly ajar. Emery gave a courteous rap before entering.

The scent of camphor hit James when he entered, a cloying, stifling scent that thickened the air. When he saw Sir Piers sitting by the hearth, James halted, startled at the change in the man. Once bluff and hearty, Sir Piers now appeared shrunken, lost within a velvet robe and wrapped in an embroidered blanket. Beside him, a steaming bowl of broth rested on an oval table.

"My lord." James struggled to hide his dismay.

"I have a quarrel to settle with you," Sir Piers said, his voice harsh and rasping. "What sorry manners did you learn in that Royalist army? I sent that letter weeks ago. Did you forget where Bideford was, or did something better occupy your time?"

The years fell away, and James was once again a young clerk reprimanded for his tardiness. "I couldn't think of your purpose."

Piers snorted and waved his hand in the direction of a chair. A wracking cough seized him, and it took a few moments before it subsided. "That is why the most prudent course would have been to come sooner. Answers are not divined otherwise." He took a sip of broth and sighed, cradling the bowl in his lap. James noticed the purple veins and spots colouring the man's hands. He thought he saw a small tremor, though it might have been a trick of the firelight. "I'm not sure why I ever put up with your unpredictable temperament. You made a poor clerk. Brilliant head for sums and figures but careless in your recording of them."

James recalled Piers shaking his ledgers at him and thundering, "Od's oath, lad! Good enough is not good enough for Bideford."

"As it happens, I've improved," James said. He glanced at the empty writing table, once covered with ledgers and quills. The Bideford crest, a pair of stags rising on their hind legs, was carved in the side panels. Above the desk hung the dour portrait of Sir Piers's grandfather, a stern figure placed there for the sole purpose of frightening the beholder into sobriety. "You successfully beat it into my head."

Piers grunted and drew the blanket to his waist. "You deserved several thrashings, if not a dozen. But I was too indulgent. I wonder at your father's wisdom in entrusting me with your education. Edward Hart always had high hopes for you."

James stiffened. "You honoured him when you took an interest in my future. You must regret that kindness now."

"For you or your father?" Piers asked. The corner of his mouth quivered into the first hint of a smile. "He begged me to consider you for my stables as a reward for your rebellious nature. I thought better of your abilities than mucking horses."

"And yet that is where I am now."

"So they tell me," Piers sniffed. "I hear you earned your commission in Northumberland's cavalry."

James exhaled. *Best get through this.* "Aye, my lord honoured me as third captain."

"He could have shown *me* more courtesy. He had no right poaching my household," Piers said. A frown gathered on his brow. "Inconsiderate whelp. Your duty was to me."

Duty. James chewed on the word. "A man must follow his conscience. You promised treason while my lord Northampton offered a king's favour and my honour intact."

Piers shrugged away the barb. "I passed your father in town the other day," he said, holding James's gaze. "I understand you haven't spoken to him since the war."

"I thank you for your interest, my lord." James curled his hand around the end of the chair's arm. "A man of your standing should not concern himself with the troubles between a yeoman and his son."

"Are you not prepared to make amends with him?"

"I'm afraid the matter is impossible."

"And yet we are here together, enjoying this late evening and a conversation, proof that men can settle their grievances—even I, a more staunch supporter of Parliament than ever your father was."

"Not in the beginning," James said, and his gut tightened. Every one of his father's rages against the late king remained with James like an infectious scab. *Damned ship's tax*, Edward would say between gritted teeth. *Do you see any harbours in Coventry? Despicable, greedy whoreson of a king.*

"You know he's been ruined—forced to sell off half his land to settle his debts. He never recouped the rents owed to him. Shunned by those who could have helped. 'Tis a shame to see him working the plough on his own."

James searched for a way to change the topic.

"Found himself neither here nor there," Piers continued. "You're not terribly different from your father, James. I wonder that you don't see that."

James felt as though he had been slapped. "Did you invite me here to discuss Edward Hart?"

Piers opened his mouth to reply, and instead a spasm seized him. He started to cough, a rattling deep in his chest. He reached for the now cool broth and took a sip.

James regretted his sharp tone. "You're ill."

"Aye, I admit I'm not well." Piers took a steadying breath. "Haven't been this past year. They offered me the mayorship of Coventry, but I turned them down. It is quite beyond me. Besides, I have no further interest in their politics."

James did not miss the trace of bitterness. "They were once yours."

Piers rested his head against the back of his chair and closed his eyes. James wondered if his chest pained him. When he spoke, his voice was little better than a rasp. "I did not support Parliament so the King could lose his head. Many of us had thought to demonstrate our desire for reform through unrelenting resolve. We hoped that the King, when faced with our remonstrance, would turn against his cravenly advisors and see reason."

"You could have trusted that the King knew his mind."

"Let's not argue that point," Piers said. He tipped his head to stare at the coffered ceiling. "The King should never have met his end on a scaffold. 'Twas an evil day for us all." Piers lifted his hand and rubbed his left temple. "I refused to judge the King. I exercised my privilege and announced that the seat of Coventry would not vote for such a travesty. For a reward, I found myself purged from Parliament and bundled off to the gaol with others who refused to sign. Though no one dared say that 'twas Cromwell who gave the order, it reeked of his politics." His lip curled, and he started to cough again. He waved James away when he rose to give him a hand. Finally, the spasm subsided. "A gift from the gaol, courtesy of that tyrant."

Anyone else and James would have felt vindicated. But with Piers, his sympathy increased with every moment. He had known Piers as a fair and honourable man, and he had been deeply disappointed when the man chose Parliament.

"You give too much credit to one man," James said.

Piers leaned forward, the rims of his eyes bloodshot. "If nothing else, heed me in this. Cromwell is not to be trusted. He speaks the golden words of an orator, and men are taken by the glory of his vision, but do not forget for a moment that he has the army at his back. If tested, who will they support, Parliament, who quibbled over their wages until the eleventh hour, or the man who marked the bill paid?" Piers coughed in his sleeve and shook his head. "What have we created in our pursuit for reform? We've exchanged a true king with an unnatural despot."

"Soft, I would not see you live out the remainder of your days in the Tower," James said.

"We were all betrayed," Piers said. He stared at his clasped hands resting on his stomach. "You know Colonel Edward Massey?"

"I know of him. He held Gloucester against us. Fifteen hundred to our twenty-five thousand." Not one of their finest moments.

"We served together during the war, then as gaol-mates thanks to Cromwell's deceit," Piers said. "Good man, a strong commander for his years. He escaped to Holland and now resides in the Orkneys. Were I younger and in better health, I would join him." Piers cleared his throat. "He's made friends in high places."

"How high, milord?" James's senses prickled.

"Have you never married, James?"

Startled at the change in topic, James frowned. "Nay, I have no family."

"No one depending on you?"

Although a pair of blue eyes came to mind, he regretted that he had only one answer. "Nay. Why do you ask?"

"A man must always protect those under his care, first and foremost. A father's love. A husband's duty." Piers sighed, and when he spoke again, James had to strain to catch what he said. "I've lost everyone in the war. Neither son returned, and I returned to find my wife dead of a fever."

James looked at his feet. "My condolences, my lord. 'Tis not easy to lose loved ones."

Piers's brow lifted. "Do not forget that. It changes things, casts the world in a different light. I've vowed that I will no longer remain ignorant and in denial."

The prickling at the back of James's neck intensified. He was surprised at the direction this meeting had turned and wondered if his chronic frustration wasn't the sieve winnowing new meaning from innocuous words. "I've lately come across a curious rumour of a Royalist conspiracy in Coventry."

"Where did you hear that?"

"An inconvenient constable."

Piers cleared his throat. "Does he have suspicions about who is involved?"

"Nay."

A weak smile tugged at the corners of Piers's mouth. He reached across to the table beside his chair and nudged a broadsheet towards James. "Read this."

It was a declaration, dated 29 March 1650, written by Sir Edward Massey and signed by eighty officers. Within seven pages, Massey had written an impassioned plea to all English Presbyterians to reject the new Commonwealth in favour of Presbyterian Scotland and the King.

"Where did you get this?"

"The Orkneys," Piers said. "Once in a man's life, he is given an opportunity to choose a different path. When it comes, know it for what it is, for you won't get another occasion for redemption." He lifted his head and held James's gaze. "I have one question for you, my lad."

"Aye?"

"Will you follow me this time?"

*

117

Elizabeth couldn't sleep. After many futile hours, she abandoned her twisted quilts and slipped out to the garden for fresh air. The moon shone so brightly that she didn't need a lantern. As she walked along the garden path, she heard a scuffle and froze. Then she heard it again. The hairs on the back of her nape lifted. "Who's there?"

Three feet away, the yews shivered before a figure rose from the hedges. "Peace, mistress." The full moon revealed an old woman, her shaky hand extended. "We seek refuge. By the grace of the Blessed Virgin, help us."

Elizabeth gaped at the apparition. Papists? She had not heard the kitchen door open, but her aunt appeared at her side.

"The Knot welcomes you," Isabel said. "Pray, be at ease. You have reached safety. How many are you?"

The woman's shoulders hunched forward. "Four." She turned and motioned towards the orchard. Dark shapes shifted, and Elizabeth watched as they became more substantial—a slight woman and a burly man with a bundle in his arms. As they drew closer, Elizabeth saw that he carried a sleeping child.

Isabel touched Elizabeth's arm, and the solid contact startled her. "Elizabeth, dear, help me get these good people inside."

"Cer—certainly."

Dazed, Elizabeth followed her aunt and the strangers into the kitchen, her mind working furiously. What happened to stern, disapproving Aunt Isabel, and from where did this new version spring?

"Take your ease. We'll get you warmed up soon enough." Isabel spoke as though it were a daily occurrence for people to crawl out of the hedges. When the man took a seat on the bench, Elizabeth was reminded of the last midnight caller she had seen at Ellendale.

"Niece, stoke the fire. The kitchen is quite chilled. Elizabeth? Did you hear me?"

Elizabeth snapped out of her thoughts. The newcomers were shivering and looked like forlorn night creatures caught by the light. "Aye, right away."

Jennet bustled in, carrying an armful of linens. Without breaking stride, she handed quilts to the strangers. "'Tis a good thing, after all, that I aired these."

Elizabeth sat back on her heels. Jennet too?

"What are your names?" Isabel asked the family.

"Nicholas Giffard from Stratford at your service. This is my mother, Joan, and my wife, Margaret." His clothes were filthy—black broadcloth dusted grey and lace collar barely recognizable as such. He looked down at the dark-haired child sleeping in his arms. "Our daughter, Emma."

In the firelight, Joan Giffard appeared wizened, with deep wrinkles carved on her face. Wiry hair escaped her coif, its once white cloth begrimed. Margaret Giffard sat near her husband, hugging a torn shawl. Elizabeth noticed the anxious glances directed towards her child.

"Why have you fled?" Isabel asked.

Master Giffard appeared reluctant to go on until Isabel nodded her encouragement. "The dragoons came for us a week ago. They were no longer satisfied with the papist tax. My father sent us to hide in the attic where we keep a priest hole." He looked away, his mouth twisting as though he struggled with the words. "I would have stayed. He's an old man. 'Tis not right that he should face them with only a servant boy." He took a deep breath. "But he made me swear to see our family to safety."

Isabel laid a reassuring hand on his shoulder. "Your father spoke wisely. You'd not help them with both of you being in the gaol."

The man nodded glumly. "They searched the house for us, not heeding my father's protests that we had left for London. When the house became quiet, the boy came to release us—his own face cut and bruised." His hands shook. "They accused us of another gunpowder plot. We travelled by night and took what shelter we could by day."

Gunpowder plot? The poker nearly slipped from Elizabeth's hand.

"We passed through the home of an old friend just outside Banbury," the old woman said. "'Twas he who instructed us to make for Warwick, giving us directions to your door. He told us we would find shelter at Ellendale and help to reach our kin in Staffordshire. He told us about the Knot."

Knot? Elizabeth left the strengthening fire and drew closer. She had listened to their story with growing alarm, and the significance of the woman's words did not escape her. A million questions crowded on the tip of her tongue, but the rasping cough that erupted from the sleeping child stilled them all.

Elizabeth stooped down to examine the girl, gently so as not to startle her father. The child's face appeared chalky, and her breath rattled in her

119

chest. When Elizabeth laid her hand on the girl's brow, she drew back in dismay. The girl's forehead blazed, and her skin felt dry like parchment. "This child is gravely ill. How long has she been this way?"

"A few days—she worsened last night. Now she won't open her eyes," Margaret Giffard whispered.

Isabel stepped closer to examine the child. Her expression remained shuttered. "We'll do what we can for her. Master Giffard, take your daughter upstairs. Jennet will show you the way."

"There was no plot," Margaret Giffard said suddenly, startling Elizabeth with her intensity. "We are not criminals. You'll hear all manner of vile things—none of them are true. Since you give us shelter and risk your good name, you must know this."

"We do." Isabel gently squeezed the woman's arm.

Criminals . . . plots. All this was too much for Elizabeth—she needed a moment alone to think. While Jennet and Isabel fussed with the Giffards, Elizabeth grabbed a candle and left the kitchen. The candle sputtered in its holder, sending the shadows fleeing down the long hallway.

She reached the stillroom and released a ragged breath. The glass jars winked in the candlelight, welcoming her at this strange hour. With the windows shut against the night air, the scent of old wood fermented with beeswax.

The herbal book waited for her on the table. She picked it up and touched its leather cover. Inside were remedies against boils, gout and ague, but what of heresy, papistry and danger?

A movement at the door caught her attention. Isabel stood at the threshold. After a moment, her aunt drew closer. The skin around her eyes was like a piece of fine linen stretched too thin. She glanced at the book Elizabeth held.

"Tell me what you would do." Her tone implied this was yet another test, an opportunity for Elizabeth to prove her skill, to choose the best physic for a combination of high fever and racking cough. But Elizabeth knew that wasn't what she was being asked.

The penalty for harbouring recusants was severe, and if found, all would be lost. Crippling fines, lands confiscated—Ellendale compounded. They could expect no mercy from Parliament. Her only home would once again be taken from her.

Elizabeth's heart pounded as another grim thought occurred to her. Being new to Warwick, it would only be a matter of time before they accused her of instigating this affair. Her father's role in the Crabchurch conspiracy would surface—impossible that it should not.

But the child's waxen face burned in Elizabeth's mind. What if there was no ill child, what would she do?

Elizabeth turned the herbal book and showed her aunt the page she had found. "Ground purslane seeds, treacle water and a decoction of tormentil with scordium. This shall lower the child's fever if she is not too far gone."

Isabel nodded, some of her tautness easing. "I've given it thought, and you may be right. Add the snakeweed powder. This is a desperate situation, and there are times when it's best not to rely on convention."

Chapter Ten

By the time Elizabeth returned with the tincture, they had stripped the child down to her chemise and settled her in a bed. The girl ceased her coughing and lay still against the sheets. Were it not for the occasional fluttering of lashes, Elizabeth would have feared the toddler had passed.

Margaret Giffard refused to see to her needs, even weakened by hunger and exhaustion, and sat gripping her daughter's hand. When Elizabeth prepared to give her the medicine, the mother blocked her.

"My daughter needs the attentions of a proper healer." Margaret turned her appeal to Isabel. "Your niece is young. What does a maid know of these matters? My daughter is very ill—she is my only child." Were it not for the tremor in the woman's voice, Elizabeth would have taken offence.

"Your daughter is in capable hands," Isabel replied. "Elizabeth's mother was a skilled healer—it's in her blood. She has my complete confidence."

Margaret's hold on her child did not lessen.

The solution came to Elizabeth without thinking. "I'll need your help. Hold your daughter up so I can give her the medicine. We shall do it together." Margaret stared at Elizabeth for a moment, then nodded. She raised the girl to a half-upright position.

Isabel stood by the headboard, observing in silence while Elizabeth administered the tincture. Though initially unresponsive, the child began to cough and sputter, and the clear liquid dribbled from the corner of her mouth. Margaret looked up sharply. Elizabeth pursed her lips and tried again. She reduced the flow and continued drop by drop until she succeeded in getting a full dose into her. Pleased, she met her aunt's gaze across the bed. With a satisfied nod, Isabel left her to her labours.

Elizabeth rolled up her sleeves and threw on an old apron. She did not count the hours she remained bent over the child, applying cold compresses and mixing plasters. As she applied the warm, sticky paste on the girl's chest to loosen the phlegm, the room filled with the sharp scent of mustard and mint. When she went to wrap her with a woollen strip, Margaret grabbed her wrist.

"What is this? She's feverish as it is."

"The plaster must remain warm and cover her chest. It will help. I promise."

Elizabeth watched the little girl in her fitful sleep. Her face was expressive, frowning as though in pain, her brow smoothing when it passed. Her damp curls clustered around her head, and Elizabeth wanted to touch them.

Jennet brought a broth rich with wild mushrooms. Margaret cradled her child's head against her breast while Elizabeth spoon-fed the liquid to her. Unfocused and confused, the little girl pried open her eyes and looked at Elizabeth for the first time. She then drifted back to sleep.

Yet even with their ministrations, the child worsened.

Elizabeth tried to shut out the fear blazing in Margaret Giffard's eyes and directed a stream of soothing talk to the toddler. She repeated every prayer her mother had taught her while she stroked the girl's forehead. As the night wore on, the child's breathing became shallower.

Margaret looked on with a white, anguished face and bent over her rosary. Elizabeth had never seen one before. She stared at it, wary lest its image burn into her mind, yet resisting the instinct to turn away. Here was a piece of illegal contraband in their home, brought in the open by this woman as though it was nothing more significant than a piece of jewellery. She was both curious and repelled. Margaret looped the chain around her clenched fists. The gold crucifix swayed and danced on the end of the wooden beads.

In the wildness of the night, with the little girl failing, Elizabeth grew desperate. She could not lose this child, who lay pale under the fitful candlelight. Incomprehensible that the girl would never feel the sun on her cheeks, no longer snuggle into her mother's breast or be hoisted in the air by her father. Margaret would turn to Isabel and say, "I told you so. Your niece was too young to care for my daughter. You should have known better. You should have helped her and not left her care to a novice."

The child should be improving, Elizabeth thought in defiance. She had done everything possible, given her every medicine and said every prayer. Even Isabel had been on hand to consult over the girl's treatment. She should not be failing. What had gone wrong?

Elizabeth stared again at the rosary in Margaret's hands. The woman's Hail Mary's filled her ears, forbidden, contentious—illicit. They hung in the air, cutting like discordant waves in opposition to the natural tides. She felt like a glass nearing its shattering point. Margaret continued to pray over the rosary, her fingers clutching one bead after another. Elizabeth wanted to scream. *Cease, woman. Put away that relic.*

A coughing fit seized the girl, a violent racking that snatched her breath. Elizabeth pulled her upright and gently massaged her back as the child fought against the membrane that choked her. Margaret looked on, frozen and useless. Eventually, the spasm subsided, and the child fell limp against the bolster, her cheeks twin spots of red against a sickly complexion.

Margaret moaned and buried her face in her hands. Her shoulders shook with silent sobs, and she slowly rocked back and forth, clutching the rosary to her heart. Elizabeth felt a stab of shame. How could she have thought to take the little comfort that remained to this fraught woman?

When did I become a Puritan?

Elizabeth gathered Margaret in her arms. The woman stiffened, but instead of pulling away, she buried her face in Elizabeth's shoulder.

"Emma needs a priest," Margaret said. The rosary slipped out of her hands and fell to the floor.

"There is none," Elizabeth replied with true regret.

"Emma must be anointed. I can't bear it…" Margaret whimpered.

Elizabeth looked at this desperate woman, at a loss as to how to comfort her. What would reassure her? She bent down and picked up the fallen rosary. The wooden beads were smooth in her hands. Where the malevolence in a wooden string of beads? What difference the wooden bowl she had mixed the tincture in, praying over it as she did? Both shaped from the same material as the tree stretched outside the bedroom window, both used to direct hopes and prayers. They were only different because someone said they were.

Elizabeth placed the rosary in Margaret's hands. "I will remain with you."

Into the small hours of the night, the two women held hands and kept their vigil. Elizabeth dug deep into the farthest reaches of memory and pulled out a song she learned from her grandmother, an embracing song of comfort and love. If nothing else, it would ease Emma's passing. She continued the verses until her voice was hoarse.

When the deepest shades of night began to fade, Elizabeth sensed a difference in Emma.

"Look, Margaret." The angry flush had faded from the child's cheeks, and her breathing seemed stronger. Elizabeth bent down, and although the girl's forehead was still warm, it had lessened just enough to give hope.

The mother checked her daughter's brow, and with a ragged breath, she nodded her agreement. She closed her eyes for a moment and covered her mouth with a trembling hand.

Margaret curled up beside her daughter. She brushed the child's cheek, a tentative touch. Emma stirred in sleep, one baby hand slipping under her cheek and the other flung near her mother's chin. Margaret bent down and kissed the tiny knuckles as a tear trickled down her hollow cheeks to pool at the corner of her mouth.

Elizabeth sank into a chair, overwhelmed. She had done it. Against all odds, she had saved this girl. Then she thought of her aunt. Had these people not found their way to Ellendale, they would be digging a stony grave for their daughter. Together she and Isabel had kept this family whole.

*

Elizabeth paused outside Isabel's door. She had left Emma with her mother to get some rest. But one thing remained for her to do.

She knocked, and her aunt bid her enter. The bed curtains were open, but Isabel had not yet risen. When she saw Elizabeth, she struggled to prop herself up on her bolster. "Is all well?"

"The child is resting easier," Elizabeth replied. She wrapped her arm around one of the bedposts and traced the pattern carved in the wood. Now that she was here, she didn't know where to start.

"You did well with the child," Isabel said. "I'm not above admitting that the snakeweed made the difference."

Elizabeth nodded, grateful for this admission. A day ago, this would have been enough. She looked down at Isabel's worn hand, spotted with age, and asked the question on her mind all night. "What's happening at Ellendale?"

Isabel reached across to her side table and picked up the silver brooch that she usually wore. "Know you what this pattern is?"

"Aye, an eternal knot."

"An ancient symbol of perpetuity. Our ancestors honoured its meaning, but today there are many who scorn symbols of any kind. In their arrogance, they see this as a new world with their designs free from the past. They would unravel the fabric of our traditions."

Elizabeth accepted the brooch and turned it over in her hand. She recalled her fascination with the knot's mystery even as a child. The design was often carved on markers: a high cross, a cornerstone or a monument.

"The entwined knot has no beginning or end. Our covenant cannot be broken," Isabel continued. "Our cause may have turned a dark corner, but the road moves forward and one day will come full circle."

"Strange to hear about the evils of Parliament from one who remained neutral during the troubles."

"I speak of Puritans, child. There is a difference," Isabel said gently. "And do not mistake staying clear of war with neutrality."

Elizabeth nodded. She was discovering a world of grey in Warwick.

"My husband's health was not sound when the war started," Isabel said. "He didn't have the luxury of openly supporting the King, not when we were ringed by Parliament. He protected us with his silence, though it galled him to do so."

Elizabeth looked down at her lap, understanding for the first time the source of Isabel's objection to her father's actions.

"The true struggle begins after the drums stop beating," Isabel said. "See where we have descended. Parliament has drunk deep of power, and theirs is an alarming transformation. From a babble of discordant voices all vying to be heard, now emerges one consistent roar. These Puritans have set themselves up as pope of a new religion, and they choke us with their sacraments."

Elizabeth hadn't forgotten what her aunt had said to the Giffards. "What is the Knot?"

Isabel smoothed the wrinkles in her sheet as though gathering her thoughts. "A network—a collective, if you will—bound by sympathy and a desire to stand for what is right. We offer sanctuary to those in need, be they Royalist or papist. Then we help them reach the next link in the chain towards safety."

Elizabeth's hand closed over the brooch, and its pin pricked her palm. The first stirrings of anger finally broke through her icy surprise. "Since my arrival, you have urged caution and berated me for my rashness. Now I find you engaged in this. What am I to think?"

Isabel sighed and folded her hands on her lap. "Your letter came as a shock. I learnt of my sister's death and your need within a sentence apart. I have to admit that I hesitated. At first, I thought, 'Impossible, she can't come to Ellendale.' There are people whose lives are at risk. If we shut our doors, they will never make it to the next safe house before the dragoons find them." She glanced away. "But of course, I couldn't turn my back on Mary's daughter—blood of my blood. Not when I open my door to strangers." Isabel's mouth pursed. "What is her nature, I wondered. We help more than Royalists, as you've discovered this night. Few can put aside their ingrained beliefs of right and wrong. The conscience of an implacable soul. That would be our undoing."

"Bart," Elizabeth said. "He was no relation to Samuel, was he?"

"That poor man," Isabel said. "He had barely escaped the dragoons. You saw the shape he was in."

"What happened to him?" A thought suddenly occurred to Elizabeth. "Hammond didn't find him when he arrested Samuel, did he?"

"Nay, praise be, or it would have gone worse for Samuel. Barton had already been taken to the next safe house. Henry Grant is one of us, as is—"

"James Hart." The puzzle snapped into place. What he must have thought of her, prattling about right and wrong.

Isabel's brow lifted a fraction. "How do you know James Hart?"

Elizabeth smiled and shook her head. "Enough confidences so early in the morning. It's of no account."

Isabel took Elizabeth's hand and held it between both of hers. "What I need to know is whether you will help our cause. Speak your conscience, and tell me what you would do."

Elizabeth thought about the Giffards, lost and desperate. Decent people should never be reduced to hunted animals. "Your cause is mine."

*

127

Standing behind Piers's chair, James had a clear view of the five gentlemen collected in the Bideford study. Before they arrived, Piers had whispered, "Keep to the background, my lad. These are powerful men, and I would fain they not ill-use you."

Like vacant pigeons, three flocked close to the peacock of the group, Colonel Blount. Cavalier. The derogatory name suited the man perfectly. Blount sat in the chair across from Piers and showed off his polished boots, one positioned for good effect before the other.

But it was the fifth man who drew James's attention. Nathaniel Lewis was the prince's factor in the Midlands and a barrister of Lincoln's Inn. He stood apart from the others and resembled a brooding raven. His sleek black hair brushed his shoulders, and his dusky complexion hinted at a Welsh heritage. He wore a doublet of embroidered linen, the sleeves embellished by a row of buttons, each worth a small fortune.

"Welcome to Bideford, Nathaniel," Piers said. "Blount," he addressed the other gentleman with a curt nod.

"Rotherham," Blount replied with barely a glance at James. Addressing Nathaniel Lewis, he said, "With all due respect, barrister, I still don't see why we had to meet here."

"Bideford manor is conveniently located and has the distinction of being above reproach," the man answered. "The authorities would not suspect such a gathering in the home of a Parliament supporter, especially one as distinguished as Sir Piers."

"You needn't remind me of that," Blount said. "I had not thought ever to pay court to rebels. I would have preferred to see you in a dungeon, not a study." When he laughed, as if on cue, the others surrounding him chortled.

James gripped the back of Piers's chair. He had expected an initial show of coldness, but not this open disrespect. He burned to call them out on their rudeness, but he had agreed to keep to the background no matter how much it chafed.

"I was in a gaol," Piers coughed, offering no better proof. "This is why we are here. A government who restrains their appointed representatives is not just, and I will not continue to support them."

"Shame you didn't realise that before matters advanced as they did."

During this exchange, James observed Nathaniel Lewis. The man leaned against the mantel, impassive. Instead of defending their host, the barrister behaved as though the conversation merely revolved around the innocuous life of bugs. James had not failed to note the deference Blount paid Lewis. These lobcocks were eager to curry favour with the prince. Who better than the prince's agent to rein them in? Typical lawyer. *What do you expect from pond scum?*

"Before we start, I would know who that man is." Blount nodded to James.

Piers frowned. "He is my man and no concern of yours, save that his allegiance is beyond question."

Nathaniel Lewis toyed with a black onyx ring on his finger. "On the contrary, our enterprise depends on discretion."

"Is my word insufficient?" Piers replied with a sternness that James hadn't heard in years. He found that he missed it.

"Normally, no, but we are one slip away from the Tower and a noose."

Piers snorted. "Meet James Hart, former captain of the Earl of Northampton's Regiment of Horse."

"Indeed?" Nathaniel's brow lifted. He held James's gaze for a moment, then nodded. "An illustrious unit." He turned to their host with a slight bow. "Please accept my apologies, but these are troubled times, and we must be certain."

"And you, barrister?" James said. "How do we know that you're not working for Whitehall? You may be using the King's name in vain." The man's arrogance grated on his nerves. "These are troubled times."

Nathaniel smiled. "Excellent question." From inside his coat, he brought out a green velvet purse, then shook out a small gold coin. He held it between thumb and index finger before tossing it to James.

James turned it over in his hand. It looked like a gold unite, though shinier, as if newly minted. The late King's head was stamped on one side, and on the reverse, a pair of initials, *CS*, replaced the coat of arms. "What is this?"

"A tongue token and proof that my directive comes from the Prince of Wales himself," Nathaniel said. "Does that satisfy you?"

James tossed the coin back. Nathaniel proved equally adept at catching it. "For now."

"Now that we've established our battle lines, shall we press on to more important business?" Nathaniel said. "The prince embarked for Scotland and should land by Midsummer's Day. He has reached an accord with the Scots. In exchange with agreeing to sign their Presbyterian Covenant, Charles Stuart will be crowned King of Scotland in Scone."

James started, doubting his hearing. Scotland?

"What is this?" Blount exclaimed. "This is highly outrageous."

In this, James had to agree with Blount. The Scots had betrayed the late King by turning him over to Cromwell and his New Model Army in exchange for a Judas payment of one hundred thousand pounds. There had to be a mistake. Why would Charles bind himself to this? James stared at Nathaniel, a sour taste in his mouth. *Advisors.*

"What of the English crown?" Blount sputtered. "'Tis his birthright."

"As is Scotland," Nathaniel replied. "With the Scots backing his claim, England must soon be his."

"Are we all to become Presbyterians?"

"'Tis a reasonable arrangement," Piers said.

"Says the Presbyterian and former Roundhead," Blount sneered. "What of the Duke of Lorraine or the Prince of Orange? Surely, the French can be persuaded."

"Regretfully not. Neither Germany nor Denmark was receptive to our overtures," Nathaniel said. "We even sent envoys to Pope Innocent, but to no avail. Shudder if you will. As you can see, the Scots are our only hope."

"Are we then to bow and scrape before those turncoats?"

"There is no other viable choice," Piers said. "Ireland is being carved up by Cromwell while France offers nothing more than sympathy. Clearly, this marks our monarch as pragmatic, a trait sadly missing in his sire. We all must agree this is an improvement."

"Why? Because he's willing to negotiate his morals?" Blount said.

"Life is a negotiation; death is not," Piers snapped.

Nathaniel raised his hand to still the commotion. "No matter the alliances he forms, Charles Stuart is our rightful sovereign, and we owe him our allegiance. He is most desirous of your devotion and hopes for an affectionate welcome from his *English* subjects when he claims this throne. I assured him that I would sound out notable families for their pledge. Other factors have been dispatched to London, Scilly, Cornwall, Devon and Dorset."

"What does he need?" Piers asked.

"Men, weapons, enough gold to outfit an army," Nathaniel said. "We need to mobilise quietly, even to raise sufficient men to dispatch to Scotland—loyal men who can act as a buffer between the Scots and our monarch."

"You ask a great deal, barrister," Blount said. "We are in a difficult situation. Parliamentary militia is everywhere, cutting us off from one another."

"If you are isolated, 'tis because Parliament recognises the importance of the Midlands."

"Still," Blount pressed, "we are under extreme scrutiny. We can't scratch our balls without someone enquiring if we have a godly itch."

"And still you managed to arrive here unawares," Nathaniel said. "I compliment your resourcefulness."

"It was not easy," Blount grumbled, ceding the point. "And there are other considerations."

"Such as?"

"Family obligations." Blount tugged at his jowls. For the first time, James realised the man scoured for words. "I have lands to safeguard and pay heavy fines to keep them intact. Next time I won't be given the privilege of bankrupting myself. 'Twill all be handed over to the meanest wretch."

James couldn't take this self-interest any longer. What of the men who had marched under the King's banner, who had fought shoulder to shoulder against traitors for six long years? They had given their life for this cause without expectation of lands or riches. James had buried enough of them in blood-soaked fields. "I have a great deal more to protect than a flock of sheep," he said, stepping away from Pier's chair. "'Tis my neck, and I would not see it stretched, but I will see justice restored or risk my life in trying."

"You have an outspoken servant, Piers," Blount said.

"If he offends your ears, then you had better leave," Piers said. "He does not offend mine."

Blount scowled but remained in his seat.

James saw an opportunity to press his advantage. "Truth should not offend an honest man, my lord. Warwickshire is in the heart of England, and our sovereign will succeed or fail by the degree of support we can muster. Are we to send Master Lewis back to him with reports that Warwickshire is beaten, that our sheep have more courage?"

Blount's expression darkened. "What of the Scots, then? Will we bow to their Presbytery?"

"We bow to our King," James snapped. "If joining him in Scotland will restore the monarchy, so be it." A gust rattled the windowpanes, startling everyone. For James, it served as a reminder that outside raged the true storm.

Piers sighed. "I am the last of my line." He leaned against the arm of his chair and raised his head to the picture above the desk. "Both my sons were killed in the war. I have nothing more to lose." He coughed in his handkerchief and closed his eyes as the fit subsided. "You have my support, Master Lewis. I am past bearing arms, but you are welcome to anything else in my power to give."

Nathaniel nodded, his dark eyes triumphant. "What of yourselves?" He turned to Blount and his colleagues. "Can we be assured of your support, or should our sovereign look to others for friendship?"

Blount's mouth pursed in a tight line. The pigeons averted their eyes, waiting to gauge the direction of the wind. Finally, he nodded. "Aye, you have our support."

"Captain?" Nathaniel asked. He met James's gaze, and his expression hinted of a smile.

James drew from his coat a weighty purse and threw it on the table. "There's my answer."

*

James sat in a dim corner in Coventry's Fox and Hound. The room filled with travellers arriving in twos and threes with the dust of the road clinging to their boots. He hadn't been here since before the war. The landlord cast sideways glances, trying to place him, but the dawning of recognition hadn't yet replaced the man's curious frown. Had he changed that much in all these years? He should be more surprised if he hadn't.

A table of well-dressed rakehells drummed their fists and demanded a cure for their raging thirsts. As James sipped his ale, he considered the group. Except for their fancy waistcoats, any one of them could have been a reflection of his younger self. What was it about Coventry that brought out the worst in a young man?

James motioned for the serving maid. "Another ale and a glass of sack." A few minutes later, Nathaniel Lewis settled into the seat across from him.

"Good evening, barrister. You're late."

"Odd, I considered you early."

When Nathaniel raised his hand to hail the serving maid, James lowered it. "No need."

The wench returned, balancing the glasses on her tray. "Sack and another ale." She slipped the pale yellow drink in front of Nathaniel.

James smiled at Nathaniel's surprise and tossed the girl a threepence. He considered it worth the expense to keep one step ahead of the man.

"My thanks." Nathaniel nodded his appreciation. "Acceptable vintage." He glanced around the room, his attention lingering on the full tables. "Is there a quieter place where we can savour our drinks?"

James leaned back in his chair. "I assure you, we have more privacy here than any room the landlord might offer."

"I fail to see how."

"Plain sight, barrister," James said. "Here, we're invisible, surrounded by other patrons and with sufficient noise to muffle our words. The moment we retire to the back, we whet everyone's curiosity."

"I see—a master in deception," Nathaniel said and took another sip from his glass. "Why did you want to meet?"

James thought of a number of ways he could answer but decided in favour of bluntness. "What really brings you to Coventry?"

"Were you not paying attention?"

A wry smile twisted across James's mouth. "Solicitor, you're what—my age?"

"Likely."

"Which battles have you fought in?"

"How is that relevant?"

"Answer the question."

"None," Nathaniel admitted.

"I didn't think so." James scratched his chin. "I can't imagine you giving up your luncheons or your boating parties along the Thames."

"You have an issue because I haven't slogged alongside three thousand foot soldiers?"

"Let me tell you what will happen since you haven't lived through this first-hand." James leaned closer, no longer amused. "We won't win this through the nobles. You heard Blount. Few will risk their land unless assured of success. Men like him are bred for one goal—to pass the family estate down to the next generation."

"Ah, but you've missed something." Nathaniel carefully placed his glass on the table. "I'm a student of history and see a different possibility. This is a chance to improve one's fortune. Such an opportunity only presents itself once in several generations." Nathaniel drained his glass, then held up two fingers to the serving maid before he continued. "Now Blount is a middling landowner, his holdings scattered throughout Warwickshire. He boasts two thousand acres of land, a hundred tenant farmers and at one time, an income of four thousand a year. His sons can only hope to advance the family interests through advantageous marriages, but their prospects, frankly, are limited."

"Your math bores me. Get to the point."

Nathaniel scanned the men around them before continuing. "When our Scottish friend reclaims his father's seat, the loyal will secure their fortunes."

"Then why didn't you attempt to secure yours when the late King sounded the muster bell?"

"Does it matter? I am here now."

"It matters."

Nathaniel toyed with his onyx ring. "I thought to watch and wait. My profession is resilient and can serve either side equally well."

"Eight years is a long time to wait and watch."

Nathaniel tipped his glass to him. "I am one of the best barristers amongst the Inns of Court."

James suspected as much, but somehow, spoken aloud and confessed with such ease, the words grated like steel against stone. Charles deserved better than this.

"And you are driven by purer motives?" Nathaniel said. "Admit it, clerking for a country gentleman didn't have the same appeal as being an officer in His Majesty's army. Your time studying in Oxford, hobnobbing with the quality, must have sharpened your ambition."

James knew when someone was trying to divert his attention. He had done it often enough to good effect. "You never answered my question. Why act now?"

At that moment, a pair of dragoons arrived at the inn. They shook off the rain from their cloaks while surveying the crowd. One drew the landlord aside.

James loosened the dagger at his belt. Dragoons in an inn rarely boded well, and neither of these two appeared thirsty.

Nathaniel glanced over his shoulder. "I see." He took a sip of his drink and studied James. "It wouldn't serve for them to find the Highwayman of Moot Hill, would it?"

James drew in a sharp breath. "How did you deduce that?"

Nathaniel smiled. "I connect things that others fail to see. A beetle, a rock and a stalk of grass are all related if you know where to look."

"I'm curious to hear your logic." James glanced at the dragoons. They were still questioning the landlord.

"I had an interesting correspondence with our exiled friend when he first engaged my services," Nathaniel said. "He suggested an acquaintance with a few well-positioned families who were still in sympathy with his plight, but most curious, he also mentioned you, though he couldn't be sure if you had survived the war or not."

"Me?"

"You did a service for him once—helped him elude his father's enemies and escape to Cornwall. He hasn't forgotten it."

"Why didn't you mention this at Bideford?"

Nathaniel tilted his half-empty glass and admired the colour of the liquid. "Knowledge is currency."

James quirked a brow. "You've told me about the stone and the blade of grass, but I don't see the beetle."

Nathaniel flashed his teeth in a smile. "Along with praising you for your horsemanship and being a master of disguise, our friend referred to his Cornwall journey as a highway adventure. On its own, this meant nothing, but since I've come to the Midlands, all I've heard about is this highwayman, and I've kept dwelling on our friend's correspondence."

"That's your beetle? Looks more like an ant to me."

"I've made discreet enquiries," Nathaniel said. "I would wager my fortune on it."

A burst of laughter from the table of rakehells interrupted them. One of the dragoons nudged his companion and pointed to the young blades. They continued their drunken boasting, oblivious to the approaching trouble, until a soldier hauled the loudest to his feet. The young man balked, hurling insults at the top of his lungs. His friends tried to shield him but drew back when the dragoons drew their swords. He looked wildly around the room but found no support. As the Roundheads herded the young man from the tavern, many patrons pretended to look away.

"You asked, Captain Hart, why act now?" Nathaniel nodded to the soldiers. "*That* should never have been allowed to happen."

James met his level gaze. "I head south to Oxford tomorrow. You'll have your cavalry unit."

Chapter Eleven

Oxford stood halfway between Warwick and London but centre to the Royalist cause. During the war, James had spent his winters quartered at the Bear Inn, a staunchly Royalist establishment that sprawled along Albert Street. Though the Bear no longer publicised its political leanings, little else had changed.

James settled in one of the private rooms and waited for Maud, landlady and sole owner. A long table stood in the centre with a half-empty flagon of sack. The chamber was full of shadows made longer by the low fire in the hearth. James recalled the first time he had been in this room. The old Earl of Northampton, Spencer Compton, had sat at that very table with Prince Rupert, their commander and the King's nephew, while they mapped out the spring campaign that first year of the war. James had been forced to stand for three hours, waiting for the dispatches that would result from that meeting.

James had listened as Northampton gave counsel to the King's nephew. Others piped in with their advice, but Rupert's interest was keenest when the earl spoke.

Finally, Northampton had drawn James over to Rupert. "Lieutenant James Hart—the finest scoutmaster I have, Highness. There's none who can get the best out of a worthy steed. He'll bring a reply by daybreak tomorrow. You have my word."

"Return with a response from our governor in Banbury," Rupert had said, handing the packages to James, "and you'll be as high in my esteem as you are in Northampton's."

And he had, earning the commission of captain. Once, that had been enough—to ride under the King's standard towards a grand adventure, grabbing accolades and a coveted promotion where he could. That naive man had been left behind at Naseby.

The door slammed against its hinges and startled James from his thoughts. Maud paused in the doorway, hands on her hips. A brown braid threaded with silver hung down her linen jacket, and an apron was swathed across her hips. "You haven't changed," she said, her voice husky, calling to mind earth and peat smoke.

James rose to his feet. "And you're still a prize." Maud had always been a handsome woman with generous curves, and the years had only ripened her.

"Where have you been?" She pinched his cheeks, unabashed, as though he were an untried lad of fourteen.

"Warwick, of course," he chuckled, and she rolled her eyes. "How have you been keeping, Maud? Remarried yet?"

"And give the Bear to some slob along with my virtue?" Her laugh was deep and rich. "God rot them, no one's getting the benefit of my sweat and toil. What of you? Settle down yet?"

"I'm no catch these days." James grinned for Maud's benefit.

"Liar." She chuckled and leaned against the table. "So . . ." She traced her finger along its edge. "How's Henry Grant?"

Same Maud. "Still pining for you."

"Did he ever marry?"

"Nay, you spoiled him for it."

"A pox on him, then. He should have spoken up when he had a chance." She placed her hands on her hips again. "Are you here on Henry's business?"

"Nay, he'll split a gut when he finds out."

"How can I help?"

"I'm meeting some friends here. I'd appreciate it if you sent them back here and kept the curious away."

"When?"

"Anytime now." James smiled at her grimace. "We'll be no trouble."

Maud snorted. "How many?"

"Hard to say." James rubbed his stubbled beard. He had spread the word to his old troop, man by trusted man, yet there were no guarantees.

"We'll play it as it rolls, luv. I'll keep an eye out for you." Maud shut the door behind her.

James paced the room, pausing long enough to stir the logs in the fire. He leaned against the mantel and stared into the flames as they licked to life. He needed these men. Nathaniel had sent James a message that Parliament had appointed Cromwell as commander-in-chief and was mustering an army against Charles in Scotland. With Parliament aligning their forces, Charles needed loyal supporters. James had to win these men for him.

A lantern clock chimed, and when the seventh bell faded, three men arrived.

"Lieutenant Roger Cantrell reporting for duty." He was a lean, wiry man with an honest smile. "Ready to send these Roundhead buggers to hell."

"Cheers to that," James said and slapped him on the back. He had found Roger a week ago in Banbury, working a sleepy smithy with a lone draught horse and a rusted harrow. The man had been eager to join the moment James tossed a bag of gold on his anvil and promised to outfit a unit properly.

Roger pulled forward the other two. "Look who I found loitering by the stables."

"Jack Davis, Stephen Sheffield—keeping out of trouble?" James said, glad to see his junior officers. Roger had been confident that he could win them.

"Not if we can help it, Captain," Davis said, removing his cap and revealing his stock in trade, a crop of sunny curls. He had been trumpeter of James's old unit, the youngest officer in the troop. Davis had always looked innocent—to the detriment of those invited to a game of dice.

"You still a glover?"

"Nay, I work in the Stratford drapery now," Davis winked, adding, "And popular with the patrons."

"Nothing's changed." James turned to the other officer, their cornet. "Sheffield, good to see you."

"Captain." Sheffield nodded. A sombre man, he always gave James the impression that his head was full of gears and machinery. Once, having asked what was on his mind, James found himself sitting through a lengthy explanation of pulleys and ropes. "I'm a journeyman saddler now," Sheffield announced, still able to anticipate James's next question.

"Where's Norbreck?" James asked.

Roger grimaced. "Reconciled with his Roundhead in-laws."

James shook his head. One good man down.

Within the hour, others began to arrive, and by the time Maud brought ale and platters of beef, the last man pulled up a stool. James took stock of their numbers. Only a quarter of their former strength. The absences rankled. Far too many had accepted the new reality.

As they ate and caught up with one another, James leaned back in his chair and studied their faces; what he saw troubled him. In a few, he saw curiosity, but most held their reservations like a shield. A number even avoided his gaze.

What had happened to his old troop—the men who carried their pride as a banner? They had only come out of loyalty to him, willing to hear what he had to say yet not convinced all the same. He had to light a fire under them—to secure their loyalty for Charles. His only chance was to rekindle their hatred for the rebels.

Instead of rising, James remained in his seat. When he spoke, he moderated his voice just loud enough for the farthest man to hear. "The old Earl of Northampton, my lord Spencer Compton, handpicked many of us for his Regiment of Horse," he began. "He had been the finest horseman I knew. Before the war, the earl kept the best stables in Warwickshire, and during the war, the best cavalry."

The first smiles began to spread around him. Men leaned in a little closer.

"Who remembers our first engagement at Edgehill?" James rose to his feet. "We were eager to prove our valour, quick to charge, but unclear as to what to do after." That earned a few chuckles. "Like any good father, the earl took us in hand and taught us to focus—to win the field. We owe him a great deal, and I, my commission and the privilege of leading this troop. Most of you have been with me from the beginning."

James threaded his way around the room and met the eye of every man. "Who has forgotten Hopton Heath? Roger do you remember?"

"Aye, Captain, I haven't forgotten." Roger looked as grim as the others.

"The rebels were no match for our gunners, and our cavalry owned the field," James said. "Victory would have been complete except for one ill moment." He paused. "Sheffield, do you remember that day?"

"Aye, Captain. My lord Northampton was swept from his horse and captured."

James nodded. "The rebels demanded his capitulation—no different than today when they demand obeisance in exchange for our bread." His lip curled, bitterness sharp in his mouth. "And what was my lord's response to those scoundrels who demanded his honour? What were his final words?" James stood in the centre, surrounded by his men, whose heads were bowed. "'I scorn to take quarter from such base rogues and rebels.'"

Each man knew this. Before every battle, this had been their rally cry—their badge of honour. "My lord forfeited his life rather than bend his knee to these rebels," James said. "And instead of returning the earl's remains with due respect, the buggers tried to ransom the body in exchange for their bloody artillery pieces!" He stopped before Davis. "What did my lord's son, the third earl, do? Did he capitulate to their demands?"

"He refused," Davis said.

"And the traitorous bastards paraded his body through the streets of Derby, no better than a flea-bitten cur." James stood, shoulders squared while he raked his gaze over each of them. *No quarter.* "These are the same thieves who have stolen our country from the rightful heir. These are the same traitors who choke us with their Oath of Allegiance, who grind our self-respect into the dirt. They have held us hostage, just as they held the earl's body hostage. If we capitulate, who will restore our honour? No ransom is high enough. Our honour *will not* be corrupted by maggots."

All eyes were riveted on him.

"A week ago, our sovereign landed in Scotland. Two days ago, Cromwell set out with sixteen thousand men. He thinks to chase our rightful king."

"God save him," someone called out.

"Loyal Englishmen will save him," James said. "Cromwell marches north with a token force to prove his manhood. Mark my words—the Roundheads will be weakened and limping back before winter. Consider this our time to gather strength and make preparations to join our king in the spring. If every man recruits another trooper, his equivalent in spirit and resolve, we will show these usurpers our mettle."

Gone was their reticence. Their eyes gleamed, and every man sat straighter in his chair.

"I have never forsworn my oath to the crown, nor will I fail our true sovereign now." James braced both hands on the table and leaned forward. "Who's with me?"

A cheer of agreement rippled through the room. Someone started pounding on the table with his fists, and others immediately joined. Their steady beating sounded like a bass drum.

James smiled and caught Roger's eye. The blacksmith rose to his feet and saluted.

"Aye, Captain. The Third Company will ride again."

*

Elizabeth waited at the butcher's stall, fretting at the delay. Soldiers roamed the market, travelling in packs of twos and threes. Every subtle movement alarmed her. She had to remind herself to breathe.

Why were there so many?

An agonising fortnight had followed since the Giffard's arrival at Ellendale. Rumours of raids close to Warwick forced them to arrange for the family's departure, even though Emma still needed attention.

The butcher's line moved slowly. Elizabeth shifted from one foot to the other, trying to peer past the shoulders blocking her view.

"Good morrow, mistress." Henry Grant appeared in the line behind her. He had switched his apron for a hat and coat, and both looked ill-placed on him.

Elizabeth smiled, relieved to find a friendly soul. "Do you often come to market? I have not seen you here before."

Henry snorted. "Not if I can help it. I'd rather stay with my paying customers than part with my hard-earned coin. My ostler usually undertakes this mission of pity, but he's only just back from Oxford."

Elizabeth itched to press Henry for more information, but the innkeeper had already moved past the subject.

"Lines make me tetchy." Henry craned his head and raised his voice for all to hear. "Others may enjoy waiting on *caw*-handed blunderbusses, but Henry Grant is not one of them."

The butcher's head popped up. His bushy eyebrows drew together and merged in the middle.

"You included, Merrell." Henry waggled a finger at him. "Step to it, man, I haven't got all day."

"Mind your manners, Grant."

Henry waved his hand as though swatting a horsefly. He turned again to Elizabeth, his half-moon eyes appraising. "I heard your aunt was very ill this past fortnight with the fever. I hope she's recovered?"

A few people shifted closer to catch Elizabeth's reply. She measured her words carefully. "Thank you for your concern. The fever came upon us like an unexpected guest and alarmed us greatly." A few people didn't even bother to feign discretion. "She is still quite weak and will not be able to take a turn beyond our kitchen door for several more days."

"Glad to hear she's on the mend. Your aunt expressed a desire to visit friends in Worcester. Let her know that I'll call on her at week's end. Depending on the clime, the trip may suit her."

So the Giffards were for Worcester. "That will favour us well."

"In the meantime, come by the inn, and I'll send you home with a dish of marrow." Henry had managed to send extra victuals to Ellendale, as it would not have served for the butcher to wonder at their need for additional meat. Henry's attention shifted to the eavesdroppers standing close. He tipped his hat to them, and they finally turned away.

Finding herself next, Elizabeth stepped up to place her order. "A link of sausages, if you please."

Henry crowded beside her. He braced his hands on the counter and glared at the butcher. With Henry leaning in and Merrell planted behind the stall, they resembled a hoary lion squaring off against a grizzled bear. "What's the meaning of this delay, Merrell? Where's young Boddington? Not like you to indulge your apprentices, being the cheap bastard you are."

"Piss off, Grant."

"I don't think I will." Henry dug his heels in. "Go on, explain why you've done away with your help. Don't we pay enough for your mutton shanks? I know I do. Shaving off a bit more profit, are we?"

The butcher growled. Elizabeth would have taken a step back were it not for the people crowding behind her. She was aware of the meat cleaver that Merrell clutched and the fresh blood muddying his apron. He slammed the cleaver down.

"For your information, Grant, they called the lad to attend an emergency. His mother was in a nervous distress after dragoons ransacked their lodgings last night. Tore apart their parlour and made a shambles of their storerooms. *That* is why I am short an apprentice and why you, meddling old goat, must wait your turn."

A coldness curled around Elizabeth's heart.

Henry's bluster evaporated. "Dragoons, you say? What happened at the Boddingtons'?"

"Damned if I know—beggin' your pardon, mistress." The butcher nodded to Elizabeth, finally remembering his manners. "Will that be all?"

"Aye." Elizabeth fumbled the coins when she handed them over. She tucked the sausages in her basket without a second glance.

"Remember me to your aunt," Henry said, and their eyes met.

"I will. God save you both."

Elizabeth stepped away from the stall, now in a greater hurry to return to Ellendale than before. She hastened through the market, not even pausing to exchange a few words with the bookseller, Master Ward, who tipped his hat to her as she passed. Soldiers congested the haberdasher's market, slashes of russet blazing against the grey and brown cloaks of the citizenry. Elizabeth weaved her way against the current of people going about their business.

The raids had reached Warwick. Were they searching for the Giffards? It hardly mattered—a search for any reason did not bode well when there were papists at Ellendale.

Elizabeth reached the main square and spied Lieutenant Hammond at the centre of an eddy of dragoons. He had often sought her out after church, wanting to hear what she thought of the sermon. Between his warm attention and the craned heads turned in their direction, Elizabeth suspected that the man harboured an affection for her. It occurred to her now that instead of hurrying past him, she might glean valuable information. She owed it to the Knot to try.

When Hammond saw her approaching, his expression lightened, and he closed the distance between them.

"Mistress Seton. A pleasure to see you this day."

Elizabeth willed her hammering heart to settle so her voice wouldn't tremble. She returned the smile. "And you, sir."

"I am looking forward to Sunday next. I trust you are as well. The vicar promised more on the subject of original sin."

"Yes, yes, of course," Elizabeth said. "We should all guard ourselves against temptation and trust in the Lord." How she hated these platitudes. The words were chalk in her mouth.

"I am so encouraged to hear you say this, mistress," Hammond said, inching closer. "A godly man is a prize, but a true godly woman is wealth untold."

Elizabeth's mind churned as to how she could turn the conversation back to Hammond's investigation. "The fine weather has brought everyone out to market. Even the garrison has emptied, it seems." She made a show of looking around. "Has anything happened, Lieutenant?"

"Nothing to concern you." He didn't bother to look over his shoulder. "How is your aunt? I understand she is ill."

Elizabeth lowered her lashes. "She's recovering, but slowly. Already she misses having news of the community. I try to keep her apprised as best I can." Her gaze lingered on the dragoons who passed them. When she turned again to Hammond, her smile deepened. "I'll be most grateful to hear what is afoot."

Hammond coloured. "It would not be appropriate to discuss it here. Perhaps I can call on you and your aunt. It would be my pleasure to engage in stimulating discourse for her convalescence."

Elizabeth realised her mistake too late. "I'm afraid my aunt is still too weak to receive guests," she said quickly. "But thank you for the offer. I know how busy you are. The garrison would be wandering the wilderness without you."

Hammond squared his shoulders, clearly pleased by the compliment. "My duty is to Warwick. The county will be a paradigm for the Commonwealth, second only to the capital."

As Hammond spoke of his achievements in London, Elizabeth wondered how to steer him back to the searches. Her attention wandered past him, and with a start, she locked eyes with James.

He leaned against a stall, arms crossed across his chest. The intensity of his gaze sliced through her. Though a bustling market separated them, they may as well have been alone.

"Mistress?" Hammond brought her back to the present. "Are you well? You appear flushed."

"Aye, perfectly well." She touched her warm cheeks. "I thought I saw Jennet. I'll need to find her soon or—" She was about to say she would have to walk home but then feared he might offer her a ride. "Or risk aggravating her." Elizabeth snuck a peek to the stall. James was still there. She longed to stare openly but was conscious of the officer between them.

"Jennet is a servant, is she not?"

"Aye," Elizabeth said, frowning. "Am I to be discourteous with her time because of that?"

"I meant no offence." Hammond glanced over his shoulder and stiffened when he noticed James. Currents of animosity passed between the two men. A moment later, James left the stall and walked away.

Hammond turned his attention back to Elizabeth. "How does Friday next sound?"

"I beg your pardon?"

"Surely, in another week your aunt will be grateful for callers, though she does have your charming company."

Elizabeth scrambled for a response. "We're unable to commit to a time. Perhaps when my aunt sufficiently recovers, we can send you an invitation."

Hammond looked as though he might press his suit but instead tipped his hat. "Until a better time presents itself. I'll look forward to hearing from you, mistress."

Elizabeth should have been relieved when he finally walked away, but an uneasy lump settled in her stomach. Rather than being the fox, she had become the hare.

*

Elizabeth snuggled Emma on her lap while her aunt and the Giffards prepared for the family's departure at week's end. Henry had made it his business to speak to all who passed through the Chequer for any murmur of trouble. For the time being, the garrison had ceased their harassments, but Isabel preferred a course of safety.

Margaret kept as close to the window as she dared to catch the fading light for her sewing. She bent over a shirt and worked her needle in small, neat stitches. Joan sat next to Isabel on a bench with satchels of dried powders between them while Nicholas kept to his corner reading a catechism.

The sound of running footsteps preceded Jennet, who burst into the dining hall, gasping and out of breath. "Hammond—here—he's here!"

The Giffards scrambled to their feet, and Margaret scooped up Emma.

"Good Lord." Elizabeth thought she had fobbed him off—she was certain of it. A knot twisted in her stomach. "Is he alone?"

"Aye, mistress."

"Jennet, take them to the root cellar." Isabel ushered the Giffards into the passageway. "'Tis the best we can do since there are no priest holes at Ellendale. Niece, stay with me." Isabel faltered and leaned against the wall for support, her face chalk-white.

Elizabeth steadied her, alarmed at her aunt's condition. "Are you all right?"

Isabel nodded and pursed her lips. "I'm practicing—for our constable."

Elizabeth looked at her sharply. "As long as it's only for Hammond's benefit." She snatched the quilt that she had wrapped Emma in. "Here, you'll need to play the invalid."

"A role I hate." Isabel settled in the chair while Elizabeth spread the blanket over her.

A sound rap on the door made them both jump. They didn't dare answer it until Jennet had secured the Giffards. Time strained. Another knock, this time louder.

"Hurry, Jennet," Elizabeth muttered and wrung her hands.

Bang, bang, bang.

They couldn't delay any longer. Elizabeth moved towards the door just as Jennet hustled past. The Giffards were hid.

As Elizabeth returned to her seat to wait for Hammond, she spotted Margaret's sewing puddled on the floor. *A man's shirt*! She leapt for the garment and tossed it to her aunt, who hid it beneath her quilts. Elizabeth hurried back to her seat and scooped up her aunt's herbal book just as the constable entered the room.

"Lieutenant Hammond, what a surprise to see you today." Elizabeth rose. She sounded breathless.

"God save you, ladies." He removed his hat and smiled. "I happened to be riding past and thought you might welcome guests."

"We had not expected callers this eve, sir, and have nothing prepared to offer you." Elizabeth frowned her discouragement.

"I won't trouble you for refreshments. I am quite comfortable." He dismissed Jennet, who hovered by the door. "My only desire is to assure myself of Mistress Stanborowe's convalescence and to pay my respects." He smiled again.

"My aunt is still quite unwell, sir." Elizabeth's heart pounded in her throat, but she forced herself to breathe. "I prefer not to tire her with callers."

"Your concern for your aunt commends you, as does your duty and devotion. The Good Lord does not mean for us to shoulder our burdens alone," he said with warmth. "The right society may yet raise her spirits."

Elizabeth sat on the edge of her chair. Either the man was a boorish clod with no sense when his company was unwelcome, or he remained for other reasons. Not knowing which, she chose to say as little as possible. The silence grew, the only sound being the persistent clicking of the chamber clock.

"I have brought you several inspirational tracts I thought you would enjoy," Hammond said. "They will edify your aunt's soul and bless her with fortitude." He removed a small packet of papers from the inside of his jacket.

As he shuffled them into order, Elizabeth spied Nicholas Giffard's catechism lying open on the stool. Her eyes widened, and cold panic coursed through her. Hammond only needed to turn his head to see it. What better evidence against them than a volume of papist teachings?

She had to hide it.

"Here is a good one to start with." Hammond selected a tract and began his reading.

Elizabeth's mind raced. She rose and walked over to Isabel. The lieutenant raised his head, and Elizabeth smiled, encouraging him to continue while she pretended to adjust her aunt's quilts. Isabel gave her a quizzical look, but when Elizabeth lifted her brows in the direction of the stool, the last of Isabel's colour fled.

Hammond warmed to his subject. The catechism was steps away. Elizabeth edged closer, praying he wouldn't look up. She finally reached the catechism and slipped it within the folds of her skirt. On her way back to her seat, she passed the contraband to Isabel, who tucked it safely away.

Hammond read without pause. He droned on in a level tone except when the passage moved him to passion, and then his voice trembled.

How long would he stay? Elizabeth began to worry about the Giffards huddled in the damp cellar. The cold could prove dangerous for Emma.

The child didn't have the strength to withstand another fever. Elizabeth squirmed in her chair, racking her brains for how she could hurry him on his way.

A sound pricked her ears, a thin intermittent wail. Elizabeth froze. *Was that Emma crying?* The blood drained from her face. *Let it be my imagination... it's not happening.* She exchanged a fearful glance with a wide-eyed Isabel. *Dear God, it is real.* Elizabeth gripped the arms of her chair. Somewhere in the dark cellar, Emma was crying, and Hammond would hear.

Elizabeth prayed the child would stop, that someone would soothe or muffle her. If Hammond heard, all would be lost. She had to cover the sound—a song or a tune? Hammond hated music. So she began to cough, delicately at first, then with more force.

"Are you—" Hammond paused then canted his head. "What was that?"

"A cat," Elizabeth blurted. Her mouth was dry, and it came out like a croak. "In heat." She forced an embarrassed laugh. "How indelicate of me, Lieutenant."

The cries suddenly ceased. Elizabeth's heart hammered in her chest, and a rush of blood pounded in her ears. She prayed that Hammond wouldn't choose to investigate. "Will you not continue, Lieutenant?"

Hammond hesitated. He cocked his ear and waited. Nothing. He shrugged. "I do have another selection."

Elizabeth sat in misery for the next half hour, fearful that Emma would start crying again and anxious over the time they remained in the cellar. Finally, Hammond closed his volume.

"That was very instructive, sir," Elizabeth said, rising.

"Thank you for taking the time from your day," Isabel said. "I fear I'm weakened."

"We've had enough excitement." Elizabeth dropped a hand on Isabel's shoulder. "I should like to settle my aunt now, Lieutenant."

"Absolutely. I've enjoyed my visit immensely," Hammond said. "By your leave, I shall return tomorrow. Master Ward has promised me a copy of a Thomason tract, which I believe you'll find thoroughly enlightening."

"We'll look forward to it," Elizabeth said in a thin tone.

Unbidden, Jennet appeared at the door with the man's cloak draped over her arm, but Hammond ignored her. Instead, he hovered close to Elizabeth.

"It would please me greatly if you would accept this gift," he said, presenting her with a book of Psalms.

Elizabeth had become trapped by her own cleverness. If she accepted his gift, she was acknowledging his feelings for her; but if she declined, the sting of rejection might prompt him to look more closely into their affairs. "Thank you, Lieutenant," she said and took the book.

"Until the morrow, ladies." He bowed to Elizabeth. "God save you."

Elizabeth strained to hear the sound of the door close behind him. When it came, she sagged against the doorjamb, and her legs buckled. "God help us."

"The Giffards must leave tonight," Isabel said. "No use involving Samuel after that unpleasantness with the stocks. He's bound to be marked. When it gets dark, hie yourself down to the Chequer and get help."

Chapter Twelve

James worked on the hoof of a chestnut mare with only half a mind to his task. He had been in a foul mood since seeing Elizabeth in the market with Hammond. The bastard was no doubt plying her with mild words and the loftiness of his position.

The mare shied when the horse pick slipped and touched a sore spot. "Sorry," he muttered and tried to refocus. A scuffling from outside, like the tumble of rocks, made him pause. He strained to listen. Just as he decided it was nothing, he heard the shutters creak.

James grabbed a sharpened file and slipped outside through the postern door. He crept along the length of the stables. Upon reaching the courtyard, he hung back in the shadows. He saw nothing at first and then spied a cloaked figure hovering by the stable door.

James stole closer, balancing the file in his hand. He shortened the distance, gauging a plan of attack, then his boot scuffed the edge of a raised cobble.

The figure whirled around, and James braced for a fight. When the hood fell away, he halted in surprise.

"Elizabeth?"

Her hand flew to her throat, and she gaped at the weapon in his hand. "James!"

"What the devil are you doing here?"

She stepped forward, her voice low and urgent. "I understand that you are knowledgeable about *knots*..."

Knots? *The Knot*. Before he could answer, the shutters from an upstairs room opened. A chorus of laughter erupted over the clinking of glasses.

"Come with me." James drew her along the side of the stables and inside through the postern door, guiding her by the small of her back. "You know?"

"I've learned."

"I can't believe they've sent you here alone. Any manner of evil could have befallen you." His imagination fuelled his anger.

"I had no choice. We must arrange passage for particular guests of ours—this very night. The morrow will be too late."

James glanced down and realised that his hand still rested on the curve of her waist. She realised it at the same time. His fingers fanned out, and he had a desire to draw her closer. Elizabeth's blue eyes widened, appearing nearly black. He was disappointed when she pulled away.

James cleared his throat. "Why? What do you expect on the morrow?"

"Lieutenant Hammond called on us this afternoon. He intends another visit."

Another one? "Indeed." Twin demons of rage and jealously roared in his head. "Aside from your recusants, is that situation unwelcome?"

Elizabeth pursed her lips and looked somewhat queasy. His internal demons multiplied. "I see," he said.

"Nay, I don't think you do," she replied quickly. "Hammond's attentions are most definitely not welcome, but..." her voice trailed, and she winced, "he might *believe* they are."

James's brow lifted slightly.

"It's not like that," she rushed on. "The Giffards were hiding in the cellar—I may have allowed him to think he was welcome to return."

"That is hardly the strategy I would have employed."

"I was trying to avoid an unpleasant situation and inevitable scrutiny had I cruelly dashed his hopes before witnesses," she said with a touch of impatience.

This was a dangerous game she played. "Never coddle these Roundheads. They're like feral beasts and will turn for no reason."

"Fine, fine," she said with a wave of her hand. "The pressing concern now is the Giffards. Will you help?"

"Aye. Truce?"

"Truce." She offered her hand. "We are allies, then."

James smiled. He took her hand and gave it a light squeeze. "There are worse things, yet I can think of better." Reluctantly, he let it go. "Who are they and how many?"

"A papist family. Four in all."

James considered the late hour. If only he had more time. "The closest house lies near Solihull, but I won't make it back before dawn." Then an idea struck him. It was either a brilliant inspiration or sheer lunacy. "But

I know of a home in Coventry where they'll be safe. Wait here while I get a few things."

From the hidden compartment, James brought out his doglock pistols and cartridge bag. Last, he dug out his highway gear—hat, scarf and worn cloak. In no time, he returned leading Sovereign by the halter.

Elizabeth stopped her agitated pacing when she saw him.

"The highwayman returns," she said.

James had been chewing on this for some time. All she saw was the outlaw. Could he make her see the man? "You asked me why I do it. Now I ask you the same thing." He stepped closer until only a foot separated them. "Why are you here?"

"What?"

"You've set out alone during the night, risked your personal safety and reputation to harbour papists? Why do it?"

"What would you have us do? Turn them out of doors?"

"There are those who would, believing their soul takes precedence."

"We are not those people."

"Tell me, then, is it worth helping this one family though there are many others who can't be saved?" When she didn't answer, he said, "It's easier to learn to live with the hypocrisy, but it demeans us all. There are times when we must cut our own path." He leaned in closer. Her blue eyes widened, but she held her ground. "You and I, Elizabeth, are no different, whether you admit it or not."

She didn't reply, nor did she look away. The ghostly scent of lavender hung between them. He stared at her half-parted lips and wondered how they would taste. With a mental jolt, he reined in his wayward thoughts. *Concentrate, man.*

"The hour is growing late." Her voice sounded strained.

"Agreed," James said and drew a deep breath to clear his mind. He lifted a saddle from the rack and settled it on Sovereign's back. "Four people, you said?"

"One is a child."

"You didn't come here on foot, did you?"

"Nay, I tethered the mare in the Cornmarket. I didn't want anyone seeing me arrive."

"Good. Two horses will need to serve as I have no spare. The others are needed at first light. You'll need to ride with me to the Cornmarket."

Elizabeth looked unconvinced. "I have never ridden thus before."

"I should think not, but I have no intention of walking, not when time is of the essence," he said. "'Twill be our secret."

"Very well. My reputation can hardly be held to account by a highwayman. We will each have our secrets."

James chuckled. "Indeed, we will."

She slipped her foot in the stirrup, and James placed his hands around her waist to help her up. The curve of her waist fitted his hands, and his fingers lingered for a fraction longer than necessary. A small treat, but one he was not above enjoying.

James settled behind her. She felt good in his arms, and it took all his willpower not to bend down and kiss her. When she looked up at him, her expression was unreadable.

"Ready?" he asked, clearing his throat. He was aware of the pale curve of her neck and the enticing dip at the base of her throat.

"Aye, ready."

He leaned in closer and urged Sovereign into a trot. At first, she tried to maintain a discreet distance between them, but by the time Sovereign sped to a full trot, she gave up and pressed against him. James grinned and gave serious thought to increasing their gait to a gallop.

*

Elizabeth realised that James was not taking the direct route to the Cornmarket. Instead of turning east on High Street, he rode towards the West Gate. She twisted slightly and asked, "Where are we going?"

"Soft, love. The Cornmarket, but by a safer route. These Roundheads keep strange hours. Best approach with caution."

Elizabeth settled against him, oddly comforted yet excited at the same time.

With the West Gate rising in the distance, he turned down a narrow lane, one that Elizabeth could have easily missed, and continued until they reached Brook Street. They passed the Swann Inn, silent and shuttered, and once more slipped into another side lane. He followed this to the end, where they got their first view of the Cornmarket.

A patrol of three dragoons clustered around the Ellendale mare. Elizabeth's stomach dropped.

"Damn," James muttered.

"We must get to Ellendale before them," she hissed. How much time did they have?

"Not without that horse," he whispered in her ear.

"But they must know that it belongs to my aunt."

"In the dark, that beast is as common as fleas."

"'Tis a fine horse."

James's arms tightened around her. "Aye."

Elizabeth heard the amusement in his tone. "Can we distract them?"

James didn't answer. He leaned back slightly and backed Sovereign down the lane until he could turn the horse around. He kept his hands low and worked the reins with the lightest touch. "Aye, they'll be distracted soon enough," he finally said. "I'll lead them away from the square to give you time to get the mare. Make for the East Gate and don't stop for anything. Meet me in the woods along the river road. I'll join you as soon as I can." He helped Elizabeth down. "Clear?"

Elizabeth bit her lip. *What if you're caught?* "Aye."

James handed a dagger to her. "Just in case."

"I don't know how to use this." But she accepted it nevertheless.

"You will if you have to." His fingers brushed her cheek. "Good luck."

"And you. Be safe."

James winked and raised his scarf to his face. The highwayman returned, but this time Elizabeth would not fault him for hiding behind it. He lifted his hand in a final salute and rode back the way they came.

Elizabeth crept down the lane, hugging the shadows. When she reached the end of the building, she peered cautiously into the square.

The dragoons were still there. Two argued while the third attached a lead to the mare's bridle. Their voices carried in the still night.

"I say we keep it," the first said.

"Hammond will knock our heads if he learns of this," said the other.

"He don't need to know."

"I want to know what the beast is doing here," said the soldier with the lead.

Elizabeth looked around for a sign of James. *Hurry.* The dragoons didn't look as though they'd be there much longer. Then she heard a rumbling—a pounding of hooves. The dragoons whirled around.

James charged into the square and halted a hundred feet from the dragoons. Horse and man were as intimidating as when she had first seen

155

them on the highway. "Baseborn rogues and scoundrels," he shouted. "You've not one wit to share betwixt the lot of you. Return to your master and have him beat you soundly."

The soldiers scrambled to reach their horses, yelling, "Bloody highwayman!" and, "Ten pounds to catch him!"

Elizabeth grinned. Their plan was working.

Two dragoons mounted their horses while the third hastened to his. Elizabeth's heart sank when the leader turned to him and ordered, "Stay here in case he returns for this one."

The man started to protest, but his companions were already barrelling down the street, leaving him no choice than to obey.

Damn you! Elizabeth clenched her fists. *The highwayman is worth more than that horse!* How was she to get the mare now? *Think.* She looked wildly around. Naught but dirt and rocks. *And a dagger.* Elizabeth bent down and scooped up a handful of pebbles. It's all in the angle, James had said. Taking aim at the adjacent street, she threw the stones as far as she could. The dragoon whirled around. He peered in the direction of the clattering. Elizabeth flattened against the wall.

"Who's there?" The soldier cocked his pistol and walked towards the sound, passing where she hid.

Elizabeth drew up her hood and gripped the hilt of the dagger, pummel down. She measured each footstep, fighting the urge to rush forward and possibly give herself away. If he turned around, he'd see her. She lifted the dagger and focused on the back of his head. The soldier paused and shifted his stance.

Elizabeth steeled herself and smashed the pommel against his head. *Whack.* He jerked backward and dropped to the ground. His pistol bounced twice before discharging. The shot echoed through the empty street.

Elizabeth ducked and covered her head. *Am I shot?* She snuck a glance at the prostate dragoon. *Have I killed him?* She saw the rise and fall of his chest.

The sound of the pistol would draw them back. Elizabeth leapt over the dragoon and dashed towards the mare. The horse backed away nervously. Elizabeth grabbed the lead and tried to calm the skittish animal. "Hush." She tried to put her foot in the stirrup, but the horse sidestepped.

In the distance, she heard the drumming of approaching hooves. She tried another attempt to mount the mare. Again the animal tossed its head and would have none of it.

"Damn you." She grabbed the horse by the bridle, but as she was in such a panic, the mare became more nervous.

The sound of hooves rolled like thunder. They were nearly upon her. Elizabeth looked for a place to hide. She whirled around to dodge into a laneway when she saw Sovereign burst into the square.

James pulled up beside her. "I heard a shot—are you hurt?"

Elizabeth shook her head, incapable of speech.

"Take my hand!" He reached down to help her.

Elizabeth placed her foot on his boot and scrambled up. Hiking up her skirts, she threw her leg over.

"Hang on." James made a pass alongside the mare and scooped up the lead. He handed it to her. "Don't drop this." He kicked his heels and they charged down the street with the mare running alongside them.

Elizabeth clutched Sovereign's mane with her free hand. James's arm tightened around her waist to steady her. When they turned onto High Street, James swore and pulled up short. A hundred yards away, the dragoons were returning to the Cornmarket.

He wheeled the horses around and retreated the other way. Too late. Excited shouts sounded the alarm.

A crack of a musket whizzed over their heads, and James hunched forward, shielding Elizabeth. With a sharp turn on Swann Lane, they dashed towards the inn. Just before they reached the building, James pulled to the right and pressed his left thigh against the horse's flank. Sovereign slipped into a narrow lane, smooth as glass. Elizabeth tightened her hold on the lead, and the mare followed without balking.

James halted Sovereign halfway down the lane while Elizabeth roped the mare closer. She looked up at him, heart pounding. He held his finger to his lips and watched the main road. The clatter of hooves drew closer. Elizabeth held her breath and pressed against him into a tight ball. The dragoons raced past and continued down the street. The sound of pounding hooves faded.

Elizabeth's relief came in a rush, and as though he had read her mind, James said, "Not clear yet."

He clicked on the reins and turned both horses around to double back from where they had come. Elizabeth craned over her shoulder to look for the dragoons. When they turned on High Street, James leaned forward. "Hold on."

He sent Sovereign into a full gallop, and Elizabeth wobbled. She gasped and grabbed a fistful of Sovereign's mane. James's arm locked her in place. The East Gate loomed ahead. The spires of the adjoining chapel rose sharp against the moonlit sky. Before reaching the gate, James eased their speed. The clattering hooves bounced off the arched walls as they rode through.

James spurred Sovereign past the last row of buildings, rushing southeast to the cover of trees. A hundred yards to the tree line. Now fifty. They finally reached the shelter of the woods. James slowed to a trot before circling around to look behind them. He pulled down his scarf.

Elizabeth strained to see through the darkness. No sign of them. They had lost the dragoons. She sagged against him.

James swung down from the horse and held out his arms for her, a wide smile on his face. She placed her hands on his shoulders and slipped off the horse.

"We did it!" she cried. Without thinking, she flung her arms around his neck and started laughing—from relief and sheer exhilaration.

James whirled her around in a circle. "Christ's teeth, you are a prize."

His hold loosened, but instead of stepping away, he swooped down and kissed her. His mouth parted and slanted across hers, demanding and insistent. The kiss shocked then awakened sensations that Elizabeth had no idea she was capable of. Her lips parted in response, his scent and touch filling her head. He drew her closer, crushing her against his chest. His tongue probed her mouth, turning her insides to a puddle. She leaned against him for support and, without realising, began to answer him with her own unstopped passion.

Then the first rational thought intruded into her kiss-soaked brain. *What am I doing?* Her senses screamed, *Hush!* But cruel reason asserted itself. Elizabeth pressed her hands against his chest and pushed away. Her lips felt bruised yet alive, and her knees had grown weak.

She stared at him, trying to catch her breath. In the moonlight, he looked fierce, his chest rising and falling. It wouldn't take much to throw herself back into his arms.

"I can't," she said. "I shouldn't—" She covered her mouth, confused.

James made no move to touch her. Instead, he ran his fingers through his hair. When he spoke, his voice sounded strained. "Right."

"We have to go." She backed up. "The hour is late." Without waiting for help, she mounted the mare.

James tilted his head to the sky and released an audible sigh. He gathered Sovereign's reins. "Aye, Coventry awaits."

They reached Ellendale in silence. The painful, unresolved yearning nearly crippled Elizabeth. By the time she and James circled to the back, the Giffards, her aunt, and Jennet were waiting outside.

Isabel rushed up to them. "You were so late, we were worried."

James helped Elizabeth down from the mare. His touch lingered on her waist a fraction longer than necessary. "Naught but a small complication."

Chapter Thirteen

At dawn, Elizabeth stole to the barn to see if James had returned and instead found the mare already bedded in her stall. A mixture of emotions churned: relief that the Giffards were obviously safe and a perverse disappointment that she had missed seeing him.

Three days later, Elizabeth spied James in the market. He stood by the horse pens amongst a small group of men. They were leaning over a split rail assessing the horses for sale. Most of the questions were being directed to James, and his answers triggered a round of nodding and general agreement. He didn't notice her at first, but he eventually turned his head, and their eyes locked. Elizabeth's cheeks warmed. His expression softened, then one by one the others turned to see what had diverted his attention. Before she could make a further fool of herself, Elizabeth hurried away without a greeting.

Determined not to act like a mooning maid, Elizabeth turned her mind to industry. For the remainder of the week, she launched an attack on the weeds in her kitchen garden, piling them up like casualties. Finally, she sat back on her heels to survey the carnage, and a movement down the lane drew her attention. A horseman approached on a black horse with a packhorse in tow. *James.*

He passed from view, having continued his progress to the front of the manor.

Elizabeth was on her feet in an instant, brushing the dirt from her hands as she hurried to the side door. Cutting through the kitchen, she approached the parlour and heard her aunt's voice.

"It's such a relief that the Giffards are safe, James. Thank you for managing that."

"I need your help on another matter..." His voice trailed off when he noticed Elizabeth at the door.

Isabel turned her head. She was settled in one of the armchairs, recovering from another of her spells. Though her colour had improved, she still looked wan. "Anything in my power, James. What can I do?"

"I was at the Norton farm yesterday attending a lame horse. Rose Norton isn't well, and I thought you might have a look at her. I'm on my way there now."

"What's the problem?" Isabel asked.

"Liver stones, I'm told."

Isabel nodded. "Poor Rose. She's had this problem off and on." Isabel leaned her head back and closed her eyes. "I couldn't possibly manage it at this time—I'm feeling poorly myself. But I'll send Elizabeth in my stead. Niece, can you handle this?"

"Of course," Elizabeth replied quickly.

James's expression remained neutral. "I'll ready the mare," he said before leaving.

His coolness dismayed Elizabeth, but she didn't have an opportunity to dwell on it as Isabel had started rattling off a list of supplies she would need.

"Bring birch bark and hazel rind. Strong vinegar and camomile for comfort."

"I'll gather everything," Elizabeth said, but before she left, Isabel stopped her with one last piece of advice.

"I beg your discretion, not only for my sake but for the Nortons. They are tenants of Sir Richard, and it would not do for him to know I've been meddling in his affairs."

"Are you not to help if they are ill?"

"Richard is touchy about what is his. Trust me, it's better he doesn't know."

"Very well. He shan't hear it from me."

Elizabeth gathered a satchel and filled it with herbs and vials and a few more items—just in case. When she walked out to the forecourt, she found Jennet waiting by the gate while James strapped the basket of provisions to the packhorse.

"If Rosie hasn't been well, I don't know what her children are eating," Jennet said to Elizabeth. "Give her my best."

James held the mare's bridle so Elizabeth could climb up. He waited patiently as she adjusted her seat, then handed her the reins with the detachment of a groom.

"We've a league to travel, mistress," James said as he mounted Sovereign. "I hope to be there by mid-morn."

His formality disturbed her far more than she expected. "Very well, Master Hart," she said and started down the lane.

As they left Ellendale behind, the steady clip-clop was the only sound between them. James rode straight in the saddle and gave no signal that he wanted conversation. Elizabeth didn't know how to behave. Should she lock her gaze on the road or allow her attention to casually drift to the man riding beside her?

"Did Hammond pay you a visit as he threatened?" James asked.

The unexpected question surprised her. "Aye. He prides himself on his punctuality and single-mindedness."

"Bloody-minded, I'd say." He held his reins loose in his gloved hands. "In what manner does his courtship take?"

"We're not courting."

"That isn't what they say in Warwick."

Elizabeth stiffened. "What *are* they saying?"

"That you're courting." A hard edge sharpened his tone. "They call you fortunate for having attracted someone with such excellent prospects."

Elizabeth squirmed. Her own cleverness had created this mire—thinking she could blunt Hammond's vigilance with a winning smile. Now that the Giffards were no longer hiding at Ellendale, she'd have to find a way to cool his interest without alienating him. "They're wrong. You know what was behind that and nothing more."

After another pause he said, "You may have had second thoughts."

Elizabeth's cheeks burned. Her own participation in their kiss and subsequent rejection mortified her. "You must think I'm a fickle creature."

"I don't." James paused another moment and added, "You must think I'm an unprincipled scoundrel."

"Nay, I don't."

Elizabeth felt the mood between them lighten, though neither engaged in more conversation. After two more miles, James turned down an old laneway, rutted and overgrown, that hadn't seen a cart in ages. A canopy of trees provided a dappled screen from the sun while along the side of the trail lupins and daisies nodded in the light wind. They passed more fallow fields than cultivated, and all the fields of clover and brome still needed to be cut.

"Who are the Nortons?" Elizabeth asked.

"Hugh Norton died during the war," James replied. "He fought with the King's Foot. His widow, Rose, was left to raise their five children. The oldest, Matthias, does what he can about the farm while Rose takes on a bit of weaving to pay the rent to Sir Richard."

"Could she not appeal for a reduction? Surely—"

James snorted. "You do remember Sir Richard? He'd like nothing better than to rent the cottage to another family—preferably not Royalist. The moment she falls behind in the rent, he'll evict them." His jaw tensed. "But I'll do what I can so that doesn't happen."

Elizabeth studied James as he rode. Few people would have bothered with the Nortons for fear of displeasing Sir Richard. But not James. He gave up his time, and likely his wages, to help this family. More than anyone, Elizabeth keenly appreciated what this meant for the Nortons. She had not forgotten the gnawing worry of living day by day, nor the relief when Old Nick dropped by to see how they were getting on. It had been a great comfort knowing that someone looked out for them when no one else did. The thought struck her. *He is a decent man.*

"Elizabeth?"

Her thoughts scattered like starlings. "What?"

"Is aught the matter?"

"Nay, nothing," she said with an embarrassed smile. "Mistress Norton must be grateful, I'm sure."

When they crested a hill, a small cottage came into sight. The thatched roof badly needed repair, and a small herb garden had been left to ruin. A few chickens scratched at the ground while two lads, around twelve and eight, watched from the top rail of a fence. The moment they saw James, they jumped down and ran to greet him. A pair of hounds joined the fray. By the time James dismounted, boys and eager dogs swarmed him.

"Captain James, Captain James," the boys chanted. "You've brought another horse."

James grinned openly at the lads. "Did I not say I would?" He tousled the hair of the youngest boy, then handed the packhorse's reins to the other boy. "How is the horse, Lukas?"

"Not a bit better," he answered. "Matt's in the barn with it now."

Elizabeth watched a little awkwardly, feeling very much an outsider. Rather than asking for assistance, she started to dismount, but before she could, James offered his hand. A frisson of energy passed between them.

"Captain James!" a young man called out from the direction of the barn, diverting their attention. He hurried over to join them.

"Matthias, well met," James said, offering his hand.

"I didn't look for you until the evening." The young man grinned. His cheeks were still downy, with scruff growing in patches under his chin. Elizabeth guessed him to be about seventeen.

"Who's this?" the younger boy asked, pointing to Elizabeth.

"Zachary, you really need to learn more subtlety," James said. "This is Mistress Seton from Ellendale. She's here to see your mother."

Elizabeth smiled, feeling a thrill from his words. She *was* from Ellendale. "Pleased to make your acquaintances."

The two younger lads gaped sheepishly, but Matthias remembered himself. "God save you, mistress." He snatched his brothers' hats from their heads. "Show your manners."

"God save you, mistress," they both chimed.

James's grey eyes crinkled in the corners. He turned to Matthias and said, "The horse hasn't improved?"

Matthias shook his head. "Not that I can tell."

"It'll take some time."

"Another thing we don't have," Matthias grumbled.

"Don't worry," James said, squeezing his shoulder. "We'll get those fields ploughed, and by the time the corn is ready, the horse will be well enough to pull a wagon." He gave the boys the reins to the three animals and unfastened the basket from the packs. "I'll meet you in the barn right after we see to your mother."

Matthias muttered his thanks and headed towards the barn with Sovereign while his brothers followed with the other two horses.

"This way." James led Elizabeth to the cottage. "I'm sure Rose has heard the commotion by now."

He rapped on the door, and it was answered by two little girls—a dark-haired child with large blue eyes, looking shyly through tangled lashes, and her younger sister, a saucy girl with fair curls. Though both children were tidy, their clothes were patched and worn.

The youngest squirmed past her sister. "Captain James, Ma's much worse. She's moaning. Can she be . . . dying?"

"Hush, Alice," her sister said, though she couldn't entirely hide her fear.

James sat on his haunches and looked both girls in the eye. "Grace, Alice," he addressed them, "no one is dying today. I've brought Mistress Seton to help."

"Where's your mother?" Elizabeth asked.

"Upstairs in her bed, mistress," Grace answered. "Will you take away Mother's pain?"

Elizabeth touched the top of the child's dark head. "Aye. Will you help?" The girl nodded eagerly. There was something about this child that reminded Elizabeth of her younger self. When she looked up, she caught James looking at her with an unfathomable expression.

She settled the basket on the rough-hewn table, and the girls sidled up to peer inside. Their eyes widened when they saw the bread and jars of preserves tucked inside. "I've brought a few treats from Ellendale for you."

As they were exploring the contents, Elizabeth stole a glance around. The main living area had few pieces of furniture and a generous stone hearth at its centre. The scattered rushes on the floor needed sweetening. Oilskin covered most of the windows, leaving the interior dim. As feared, the shelves were mainly bare. Elizabeth was glad of Jennet's foresight.

"I'll take you to Rose," James said.

They climbed the rickety stairs to the upper chamber. A sour, bitter scent hit Elizabeth the moment she entered the stifling room.

Rose was curled in a ball, clinging to the edge of her bed. Her face was a sickly shade of yellow and her cheeks pinched and sunken. She lifted her head a fraction.

"Rose," James said, stepping closer. "I've brought Isabel Stanborowe's niece to take a look at you." He glanced at Elizabeth. "You're in good hands."

"Thank you for coming," Rose spoke between gritted teeth. "Your aunt usually boils some special bark for me. Eases the pains."

Elizabeth sat at the edge of the bed beside Rose and took the woman's hand. It felt hot and dry. "Are the pains sharp?"

Rose nodded, her lips pursed and her whole body stiffened as though gripped in another wave.

"Your back, does it hurt?"

"Even to my shoulders," Rose gritted.

Elizabeth glanced over at the chamber pot positioned near the headboard. She could smell the bile coating it, although it appeared to have been recently emptied. She asked a few more questions and felt assured that it was as Isabel expected. "I'll be right back."

She walked downstairs with James. "It is as they said—stones of the liver."

"Can you help?" he asked when they returned to the kitchen.

Elizabeth nodded. "I'll get started." She tied her apron around her waist and sent the girls off to the well for fresh water.

"I'll leave you to it, then." He laid his hand on her arm. The warmth penetrated her linen sleeve. "Thank you."

Elizabeth watched him leave with a conflicting, wistful churn of emotion.

*

After Elizabeth had dosed Rose with a couple of rounds of vinegar and bark infusions, Rose fell into an easier sleep. Careful not to wake her, Elizabeth padded silently to the open window. A light breeze drifted in, and she leaned on the sill to look outside. The sky was a crystalline blue with only a scattering of fluffy clouds skimming its surface.

From the window, she could see James and Matthias ploughing one of the fields. The two worked in tandem, Matthias leading the horse along a straight line while James guided the plough. They had already done half a furlong, readying the soil for the fall planting. Though it was still high summer, this job should have been done weeks ago.

James had his sleeves rolled up, and his unbleached linen shirt was plastered to his back. He wore no hat under the hot sun, and his nut-brown hair hung down to his shoulders. When they got to the end of the next row, they stopped to let the horse take a brief rest. James showed an easy manner, laughing openly at something Matthias said. The other two boys joined them and took turns leading the horse.

Elizabeth watched, fascinated, before she gave herself a mental shake. They'd be finished soon, and the least she could do was ensure that they had something nourishing to eat for their evening meal. With a last look at Rose, she closed the door behind her and went downstairs.

Grace stood before the hearth stirring a pot of simmering pease with one hand and holding her skirts away from the fire with the other. Alice sat at the table sorting through the beans and leeks that Jennet had sent. Both girls looked at her, expectant.

"Your mother is feeling better," Elizabeth answered their unspoken question.

Alice squirmed happily on her stool while Grace smiled and continued stirring.

Elizabeth checked the pot and tossed in a few sprigs of fresh summer savoury. The scent filled the kitchen.

"That's wonderful, mistress," Grace said.

Elizabeth took the ladle from her and tested the stew. Chunks of meat were sprinkled through the mixture. Like chicken but with a gamey taste. She threw in a bit of rosemary to balance it out. "What meat is this?" she asked the girl.

Grace evaded her eyes. "Matthias found a plump bird, mistress."

Elizabeth decided not to ask further. "You have this well in hand," she told Grace. "If those beans are ready for the pot, I'll take Alice down to the fields. The boys could use something to eat." She gathered a loaf of bread and a round of new cheese and wrapped both in a towel. "Lead the way, Alice."

The little girl ran ahead with a half-skipping gait and headed towards the fields. Along the way, Elizabeth saw so many instances where the place needed work. An old harrow lay rusted and looked like it needed sharpening; a small cart was missing a wheel. A single cow grazed in a small fenced-in pasture.

When they neared James and Matthias, Alice shouted a greeting, prompting them to stop their work.

"Look, Captain James—the bread's not coarse."

"They're very clever at Ellendale," he answered with a wink.

Alice took the bread to her brothers. James didn't bother to join them and stayed with Elizabeth.

"How's Rose?"

"Better." Elizabeth's attention kept drifting to James's open shirt. His skin was starting to darken by the sun, and a sheen of sweat coated it. He didn't seem to notice as he wiped his hands on a cloth. "You'll be finished with the field soon," she said.

"Aye, this one, but there are two others," he said glancing over at the fields. "Thought I'd have time to repair the thatch, but I may need to just show Matthias. He's a clever lad—he'll pick it up."

"You've experience in working a farm."

James shrugged. "Aye."

"Captain James," Alice called out to him. "They're even clever with the cheese."

James chuckled. "She's a sharp one."

Elizabeth smiled. "Why do they call you captain?"

"Because I am. Received my commission during the war."

"You were an officer?"

James tilted his head and looked at her. "Aye. Does that surprise you?"

Elizabeth thought about it. This should have, and yet it didn't. It suddenly occurred to her that James Hart was the sort of man to take charge of a situation—even a bad one. "It explains a great deal."

"I will take that as a compliment, Mistress Seton," he said with warmth.

Elizabeth's stomach fluttered, and she returned the smile. "I had better get back to the cottage." Trying to feign a casual indifference, she called out to the little girl. "Come, Alice, it's time to head back."

As they walked away, Elizabeth looked over her shoulder to find James still staring at her.

*

The sun had nearly sunk below the horizon, casting long, slanting rays. Elizabeth left Rose to rest after working her up to a cup of light broth. Her fever had abated.

She checked the kitchen window to see if James and the lads had finished and spied them heading towards the barn. Matthias led the dray horse by the halter while Lukas rode bareback. Zachary darted around James, who scooped up the boy and tossed him over his shoulder like a grain sack. Zachary thrashed and squealed while Lukas hooted. When they reached the barn, James deposited the laughing boy on the ground.

Elizabeth found herself smiling. "They'll be here soon," she called out to the girls. By the time James and the lads drifted in, the table had been set for the evening meal.

James's hair looked wet, as though he had dunked himself in the creek. He smelt fresh, of water and rocks and earth. The others were equally damp.

Elizabeth ladled stew into the bowls, and the girls set them down on the table. Before long, bread was being passed around the table and the children were tucking into their meal with a vehemence that tugged at Elizabeth's heart. She caught James dividing his bread and handing a piece each to Zachary and Lukas on either side of him.

She met James's gaze, and this time she didn't turn hastily away. The conversation flowed easily across the table.

Matthias watched Grace dipping bits of bread in her bowl. He picked at his own stew.

"Is it not to your liking, Matthias?" Elizabeth asked.

"It's very good," he assured her. "Thank you."

"The wheat is ripening nicely," James said to Matthias. "By the end of the month, you'll need to cut the hay."

"Aye," Matthias muttered into his bowl.

"I'll come by next week to help. The inn should be able to spare one of the lads as well."

Matthias rubbed the back of his hand across his mouth. "It's still not enough," he muttered under his breath. When he caught James's questioning glance, he flushed. "We have one cow, and that creature eats better than we do. What we need is more than eggs or a bit of cheese."

"When your mother gets back on her feet—"

Matthias rose from the bench. "There's only so much one woman can do. Excuse me." He left the table and made an excuse about going for a walk before dark set in. He whistled to one of the hounds, who followed him out.

James watched him go with a troubled expression.

After the meal was done and the bowls were scrubbed and cleared, Elizabeth sat near the hearth trying to mend the girls' clothes. Zachary brought out a backgammon board and entreated James to teach him the game.

"Lukas has no patience for me," the lad said. "He only wants to beat Matt."

Elizabeth watched as James taught the boy to play, from where the draughts were positioned to different strategies to beat his opponent. She never knew how Irish was played and found the instruction fascinating.

When they finished a round of the game, James looked up and noticed her interest. "Did you want to learn too?"

Elizabeth shook her head. "Another time."

James nodded, but a smile flitted across his lips. "I'll hold you to that."

Elizabeth lowered her head, hoping her flushed cheeks weren't noticeable in the candlelight.

"Captain James, did you fight at Naseby?" Zachary asked, his chin cupped in his hands.

James frowned and carefully put the draughts in the board. "Aye."

"Our father was captured there," Zachary said.

"And marched back to London," Lukas added.

James picked up a draught and rubbed it between thumb and forefinger. "I'm aware of it—he was a pikeman."

"He's still in London," Zachary said, "only in the ground somewhere."

"Aye, I heard."

Elizabeth noticed the hardness in his expression, and it occurred to her with sudden clarity that he had been at that battle. She had heard about Parliament's victory through the news sheets, but as the publications sided with Parliament, they only crowed at their jubilant success. But there was another side to it, one she was aware of as a Crabchurch orphan. Just because one appeared unscathed from the war didn't mean there weren't internal scars.

*

James slipped outside alone and sat on the doorstep. The first stars were coming out, and a sliver of a moon rose in the evening sky. He was tired after a long day in the fields, but he felt more at peace than he could ever remember.

Elizabeth's voice drifted from the second floor as she readied the Norton children for bed. Already she had made a difference. It wasn't lost on him how the Nortons hung on her every word—he couldn't blame them; he did too.

On the morrow, he would take Elizabeth back to Ellendale. He'd have to return to the Chequer, and his normal life wouldn't have the same

170

flavour it once did. She had a soothing way about her, and he didn't realise how much he craved this serenity until now.

Though there were a number of chores he needed to finish in the barn before he turned in, he couldn't muster the will to leave. Instead, he picked up a long twig and started drawing shapes in the ground with its tip. It was only when the door opened and Elizabeth stepped outside that he realised he had been waiting for her.

She took a seat beside him. The faint scent of lavender teased him. "Zachary insisted on taking the game board with him to bed," she said.

"I used to do the same thing," James said, remembering how he used to shield his candle so his mother didn't realise he was still up playing. "It takes practise to get the rhythm of the game."

"Your father must have taught you?"

"Aye." James continued scrolling in the dirt.

Elizabeth hugged her knees. "The lads had a lot of questions about the war."

"They're curious. It's understandable."

"Did you want to talk about it?" she asked softly.

The question surprised him. "About what?"

"Naseby."

James lowered his head and continued to trace a circle. She didn't really need to hear what happened. "It's over."

"I don't think it is."

James didn't look up, but he could feel her gaze on him. "We had the field, and then we didn't," he replied as lightly as he could.

She didn't answer, and the expectant silence became a physical weight.

James took a slow breath and tipped his head to the darkening sky. "It does no good to dig these things up."

"You've spent the day furrowing that field. There's value in turning things over."

James shook his head. "The devil spurred the Roundheads that day. Let's just leave it at that, love."

Elizabeth looked as though she debated questioning him further. After a few moments of silence, she said, "You've done well with the fields. Are your people farmers in Coventry?"

James groaned and dug the stick an inch into the ground. Was she shooting blindly, or did she have the skills of a marksman? "You are wounding me, Elizabeth."

"I'm sorry," she said. "I seem to be saying the wrong things, and here you've come outside for a bit of peace. I should leave." She started to rise when James took her hand and held her back.

"Don't go," he said. Her hand was soft in his own, and he didn't want to release it. "This has been a good day for me—the first one in a long time." Instead of pulling away, she slipped beside him. Though she looked at him searchingly, he couldn't open up about this. She would think less of him if she knew. "My father was a hard, implacable man. I haven't been back at Stoneleigh for years. That's all there is to it."

"He sounds fearsome," she said, "for one implacable man to say of another." A dimple flirted at the corner of her mouth.

James smiled wryly. "Alarming, isn't it?" He chuckled and squeezed her hand.

"You forget that I'm Dorset born."

"Aye, I haven't forgotten. Nothing daunts you, does it?" James said. He truly hoped so.

*

James finally parted from Elizabeth after another hour on the step. She had been more open to sharing about Weymouth than he had of Stoneleigh. She was animated when she spoke of her old home, but there were times when he sensed a deep-seated hurt. Still, she held nothing back, which made him feel guilty over his reticence.

When he returned to the barn, he found lamplight shining through the open doorway. Matthias must have returned. The lad was in the corner with his back to him, hunched over something in the straw. The hound was intent on what he was working on. As soon as Matthias heard James enter, he whirled around.

"Where have you been?" James asked, coming closer. "What's that?"

"I had business," Matthias said.

James could see a twig and stick box with tail feathers peeking out. He recognised it as a partridge trap. "Does your business include poaching?"

Matthias flushed. "I found it in the woods."

172

James crossed his arms against his chest. "Don't mistake me for a fool. There are no partridges nearby, only in Sir Richard's woods. Did you get leave from his warren keeper to hunt his birds?"

"You don't understand."

"Indeed?"

"He's done nothing for my family except raise our rents." Mathias was nearly shouting. "Sir Richard made it very clear that he owes no loyalty as lord to our family, not after my father fought for the King against him."

James wanted to curse Sir Richard but chose not to fuel the fire. "I know you're frustrated at not being able to provide for your family. You worry about there being enough food on the table, but poaching on Sir Richard's lands is dangerous."

"You're defending his property?"

James snorted. "That's the last thing I would do. Nay, think for a moment. Who will look after your sisters? What of the boys? Do you expect Lukas to shoulder the burden?"

"I am thinking of them," Matthias's voice cracked. "I have to provide for them—there is no other."

James rubbed the back of his head. Who was he to lecture this young man to stay within the law? "Do what you must, but don't get caught."

Matthias blinked. He didn't look as though he trusted his ears. "You won't tell?"

"Of course not."

"Not even to Mistress Seton? Her aunt is kin to Sir Richard."

"I won't say a word, but she'd not turn you in even if she knew." He didn't doubt it for an instant. "I'd trust her with my life."

Chapter Fourteen

Elizabeth found it difficult to get back into the routine after she returned to Ellendale. Though the stillroom occupied most of her time, and her aunt had rewarded her by giving her a key to the room, contentment eluded her. She missed the children's high-pitched voices and the tangle of dogs and boys. Though she had never been more tired as she had during her time at the Nortons, she had never been happier. Elizabeth knew that the source of that wellspring was James.

She missed not having him close and felt keenly the absence of his wit and easy laughter, and she brazenly wondered what excuse she could conjure to visit him in town. In the end, she didn't need to do anything. An epidemic of ailments suddenly swept through the Chequer. Minor problems like rashes, fussy livers and digestive troubles all required immediate attention, and James arrived almost daily with a list in hand.

On the third consecutive day, Isabel chose to greet him herself. "Since when does Henry have gout?"

James shrugged. "Henry is a stoic man and rarely complains."

"I see," Isabel said. "He's fortunate that he has you to mind his health."

"Indeed."

To Elizabeth's disappointment, her aunt's few words were more effective a physic than any remedy Elizabeth could concoct. The pall of plague and stomach complaints eased from the Chequer. Then Isabel made sure that Elizabeth did not lack for industry, deciding that their stores were getting low. She set Elizabeth to grinding, drying and distilling from dawn to dusk.

Elizabeth stood over her mortar, working the pestle to break down a hellebore root, a tedious and thankless task. At the sound of footsteps, she lifted her head.

James appeared in the open doorway, his hair slightly tousled, as though the wind had snatched through it. He leaned against the doorjamb and smiled.

A rush of gladness washed over Elizabeth. "You've returned." The pestle slipped from her hand, and she scrambled to catch it. "We wondered at your absence, believing the worst—that you all had succumbed to the falling sickness, and none had been spared."

James chuckled and stepped into the room. "Even then, I wouldn't have stayed away."

Elizabeth willed her heart to stop its frantic patter. "What ailment do you have for us today?"

"Naught for the Chequer. Nay, this in truth is for my old master, the gentleman who sheltered the Giffards. His man, Emery, has drawn up what they need." He handed her the sheet. "I'm hoping you have everything."

Elizabeth read over the list: sweet chervil root, decoction of willow, hyssop with rue and honey and finally king's claver. Each item on its own was innocuous, but collectively, they spoke of a different matter. She lifted her head. "Consumption."

"What?" James's smile faded.

"This physic is for consumption," she said. "With king's claver, he must be in the late stages of the disease."

James frowned, clearly troubled. "How soon can it be ready?"

"No time at all," Elizabeth said. His troubled expression tugged at her. "I'm sure it will be fine."

Jennet appeared in the doorway, her manner grim. "Mistress, Lieutenant Hammond is here. He's arrived with a stack of books, and he looks to sit out the afternoon."

Elizabeth cringed. "I'll be right there." When Jennet left, she turned to James and said, "I can have it ready in the morning."

James's expression was inscrutable. "That won't be a problem."

"I'm sorry, I have to go."

"Lead the way."

"What do you mean?"

"I've come to see you," he said, triggering a quickening of her heartbeat. "Damned if I let that Roundhead chase me away." By the stubborn set of his jaw, Elizabeth knew it was useless to argue. He stepped aside and winked. "After you, love."

This wasn't going to end well.

When Elizabeth entered the parlour, Hammond jumped to his feet but froze when he saw James. Isabel looked up from her place by the hearth, and her eyes widened.

"Lieutenant Hammond, I believe you know James Hart?" Isabel said, breaking the awkward silence. She motioned for Elizabeth to sit beside her.

"We are acquainted," Hammond said. "I was not, however, made aware that the ostler was a regular caller at Ellendale."

The man's tone jarred Elizabeth. The implication that he needed to approve their visitors deeply offended her. "Lieutenant, I wasn't aware that we required passes to accept callers," she said with a brittle smile. "Pray, how must we petition for one, through yourself or the garrison?"

Isabel touched her hand in a silent warning. "Master Hart," she said, "did my niece have Henry Grant's… gout powder ready?"

"Aye," he said. "The rest will be ready tomorrow."

"Very good," Isabel said. "You're welcome to stay, though I suspect Master Grant will be anxious for your return."

"Thank you, mistress," James said, selecting a chair. "I have time for a visit."

"You are welcome, then," Isabel said flatly.

Hammond watched the exchange with the dogged interest of a bear. He selected a chair closest to Elizabeth and settled into it with a stack of books on his lap. Given his proximity, Elizabeth expected to have been the subject of his unwavering attention, but instead, he remained preoccupied with James. This made her even more anxious.

"Will you be entertaining us with your entire library, Constable, or is this only a sample?" James asked. A quirk of a smile tugged the corner of his mouth. Elizabeth tried to catch his attention, to dissuade him from baiting the man.

Hammond scowled. "You may enjoy the instruction, ostler, although I have brought nothing about the breeding of horses."

James smiled. He reminded Elizabeth of a hawk moments before it dove for its prey. "I suspected as much," he said. "Fear not, Constable, I am considered an adaptable fellow. There's nothing quite like John Earle for the keen observation of a man's character. One of my favourites is *A Vulgar-Spirited Man*. Perchance are you familiar with it?"

Elizabeth winced.

"I do not subscribe to the scribblings of a disgraced Anglican clergyman," Hammond said.

"Disgraced in whose eyes, Constable? Surely not before the late King or his son, who took fond instruction from the good bishop."

"Perhaps Lieutenant Hammond would care to grace us with a reading?" Elizabeth interrupted, alarmed at James's audacity. She had a sudden vision of the two men coming to blows. Though she had little doubt that Hammond would end up on the floor, she was keenly aware that the man yielded the greater power through the garrison. "I would be most interested in what you have brought us, Lieutenant."

Hammond gripped the arms of his chair, and he looked as though he were about to heave himself to his feet, but Elizabeth's coaxing words seemed to reach him. His shoulders eased, and although still sullen, he appeared somewhat mollified by her encouraging smile.

Hammond examined his pile of books, and his countenance changed. A cagey gleam replaced the scowl, and he plucked out a book from the middle of the stack.

"Ah, let us start with a lesson from Exodus, my personal favourite." He licked his finger and flipped through a few pages. "I take great comfort in this verse, for it guides me through all the choices I make. 'Tis a reminder that the Lord is ever watchful, and the seeds strewn will mature and demand a reckoning." Hammond cleared his throat and began reading.

"You shall not bow down to them or worship them; for I, the LORD your God, am a jealous God, punishing the children for the sin of the fathers . . ."

Elizabeth listened to his reading with an increasing sense of confusion. She felt the growing tension in the room, but didn't understand its source. Hammond's voice cut like the lashing of a whip while James's expression darkened as the reading continued.

Hammond lingered over the final words, then shut the book and leaned back. James sat rigid. A muscle twitched in his jaw. Elizabeth felt cold rage radiating from him.

"What think you of the selection, ostler?"

"Illuminating," James replied. "But there are flaws with the reasoning."

"I would be most curious to hear them," Hammond said with a cheerless smile. His fingers drummed on the stack of books on his knee.

"Free will. A man can overcome the defects of his birth and select his own path."

"Or be predestined to betray."

James did not respond. The tension in the room pulsated like sullen waves. Elizabeth understood none of it.

"I was in Coventry recently," Hammond said as though the conversation was somehow connected. "You are from there, are you not, ostler? I understand the name Hart carries little respect." He paused, savouring the attention. "I heard all about your father. He pledged his support to Parliament in plate and gold but then dishonoured himself by reneging on his oath." The only sound in the room was the tapping of Hammond's finger against his books. "Naturally, he is an outcast, for honest men place no faith in a neighbour who does not stand by his word. Those who break their vows will reap the Lord's vengeance. You are twice cursed, ostler. Not only did you support the wrong side, but you have a sire reviled by all."

For an unguarded moment, a flicker of pain crossed James's features. It was a fraction of a second and subtle, but Elizabeth caught it. She pressed her hand against her mouth. Having lived under the pall of "traitor's daughter", she knew how sharply that knife cut. But for James, this must be worse than a festering wound, being divided from his father both in politics and character. She ached for him.

James's expression hardened. He rose to his feet, his anger barely contained. "As always, your information is inaccurate. I did not support the wrong side."

He bowed to Isabel, but would not meet Elizabeth's gaze. "If you'll forgive me, I must be leaving. I'll send a boy tomorrow to pick up the last of the medicinals."

With that, he turned and left.

*

James raced along the highway under a dark moon, crouched over Sovereign's bare back. The wind ripped through his hair, and his cloak snapped behind him. Barely touching the ground, the horse galloped in a fluid motion, muscles bunching then exploding as he devoured the road. A wildness had seized him, and he unleashed it on the strip of highway beneath Sovereign's pounding hooves.

Outcast. Twice cursed. Hammond's slurs pounded in his head. Elizabeth had heard it all.

James kept at this speed until Warwick Castle melted away into the horizon, a dark blur against a midnight sky. Blood coursed through his veins, and a thin sheen of sweat beaded his brow. He reined in Sovereign, slowing the horse to a brisk trot. They turned off the main road and struck for the river road.

Without a destination in mind, James set his course by the stars and kept the flowing river on his right. Though they had travelled down this path countless times, he kept a sharp eye on the road and a tight hand on the reins. A low overhang of branches snatched at his cloak, but he brushed past them. Underfoot, thick mulch muffled Sovereign's hooves. They continued along the trail, and the farther they descended into the woods, the richer the scent of resin that filled the warm air.

The woods were alive under a dark moon. A small creature scurried across their path, and James checked Sovereign. Pausing, he heard the frantic clicking of nails scrambling up the bole of a tree and the enraged shriek of an owl missing its catch. James was in sympathy for the offended bird. Pressing the horse's flanks, he urged Sovereign on his way.

When they reached the edge of the woods, James drew to a halt, reluctant to move forward yet unwilling to turn back. A wide swath of meadowland stretched before him, its grasses rippling in the night breeze. He recognised this pasture and knew where it led. If he were to cross the meadow, he would test the fine edge between recklessness and daring. If he were to proceed, there could be no retreat. A prudent man would return to Warwick and deal with his troubles another day.

James struggled against the raging conflict. A hard knot lodged in his chest. He could think of a million reasons to withdraw but only one to press forward. Finally, drawing a deep breath, he pressed his knees against Sovereign's flanks and urged the horse onward.

He found Ellendale shuttered and dark and as daunting as a thirty-foot wall.

Pathetic fool.

Madness carried him here this night—what was he hoping for? Reassurance that she didn't think less of him for what she heard, that against all odds she cared?

He rode to the guest wing, wondering which window was hers. One of the casements was slightly ajar. He couldn't imagine Isabel or Jennet risking a chill—it had to be hers. He dismounted and tethered Sovereign to a birch tree.

James stared at her window with the intensity of one warring with his demons. He needed her, this night more than ever.

He scooped up a handful of pebbles and rolled the stones in his palm while he gauged the distance to the window. He selected one, took aim and threw. The pebble tapped the centre of the glass and bounced against the sill before dropping to the ground.

A light flickered, and a wavering shadow took shape in the candlelight. Then he saw her at the casement. Elizabeth leaned out, dark hair tumbling in heavy waves past her shoulders. James watched her in silence, his heart open and raw. Would she turn away?

Their eyes met. She didn't raise her hand or call out, only stood there. In the next instant, she disappeared from the window, and the light was snuffed out.

Right, then. He had his answer.

James turned his back on the manor and returned to Sovereign. *It's better this way*, he thought as he tightened the horse's girth and prepared to leave.

A sound like the scatter of leaves made him pause. He whirled around to find Elizabeth running to him. When she reached the birch grove, she stopped, breathless. Her expression was questioning; her lips parted, but she didn't speak.

Some things were beyond words.

James held out his hand, and she stepped into his embrace.

Chapter Fifteen

"Have you stirred that broth long enough, Elizabeth?" Isabel asked from the bench in the kitchen. "I should think that it's as mixed as it ever will be."

Embarrassed at having been caught daydreaming, Elizabeth dropped the ladle and scrambled to fish it out before it sank to the bottom.

"What's the matter with you this morning?" Isabel asked. "It's not like you to be so distracted."

"I hardly slept." Elizabeth averted her blushing face.

She and James had lingered at the riverbank until the early dawn crept over the hills. Elizabeth had watched as he rode across the fields. Before he had passed from sight, he paused and gave her a final wave. When she had finally crept inside, she stopped to smile at her reflection in the Venetian mirror. The rasp of his stubbled beard had tingled on her face, and her eyes were bluer than they had ever been.

Collecting herself, Elizabeth ladled broth into two bowls and took a seat across from her aunt. They preferred to break their fast in the kitchen.

"Where's Jennet?" Isabel asked but received her answer when the maid bustled into the kitchen.

"Right here, mistress." She laid a basket on the table. "I thought I would get an early start on gathering the eggs."

Elizabeth barely paid attention to the two women. For her, the world had shifted, and yet they spoke of eggs. She dwelled on the memory of James's lips slanting over her own and the taste of his mouth. As she sipped her broth, she smiled to herself.

"Will you have James's order ready, or do you need assistance with it?" Isabel asked.

Elizabeth looked up, startled to hear his name spoken outside her thoughts. "I'll have it ready. I thought to take it myself before the noon hour. That is, unless you have any objections?"

"Objections? Why should I?"

"You were rather cool with Master James yesterday," Elizabeth replied. She savoured his name on her tongue and had a desire to repeat it like a magpie.

Isabel leaned forward on her elbows. "That was for the benefit of Lieutenant Hammond. He is quite taken with you."

"Hammond?"

"Were you thinking of another?"

The butterflies lurched in Elizabeth's stomach. "Of course not."

"Good, because I happen to know what James Hart does at night." Isabel's eyebrow arched slightly.

Elizabeth's eyes flew to her aunt's face. She must have meant the Knot, or did she suspect the highway robbery? Her aunt's expression gave nothing away.

"I prefer as few complications as possible," Isabel continued. "There's enough talk in town about the lieutenant's courtship and your impending betrothal."

"What?" Elizabeth knocked her bowl and fumbled to keep it from tipping. The broth sloshed over the sides, making a small puddle on the table. She faced her aunt in growing dismay. "*Betrothal?*"

"I am merely repeating what I've heard."

A maggot of a thought came to Elizabeth. "Are you suggesting I encourage the lieutenant?"

"I am not," Isabel said. "Dash his hopes, by all means, but take care that he does not associate his disappointment with James. The lieutenant has a strong rancour against the man, and he's in a position to inflict a great deal of damage to us. To James most of all. Tread carefully."

*

Hammond's cat-and-mouse game persevered through Warwick market. Partially screened by an awning, Elizabeth monitored Hammond's advance. He was closing in on her position.

"Is there anything the matter, Mistress Seton?" Master Ward asked.

"Nothing at all."

Lately, whenever Elizabeth came into Warwick, Hammond appeared at her elbow and insisted on escorting her through the market. He deftly sidestepped all excuses and turned a deaf ear to her terseness. Worse, his preference was to parade her past the Chequer, dangling her like a baited hook. As intended, James usually appeared at the door of his stables.

Elizabeth could feel his rage and sensed he held himself back only by the whisper of a thread. She was certain Hammond knew it too.

Hammond drew closer and reached the cutler's stall.

"That will be two pence, mistress," Master Ward said.

Elizabeth started. "Of course." She fished into her purse to find the coin and, in her haste, dropped it. Crouched low, she peered over her shoulder, through the legs of milling people.

"Here—" She practically threw the coin at Master Ward. "I must be off." She backed away and merged into the crowd.

"Wait! You forgot your broadsheet!"

Elizabeth didn't dare return for it. Hammond finally reached the bookseller's and looked around the stall for her. *A pox on that man.*

A sizeable crowd had gathered around the haberdasher's. Delicate laces, newly arrived from London, had been causing a sensation all day. Elizabeth squeezed past the other women to reach the front. A gossiping clutch of shoppers buffered her from sight. She pretended to be taken by the delicate stitches while she cast anxious glances over her shoulder.

"Did you want a length of ribbon?" Mistress Rathbone appeared with her shears.

"I'm . . . admiring the lace."

"These good women are here to make a purchase. If you don't wish for anything, may I ask you to step aside?"

Elizabeth was more prepared to face a disapproving haberdasher than a determined Hammond. She just needed a few moments. "As a matter of fact, I'd like half a yard of this." She flipped a mustard ribbon with her fingertip. It had a hard, flat colour with nothing to recommend it beyond the fact that it was closest at hand.

"A length of that? The colour doesn't suit you."

"On the contrary," Elizabeth replied with a forced smile. "It's a winning shade."

While Mistress Rathbone measured and cut the length for her, Elizabeth's eyes darted around the crowd. Nowhere. He must have given up. Her shoulders eased in relief.

"Here you go. Give my regards to your aunt."

"Thank you, mistress. God save you."

Elizabeth pushed through the knot of women pressing to take her place at the stall. "Excuse me," she gasped, and they cleared the way for her and the ugly yellow ribbon.

Just as she reached the last matron, a demon in the form of a Puritan Roundhead materialised in her path.

"Good morning, my dear," Hammond drawled.

She pressed her hand to her chest. "Lieutenant—you surprised me."

"A pleasant one, I trust," he said. "I'm glad I found you. There is something I thought you might find of interest." Without waiting for a reply, he took her by the elbow and led her away from the haberdasher's stall. "A godly woman does not gild herself with laces and frills."

Elizabeth's expression hardened. She had every right to visit any shop she desired. Next he would criticise her for frequenting the bookseller's. Would they hang her for choking a constable with a mustard-coloured ribbon?

"I would lower your voice, Lieutenant. Mistress Rathbone will not thank you for your comments."

Hammond led her to the draper's with bolts of broadcloth laid out in display—various shades of grey, charcoal, black and mud brown. He held up a corner of the wool. "Plain, simple fabrics—these are pleasing to the Lord. We must not draw attention to our corrupt body."

"And what of your russet feathers, Lieutenant?" Elizabeth pointed to his coat. "Methinks that this colour draws sufficient attention to the material world."

Rather than take offence, he smiled. "A banner for the godly. My lord Cromwell has seen fit to garb us in this fashion. Come."

Hammond led her away, but to her relief, he did not head for the Chequer. "I should tell you that I'm leaving Warwick for apace."

Elizabeth choked down her excitement. "Indeed? The town will not be the same. Are you returning to London? I recall that you missed it keenly."

"Nothing of the sort," he said. "I shan't be leaving the county. Sir Richard has entrusted me to oversee a particularly delicate enterprise."

Elizabeth's instincts prickled. This sounded ominous, and anything that made Hammond look smug as a cat in cream could not be good. She feared it might have something to do with James. "Might I enquire as to the nature of this business, Lieutenant? I hope it shan't be a dangerous enterprise?"

"Your concern warms me a great deal, my dear."

The softening in his expression made Elizabeth squirm. She hated to encourage the man, but if it could protect James…

"Unfortunately, I'm not at liberty to explain," Hammond said. "Suffice it to say that if we are successful, a mortal blow will be struck to the Commonwealth's enemies."

Elizabeth's worry increased. The only enemy to the Commonwealth that she knew had stolen her heart. She had to warn James. "I wish you joy in your mission, Lieutenant. I must take my leave of you. My aunt wasn't feeling well this day, and I'm anxious to return to her side."

"But you haven't seen my treat."

"A treat?" The hairs on the back of her neck lifted.

Hammond led her down a side street lined by a row of town houses and away from the din of the market. A waiting company of dragoons clustered around the glover's house. Hammond watched her as though savouring her reaction.

"Why are we here?"

"I promised you something of interest."

One of the dragoons presented himself to Hammond. "Everything is secure inside, Lieutenant."

"Very good." Hammond looked around. "And the wagon?" Before the man could answer, a conveyance with thick bars turned the corner and rumbled to a halt before the house. "Excellent timing."

"Why is the gaol cart here?" Elizabeth asked.

"Patience is a virtue, mistress."

A piercing shriek and shattering glass broke the expectant hush. Barked commands drowned out a series of angry shouts. The front door flew open, and a pair of dragoons burst from the house dragging a young woman. Tears streamed down her face, and she clutched a sheet to cover her nakedness as the soldiers marched her to the cart. Elizabeth recognised her as the glover's maid.

The woman stumbled and spilled to the sidewalk, exposing small, quivering breasts. "Please!" she cried as they hauled her to her feet.

Shocked, Elizabeth watched them push the naked woman into the wagon. One of the soldiers tossed the sheet back to her.

Next the dragoons marched out the second prisoner—the glover. The man stumbled out of his home, clad only in a shirt. The garment barely covered his naked loins. Normally fond of gawking at the young maids, he no longer leered.

"Distressing, isn't it?" Hammond said.

Elizabeth started. "What—?"

"Adultery and fornication," he replied. "They will spend time in the arms of the stocks. We must prepare to don the mantle of the New Jerusalem. There is no room for heretics and the ungodly in this new order."

Elizabeth's stomach turned. By now, a small crowd had flooded in from the market. A few of the bolder men hovered near the wagon to get a good look at the prisoners. Laughter and jeering rippled through the crowd. Elizabeth found it difficult to watch. "What of mercy?"

"Mercy? Would that please you?" Hammond's smile widened. "I have shown them mercy. Had we arrested them in another fortnight, they'd both be in the gaol."

"The *gaol*?"

"The new act against adultery and fornication. I have shown them ample mercy." Hammond smiled. "Let this serve as a warning."

*

James waited by the riverbank for Elizabeth. Twelve stones placed in a circle at the base of the birch tree—a sign to meet at midnight. Moonlight sparkled on the running river, and the air was balmy and calm. A fever drove him to see her before he left for Coventry in the morning. He debated telling her about Sir Piers and his pledge to help Charles, but thought not yet.

Elizabeth came running down the trail and didn't stop until she launched herself into his arms. James held her with a fierceness that surprised even him. Their lips met in a fevered kiss, slanting, devouring, their breaths merging. She drove him wild, and he felt a tugging regret when she pulled away.

"You're safe," Elizabeth said, cradling his face in her hands. "I came by the Chequer, but I couldn't find you or Henry."

"What happened?"

"Hammond is on some business—I don't know, but it must have something to do with you."

"He cornered you in the market *again*?"

"It's of no account—"

"Elizabeth, do not let your guard down with that one—with any of his kind," James said hoarsely. He could tell she thought him half-addled by jealousy—he had to make her understand. "You think he plays a harmless game, but I know better than most what they're capable of."

"James, he's determined to cause you mischief. If you don't rise to the bait, he'll lose interest."

"And in the meantime, shall I meekly stand while he sniffs around your skirts?" The anger pounded in his temples. "If nothing else, I have the right to court you openly."

"Please—no one must know, him least of all. Not yet. I fear for you." She clutched his hands, her eyes wide with alarm.

James willed his anger to dissipate. Their time was precious, and he wasn't going to squander it with arguments. He gathered her in his arms and kissed the top of her head. "Forget Hammond."

"What if—what if you're captured?"

"By him?" He laughed, hoping to coax a smile from her. "He'd have better fortune finding a papist catechism in the Scottish Kirk."

No smile, only a deeper frown. "I'm not amused."

James grinned. "Be at peace, love. Truthfully, our paths will not cross. I'm for Coventry in the morning."

"Coventry? James, what are you—"

He laid his finger against her mouth to still her rush of words. "Trust me." His thumb brushed her bottom lip, and her mouth parted. He drew her against him and bent down for another taste. He felt the crush of her breasts against his chest, and his heart pounded. The desire to spread his cloak and lower her on the soft ground tempted him. He stopped kissing her and stared at her flushed face.

Patience, man.

"Come, walk with me for a space." He needed the crisp breeze to clear his head and more besides. As he brushed his lips on the inside of her wrist, the faint scent of lavender stirred his senses.

She searched his face, and then a hint of a dimple flitted at the corner of her mouth. "Aye, lead on."

They walked together for some time, following the running brook into the forest until they came across a small ridge where the trail fell away.

The streaming water played soothing music above the rustling of the leaves. The scent of sweet meadow rue filled the air, and they found a patch of moss to sit on.

Elizabeth settled beside him and hugged her knees to her chest. James caught a glimpse of her bare leg before she smoothed her shift. Dropping one hand, she toyed with the moss, a full sleeve trailing at her wrist. Her dark hair spilled over her shoulder to her narrow waist. Occasionally, she reached up and brushed away a stray lock from her face. He imagined how her fingers would feel tracing down his back. His loins tightened again. Perhaps this was not a good idea after all.

James cleared his parched throat. "A cure for melancholy, do you think?" He indicated the moss.

"Ground moss?" she tilted her head and smiled at him. "Nay, but a good guess as 'tis ruled by Saturn. Have you any aches? I could brew you a cup of stewed moss."

James grinned. "I have aches, but I doubt that would effect a cure."

Elizabeth averted her gaze and smiled. "If you seek a remedy for lassitude, 'tis the tree moss you need."

James rubbed his stubbled beard and looked at the trees crowding the river. He stared at the river flowing towards Coventry, then back to her upturned profile. He knew of no other cure for weariness than sitting beside this woman. The tree could keep its moss.

He could almost forget the world that awaited him beyond the ridge. How easy it would be to turn his back on everything and take her away with him. Maybe he should have listened to Henry—start fresh, put the past behind him.

James grimaced. He couldn't. Men and arms would need to be raised, and he was the one to do it. He'd have to be content with a few spare moments.

He touched her shoulder and drew her against him. She leaned against his chest, moulding herself into his arms. He rested his chin on the top of her head, felt her shoulders rise and fall with each breath. His gaze lingered on the curve of her breast beneath the linen of her shift.

James lifted her chin and pressed his lips to her own. She turned slightly in his arms, her mouth sweet and responsive. He cupped her breast through the cloth and teased her nipple with his thumb. She drew back slightly, her breath warm against his mouth, before she leaned into him, looping her arm around his neck.

His hunger flared, and all thoughts of restraint scattered. He shifted and lowered her to the ground. The top of her shift eased from her shoulders, and his hand slipped under the fabric to stroke one rounded breast. A soft moan escaped her parted lips. Her tongue, her kisses, her softness were driving him wild. His lips found her nipple and teased the pink crest with his tongue. She squirmed under him, further spurring his passion. He had abstained far too long. Lifting her shift, his hand travelled up her silky thigh until he found her seam, wet and warm.

At this touch, Elizabeth's eyes flew open, and she pulled away with a gasp. "We shouldn't—not like this." He read her conflict in her parted lips and troubled face.

James closed his eyes and drew a ragged breath. He knew what she needed—a home and family. Though his cock wanted to promise her the moon, his head knew better. He just couldn't offer her what she deserved. Not yet.

"Aye," he said hoarsely and eased from her. "We had better return." He rose to his feet and helped her up. Elizabeth's vulnerability tugged at his heart, and he brushed his lips on her forehead. "Come, love, the night is waning. I leave at first light."

*

A furtive scurrying woke James from a deep sleep. After a second of disorientation, his soldier's instincts kicked in. He rolled to his feet, and in one fluid motion, lunged for the dagger beside his bed. Crouched and ready to spring, he froze when he found Henry standing in his room. The innkeeper took a step back and held up his hands.

"Easy, lad—didn't mean to startle you."

"Christ's teeth, Henry," James exhaled. He started to relax until he noticed who accompanied him. "Emery?" James's stomach twisted. "What's wrong?"

"They came for Sir Piers last night—a troop of dragoons. So terrible, poor Master, and him still in his bed clothes."

"What?" A cold dread seized James.

Emery sucked in a ragged breath. "Shortly before ten, the dragoons came with a writ of arrest signed by Sir Richard. Accused my lord of agitating against Parliament."

Christ's teeth. James started pacing. How much did Sir Richard know? *Think*! How had this happened? "Did they mention any names— accomplices?"

"Nothing. Sir Piers said nothing, not even to answer their accusations," Emery said. "They were alerted to suspicious activities at Bideford. The lieutenant bragged that they would cut off the serpent's head."

James raked his fingers through his hair. *Great, another one like...* A cold chill snaked down his spine. "Who was he—this lieutenant?"

"Ezekiel Hammond."

James fought the urge to bellow his rage. How had he missed it? The signs were all there. Coventry. Royalist plot. Hammond had been prattling about this before, but James hadn't seriously believed the Roundhead was capable of uncovering an earthworm. Even Elizabeth had warned him. Piers had been counting on him, and James had failed the first test.

Emery's eyes widened. "James? You know him?"

"Aye, I know him for a bastard." His hand tightened around the dagger until his knuckles were white. Had the bastard been within reach, the blade would have been plunged into his throat. "A fine fish he's caught. A high-ranking Parliamentary officer turned King's man. That will secure the devil's future."

"What are we going to do? Master won't survive this. The last time nearly killed him." Emery swayed on his feet.

James struggled to cool his anger. He must think clearly. "What hour is it?" he asked Henry.

"Near daybreak."

"Have we a spare room where Emery can rest?"

"Aye."

"I don't need rest," Emery protested.

"You'll be useless to us before long," James replied.

"What of my lord?"

"Leave this with me," James said. "I'll get him out."

Chapter Sixteen

Thunder rumbled in the distance while clouds scudded across the night sky. A flash of lightning illuminated a stone building on the banks of a river. Another streak of light and James made out the water wheel. He kept checking the road behind him.

James sat astride Sovereign in Conduit Meadow, outside Coventry. The place was abandoned at this hour. He had often escaped here in his youth. The damp smell of river mud stirred memories of running barefoot and hunting for tadpoles amongst the rushes. He'd often clamber up the thick spokes of the water wheel until he reached as high as he could, scrambling from one safe footing to another. He had been able to see for miles and fuel his dream of what lay beyond Coventry.

From a distance, he heard the pounding of hooves and the creak of carriage wheels. James drew his pistols and focused on the empty road. A squat carriage and a lone rider materialised. He cocked his pistols and took aim. With another streak of lightning, the company came into sharp relief, and he lowered his weapons.

Henry pulled up in the inn's carriage with Emery seated beside him. Its panels had been stripped of all markings. Nathaniel reined in his bay beside the stopped carriage.

"All right, lad?" Henry called before jumping down from his perch. He wore a dark overcoat, and a knit cap hid his tawny head. "These roads are in sad shape. Nearly bust a wheel a mile back."

"You took a bloody long time," James said as he dismounted. "I began to think you lost your way."

"Your directions were a bit hodgepodge. Emery kept us from ending up in Birmingham."

James walked up to the carriage. "What are you doing here, Emery? You were to wait for us in Warwick."

"I serve my master, Hart."

"He'll stay with me, lad," Henry said. "One more minding the horses won't matter."

James shook his head. "See that he doesn't leave, not for any reason." He turned to Nathaniel, who had yet to dismount. He, at least, had followed James's instructions, exchanging his fine brocades for a dark woollen cloak and plain hat. "Barrister, we go on foot, not horse."

Nathaniel dismounted and handed his reins to Henry. "I'm not fond of gaols."

"I don't plan to make this a habit," James said, adjusting the scarf around his neck.

"With your profession, Captain, you might consider leaving room for that possibility."

James gave Nathaniel a hard look. "Let's get going."

They left the horses with Henry and travelled the quarter mile to town on foot. Even in the dark, James knew every boulder and ditch. The wall loomed ahead, a stone-and-mortar barrier filled with lichen and trailing vines. James walked several paces and halted. He groped the rough surface and hesitated when all he found was unbroken stone. There had once been a gap in the wall, but that had been over ten years ago.

"Anything the matter, Captain?"

James didn't reply and instead continued for several paces. Another flash of lightning illuminated what he searched for. The tangled vines had grown thick over the stone, but the crumbling break was still there, though barely wide enough for a grown man.

"I seem to remember it being larger," James muttered as he squeezed through. He scraped his hand on the stone and grimaced.

"Memories can be false." Nathaniel prepared to follow after him. "I've built a living on that premise."

On the other side of the wall, James paused and looked around. The street lay deserted. Nathaniel grunted and swore under his breath at the tight squeeze until James motioned him to silence. They stood in a muddy lane behind a row of houses. James signalled for Nathaniel to follow.

They shunned the main thoroughfare and kept to the back lanes. Nothing had changed. The streets still reeked of piss in the gutters and the offal of nesting rats. Packs of dogs called out to one another, forlorn howls that lifted the hairs on James's nape.

As they were about to cross the main street, the clip-clopping of approaching horses alerted them. The slipped into the shadows and waited while a small patrol passed. After the company disappeared, the two men pressed on.

They arrived at a large three-story wooden building. Its white daub panels stood out like ghostly squares in the night. A wall ran along its perimeter, and the few windows that faced the street were dark and shuttered. The building huddled on the corner like a sleeping beast.

A bell began to toll, its sombre peal breaking the silence with a series of echoing chimes. Eleven bells, then no more. By now, the gaoler should have left for the night. James lowered the brim of his hat and raised his scarf. "Time to play."

Nathaniel nodded and pulled up his hood.

They circled to the rear of the building and found the postern gate. A row of spikes topped the iron grill, and the wall, weathered over time, provided few footholds.

"How do we—?"

James reached through the bars and unlatched the gate. "Two gold crowns for an unlocked gate."

Nathaniel shrugged. "Fair trade."

Without another word, they passed through an empty courtyard and made their way to the rear door. As with the gate, it had been left unlocked. Before they entered, James examined the door with a critical eye. Half-rotted, it would be nothing to break. That should place further distance between the gaoler, Caleb, and the enquiries that were sure to follow.

Inside, they stepped into a darkened corridor. James unsheathed his sword and paused. The burnt smell of snuffed rushes lingered. *Five gold crowns for a gaoler gone.* Satisfied, James led the way to the guardroom, guided by Caleb's directions. There, the banked fire provided meagre light, but it was enough to find what they needed—a spare set of keys hanging on a hook. James snatched the ring while Nathaniel lit a candle.

They climbed the back stairs to the top floor. James paused to survey the corridor of locked cells, recounting the gaoler's instructions: eight prisoners—one on the top floor. Fifth one from the stairs. They reached the cell and peered through the barred grate. Black as Hades. Nothing to suggest they had the right one. James fiddled with the lock until they heard a sharp click.

"Who's there?" Sir Piers's voice sounded feeble. A cot creaked.

"Friends, my lord," Nathaniel whispered drawing closer.

James took a step into the cell and shivered. It took a few moments for his eyes to adjust to the gloom. He found Piers sitting on his cot. The cell was dank and cold with the walls crowding close. James had no desire to stay any longer than necessary. "You're coming with us."

"Ja—"

James covered Piers's mouth with his hand. Understanding, Piers nodded, and James released his hold.

"'Tis foolish, my boy. Foolish to risk your neck for me," he whispered. "Leave me to my punishment."

"Nay, I'll not leave you here."

James helped him to his feet and, together with Nathaniel, ushered him out of the cell. They rushed down the corridor towards the stairs. James took the lead with his blade drawn. Partway down the staircase, Piers stumbled. Nathaniel caught him before he plunged down the stairs.

James slowed. Something felt off, as though the very walls held their breath. Too silent. They had passed the second floor when James heard the protest of a rusty door and an echoing clang. Cold air rushed past them and nearly snuffed out the light. He held up his hand, and the others stopped. A bump and rattle, then the steady pounding of boots and muffled voices headed their way.

"Curse that Caleb," James hissed under his breath. He thought quickly—flight or brazen it out? He looked back at Piers whose shoulders slumped. "Back—up the stairs."

By the time they reached the upper landing, Piers was bent over and wheezing. Nathaniel and James each grabbed him by the arm and half dragged him into his cell.

"Flee, lad. Go," Piers urged between hacking coughs. "There's still time."

"Not without you." James drew from his belt his pistols and held one out for Nathaniel. "Stay or flight? Your choice." The heavy footsteps grew louder—two men by the sounds of it.

Nathaniel accepted the pistol. "You have a plan?"

"Aye. Master, lie down on the cot." James extinguished the candle and pulled Nathaniel to the hinge side of the door. Their pistols were cocked and primed. James adjusted his scarf and waited.

Voices drifted in the corridor. Caleb spoke in a nervous, pleading tone. The gaoler stopped outside the cell. Flickering rush-light spilled through the grate in the door. "Can't this wait until morning, Lieutenant? The hour is late. If you like, I'll admit you at first light."

James's ears pricked. Nathaniel lifted his head, and they exchanged looks. The gaoler had not betrayed them after all. They flattened themselves against the cold wall.

"Simple laggard, this can't wait until the morning."

James nostrils flared. *Hammond.* He gripped his pistol tighter.

"Whitehall's lackey arrives in the morning to wrest the truth from the traitor," the lieutenant continued. "That duty should fall to me."

Caleb fiddled with the lock and made a convincing pretence of unlocking an unlocked door. "One moment."

"Hurry up."

Caleb opened the cell door, tentatively at first, as though nervous as to what he would find. He held up the torch. "My lord? Have we disturbed your sleep?"

Piers turned over in his cot. "What is the meaning of this, Master Gaoler?"

"He's a traitor. What care I for his comfort?" Hammond pushed past the gaoler to confront Piers. He stood with his back to James.

Caleb stepped inside and peered around. He started when he saw James and drew Hammond's attention. As the lieutenant turned, James smashed his forearm into Hammond's face, connecting hard under the chin. Hammond's head snapped back, and he stumbled backward with a half twist before crumbling to the floor. He lay there as motionless as a scarecrow cut from its post.

James grunted. "I've wanted to do that for a very long time."

Nathaniel bent over the unconscious man, lifted an eyelid and checked his breathing. "You'll not be wanted for murder, Captain. He yet lives."

"Pity." James felt a grudging respect for the solicitor's ability to remain unruffled. He had not expected this from a pampered London lawyer. If only Caleb displayed more presence of mind.

The gaoler had not moved, only stared at the unconscious lieutenant with round, terrified eyes. "Caleb?" James flicked him on the cheek to get his attention. "We need a pair of manacles." When the gaoler still appeared stunned, James slapped him. "Manacles, Caleb. Not tomorrow—now."

The gaoler shook his head to gather his wits. "Aye, I'll get them."

"He won't return," Nathaniel said, helping Piers to his feet.

"He will," James said. "Take Sir Piers and get to the meadow. I'll follow as soon as I can. If you don't see me within the quarter hour, leave."

On his way out, Piers grabbed James's hand with surprising strength. His eyes were bright, and he struggled to speak.

A lump formed in James's throat. "Go on," he said. "I'll catch up." Nathaniel led Sir Piers down the hall.

James paused over Hammond. Still unconscious, the Roundhead's mouth gaped open, and his throat was exposed. With a single slice of a dagger, this problem would be solved. In cold blood.

"Damn my morals." Instead, James dragged Hammond's limp body to the far end of the cell, surprised at how heavy the man was. "You've fed on too many puddings."

Caleb returned, clutching the irons. James grabbed one pair, looped them around the foot of the cot and snapped a manacle around each wrist. The sharp click of the latch gave him intense satisfaction.

"Sleep well, Roundhead." James then snatched the second set from Caleb and pulled the gaoler towards the same cot.

"What are you doing?"

James grabbed the gaoler's hand and slapped the other manacle around his wrist. "You will thank me later."

Caleb struggled to pull away. "This wasn't our agreement. You can't leave me trussed up in my cell."

Without warning, James threw a punch and hit the gaoler square on the face. Caleb stumbled back, blood spurting from his nose. "What the hell?" His free hand flew up to protect himself.

James yanked the gaoler towards him. "Don't be a fool. If I don't do this, you'll be left to explain to the codfish why you are unharmed and unrestrained."

Caleb ground his teeth and swiped at the blood. "Argh! At least leave me some comfort."

"Of course, you can have the cot, courtesy of Sir Piers, who paid and warmed it for you." James chained him to the cot as well, then pushed

Caleb down on the bed. When he finished, he sat on his haunches, eye level to Caleb. "Try to have a restful evening."

Before he left, James tipped his hat to an unconscious Hammond.

*

Elizabeth turned on her side and drew the quilt over her shoulder. She lay between sleep and awake, lulled by the sound of thunder and the splattering rain against her window. *Rap, rap, rap.* The wind sounded odd as it rattled against the panes. Outside, jagged lightning illuminated an ink-black sky. *Rap, rap, rap.* She came fully awake. Not thunder. Someone was pounding on the door. She scrambled out of bed and grabbed the fireplace poker.

Her feet made barely a sound on the stair's wooden treads. A gust of cool wind lifted the hem of her shift. Muffled voices came from the kitchen, and she heard Jennet's. Then Elizabeth recognised the deep timbre of another, and she rushed into the kitchen.

James spun around. Sopping wet, his dark hair lay flat against his head. A puddle of water collected beneath his boots. Henry stood behind him with three other strangers—a servant, an old man in a filthy coat and a slender man plucking at his sodden clothes.

"What happened?" Elizabeth asked.

James glanced at the poker in her hand and grimaced. "A bit of trouble in Coventry. We had nowhere else to go. The roads are washed out from the storm, and there's no making the Chequer. We can't go another twenty yards, never mind two miles."

"A bit of trouble?" She looked at the bedraggled men. Henry took a sudden interest in the rafters.

"Aye, in the gaol," James replied.

"The *gaol*? You were in the gaol?"

"We paid our respects to Hammond."

"Hammond? You came up against *Hammond*?" Elizabeth tightened her hold on the poker, unaware that she held it aloft like a sword until Jennet pried it from her grasp.

"Actually, he came up against me and is the poorer for it," James said with a sudden grin. A wet lock fell across his brow, and for a moment he reminded Elizabeth of a naughty child having escaped with a robin's nest. "We left him at his leisure in one of the cells." Behind him, one of the men coughed delicately in his sleeve.

197

Elizabeth groaned. *Worse and worse.* "And now he'll be hunting for you—for all of you." She corrected herself in time, conscious of everyone's attention. "We're lost," she said under her breath.

James sobered. "He didn't see us."

Elizabeth couldn't decide whether he spoke the truth or said it to placate her. The others looked weary, but not desperate. Dared she hope?

"I will swear by it. All is well," James said.

Elizabeth searched his face, then nodded. "Except that you're dripping on our clean floor." She turned to Jennet. "We'll need some dry linen."

"Aye, and I'll have to unpack the great chest by the looks of it," Jennet said. "Should I wake up your blessed aunt, do you think?"

"She should be told."

The old man released the arm of his servant and hobbled to Elizabeth. He cleared his throat, and a rattling cough seized him, but he fought it down. "Our apologies for bringing trouble upon you, mistress. The fault is mine." Although frayed and dishevelled, he had the speech of a gentleman. "All this was for my benefit. If you are to be cross with anyone, blame me. James, you didn't need to go through all this bother."

"We've discussed this."

"Mistress, you should know the truth before agreeing to open your doors to us. I was, of late, a prisoner in Coventry gaol." A flush of colour appeared on the man's sunken cheeks.

James rubbed his forehead with the palm of his hand. "You make it sound as though you were a criminal."

"Parliament would disagree, my lad. They've taken a dim view on my attempts to restore the Prince of Wales to his rightful throne, even with my past service record. Most especially because of it, in fact. Treason, they'd call it, not reparation."

"You had no business being there, and if I have to break into thirty more gaols to keep you out, I will." He took a deep breath before turning back to Elizabeth. "This is my former master, Sir Piers Rotherham, and his manservant Emery Yardley. Nathaniel Lewis—"

"Barrister of the Inns of London." The slender man stepped forward and gave Elizabeth a courtly bow.

James cleared his throat, and the two men exchanged a glance. James turned his back on the barrister and faced Elizabeth. "We must hide Sir Piers until things quiet down in Coventry," he said. "'Twill only be for a short time until we can make other arrangements. They have no cause to search for him in Warwick as the Rotherhams have no close connections here. Trust me, Ellendale will be safe. I would not ask otherwise."

Elizabeth considered the gentleman. She noted his pallid complexion and telling cough, remembering the physic James had once asked her to prepare. There was no question about offering shelter. "Welcome to Ellendale, my lord."

James smiled his thanks, and its warmth touched Elizabeth to the core.

"I understand I've nearly missed the adventure," Isabel said, appearing with Jennet. "Fortunately, you all make enough noise to wake an old woman." While Jennet passed around dry towels, Isabel sized up the dripping men. "James, I admit no surprise to find you're involved in this mayhem, though I had hopes for Henry."

James grinned. "Consistency is a virtue."

Isabel harrumphed. "'Tis chilled in this room, or is it just me?" Her head canted ever so slightly as she considered Elizabeth. "Niece, be a dear and get the fire going."

"Right away."

Elizabeth knelt by the hearth to stoke the banked embers while exchanging stolen glances with James. Soon the fire sprang to life, orange sparks hissing. The wind blasted the windows, and more flashes of light lit the black night.

"There's only one spare room fit for use this night," Jennet told Isabel.

"I'm sure it will do for Sir Piers," Isabel replied and looked over at the others.

"A spot by the hearth will suit us proper," Henry broke in. "No worry, we leave as soon as the storm passes."

"I'll return to the barn and see to the horses," James added as he towelled his dripping hair. "Forgive me if I don't return, Henry Grant. Your snoring is legendary."

Elizabeth smothered a smile and laid another log on the fire. She watched the men and perceived their relief. Their initial wariness thawed, and the occasional low chuckle replaced their silence. James stood in their midst, his legs braced apart and shoulders squared, reminding her for all the world of a king upon the hill. His eyes glowed, and he wore a hawkish triumph. A rush of love for his daring and courage flooded her. She hovered close, drawn to his flame.

Though he appeared unconcerned with this night's adventure, she knew it would not end here. An icy shiver ran down the length of her spine. The highwayman would continue to ride until Hammond finally caught him. What would she be left with except empty arms and an abiding regret? Deep inside, she knew their time was precious, but she feared that one day she'd be left with nothing—not even treasured memories. Regret cut both ways.

The men sorted out their makeshift pallets, but Elizabeth no longer paid attention. Her focus centred on James. She watched him through lowered lashes as he shrugged out of his wet coat. His shirt clung against his skin, nearly transparent, and defined every muscular line of his chest. She imagined lifting the shirt over his head then pressing her lips against the base of his throat. Her mouth went dry. Before she could tear herself away, he lifted his gaze and met hers with an intensity that shot through her.

A question burned in his slate-grey eyes, one she was ready to answer.

*

The house had grown silent when Elizabeth heard a scratch at her bedroom door. She opened it, and James joined her inside. A cool breath of air clung to his coat from the stables, where they all believed him to be. She shivered.

James tossed off his coat and drew her into his arms. Elizabeth no longer thought of the cold. "Was I wrong to come?" he asked, his words soft against her ear.

Elizabeth tightened her hold around his waist and laid her cheek against the hollow of his chest. The beating of his heart echoed in her ears. Borrowed time, she knew; every moment to be held fast and cherished. She would not winnow it away. *If nothing else, I will have this.* She tilted her head and met his searching gaze. "Nay. Stay the night."

James threaded his fingers through her hair. His mouth slanted over hers, exploring with a thoroughness that left Elizabeth breathless. Gone his self-restraint. He no longer reined in his passion and instead tested the depths of her resolve. Her arms curled around his neck, and she answered him, holding nothing back. Only thoughts of this man filled her senses.

Elizabeth felt her shift lift over her thighs, a soft whisper of cloth against her skin. James's hand cupped her bare buttock and pressed her against him, and she gasped at the blunt hardness straining against his breeches. She tilted her head as his mouth traced a hot path down the curve of her neck and savoured the shivers that his breath stirred against her skin. James drew the shift over her head, and the cloth drifted to the ground to lie in a discarded puddle at their feet.

"Ah, my love," he murmured against her lips. "Beautiful beyond belief." He caressed her bare breast, his thumb stroking the peak until it hardened.

Elizabeth melted against him, impatient and awash in sensations she had never felt before. She slipped her hands under his shirt, revelling in the feel of his unyielding chest against her questing fingers. James yanked off his shirt, and it joined her shift on the ground. Elizabeth held her breath. His hair fell in waves to his broad shoulders, and his bare chest tapered to a narrow waist. She traced her finger along the line of dark hair that trailed down below his stomach. His eyes darkened. Emboldened, she undid his laces and loosened his waistband. James captured her lips in an impassioned kiss, and she clung to him as her world canted. With a groan, he dropped his breeches and carried her to the bed.

Elizabeth opened her arms to him, and he knelt above her, skin brushing against skin. He bent down and teased her with his mouth, his tongue tracing circles around her pink nipples until she squirmed with the agony of it. She threaded her fingers through his hair and cradled his head in her arms. Moving downward, he explored the curve of her hips and spread fevered kisses along her stomach. Her breath caught in her throat, and she shuddered when his fingers slipped between her thighs. She unfolded like the petals of a rose, writhing at the strange sensations. Elizabeth pressed closer, greedy for his touch. A languid heat spread between her legs.

"There's no turning back," he whispered hoarsely. "I can't turn back."

Elizabeth shook her head. Easier to reverse in mid-flight. His every touch was a torment, and she hungered for him to show her more. "Prove me your love."

James rose between her legs, and Elizabeth felt her softness yield to his hardness when he penetrated her. A slight tugging, a quick pain and a spreading warmth as his manhood buried deep inside her. James moved slowly at first, and when she shifted beneath him, he settled in a steady, long rhythm. She arched her hips and wrapped her legs around his. They were caught in an ancient dance where her body moved instinctively in response to his.

She ran her palms down the length of his back, and his muscles rippled under her fingertips. He tormented her with scalding kisses along the curve of her neck. Closing her eyes, she licked her suddenly dry lips. His long hair brushed her shoulder as he found the soft hollow of her throat. Elizabeth savoured every touch, thrilled to every new sensation until she felt herself soar.

James hungrily claimed her lips, and she rose to meet him, pulling him closer. Spreading warmth infused her limbs. Elizabeth poised on the cusp until the storm broke. Waves of pleasure coursed through her body, so intense it bordered on exquisite pain. A cry escaped her, but she bit her lip and buried her face in his shoulder. She held on, digging her nails into his skin. *This is death. I am reborn.* James groaned and with a final thrust, shuddered and collapsed, his breathing hoarse in her ears. She felt his pounding heart against her breast.

Gathering her in his arms, James kissed the damp strands of her hair. She snuggled closer, revelling in the feel of him still inside her. He was hers, and she did not want to let him go. A pulse throbbed in the base of his throat, matching her erratic heart. She pressed her lips against his neck, tasting the salty sheen of sweat coating his skin.

James ran his thumb along her jawline and tipped her chin so that his eyes searched hers. "My love." He settled her in his arms, and she lay against him, their legs entwined.

For a time, they dozed. Elizabeth awakened with James's arms still encircling her. Her head rested on his chest, and his breathing was deep and rhythmic. She lay still, watching the black night soften through her bedroom window. The storm had nearly spent itself, and rain no longer lashed against the windows. She spared no thought for those who would have been shocked to find them together; less for their enemies who hunted him and forced them to remain in the shadows. Her world revolved around this man, and she trembled at the love that welled in her like a tapped spring.

James awoke and stretched. Inhaling deeply, he turned on his side and propped himself on his elbow. "Did you sleep?" He traced a path with his finger along her bare arm, then toyed with a lock of hair that curled over her breast. His hands were warm against her skin.

"I dreamt." Elizabeth traced his mouth with her fingers and held her breath when his tongue flicked out to kiss each tip. A sweet ache spread between her legs.

"Come, my love," he said, "I'll show you a new dream."

Chapter Seventeen

Elizabeth paused, the sensation of being watched strong. The men were gathered at Ellendale, discussing plans for Piers's eventual departure. No one faced her direction, not even James. Instead, he stared at the Venetian mirror hanging on the wall. Elizabeth followed his gaze and, to her surprise, saw his reflection. His eyes were locked on hers. She wondered if he truly saw her or if it was a trick of the glass. She glanced again to where he sat. The others debated a course of action, but James remained silent.

Elizabeth returned to the mirror and feasted on the image like a guilty treat. When she smiled, the corners of his eyes crinkled in response. She relaxed in her chair, needlework forgotten, and enjoyed the unexpected opportunity to drink her fill of him in a room full of people. Always she had to avert her gaze when all she wanted to do was memorise every contour of his face, from the arch of his brows to the strong hawkish nose and the sensual line of his mouth. Her smile deepened as she remembered the pleasures that same mouth had given her a few nights ago.

An intense fluttering tickled her stomach, and she bit her lip. James lifted his brow a fraction, and his eyes narrowed. A languid feeling spread through her. She stared greedily, knowing that any moment they would be forced to return to unsatisfying, furtive glances.

"Four days' travel and Sir Piers can be in London—a few more and his passage to Holland secured," Nathaniel said. "With all due respect, Captain, 'tis foolhardy to attempt anywhere else. Captain?"

James sighed and turned his head. "The Rotherhams have family connections to the north in Lancashire, where Royalist sympathies remain strong. Sir Piers could make Warrington in six. You speak of a difference of two days."

"He could sail for the Continent in that time."

"I am not leaving England, Master Lewis," Piers said. "I am in the twilight of my years, and night approaches. I will not abide with strangers. Sir Anthony Birchall of Warrington is a distant cousin, both in lineage and politics, but he has a clannish heart and will not turn me away."

"Why stop in Lancashire?" Nathaniel said impatiently. "By all means, press on to Scotland and join the King. No need to wait for the spring campaign."

"I understand your situation, Master Lewis," Piers said. "I don't envy you the task of recounting these unfortunate events to His Majesty."

"This is but a complication," Nathaniel said, toying with the cuffs of his jacket. "Though we've lost the advantage of Bideford, our efforts continue. We will be ready in the spring—true, Captain?"

Elizabeth frowned.

James met her gaze in the mirror. "Aye," he said in a low tone, then turned to Piers, "I'll send a messenger to Lancashire in the morn. All will be set for you to leave within the fortnight."

"My coach is at your disposal," Nathaniel said. "I admit that my plans included travelling north, though not for at least another month. We'll have to devise a strategy to avoid unfriendly patrols."

"Leave that to me. We'll skirt Warwick from the south, then strike westward along the Henley road to cross into Worcestershire. It means an extra few hours of travel, but we'll keep clear of the patrols."

"I had not thought the Roundheads so easily confounded by circular routes."

James snorted. "How much easier if they were. Nay, barrister, I wager they'll be focused on the Coventry and London roads. I'll ride ahead and, if necessary, provide a diversion. I'll give them every reason to abandon their post."

Elizabeth sat upright, her fingers curled around the chair's arm.

"Will you be accompanying us the entire way north?" Nathaniel asked.

"Were it possible, but I dare not, lest my absence be noted," James replied. "I'll see you safely out of Warwickshire, but no farther. You'll be secure enough then." He glanced in the mirror. "Besides, I have matters to attend here."

*

A drowsy haze filled the loft at the inn. Sunlight filtered through the drawn curtains, shielding the room from the dying bustle of market day. A basket remained discarded by the door with its goods spilled on the floor.

Elizabeth glanced back at James where he lay stretched out on the bed with his arms propped behind his head. A sheet draped across his thighs, and he seemed content to watch as she laced up her stays.

"How do I look?" She pursed her lips and tried to gather her hair in its usual sedate knot, but her fingers kept fumbling the bodkin.

James gave her a lazy smile. "Like a woman well-ravished by her lover."

Elizabeth's stomach fluttered. If only she could while away the rest of the afternoon in his arms. She barely paid attention to the workings of her hairpins and winced when she scraped one against her temple.

James rose from the bed and crossed the room, sleek in his nakedness. He took her into his arms and gave her a lingering kiss. "Don't leave yet."

Elizabeth gathered her willpower. "Market day is nearly over. They'll be wondering."

James sighed. "I can steal many things, but time seems to elude me." He gave her a last, tender kiss before releasing her.

As he got dressed, Elizabeth gathered the rest of her things. A growing melancholy slowed her task. She crouched down to pick up the contents from her scattered basket. Stolen moments. "When were you going to tell me?"

"What?"

She wrapped the apothecary's tincture into the worsted yarn so the glass wouldn't shatter. "Your plans with the King." There, she'd said it after debating when or if to ask. Later, she kept promising herself. Later became now.

When James didn't answer, she looked up. He stood close, his expression troubled. She was grateful that he didn't try to smile and shrug it aside.

"I didn't want to worry you," he said. "These things can brew for years."

"Nathaniel mentioned a spring campaign."

James crossed his arms. "Aye." He could have answered that it was just talk, that he didn't really know—any number of ways to bless, or curse, her with ignorance.

Elizabeth placed the last of her purchases into the basket. She squared her shoulders and rose to her feet. "You needn't shelter me. I'd rather hear the truth from your lips, however dark it may be."

The intensity in his expression prevented her from turning away. "I love you," he said.

Elizabeth blinked at her sudden tears. She touched his cheek and traced the lean contours of his jaw. "I love you, too," she whispered thickly.

He wrapped her in his arms, and his lips brushed the top of her head. She could feel the fierce beating of his heart.

"I have to go," she reminded him.

"Aye. I'll see you safely out."

Elizabeth followed James down the back stairs, one hand tucked in his and the other holding her half-full basket.

Before they reached the first floor, he pulled up. "I'll make sure the mews is clear, love," he whispered and squeezed her hand. "Remember, follow it to its end, and it will bring you to another lane. From there, Jury Street."

Elizabeth nodded. She had left the mare stabled behind the apothecary's. He was a quiet man with a healthy regard for Isabel, but beyond that, oblivious to the world around him. He would not have noticed how long the Ellendale mare stayed with his old cob. "I wish you were coming with me."

"I wish you weren't leaving at all." He snatched a last kiss before moving away.

Elizabeth hung back on the stairs and waited for him. Within a few minutes, James returned and motioned for her.

The door leading to the back was warped, and James gave it a hearty budge to open it. Outside, the sky had clouded over and hinted at rain. Elizabeth drew her cloak around her. "When will I see you?"

"Look for me tomorrow night." He pulled up her hood and tucked in a stray lock. His hand lingered a moment on her cheek.

Before she could reply, they heard the rattle of the back door. Elizabeth froze, and James looked around for a place to hide. Twenty empty barrels were stacked tall and wide along the back with a foot gap between them and the building. He managed to pull her down just as the back door swung open.

The crunch of boots on gravel approached where they hid. Through the slight gaps between the kegs, she saw two men in russet coats. She tensed and turned to James, but his hard expression proved he already knew.

The soldiers stopped in front of the kegs.

"Bloody hell, man," one said to the other. Elizabeth heard a stream of water, followed by the sharp scent of urine. "Not on the kegs. The landlord will have your nuts for pudding."

"It ain't like I'm taking a piss in the barrels," the man grunted. "A bit of seasoning won't hurt them none."

The other snickered.

"What's so funny?"

"Did you see Hammond's jaw? More swollen than a Twelfth Night goose."

"I'd gladly shake the hand o' the cheeky bugger who gave him that." The man spit on the ground.

"Don't let anyone hear you say that. They're all put out over that business. Hammond tried to explain to the Whitehall cully how he lost the man. Near choked on it."

Another spit. "Did you believe that clanker about a highwayman storming the gaol?"

A derisive snort. "Brains to jelly."

"Come on, one more cup before we head back to the garrison." The man kicked a rock against the empty barrels. "We have an early start in the morning."

"Rank nonsense searching Warwick for an escaped Coventry man. The man's long gone, I wager. I'd have flown to London by now. But Hammond won't listen to reason. Swears he couldn't have gone far."

"Lobcock has to salvage his manhood." Another wheezing laugh. "Sir Richard ain't best pleased with him."

Their voices faded as they returned to the inn. James waited for the door to slam shut before rising to his feet. He offered Elizabeth a hand, though his attention was elsewhere.

"Go straight home, Elizabeth," he said. "I'll collect Nathaniel and meet you there."

She nodded and adjusted her hood. "We'll have Piers ready."

When Elizabeth crossed the alley and looked back, James had already disappeared into the stables.

*

The first stars littered the night sky when they finished preparing Nathaniel's coach for Piers's departure. James gave instructions to the coachmen.

"Keep your muskets ready and a sharp eye on the road," James said. "Fail, and answer to me."

The driver nodded and headed back to ready his team.

James seized the opportunity to watch Elizabeth as she helped Piers to the waiting coach. Her hand was tucked in the crook of the old man's arm, as though it was he who offered her support, but Pier's sloping shoulders told a different story. The women had dressed him in Isabel's late husband's clothes, and he now looked every bit a yeoman farmer. Elizabeth's idea, clever woman. A rush of love made James smile. Her lithe grace fascinated him—the way she moved, the charming tilt of her head, even the way she brushed the loose strands of hair from her cheek. When Piers lifted Elizabeth's hand to press a light kiss upon it, James stifled a groan of envy and frustration. *One day…*

Emery rushed forward to assist his master, leaving Elizabeth standing alone. As though drawn by the intensity of James's stare, she left the others to join him.

"All ready?" She drew her woollen shawl over her shoulders.

James nodded and stared at the gravel. The dragoons' talk bothered him. "Hammond will come. His pride is smarting and his position tenuous. He'll try to salvage what he can."

"I can manage Hammond," Elizabeth replied, her blue eyes steadfast.

"Of that, my love, I have no doubt. No baiting of the man, no matter how much he deserves it." James grinned when she tilted her chin and a dimple flirted. He had an overwhelming desire to cup her face and claim a kiss, to feel her pressed against him. With a ragged sigh, he glanced back at the others. Sir Piers leaned out of the window of the coach, deep in conversation with Isabel.

"James," Elizabeth said, "for my sake, take no unnecessary chances. The dragoons will be extra vigilant."

"I know."

209

She wrapped the shawl tighter around her shoulders and looked straight ahead towards the coach. "You can't risk coming now that the garrison will be swarming Warwick."

"Elizabeth Seton, look at me," James said, his tone uncompromising. "Do I look like a man easily deterred? I don't give a damn how many dragoons are stationed between us. I *will* find a way to see you. Let the devil take the hindmost."

"I need you," she admitted in a whisper. "Be careful."

James heard the catch in her voice and closed his eyes. "I won't be caught, not by Ezekiel Hammond." A shout from the coach interrupted them. He cleared his throat, and his voice sounded hoarse to his ears. "I better go."

"Godspeed, my love. Return soon."

When he returned to the others, he swung atop Sovereign and took the lead. His last view of Elizabeth was of her standing in the dark, the wind bending the grasses at her feet.

*

Hammond arrived at Ellendale the following morning with a company of dragoons. Startled by the sudden pounding on the front door, Elizabeth knocked over a bowl of seeds.

Jennet's voice sharpened in protest as the sound of heavy boots thumped across the entry. Elizabeth rushed down the passageway and found Jennet, feet planted and prepared to fend off the entire company. Six men stood behind Hammond and another dozen outside.

"Mistress," Hammond said. "My apologies for the intrusion at this early hour, but we are making a search of homes in the area for a wanted traitor."

Elizabeth's eyes darted to the ugly bruise on his chin, purple spreading to yellow across his cheek. "Traitor in Warwick? Do you believe Ellendale to harbour fugitives?"

Hammond smiled. "Assuredly not, but for everyone's safety we are here. This fugitive may have pressed innocents to hide him, by threat or by force. I came here right away to satisfy myself of your safety."

Elizabeth forced a smile. "We have no such person here at Ellendale and are quite safe, but thank you for your concern." She glanced at the men collected in the hallway, their boots caked with mud and muskets in hand. They cast knowing looks between Elizabeth and Hammond, further deepening her discomfort. "However, you are welcome to have a look around to satisfy your superiors."

"I appreciate your understanding." Hammond motioned to the men to spread out. The soldiers respectfully stepped past her and headed for the back of the house. Jennet chased after them.

"Take care, men. Conduct yourself as befits soldiers of the Commonwealth." Hammond turned to Elizabeth and smiled. "My dear, is there somewhere we may sit until they finish?"

Elizabeth's stomach twisted, but she merely nodded and led him to the parlour. Hammond settled in a chair, and to delay joining him, she fussed with the fire. She heard them trampling upstairs and knew that they reached the guest chambers directly above. She chewed her lip and hoped Jennet hadn't missed anything when straightening the room after Pier's departure. After all, the hour had been late and everyone rushed.

It was up to her to dull Hammond's vigilance. James's words rang in her head. She turned to the lieutenant with a smile and selected a seat across from him with as much composure as she could muster. "I thought you were in Coventry. When did you return?"

"Recently, mistress." Hammond leaned forward in his chair. The bruise on his cheek looked worse in this light. "The traitor we chase is a Coventry man, but we've expanded our search into neighbouring towns."

"First a highwayman, now a traitor. I didn't realise Warwickshire was so dangerous." Elizabeth cursed herself the moment the words left her mouth. The urge to dig at the man had overridden her good judgment.

Hammond's expression hardened. "'Tis a lawless society. I will rectify this even if it takes me to the end of my years."

A chill spiralled down Elizabeth's spine. "This traitor, what has he done?"

"I'm not at liberty to say, other than his cohorts attacked the gaoler."

"How dreadful." She stared at his bruise. "I can't help but notice your cheek. Perchance did you also have an altercation with the villain?"

"An unfortunate accident, nothing more," he said. "I had hoped you might have a salve to take the swelling down. Another reason for my call."

"Certainly, I have something."

"Shall I accompany you to your workspace?"

Elizabeth shook her head, not warming to the thought of Hammond intruding in her space. "My aunt allows no one into the stillroom."

"Surely, there is no better place for a patient?"

"This is her home and I abide by her rules."

Hammond sniffed and looked away. "One day, 'twill be time for you to manage your own household."

Elizabeth panicked at the direction of his thoughts. "My aunt is not well, sir. While she has need of me, I will not forsake her." She rose quickly to her feet. "I'll be a moment to fetch the salve."

She hurried out of the parlour and tried to collect her routed thoughts. *Think physic.* She willed her heart to slow down. The last thing she needed was to give him a wrong salve.

Presently, she returned carrying a tin with an ointment of nightshade. Hammond had unbuttoned his russet coat and now sat in her aunt's place by the hearth.

"Does this give you enough light to work from, mistress?"

"The salve may discolour your coat, Lieutenant," Elizabeth said, clutching the tin. "You may prefer to apply it in the evening when you have completed your duties for the day." The thought of touching him made her stomach churn.

"Show me how to apply it."

Elizabeth hesitated. When had she become the fly to his spider?

"Come, mistress. You will spare me the tedium of assisting my men in their duty."

"Very well." Elizabeth pulled up a stool and perched on its edge. Her hands shook as she pried the lid open.

The salve was cool against her fingertips, and she began to apply it to his chin. His mouth twitched as she worked in the cream with circular strokes. The dusty pea scent of the nightshade mingled with crushed rose petals, infusing the ointment with an unsettling odour. His skin was hot beneath her touch, the fault of the collected blood under the bruise.

Hammond's gaze bored into her, but she kept her eyes averted. She felt naked under his stare—and vulnerable. His breathing became shallower, and he leaned in closer. She read his desire in those pale blue depths. He made her feel smothered and unclean.

Elizabeth hurried her ministrations and, in her haste, scraped a fingernail against his bruise. He winced and drew back. "That should do it," she said and jumped to her feet. "Twice a day, and the worst of the swelling will go down by tomorrow evening."

Elizabeth spied Isabel coming slowly down the stairs. But there was something strange in her aunt's manner—her movements were uncertain and shaky. She frowned and approached her aunt.

"Are you well?"

Isabel's skin had taken on a grey pallor. When she tried to speak, no words left her mouth. Then her eyes clouded and shoulders sagged. To Elizabeth's horror, her aunt began to crumple. Elizabeth caught her before she hit the ground and eased her to the floor, cushioning her in her arms.

"Jennet!" she screamed.

Isabel's skin was clammy to the touch. Elizabeth checked her heartbeat—faint and erratic. Under parchment-thin lids, Isabel's eyes darted back and forth.

"Aunt . . . Isabel . . . wake . . . up." Elizabeth slapped her cheek.

Jennet rushed down the hallway and gasped when she saw her mistress lying prone. Her small black eyes widened, and she clapped her hand over her mouth. "Grace and mercy—"

"Come quick. Stay here with her."

When Jennet took her place, Elizabeth scrambled to her feet. She flew to the stillroom and pushed past a soldier. She snatched a vial of foxglove from the shelf, grabbed a dropper and raced back to her aunt. By now, a number of soldiers had collected around her aunt. Hammond stared at Isabel impassively.

"Lift her head," Elizabeth instructed Jennet. She pried open her aunt's mouth and wormed her finger beneath her tongue. Two drops. Did she dare give her another? Death to give her too much. Elizabeth massaged Isabel's limp arms. After a few minutes, the waxy grey pallor faded, and colour returned to her cheeks. Isabel's eyes fluttered open, though still unfocused.

Jennet sobbed in her apron and Elizabeth released a shaky breath. When she finally looked up, she met Hammond's pale eyes. Elizabeth didn't miss the flicker of disappointment.

Chapter Eighteen

"For the grievous crimes of absconding with Sir Richard Crawford-Bowe's property and disparaging the laws of Moses, the perpetrator will be hanged today in Market Square . . ."

The placards were posted throughout Warwick, and word had spread beyond. Elizabeth drove the wagon into town, numb with shock and grief. Isabel and Jennet sat on either side of her. This couldn't be happening. She prayed mercy would stay Hammond's hand—that he really didn't intend to go through with it.

Hammond had caught Matthias Norton poaching partridges on Sir Richard's land. As quickly as the notices were nailed, the gibbet was erected. There hadn't even been a trial.

Elizabeth couldn't fathom the depths of Rose's despair.

The streets leading to the market were clogged with carts and wagons. Elizabeth squirmed in her seat. They'd never reach Market Square at this pace. Elizabeth turned down Jury Street and pulled into the Chequer's courtyard. The stables were deserted.

Elizabeth hitched the mare to the post. "We'll have to walk," she told her aunt and Jennet. "We're not far. Can you make it?"

"Don't worry about me," Isabel said as Jennet helped her down from the wagon.

Elizabeth led the way towards the square. She pressed through the slow-moving crowd as though it were a sluggish stream. "Let us through," she called out.

The square was crammed with people, and half the garrison was positioned along the parameter like roosting vultures. In the centre of the market stood the gibbet, looming atop a raised platform. Blackened timbers contrasted with a single white rope that swung in the wind. Elizabeth, Isabel and Jennet arrived just as the gaol procession came rattling down the street.

Hammond rode in the lead, followed by four dragoons. A thick black belt cut across his crisp russet coat with his sword strapped to his side.

Elizabeth caught a brief glimpse of Matthias strapped to a trundle. She clamped her hand over her mouth. Isabel linked her arm through hers and held her tight. Matthias's feet pointed upward while his head slapped against the base of the board that scraped along the uneven cobbles.

Elizabeth stood on her toes and craned her head, but she couldn't see past the hats and shoulders. She had to find Rose—she couldn't let the woman suffer this alone. "Do you see her?"

Isabel shook her head. "Maybe near the front?"

Elizabeth felt a light touch on her back. James came up beside her. Hidden by the folds of cloaks and the press of the crowd, he clasped her hand for a moment, giving it a reassuring squeeze. She closed her eyes, grateful for his presence.

James gave no other sign that he knew she was there. All his attention was centred towards the gibbet, his angular jaw set in a grim line. The next moment, he brushed past her and headed towards the front.

Hammond ascended the platform and stood in front of the masked hangman. The lieutenant motioned to the dragoons at the trundle. They unstrapped Matthias and hauled him to his feet. He tried to pull away from the guards, but it was useless. His arms were still tied behind his back.

At that moment, a broken wail rose. It hung in the air like a wounded thing. Rose Norton had seen her son.

The soldiers harried Matthias to the platform. He stumbled up the steps, but they continued to march him to the top. Matthias faced the crowd, flinching and dazed. His shoulders were hunched over, and Elizabeth suspected that it took a great effort for him to stand on his own.

The dragoons pushed Matthias to the crate and forced him to step up. One soldier grabbed the noose and placed it around Matthias's neck. With a quick jerk, he yanked it tight.

"Nooooo—" Rose cried out. "Not Matthias! Please."

Elizabeth left her aunt with Jennet and made her way through the crowd towards Rose. When she got close enough, she saw James trying to comfort Rose. He held the hysterical woman in his arms and tried to prevent her from rushing the platform. Rose was at once clutching his shoulder and trying to slip away from him. Even if she had broken free, she wouldn't have made it. Dragoons were posted before the steps, brandishing cudgels and muskets.

A few feet away stood Lukas and Zachary. Elizabeth was relieved that the girls had stayed behind. Lukas tried to remain stoic, but Zachary cried openly. When he saw Elizabeth, the lad launched himself into her arms. She wrapped her arms around the sobbing boy. Her heart wrenched for him. Elizabeth sensed eyes on her and looked up to meet Hammond's displeased frown. He motioned for her to step away from the boy, but Elizabeth turned her head. *Devil take him.*

After a moment, Hammond finally lifted his voice to the crowd. "The laws of the Commonwealth must be upheld. This man stands before you guilty of theft."

Someone shouted, "With what trial?" It sounded like Henry.

Hammond raised his gloved fist. "I witnessed the crime with my own eyes."

"Trial!" another shouted. "He deserved a trial!"

"Trial! Trial! Trial!" people chanted.

Hammond barked, "To that I say, when Moses returned with the commandments and witnessed the idolatry and lawlessness with his own eyes, did he stop and demand a trial? Nay. He served the Lord's vengeance."

Elizabeth looked around, her anger growing. Where was Sir Richard? He should have been up there on the platform to answer for this travesty. Instead, he had washed his hands of it quick enough. She couldn't remain silent any longer. "Mercy!" she shouted, then again louder, "Mercy!"

More people joined in. "Mercy! Mercy! Mercy!"

People started stomping their feet and banging on anything they could find. They lifted their voices to shout Hammond down. Now the chant changed to "Murder! Murder! Murder!" Waves of mounting anger rippled through the square, stoking the latent discontent.

The crowd surged like a raging tide. Men rushed towards the platform, and Elizabeth fought to keep hers and Zachary's balance. She looked wildly around for her aunt, fearful that the frail woman would be swept under the press of the crowd like a leaf. "Aunt Isabel!" she shrieked. She couldn't see her aunt or Jennet anywhere.

Someone drove their elbow into her side as they pushed past her. A flare of pain made her suck in her breath. They were being squeezed on all sides. She had to stay on her feet or be trampled underfoot. Elizabeth searched for a way through the crowd and finally spied a gap. She gripped Zachary's hand and pulled him behind her.

The garrison soldiers moved in to drive the protesters back. They swung their cudgels and cracked the butt ends of their muskets over heads. Rather than dampening the protestor's rage, the attack only fuelled it hotter.

Elizabeth looked around in panic for her aunt and finally spotted Jennet leading Isabel away.

A shot exploded. Elizabeth flinched and instinctively shielded Zachary. When she opened her eyes, she saw Hammond centre platform, holding a smoking carbine in the air.

"That's enough," Hammond snarled. "I will not suffer disobedience." Behind him, a troop held lit matchlocks on the crowd. The resistance sputtered into glum silence. Elizabeth had no doubt that many considered rushing the gibbet, but no one was foolish enough to do it.

Hammond lowered his carbine and motioned to Matthias. "Have you any last words, wretch? Now is the time to repent your sins."

Matthias tried to work his mouth, but no words came. He tried again and croaked a reply, but the sound didn't carry. The vicar climbed the platform and hurried to reach him. The troubled minister laid his hand on the young man's shoulder and said a few words to him. Tears started to stream down Matthias's face.

After a few moments, the hangman nudged the vicar aside and yanked a black hood over Matthias's head.

Rose broke away from James and hurtled towards the platform. "Please, not my son—he's my boy—just a boy. Please!" Her sobs overwhelmed her.

"Silence, woman."

"Please, no—Matthias—Matthias! Let him go!"

The dragoon drew his fist back to strike her, but James stepped between them. Elizabeth's blood froze. Even if James defended himself, Hammond would use that as provocation to seize him for the hangman. The lieutenant moved in closer, eager for the kill.

Step back… take a step back, James.

But James Hart had never been a Roundhead's fool or easily goaded. He didn't lift a hand to the man, even when it looked like he'd be struck. Instead, he said something and drew Rose back a few paces. The dragoon crossed his arms and returned to his position. Elizabeth released a ragged breath.

Scowling and clearly disappointed, Hammond gave the hangman the signal. The masked man hesitated a moment, then with a swift kick, knocked the crate away.

Matthias dropped; his legs scrambled for support but found only empty air. Rose's screams shattered the square and mingled with the creaking of the rope against the struts and the gurgling behind the mask.

Elizabeth wanted to vomit. She'd never forget that sound in her life. Turning her head, she shielded Zachary from the sight. Matthias's legs kept twitching.

Dear God, when would this end?

Finally, the hangman took pity and yanked on Matthias's legs. Elizabeth heard a snap, then all struggle stopped. Matthias was dead.

Hammond stood bigger than life on the platform. Like a great carrion beast, he surveyed the crowd without bothering to hide his fierce satisfaction.

*

Three days after the hanging, an impatient knock sounded on Ellendale's front door. When Elizabeth answered it, she was surprised to find Sir Richard. She had imagined what she would say to the man when he next turned up at Ellendale. Base coward. Plague-sore. But instead of slamming the door on his face as she itched to do, she coldly asked, "Can I help you?"

"Step aside, girl," Sir Richard said, oblivious to her tone. "I don't have time for this. Where's your aunt?" He was halfway down the hall to the drawing room when Jennet came hurrying from the kitchen.

Elizabeth nodded to the maid and said, "Jennet will fetch her. Why don't we wait in the drawing room?"

Sir Richard settled himself in his favourite armchair. He appeared agitated, tapping the bottom of his cane on the floor in an irritated tattoo.

Elizabeth took the seat across from him. She perched rigidly at the edge of the chair. "The first time we met, my lord, you had fined a poor farmer more than half his annual income for having pastured his sheep on church lands. On another occasion, a man spent a day in the pillory for having dared drive on the Sabbath. His health is ruined. Now a young man, not yet eighteen, has swung for catching a partridge to put food on the table. What next, my lord? Shall we hang, draw and quarter those who are caught uttering profanities?"

Sir Richard's face grew beet red, and he nearly launched himself to his feet. "You dare speak to me like that, you ungrateful chit? A man of my stature? I told your aunt that she should never have brought you here, stirring mischief like a—"

"Richard," Isabel interrupted when she came through the door, her tone sharp. "What are you on about?"

"Madam, you have a viper in your nest," he sputtered.

Isabel lifted her chin. "You are mistaken. If she speaks boldly, it is understandable, considering the travesty of what we recently witnessed."

Sir Richard made a show of brushing the dust from his sleeves. He ignored Elizabeth and directed his comments to Isabel. "I would have a word with you... alone."

Isabel took the seat beside Elizabeth. "Elizabeth is my niece, and this is her home. Anything you wish to discuss with me, you can do so before her."

Sir Richard folded his arms across his chest. "I don't believe I can. Her loyalties may compromise me."

Isabel's eyebrows shot up. "Loyalties? What are you referring to?"

Sir Richard's brow darkened. "To Lieutenant Hammond."

"I have no loyalty to Hammond," Elizabeth ground out.

Isabel touched her arm to silence her. "Really, Richard, don't tell me that you believe those rumours? My niece has better judgment than that." She sniffed. "But since you brought that up, what happened with the Norton boy? Hanged without a trial? This is an outrage. What has happened to Warwick when our very laws are not followed?"

"This is exactly the problem, Isabel." Sir Richard rubbed his temples. "I have just returned from Stratford only to find *this*. Blessed God, I swear I was not consulted or advised."

Elizabeth and Isabel looked at each other.

"What do you mean, Richard?"

"I... was... not... consulted." He gripped his cane as though he wanted to strangle it. "Do you have any idea what position Lieutenant Hammond has put me in?"

Position? At least your neck wasn't stretched. Then a thought occurred to Elizabeth. "If this was an unlawful hanging, does this not mean Hammond is guilty of murder? Without the mantle of the law—"

"It's not that simple," Richard snapped. "Hammond is an officer of the law, appointed by me. I invested him with authority."

"Then sack him," Isabel said sternly. "He's overstepped his bounds—surely, you can see that?"

"I can't, Isabel, I can't." He buried his head in his hands and made a low noise of frustration. "What am I to do, send Hammond back to Whitehall, so he can tell his superiors—Colonel Harrison and Oliver Cromwell—that Sir Richard Crawford-Bowes is soft on criminals—Royalist thieves at that? By God, Hammond found that boy with the goods. How can I have found him not guilty even if he did come before my bench?"

"That is a poor excuse, Richard, and I am frankly appalled that you are trying to evade your responsibility," Isabel said with a sharp tone. "For once, put what is *right* before political expedience. These festering distinctions between Royalist and Parliamentarian ensure we will never heal. To win Harrison's approval and elevate your own profile, you have prostituted your reputation to tiptoe around a man who makes his own law. Hammond has overstepped his bounds, and I'm not sure what is more terrifying—that he bloody does what he wants, or that you are too intimidated to check him. Either way, you have fostered this egotism."

Sir Richard's cheeks puffed out, and he looked close to having a seizure. "You go too far, madam! You blame me? The Nortons are a shifty family, incapable of making anything of themselves. The boy is no different than his father, a lazy knave who has been a thorn in my side for the past twenty years. I tell you, I was not saddened by the father's death, even if he did not provide for his family."

"That's not fair," Elizabeth said. "They are doing what they can. Those children—"

Isabel took her arm and motioned for her to regain her chair. "What will it take, Richard, for you to get rid of Hammond? For surely you must see this is needed before anyone else is hurt?"

Richard slumped in his chair. "Nothing shy of treason."

Isabel released a heavy sigh. "God help us all."

Chapter Nineteen

James waited astride Sovereign by the hollowed tree stump along Moot Hill. He wrapped his cloak over his buff coat against the autumn wind. The setting sun slanted through the thinning tree canopy.

Nathaniel should have been here by now. The barrister had sent a note requesting this meeting. Discretion mandatory.

James heard the measured clopping of a trotting horse. He primed his pistols and adjusted his scarf. When Nathaniel came into view, James tucked away his weapons and pulled down his scarf. "You're late," he called out.

Nathaniel reined in his horse. "I'm precisely on time."

"What news from London?"

"Is there a less exposed place? We're not far from the main road. Or is this another clever way to remain inconspicuous?"

"Hardly," James said and tugged Sovereign's reins to turn him around. "This way."

He picked up a rough trail that was no wider than a deer run. Trees clustered thickly, their boughs twisted and bent. He rode low over the horse's neck to avoid the low-arching branches and kept an eye on the ground, cluttered with roots. Behind him, Nathaniel struggled with the grasping shrubs that snatched at his cloak.

As they rode deeper into the forest, the trees thinned. James continued until he reached a hollow, a slope of earth carved like a bowl. A riot of ferns and young saplings covered the parameter, and at its centre was a cold campfire. James tethered Sovereign to a sapling.

Nathaniel looked around. "So this is the underbelly of Moot Hill?"

"It serves its purpose." James kicked a loose stone into the campfire. "Out with it. What's so important?"

"You've heard about Cromwell's surprise victory against the Scots at Dunbar three weeks ago?"

"Everyone heard about that disaster." James shook his head. When the broadsheet *Mercurius Politicus* flooded the streets of Warwick, the taproom at the Chequer exploded with the news. The losses at Dunbar were significant—thousands killed or taken prisoner. Cromwell had finally secured a foothold in Scotland, and his New Model Army wasn't returning to England anytime soon. "Damned Scots—can't be counted on to wage a proper war," he said.

"How many have you recruited?"

"Fifty," James said. He rested his hand on his thigh as he bent down to pick up a stick. "Maybe fifty-five. I'm returning to Oxford at the end of the month."

Nathaniel's mouth disappeared in a tight line. "I had hoped for more."

"The King will have his men come the spring," James said, his irritation rising.

"We need those men now," Nathaniel said. "Spring is too late."

"I don't think I heard you correctly."

"You did."

"You expect us to leave now? That would mean overwintering in Scotland." James waited for a quip, but none came. "You're mad."

"I assure you, I'm not," Nathaniel said. "I've uncovered plans for a great push by Cromwell in early spring. The source is undoubted."

James shook his head. He balked at having his troop's policy dictated by a man who had never donned a campaign coat. "We've discussed this. You know the plan—"

"Every day, more English troops are sent to occupy the border," Nathaniel said. "Come spring, a squirrel won't be able to cross without a pass. Meanwhile, Cromwell's troops are encamped within striking distance of Stirling."

"Cromwell is the foreigner there. You can't convince me he has any advantage."

"The Scots will take comfort to hear that," Nathaniel said. "Clearly, no one explained this to them before Dunbar."

James seethed over the man's wit. "'Twas not Cromwell who won the day—the bloody Scots with their damned Kirk and Covenant threw it away."

"And these are the men you expect to protect the King's back?" Nathaniel asked. His voice betrayed an edge of steel. "I'll be blunt. You swore to support the King, and his hour is nigh. Will you honour that oath, or will you renege?"

James's arm shot out and gripped Nathaniel by the throat. "I will *never* renege. Suggest that again and I'll rip your throat out." He released the solicitor and said, "Nothing has changed, pond scum. I will be there."

*

James's borrowed time had run out. As he paced in the Ellendale barn, dry straw crunched beneath his boots. How was he going to tell Elizabeth?

He raked his fingers through his hair. If a hanging death was preferable to reneging on his oath, breaking the news to her was worse than being quartered. He had faced enemy charges, survived gunshot and sword blade, but this would rip him apart. There was no choice—he had to face this like a man.

James halted his pacing in mid-stride when he heard running footsteps. Elizabeth raced inside and threw herself into his arms. The scent of lavender hit him before she pulled him down for a long kiss. He closed his eyes and drank deep, his hands gathering the folds of her cloak in fistfuls. The tightness in his chest nearly crushed him.

"My love—"

"I couldn't wait to see you," she said almost shyly. She toyed with the laces of his shirt as though she had something on her mind.

"Is everything all right?"

"Of course," she said, then smiled. "My—my aunt had a good day and now the household is safely tucked abed." Her arms encircled his neck. "No one will be looking for me. You'll have most of the night to show me your love."

James stifled a groan. *Brace up, man.* He touched his forehead to hers. "Elizabeth, you once told me that you would rather hear the truth from my lips, dark though it may be."

Her expression became wary, the first stirring of unease. She lowered her arms. "I did. You answered that you loved me."

"More than my very life."

Elizabeth stared at him, frozen. "You're leaving."

James searched for the right words to give hope and soften the pain, but they eluded him. "We go to the prince's defence. I'm pledged to him." He touched her shoulder, but she pulled away. "Please, my love." He ached when he saw her struggle to hold back her tears.

"Why now?" Her voice was hollow.

"Our king is facing Cromwell's Ironsides, and unless he receives support, he will end like his father."

"Now? Why now? Winter is approaching. Surely, you can wait until spring?" She swiped away a stray tear and laughed bitterly. "Though why spring would be better than now, I can't say. It isn't. Truly, this is madness."

"I have no choice," he said in a low voice.

"Choice? What choices have I?" She choked and held her fist against her chest. "If I say nay, will you stay?" He averted his head. "As I thought. So do not speak to me, then, of choice." She hugged herself and added in a barely audible voice, "I made mine."

"Please understand." However hard he found this, however torn and conflicted over leaving her, he would not betray his pledge. This Hart would not turn his back on his cause.

Her face blazed white. "I understand more than most. I have sacrificed and lost enough. No more—I can't—no more to this senseless war. Everyone who meant the most to me, and you—" Her voice caught, and she clapped a hand over her mouth. "You want me to let you go."

"I will return, my love."

"Truly? Is that a promise? Forgive me if I don't find comfort in it."

James lifted her chin and forced her to look at him. "I will. Though the whole Roundhead army lies between us, I will return."

"But why must you go?" she pleaded. Tears sparkled on her lashes.

"It's my duty—"

"Duty?" she cried, blue eyes nearly black. "What of those you love?"

"I have not forgotten my duty to you, Elizabeth." James tried to take her in his arms, but she blocked him with her hands.

"There are no ties between us, James, only affection. You could have left without telling me. I will give you that." Her words tore into him.

"*Affection*? Is that what you think?" James said. "I love you, Elizabeth. Though this world is an uncertain mess, do not think for one moment that what I feel for you is mere affection."

"Then please stay."

"I can't." James's insides twisted.

Her shoulders slumped, and she turned away. "When?"

"In a fortnight—before St. Crispin's day."

"St. Crispin's? Of course. How appallingly appropriate." Elizabeth wrapped her cloak tighter around herself. "I have to go."

James reached to draw her to him, but she eluded his grasp and hurried to the door. For a moment, she paused and opened her mouth as though to say something, but remained silent. She whirled and ran back to the house.

James released a ragged breath. It didn't ease the hard lump lodged in his ribs. He didn't even have a chance to tell her everything.

Reaching under his cloak, he pulled out a scarf of red muslin. It slid over his hand, silky to the touch but useless now.

He shoved it back into his pocket.

*

Elizabeth sagged against her bedroom door. She had extended too much energy fending off her aunt's concerns during the past fortnight. When she fumbled a vial and it splintered at her feet, she claimed, "Nothing is wrong, I slept poorly. Nothing at all."

Everything was wrong. In two days, James would leave for Scotland, and Elizabeth was pregnant.

She slid to the floor and hugged her knees to her chest. Twilight deepened, turning the sky purple. She didn't bother lighting a candle. At the sound of someone approaching, she scrambled to her feet and backed away from the door. Let them think her abed. She could not face their questions. A tentative knock sounded.

"Mistress?" Jennet called out softly.

Elizabeth slipped into her bed and drew the quilt over her shoulders.

"Mistress?" The door squeaked open, and the candle's glow intruded.

"What is it?"

"James Hart is downstairs. He's asked to see you again. I told him you already retired for the night, but he insisted."

Elizabeth curled up tighter. "I'm not well enough to receive company."

"I'll tell him to return on the morrow, then."

The door closed, and darkness once more claimed her. She turned her face into the bolster. After James had shared her bed, his scent had lingered in her sheets. For many nights thereafter, she had hugged the pillow tighter, recalling his strong arms around her. Now all she had were cold sheets.

Elizabeth thrust aside the quilt and crossed to the door. She pressed her ear against the panel. Silence. Stepping away, she paced back and forth between bed and door, taking pains to avoid the window. She hadn't seen him since he had broken the news to her. She couldn't bear it.

Elizabeth had been so excited to see him that evening—and nervous to tell him what she suspected. She imagined him transformed, sweeping her in his arms, his grey eyes alight in love and joy. What would have happened if she had told him her news first—would he have spared her this raw pain?

I have to tell him.

If she did, would he reconsider leaving? His damned honour—of course he wouldn't. All she would accomplish was to send him off with a divided heart and mind. Elizabeth could almost taste the bitterness of his conflict.

She sank to the floor and leaned her head against the trunk. Letting him go was unthinkable, a horrible void. What if he never returned? Killed in action. Taken prisoner. All these possibilities terrified her.

I can't take this.

Elizabeth hugged her knees to her chest. Did she love him enough to keep her silence?

Honour and duty defined who James Hart was—defined the man she loved. Even if she could convince him to stay, would she think lesser of him for not going? He would hate himself and blame her—maybe not right away, but the wound would fester.

Elizabeth wanted to tear her heart out—anything to stop the bleeding.

The walls stifled her. *Coward*

Could she really allow him to leave without her blessing? If anything happened to him, she'd never forgive herself.

They had two days left together, and she had squandered enough time.

Elizabeth swiped a tear with her sleeve. She had to go to him.

*

Elizabeth managed to slip out without being seen, and she raced to the barn. She grabbed a bridle but left the saddle. There was no time to bother with it. Using a bale of hay for a stand, she hoisted herself atop the mare's back.

She kept to the old river trail and reached Warwick without running into any patrols. The Cornmarket was deserted, but she knew the

Chequer would be hosting a lively crowd, so she had to be discreet. Elizabeth tethered the mare, and without a single glance back, made her way to the inn.

The mews behind the Chequer were thankfully empty. Elizabeth prayed that Henry hadn't locked the rear door. He hadn't, though she had to give it a good push to open. Inside, a single rush-light lit the corridor. Muffled laughter and the clink of tankards drifted from the main room. She dashed up the back stairs.

Elizabeth reached the upper hallway and paused before the loft door. Her knock set off muffled cursing before the door was yanked open. James's expression of annoyance changed to surprise. They stared at each other without speaking.

"I left my horse in the Cornmarket," she said breathlessly.

James searched her face. "Let's hope the Roundheads don't find it."

"I really don't care if they do."

Without another word, he pulled her into his arms and crushed her against his chest. "I didn't think I would ever see you again."

"I'm sorry," she murmured, squeezing her eyes shut. "The thought of losing you was unbearable. I couldn't face it."

"And now?" James asked, his forehead touching hers.

"Not seeing you is worse," Elizabeth said. "Are you still leaving?" She held her breath, hoping his answer had changed, but he nodded. "I've squandered enough time, then."

His fingers twined in her hair, and his lips brushed over hers. "God, I love you."

"And I you, beyond myself." She cupped his face. "Go to Scotland with my blessing. Serve the King and make me proud. But return to me." Her voice caught in her throat. "Promise me that."

"I will." He gave her a long kiss, and Elizabeth clung to this moment. "Marry me this night," he murmured against her lips. "I have nothing else to leave you except my name. When I return, 'twill be to my wife. I'll not let another have you."

Elizabeth's eyes widened. "Tonight? What of the banns?"

"We don't need them," he said. "Not for a handfasting."

Her heart quickened. "But we need a witness, my love."

"Henry will swear on it if I ask him to," James said, kissing her eyelids. "Tonight is just for us. The words are ours alone to give."

Elizabeth's heart overflowed. She couldn't speak; all she could do was nod.

"Come." James took her hand and led her to the hearth. From a wooden box, he pulled out a length of red muslin. The fabric flowed in his hand, its red tones rippling in the firelight. With their fingers entwined, he wrapped the cloth around their joined hands. Elizabeth squeezed his hand.

He smiled at her. "I, James Hart," his voice was rich and deep, "take you, Elizabeth Seton, to wife. I promise to love you deeply for all the days of my life." The firelight softened the planes of his face, and his grey eyes glowed.

Elizabeth's heart swelled. "I, Elizabeth Seton, take you, James Hart, to be my husband," her voice trembled. "I will love and cherish you always."

James's smile deepened, and he leaned in to claim a kiss. Elizabeth looped her arms around his neck and savoured the feel of his mouth against her own. Their embrace tightened. This was where she belonged.

After a few breathless moments, James bent down to lift Elizabeth and carry her to their marriage bed.

*

James rode up the rutted lane that led to his old home, Stoneleigh, and slowed down. As a lad, he had run along the lane collecting pebbles after the rain, his fingers digging into the mud. He continued on past a half-tumbled wall. Countless times he had jumped from its top, brandishing a hawthorn branch turned rapier.

As he rode, he stared at the barren fields. Once, the hills had been dotted with sheep while hired hands tilled the land. Now, most of the fields remained fallow. There was only so much a single back could plough.

When James saw the farmhouse, he pulled up. Fire had savaged half the house and destroyed most of the newer wing that his grandfather had built. Where part of a second story had once been, charred beams were exposed, and the lower daub panels still bore signs of the flames. The only part of the house that remained unaffected was the original stone structure in the rear.

James rubbed his gloved hand across his mouth. A simmering anger brewed, made worse by not knowing where to direct his rage—his father, who had brought this upon himself, or the bastards who lit the match. He clicked the reins and picked up their pace.

A thin curl of smoke drifted from a squat chimney at the rear of the farmhouse. James dismounted and hitched Sovereign to the old gate. He stared at the darkened parlour window.

The last time he had been here, he was on his way to join Northampton's regiment. His mother had been bent over her sewing, and when he rode up, she lifted her head and waved at him through the window. James's father had met him on the doorstep. Having heard that Piers was preparing to join the Parliamentary army, he assumed James was going with him.

Edward's smiles had turned to rage when he learned the truth. Without warning, he'd drawn his hand back and struck him. James's face had stung as though a thousand needles pressed into his jaw and fire spread to his temples. That had been the first time his father had raised a hand to him. The rest was a blur. James recalled his mother shrieking, and him pushing his father away, swearing he'd never return.

And yet, here I am.

James hesitated to walk through the gate. He had no reason to believe his father would welcome him, nor did he intend to beg forgiveness. He was here for Elizabeth's sake. Although Henry had agreed to watch out for her, and James had left him enough gold to see to her needs, it wasn't enough. His father should know about their marriage, just in case there was a child. James needed to settle his affairs before he left.

His feet found the familiar path leading to the orchard entrance. When he rounded the corner, he stopped. From within the brown and grey boles of a small wooded copse, his father emerged with a load of wood strapped to a leather harness on his back. The old man leaned forward as he walked with a black-and-tan hound padding at his side. He hadn't yet noticed James, but the dog halted in mid-stride.

The urge to retreat seized James. If he left now, his father would never know he had come. Before he could give into the temptation, the dog barked, and his father raised his head.

The hound ran to him, and James crouched to greet the animal, grateful he didn't have to stand in awkward silence waiting for his father to catch up. "Good girl," he said, scratching behind her floppy ears and underneath her muzzle. She had the same markings as his father's old hound, Sulis. Must be one of hers.

Edward Hart stopped several feet away. James's nape prickled as a shadow fell at his feet. He straightened and, for the first time in eight years, faced his father. Deep furrows lined Edward's face, but otherwise he remained unchanged—clean-shaven, clipped iron-grey hair, eyes still an unshakable brown. His father stared without saying a word, and James felt cut down to the status of errant boy.

"Need a hand with the wood?" James asked, clearing his throat.

"I can manage," Edward said with a grunt and moved past him. His father whistled, and the dog returned to his side. James fell in step behind them.

When he entered the kitchen, James half expected to find his mother at the hearth, stirring a pot of stew with a warm greeting waiting for him. Only shadows greeted him. His father unloaded the wood, then walked to the fireplace and checked the porridge of pease simmering in the pot. The dog rushed to the hearth and settled in her corner.

James bent down to stir the embers. When he placed a log in the hearth, his father's voice halted him. "You'll smother the fire that way, boy. Is that what they taught you in Warwick?"

"I've learnt well enough," James replied curtly. He continued to build the fire as he saw fit.

Edward settled in a chair and rested his hand on the wooden table beside him. His attention did not waver.

"Do you have help to keep house?" James asked.

"I do for myself."

James glanced around. The kitchen bore no signs of the fire, and it was as he remembered. Not as clean as his mother had kept it, but tidy enough. Tin pots still lined the brick wall, but her sewing box no longer rested on the sill. "You've managed."

"Is that what you would call it?" Edward said with a wry twist.

James folded his arms across his chest. The charred ruins were engraved in his mind. "Barely."

"Aye, I've been managing." The silence stretched between them.

"What happened?" James asked.

Edward grunted but didn't reply.

James glanced at his father's backgammon board tucked into a shelf beside the hearth. A thick layer of dust had turned the surface grey. "You don't play anymore?" He didn't know why this bothered him.

Edward didn't answer.

An old striped apron hung on a hook by the fireplace. Faded and torn in places, it looked as it had the day James had left for war. "I see you've kept her apron."

"What did you expect me to do—bury it with her?" Edward said, snapping out of his sullen silence. "But you wouldn't know because you weren't here, were you?"

James felt as though a fist drove into his stomach. *Sweet Christ*—did he really believe that he didn't care about his mother? James found out months too late about her death. All he could do, upon returning from war, was pass by the churchyard to see her grave marker, but *damned* if he would tell his father that. "I was defending my King," he ground out.

"I'm well aware of that—as was your mother. She had no peace in her final moments—worried about your sorry hide."

James kept his silence. He hadn't returned to argue.

"You just had to leave," Edward said. "Never satisfied with your lot. Always holding out for venison when plain mutton would do."

James's nostrils flared. *Keep it together.*

"You had a good living, boy—I handed it to you." Edward glared across the table. "The coin Sir Piers spent on your schooling—all for naught. How do you like mucking stables?"

James finally snapped. "And how do you like living worse than the meanest tenant?" Frustration churned in his gut. "Look at you, living in a half-burnt shell of a house, and you still find fault with me. I have less to be ashamed of than the tripe you've tried to feed me—pride, honour, respect. They're naught but empty words coming from you."

"Meaning?" Edward rose to his feet. "Go on, say it."

You are a turncoat and a coward. The thought burned in James's head. "Seems that my absence wasn't the only thing my mother had to worry about."

Edward crossed the floor and stopped a foot away. His brown eyes were nearly black, and his jaw clenched in anger. "Do not presume to know what she thought in her final hours." His tone lashed like a whip. "You weren't here."

231

"You're right. I wasn't. When my mother died, I was fighting at Naseby," he spat. What the hell was he doing here now? A mistake to think they could put aside their differences. "I've stayed long enough." James strode to the door.

"Why did you even come back?"

James continued through the threshold. "Good day to you."

*

Dawn drew near. Elizabeth touched the cold window. In the street below, the cobbles glistened with the driving rain. A raindrop splattered against the pane, capturing the flickering candlelight in its suspended sphere. How she wished time could stop. Much would change on the morrow. She had not given thought yet to what she would tell her aunt.

James's strong arms encircled her. Elizabeth closed her eyes and leaned against him. His lips grazed her temple, and her heart ached.

"I'll need to get ready soon," he said against her ear.

Elizabeth hugged his arms to her and watched the sky lighten. Unshed tears burned her eyes, and her chest was so tight the force crushed her. "You will be careful for my sake?"

James turned her around and held her by the shoulders. "Do not worry about me." He gave her a tender smile. "I can protect myself."

The corners of her mouth lifted, and her vision blurred. James cupped her face and kissed her. She leaned into him, putting everything she could not say in words into a kiss.

"You have my heart in your keeping, Elizabeth Hart," he said against her lips. "If you need anything, look to Henry." He raised her chin, and their eyes locked. "For anything, do you understand?"

Elizabeth nodded and swallowed the hard lump lodged in her throat. In her hand, she clutched a palm-sized satchel, sewn with sprigs of lavender. She brushed a kiss on it and pressed it into his hand. "Take this to remember me by." She had to keep it together. Her tears would not be what he remembered. Even if it killed her.

James kissed the satchel and tucked it in his shirt. "I will return to you, my love." He cupped her face; his look was penetrating. "I will return."

"I know." She laid her head on his shoulder and stared through the window. Dawn lightened the grey sky.

St. Crispin's day had arrived.

Chapter Twenty

One sunrise and three hours since James left. Already a lifetime for Elizabeth. She hadn't wanted to come to market and barely had the energy to hold her basket. However hard it was to move against the current, she had to wade onward. Keeping to her bed was not an option.

The bone-chilling drizzle had deterred shoppers, and Elizabeth found the cheesemonger's stall thankfully clear. She couldn't manage the vacant small talk required as the grease for polite society. *And how are you this day, mistress? I'm very well, considering that my husband has left for Scotland and, if caught, will be hanged for a traitor. But the late autumn day is quite fine, don't you agree?* She sighed. *How James would have smiled at that.*

Elizabeth reached for a round of cheese, and a switch stayed her hand. Startled, she looked up. Hammond leaned in, his collar drawn against the freezing rain. "Did you want that, Lieutenant?" she asked, withdrawing her hand. "I didn't know it had been bespoken for."

Hammond's nostrils twitched, and he smiled without humour. "Nay, mistress, I haven't the least interest in another's goods."

"Well then." Elizabeth passed her coins to the cheesemonger. "I wish you joy of the market. God save you, sir." She adjusted her hood and prepared to step from the relative shelter of the awning. Only then did she notice a pair of soldiers standing behind Hammond. The hairs on her nape lifted.

Hammond barred her way. "God will save me, for I am one of the Lord's Elect."

Elizabeth lifted her eyes. His tone rasped like steel against bone. "How comforting." She pushed against the switch with her basket. "If you'll excuse me."

"Where's your lover?"

Elizabeth froze in mid-stride. "What?"

"Your lover—you have one. Why the confusion—unless there are others?"

Elizabeth swallowed. Her heart hammered in her chest. "I don't have a lover."

Hammond glanced up at the sky and shook his head. A mocking smile stretched across his face. "I trust very little in his world, mistress, and save for the Lord's terrible splendour, I depend on only one thing—the veracity of my own sight."

He couldn't have . . .

"I saw you with him," Hammond sneered. A half-choked sound wrenched from his throat. "Yesterday, in the early hours of dawn—when I finished duty."

But they had been discreet—hadn't they? "What are you talking about?"

"As I passed the Chequer, I glanced up and, to my amazement, saw you in the loft window." He licked his lips. "As I wondered how you came to be there at such an hour, the answer presented itself," Hammond jeered, and his pale eyes narrowed. "Hart joined you at the window—you clung to each other—where he placed his hands on you—there was no doubt you both had carnal knowledge of the other."

Elizabeth's face flamed, and her knuckles whitened as she clutched her basket. *Insufferable wretch.* A multitude of scathing replies crowded her tongue, but she didn't dare. "This does not concern you, Lieutenant." She lifted her skirts to step around him.

"You err, mistress—it does." He grabbed her arm and drew her closer, his words a hiss. "Fornication is against the law."

Elizabeth drew back, aghast. "How could—"

"Do you deny it?" Fury mingled with half-pleading hope.

"Deny I was there? I will not." Elizabeth released a choked laugh and snatched her arm back. "But you are a blind fool." She smothered the warning bells and blurted, "James Hart is my *husband*. We were handfasted three days ago."

Hammond paled. "Is that so? Where is he to corroborate this?"

Elizabeth's heart drummed in her ears, and a cold dread shivered through her. From his words, he had already checked the inn for James. What would Henry have told him? "My husband is away on the inn's business. He runs the post."

"Where?" Hammond pressed.

"The landlord can answer, Lieutenant."

"Surely, a new bride would know where her husband has gone," Hammond persisted as though scenting her fear.

"I am an honest woman and speak the truth. You have no right—"

"Then tell me where he's gone, mistress," he sneered. "Has he, perchance, fled the shire—had second thoughts? Perhaps he promised you marriage and has fled to avoid making good on this?" He took a step closer, his features contorted. "Or having had a taste of your tender flesh, he's lost all interest and is now whoring his way through every brothel from here to London."

Slap.

Hammond's head snapped back, and a red welt spread across his cheek. Tiny needles of pain stung Elizabeth's hand. A dawning horror flooded her as she realised what she had done.

Hammond lifted his hand and rubbed his jaw. His attention flicked behind her. Before she could turn, the soldiers seized her.

*

Heads turned when the guard led Elizabeth into the Shire Hall on Northgate Street. Her skin crawled under their burning curiosity. A part of her hoped that James would be there. Foolish dream. He was halfway to Scotland by now. The guard nudged her forward.

Ahead, Hammond's pale gaze fixed on her with the exultance of a bridegroom. The unpleasantness of seeing him forced Elizabeth to collect herself. This charade would play itself out—Hammond had made his point. For ten days, she had waited in the gaol for this special hearing, isolated in a dank cell with poor rations and gaol-stink clinging to her pores. Let him enjoy her discomfort. As James would have said, devil take him.

Elizabeth held her head high until she spied her aunt and Jennet. She faltered, and the guard steadied her. His thick fingers dug into her arm. While she had waited for her hearing, Elizabeth dreaded facing Isabel. Though she regretted nothing with James, she hadn't wanted her aunt to discover about their marriage in this manner.

Yet another debt against Hammond.

Elizabeth met Isabel's gaze and read disappointment. As clear as though Isabel had spoken it aloud, Elizabeth knew what her aunt was thinking—*You should have told me. You should have trusted me.* The shame of her arrest was nothing to the pain she was causing her aunt.

"Aunt Isabel—" Elizabeth searched for words, but she found naught but tangled knots in her mouth.

The guard pulled her along. "This way."

Elizabeth reached the bar, grateful to have something solid to clutch. She sensed the darts of people's stares riddling her back and drew in her elbows. On the other side, a clerk continued to work at a generous table situated below the raised bench. Everyone waited with muted voices. Only the relentless scratching of the clerk's nib broke the silence.

Elizabeth glanced back, hoping to catch her aunt's attention, but Isabel had her head down. Swallowing the lump in her throat, she scanned the room for Henry. She hoped he would vouch for her, but he was nowhere to be found.

One dark figure in a far corner attracted her attention—Nathaniel Lewis. He sat apart and not once looked up, more concerned with his book than the courtroom. *Has everyone come to witness my shame?*

A latch rattled, and the antechamber door swung open. The clerk lowered his quill and rose. "All stand for the Honourable Justice Sir Crawford-Bowes." There was a sudden scraping of chairs and shuffling of feet.

Elizabeth had dreaded this moment. Sir Richard would no doubt celebrate this as the hour of her comeuppance. He'd be forever insufferable.

Sir Richard appeared with a stack of ledgers under his arm. As he walked, his robes snapped behind him like a black cloud. He climbed the few steps to the bench and settled into his chair, his expression grim. The clerk leaned forward to speak in a low tone. Sir Richard shuffled through his papers, interrupting with several sharp words before the clerk retreated. Finally, he looked straight at Nathaniel Lewis.

"Master Lewis? My clerk tells me that you've been sent from Westminster to observe."

Nathaniel bowed to the justice. "Chief Justice Blackmore has sent me to report on the application of this new statute, my lord. Your reputation precedes you."

Sir Richard's sour expression deepened. "I am honoured, barrister, particularly that my lord Blackmore has come out of retirement to comment on current legal affairs."

"He is keenly interested," Nathaniel said with a bow.

"Let us proceed, then." Sir Richard turned his attention to Elizabeth. He had never hidden his dislike for her, yet the brewing anger she saw in the set of his jaw took her by surprise. She had expected vindication and satisfaction, not this grinding vexation.

The clerk raised his voice. "My lord. Mistress Elizabeth Seton of Ellendale, late of Weymouth, is charged with fornication with one James Hart, ostler of the Chequer and Crowne."

Elizabeth shut her ears to the twitters behind her.

Sir Richard leaned forward on his desk. "Mistress Seton, since that ill-fated carriage ride, you have presented yourself as a forward chit."

"That has never been my intention," Elizabeth said. She cast a side-glance at Hammond and saw his brows furrow in confusion.

"How do you plead, young woman?"

Elizabeth raised her voice so that there would be no mistake. "Not guilty, my lord. I place my plea upon the county."

Sir Richard pushed the papers aside. "Lieutenant Hammond, you bring forth these charges?" When he turned to Hammond, there was an irritated twitch of his eye.

The lieutenant stepped forward. "Aye, my lord. I present myself as witness to this crime."

"The court awaits your account, Lieutenant."

Hammond relayed his discovery to the court, relishing elaborate details Elizabeth knew he could not have had any knowledge of unless he had taken flight and perched outside the loft window. Each time she opened her mouth to protest, the clerk shook his head in a silent warning. Hammond droned on, preaching a sermon on morality that the vicar would have despaired for. Elizabeth listened, aghast. How could he twist an expression of her love into something wicked and licentious? The blood throbbed in her temples.

Bang. The hall door swung open, and an inrush of cold swept the courtroom as Henry Grant strode down the aisle. He gave her a wink as he claimed a nearby seat.

Elizabeth exhaled slowly, relieved. *Dear Henry.* A sudden mist clouded her vision, and she bit her trembling lips.

"One moment, Lieutenant." Sir Richard turned to Henry. "Who dares interrupt the court?"

Henry rose to his feet and gave his name. "I'm the landlord of the Chequer and Crowne. I've come as witness for the accused."

"The proceedings started some time ago, Master Grant," Sir Richard sniffed. "I trust we didn't inconvenience your schedule."

"I apologise, my lord, but a company of dragoons detained me."

Elizabeth noted Hammond's smug expression and wished for a chance to scrape her nails across his face.

Sir Richard mumbled a few words, then motioned to Hammond. "Continue, Lieutenant."

Hammond's nose twitched. "I conclude by saying that this woman confessed, my lord."

"Mistress Seton? Is this true? You confessed?" Sir Richard asked.

"Nay, my lord, not to any crime. I admitted my marriage to James Hart."

"When were the banns read?"

"They were not, my lord."

"Why?" he demanded.

"We were eager to wed."

The clerk smothered a grin, and when Elizabeth caught his eye, he flushed crimson and returned to his ink pot. Sir Richard's annoyance appeared to deepen by her candour.

"Where is Master Hart to account for this?" Sir Richard peered around the court.

"He's away to London on the inn's business, my lord," Elizabeth said. "I already explained this to Lieutenant Hammond."

"Is there anyone who could speak on your behalf, woman?"

Elizabeth bit her lip. How could she ask Henry to perjure himself? But she had no witness.

"My lord, I witnessed their marriage troth and will swear upon it," Henry said.

"Is this true, Mistress Seton?" Sir Richard asked.

Elizabeth bowed her head. "It is as Master Grant states."

"If I may, my lord?" Henry strode forward. Half-turned to Hammond, he continued his address to Sir Richard. "'Tis a sad state of affairs when a man and wife are not free to enjoy the privacy of their marriage bed without wagging tongues."

"The marriage has yet to be established," Sir Richard replied. "The entire affair is questionable at best."

"My lord, if I may address the court." Hammond paused for Sir Richard's curt nod. "I find it curious that the groom has left his new bride so soon and is not here to speak on his behalf. Indeed, with the exception of the innkeeper, none stand as witness," he said. "I wonder what Henry Grant's interest is in this affair. What arrangement has he struck with this fallen Jezebel? How many others has she corrupted?"

A low growl tore from Henry's throat, and he lunged towards Hammond. The guard stepped in his way and forced him back. "I will not stand to hear this good woman maligned." A vein pulsed in his neck.

"Pity, she's done well enough on her own." Hammond smoothed his russet coat.

"Step down, Master Grant," Sir Richard said. "You are dismissed." The justice then turned to Elizabeth. "What of your family, mistress? Were they also in attendance?"

Elizabeth turned to look at her aunt. "Nay, my lord. They were not. Our decision to wed was last minute."

Isabel stood up and approached the bench. Her movements were slow, and it took a few moments for her to reach the front. She leaned heavily on her cane. The hand that clutched the handle trembled, and the blue veins were more pronounced. Elizabeth had never seen her aunt look so frail. Guilt nearly choked her.

"My lord, if it please the court. I have a few words to say on the matter."

Sir Richard looked pained. "State your name for the court register."

"I am Isabel Stanborowe, widow of the late Robert Stanborowe of Ellendale." Her voice sounded weary. "Elizabeth Seton is my sister's daughter." The clerk bent over his papers, scribbling to capture the details. "I was aware of their intent and will swear to it."

The blood leeched from Elizabeth's face as her aunt perjured herself.

"But by your niece's admission, you did not witness this. Intent, madam, is not proof."

"I have no reason to doubt her word," Isabel said. "A promise to wed fulfills the law. Insisting that a priest provide a blessing smacks of popery, my lord."

Isabel's arrow struck true. A ripple of agreement rose from the crowd, and even Nathaniel lifted his head. "Aye, what need for a priest?" someone cried from the back row. Using Puritan arguments to defend against Puritan laws proved the world had gone mad. A glimmer of hope stirred for Elizabeth.

Sir Richard's jowls quivered. "Thank you, Mistress Stanborowe, for that legal controversy. Have you anything more to say?"

"Only that I beg you to be merciful, my lord. My niece swears that her marriage is in truth, and that should satisfy the court. If there is ambiguity, then a fine will be more than sufficient to teach her the lesson that this court craves."

Sir Richard folded his hands in a steeple and regarded Isabel carefully. "That will be all, madam." He motioned for his clerk and murmured a few words. The clerk bobbed his head in agreement. Elizabeth's hope rose. She glanced at Hammond, whose mouth was set in a tight, furious line.

"My lord," Hammond stepped forward, "I must state emphatically that the laws of the Commonwealth must be followed perfectly. Only in this way may we support our glorious leaders to ensure their vision comes to fruition. We are either working together for the same end or we stand apart." With arms crossed and feet braced apart, he stared down the justice.

Sir Richard's left eye twitched. "Thank you for reminding the court, Lieutenant." Turning to Elizabeth, he asked, "Do you have anything more to say in your defence, mistress?"

"Nay, my lord, save that I am an honest woman."

"Honest?" Hammond barked an unsettling laugh. Lifting his voice so that it carried to the farthest reaches of the room, he announced, "I denounce this woman and have it on good authority that her word cannot be trusted."

A chill went down Elizabeth's spine. What was he playing at now?

"My lord, I took it upon myself to make enquiries amongst my connections in Weymouth. The former governor of that town is an acquaintance."

Blessed God. Elizabeth squeezed her eyes shut, knowing what he was going to say.

"This woman has been portraying herself as an orphan of war, a daughter of a godly supporter of Parliament. Her father was naught but a Royalist wretch, a vile conspirator who betrayed his town, thereby causing much bloodshed and misery." He turned to Elizabeth, triumph and rage etched in his expression. "Admit it, woman, you lied to the good people of Warwick."

"I spoke no lie."

"You intimated different to me, and this is a lie in spirit, if not deed," Hammond said. "Do you deny that your father was a Royalist?"

Elizabeth glanced at her aunt, who appeared stricken. The noose was around her neck, and Hammond had yanked it hard. "I do not. My father died for the King."

Hammond paced the bar with his chest puffed out. "What else have you given a convenient lie to where the truth would damn you?"

Elizabeth shut her mouth. They were getting too close to treacherous ground. Hammond must not learn the truth about James. A fevered prayer ran through her brain.

Sir Richard pointed to Elizabeth. "This is a vile matter, Mistress Seton." He looked across the room to Isabel, openly furious, as though it had been she who had betrayed him. "Madam, surely, you must have been aware of your niece's falsehoods. I'm disappointed in your judgment, vouching for this creature while knowing that she holds loose with the truth. I once regarded you as a godly, wise woman. You have put my court in jeopardy."

Everything crumbled around Elizabeth. Sir Richard's condemnation would fly throughout Warwick and seriously impair her aunt. Isabel didn't deserve this. It wasn't her fault. Everything Isabel had so painstakingly guarded against had rushed through the door because of Elizabeth's actions. Her aunt's stricken face knifed through her.

"I've heard enough." Sir Richard cleared his throat. "On this fifth day of November, the second year of the Commonwealth, it falls to us to guard against the excesses of the past and proclaim our readiness for the kingdom of heaven through our acceptance of God's laws. Only when society follows a godly path may we raise our hearts and await the Lord with true humbleness and joy."

Elizabeth's breathing became shallow.

"Mistress, you have not satisfied this court. We find you guilty of fornication."

The rest came to Elizabeth as though through a dense fog on the harbour.

"You have been convicted of a most grievous crime that threatens the moral fabric of our society. I have no choice but to sentence you to three months in the gaol or until such time that Master Hart returns and corroborates your claim."

The blood drained from Elizabeth's face, and her knees buckled. *The gaol?* Shaking her head, she prayed she had heard wrong. *Three months.* When the guard took her arm, she did not push him aside, for he was the only solid thing holding her up. As they led her away, everything blurred except Hammond's gloating face.

*

James awoke to the point of a blade pressed against his throat. Before he could move, a boot slammed against his chest.

"Quiet now, Southron." The owner of the boot spoke in a low rumble.

James swore to himself. Caught, like an unfledged pigeon, and by a Scotsman. "Who are you?" The campfire had died down to orange embers, leaving the man's face in shadow. "And on the wrong side of the border."

"A traveller, right," he said. "Aye, a bit more canny than ye."

A bloody brigand.

The crunch of boots crossing the camp merged with the low hiss of the fire. James strained to look, but the blade pinned him down. He had to alert the others.

A muffled cry was suddenly cut short. James heard furious scuffling, then a pause. A surprised shout broke the stillness, followed by calls of alarm. Just as quickly, the outcries were cut off and replaced by mocking laughter.

James's captor turned his head slightly and addressed someone beyond James's vision. "All right?"

"Aye."

James edged his hand towards the dagger in his belt and froze when the tip of the Scottish dirk pricked his skin. A drop of blood trickled down his throat.

The rogue clucked his tongue and leaned closer. A husky man, his muscles were heavily corded. Braided blond hair hung over a mottled woollen cloak. "Lie still now, and we'll nae be making any fuss, ken? Ye've a fine collection of horseflesh—seems a shame not tae share."

One of the thieves grabbed Sovereign by the bridle and attempted to lead him from his makeshift pen. The stallion pulled back and reared, hooves flailing the air.

"Back, beastie," someone shouted, then scrambled to get out of the way.

"That horse is worth your life, Scotsman," James warned.

"Aye now, says the man flat on his back." A low, rolling laugh shook him. The man lifted his head and barked over his shoulder, "Mind that one. He's mine."

With the brigand's head turned, James groped for his dagger. Instead, his knuckles scraped against a jagged rock. His hand curled around it.

"Gather the saddles," the robber said. He dug his boot into James's chest and laughed a second time. "Unless ye've an objection."

"Devil take you," James ground out.

Sovereign continued to agitate and launched himself against the crisscrossed ropes of the horse pen. The saplings bent under the pressure and finally snapped. Curses rained from the thieves, and the Scotsman's head jerked up. James seized his chance. He slammed the rock against the steel and knocked the blade away. Then with a full-blooded roar, he smashed the man's knee.

The brigand screamed and buckled to the ground. "Whoreson!"

James rolled aside and scrambled up. He drew out his dagger and scooped a fistful of dirt. As the Scotsman staggered to his feet, James tossed the rocky soil into his eyes. The robber bellowed his rage.

James whistled, and Sovereign responded with a shrill whinny. The stallion laid back his ears and charged. Spooked, the other horses bolted after him. The thieves yelled and dove out of the way.

James's men seized upon the confusion. They threw off their captors and launched into a fight. The sharp clash of steel rang in the glade.

The blond giant blocked James, cutting him off from the others. A low growl rumbled deep in the man's throat, and he brandished his dagger. "Come on at me, ye shitten bastard."

A bleak smile touched James's lips. "Let's see how you do against a man on his feet." Settling into a ready stance, he closed his ears to the brawling and focused on his opponent. He couldn't afford to lose the horses—they'd be crippled without them.

Step by side step, they circled, both crouched low. James struck fast, slashing at the Scotsman's belly. The brigand arched and jumped back, narrowly missing the knife. In the next instant, he raised his dirk eye level and stabbed downward, but James seized his arm. Muscles strained, and James braced himself against the ground. He fought to keep the weapon from plunging into his throat. The brigand's eyes bulged, face enflamed and teeth bared. James twisted the man's wrist and tried to lock it, but the brigand shifted his weight.

James stumbled over the rocky ground. The Scotsman's dirk plunged, and James blocked the thrust with the outside of his arm. The blade pierced his sleeve, biting into his wrist. James gritted his teeth and heaved him back. Without breaking stride, he slashed across the Scotsman's thigh. The man swore and tucked into a roll. When he gained his feet, a guttural sound rumbled in his throat, and he renewed his battle stance.

Again they circled each other, their breathing laboured. A trail of blood stained the robber's breeches. James ignored his stinging forearm and maintained eye contact.

With a shattering roar, the Scotsman swung his blade in a vicious arc. James jumped aside and dodged the attack. With his free hand, he grabbed the brigand's wrist and wrenched it back. The man dropped low and half twisted. With a grunt, he drove his beefy shoulder into James's side, throwing him back like a bull crashing through a gate.

The wind tore out of James. He released his hold and attempted to break free, but his boot caught the edge of a rock. Falling backward, he landed on a boulder. The bone-jarring impact missed his spine by inches. White-hot pain exploded. Groaning, James struggled to rise, but his limbs were jelly.

The brigand snarled and closed in. James lifted his forearm to protect himself—he knew he hadn't the strength for more. From behind, a loud shout stopped the brigand's advance. He looked up, and a sudden grin spread across his face. Laughing, he held his dirk in his open palm and backed away.

"Lick yer wounds, Southron." He bared his teeth, then turned to join the other thieves.

Angry yells erupted when James's men realised the brigands were escaping. "Stop them!"

As quickly as they had encircled their camp, the Scottish thieves scattered and disappeared into the forest.

Roger reached James, his face twisted in frustration. Blood smeared his forehead from a cut over his brow. "Captain—"

James struggled to his feet and bent over his thighs, working through the shattering pain. "Everyone all right?"

"Aye, but—"

"What?" James looked up. "Don't tell me they ran off with the horses?"

"Nay." Roger dropped his sword and wiped his forehead with the back of his hand. "They've taken most of the packs."

James sucked in his breath, and his nostrils flared. A high rage seized him. "Goddamn it—where were the sentries? Who pulled duty?"

"A new recruit named Murdoch."

"Haul him over here, right this minute." James looked around at the wreckage. Most of their supplies—food, rope and shot, all gone. *Hell and damnation.* With a snarl, he threw his dagger into the ground.

*

The ale did not impress James. The thin, sour brew coated the tongue and lingered like an unwholesome scent. And he had paid dearly for it, having to turn over a sizeable part of their remaining coin for a meal and lodgings in Penrith to get information. His pride still burned over being caught by Scottish brigands. Except for Roger, everyone skirted around him, particularly Murdoch. Not only had the man been on sentry duty, the pack horses had also fallen to him. Failed on both accounts.

James rubbed the back of his head and made a mental tally of their resources. Had he not stitched a quarter of their coin in his saddlebags, matters would have been more dire. Not enough to keep them in comfort until they reached the King, but sufficient to purchase oats for their horses and rough bedding for themselves in the stables. Mouldy hay and the baying of livestock didn't make for a restful night, but then he hadn't slept well since leaving Warwick a fortnight ago. Thoughts of Elizabeth gave him little peace. Last night, as he finally drifted off, he imagined the curtain of her hair falling over him and a press of moist lips against his own.

James took another swig of ale and shuddered. He pushed the cup away, deciding he couldn't stomach any more.

Roger arrived and slipped into the stool across from him and reached for a cup.

"You don't want that." James pulled it away. "What news from the landlord?"

"Soldiers are thick as fleas around Carlisle. They've set border patrols to keep the passes shut. Cromwell's orders."

"What of the roads ahead?"

Roger grimaced. "There's a company stationed here in Penrith—no more than fifty men. If we stay off the main road, we should avoid them and reach Carlisle in a few days."

"But we need to get across the border," James said, drumming his fingers on the table.

"With the borders sealed, we could ride three days east and secure a ship in Newcastle."

"With fifty-odd horses and gear? Impossible. There must be another way."

In the back, a door slammed, and a pair of serving maids rushed to the front. A sizeable crowd gathered outside. James pushed his chair aside and moved to an empty window. People spilled out on the street, their attention focused in the same direction. As he stood there wondering what the attraction was, a company of dragoons rode past, leading a group of ten prisoners whose hands were bound and lashed to their horses. James leaned in for a better look. He recognised one immediately. The man, after all, had pressed a sword to his throat.

"Do you see them?" Roger asked. "Aren't they—?"

"Aye," James replied.

"Serves them well." Roger snorted. "Too bad we couldn't petition to get our supplies back."

James drummed the sill, deep in thought. The crowd hurtled insults and pelted the prisoners with clods of dung and stone. The Scottish prisoners stared ahead without flinching.

The innkeeper sidled beside James. "Devil take them mossers," he said, his voice full of gravel and peat smoke.

"Mossers?" Roger asked.

"Aye, moss-troopers." The man folded his hairy arms across his wide chest. "Fought for the old corrupt King during the troubles, and now with him short a head, they've taken to thieving against anyone moving through these parts, no matter who they be. Off to Carlisle they go, and good riddance. May they rot there until the next assizes." Without a glance back, he rushed out the front door and joined the others in the street. Before the door closed behind him, the man's shouts merged with the cacophony outside.

James scratched his stubbled beard. When the tail end of the dragoons passed from sight, he smiled.

*

The icy wind whistled like a banshee, an eerie sound that muffled the horses. James led the way through the forest with his hat pulled low and a scarf covering his face. The others kept pace behind him, all hooded to a man. A moonless night. A snowy veil of clouds blotted out the stars above. They smelled wood smoke long before they saw the light from the distant campfire.

James held up his fist and halted his riders. He pointed right then left, and the company fanned out to encircle the glade. James drew his sword from its sheath, an eager hiss in the night. Five minutes passed before he and Roger continued forward.

They drew closer and hung back from the clearing. James waited for the signal. The hoot of an owl, then another. *All in position.* James tilted his head and mimicked the sharp cry of a goshawk. Before the last note ended, his company charged in unison against the unsuspecting dragoons huddled around the fire. Their quarry barely found their feet before being swept aside by the charging horses. A madness of confusion seized them, and they scattered in a panic.

James's sword flashed in the firelight, and he swung to disarm one of the soldiers in his path. As blade met bone, the soldier shrieked and dropped his sword. Sovereign veered to the left, and James turned the stallion to take a second pass. A dragoon aimed his musket at Roger's retreating back and cocked the hammer. Sounding a cry of alarm, James pressed his knees against the horse's flanks and charged. The soldier whirled, and his mouth dropped. He dove aside, narrowly missing the fire.

The last of the resistance faded, and the raiders herded those left standing into a tight circle.

"Drop your weapons," James barked. A collection of muskets and swords clattered at their feet. He pointed to Davis and Sheffield. "Gather everything, including their purses." He dismounted and tossed the reins to one of his men. Without glancing at the dragoons, he crossed to the edge of the glade where the ten Scottish prisoners were tied to a row of trees. He unsheathed his dagger. The prisoners watched him approach and shifted in their bonds, but James ignored them. He went straight to the one in the motley wool cloak. James crouched before him and held the edge of his dagger against his throat. With his other hand, he pulled down his mask. "Remember me, moss-trooper?"

The man nodded, his mouth twisted into a grim smile. "Aye, Southron."

"If I free you from this lot, you will owe me."

"Name yer price."

James bent closer. "Safe passage to Stirling."

The Scotsman's eyes narrowed, and he chewed his lip. "Ye'll be far from home."

"Aye, but closer to the King," James replied and watched his words sink in. "What say you?" James grabbed the corded rope, knife poised.

A slow smile spread across the Scotsman's face. "Right, then. We'll take ye."

"Your word on it?" James lifted his brow.

"By the word of a Johnstone."

James nodded and sliced through the rope.

Chapter Twenty-One

James ran the whetstone along the edge of his blade. He had smoothed out most of the nicks in the sword, all except one. He took another pass, then another, until the steel's tone changed from a grudging sigh to a sharp, fluid hiss. His men gathered around the newly built fire, keeping their weapons within easy reach. Across from them, their Scottish guides rested, wrapped in hodden-grey cloaks as muted as the Lanarkshire hills. A divide existed between the two groups, with the campfire serving as Hadrian's Wall.

James kept a close eye on Iain Johnstone. The braided giant moved amongst his own men, his dirk safely sheathed. As he passed, his mottled cloak brushed the tall grasses. The moss-trooper ignored James's men— hadn't exchanged a simple word to any of them. Whenever they asked him a question, he responded with only the mocking lift of his brow. James remained the exception, but the few words since Carlisle didn't amount to much.

The prickling between James's shoulders had intensified since crossing into Scotland. Deep, cloven valleys spanned a purple mountain range that remained remote and untouchable, no matter how long they rode. James fought against a strange edginess, an unsettling need to be elsewhere mingled with the frustration of not getting to Stirling fast enough.

Their safety depended on these Scottish outlaws. With the flood of English troops travelling north to Edinburgh, James had to rely on Johnstone's knowledge of the hidden bypaths. Though his company outnumbered the Scots four to one, James couldn't be sure if the moss-troopers were leading them straight to the nearest English patrol. It wouldn't have been the first time the Scots betrayed their cause. Refusing to remain blind to the road ahead, James had sent out a hand-picked scouting party hours before they stopped to make camp.

Another few passes over the sword and the whetstone slipped, nearly slicing James's hand. "Christ's teeth."

A sentry shattered his thoughts. "Riders approaching!"

The scouting party returned to camp with Roger in the lead. The riders pulled into the circle with lathered horses.

"Three English regiments headed this way," Roger said. "They're a quarter mile from here."

James grimaced. He had hoped to give his men some rest. "Gear up. Five minutes to disappear," he yelled. "And someone get them fresh horses."

They headed north, maintaining a smart pace to keep well ahead of the enemy vanguard. A hard rain started, and soon they were soaked through. James wrapped his cloak closer around him and lowered his knit cap. Johnstone rode in the lead with his men flanking him. None of the Scots seemed to mind the dirty weather.

They rode along a narrow valley edged by a ridge of hills. The flicker of Sovereign's ears warned James before he heard the low rumble. It strengthened into a steady, unbroken drumming coming from the direction of a distant hill.

It took a few heartbeats to see them. Their bobbing helmets were the same colour as the leaden sky, but they coalesced before his eyes, revealing a swarm of cavalry. More and more crested the hill, swelling over the top like red hornets pouring from a hive. A cross of St. George snapped in the wind.

In the distance, a blare of English trumpets rang. As one, the enemy Horse fanned out, cutting them off from the north.

James's jaw dropped. *Sweet Christ Almighty.* "Run!"

The company bolted—straight into the teeth of the storm. James looked over his shoulder. Four regiments—over a thousand horse. He yelled to his men, "Keep up!" Damned if he was going to get caught less than a month after leaving Warwick. He refused to rot in a dank cell.

Johnstone drew alongside James. The rain streamed down his whiskers. "There's a crossing seven miles from here—our only chance tae lose them."

Mile after mile, the moss-trooper led them along a wooded defile, and they rode as fast as they dared. The rain angled in slanted sheets, making visibility poor and the ground treacherous. Their pursuers had not dropped off and, with every mile, managed to narrow the gap.

"Five more miles," Johnstone cried over the roar of the wind.

The horses laboured in the cold. It became a test of every man's skill to remain in the saddle and not fall behind. James loosened his reins to give Sovereign his head, counting on the horse's instincts to get them through this.

The sky was getting darker when they finally reached a swollen river. As they continued, the river widened, and its churning water became angrier.

"This is your plan? Trap us at a river?" James shouted.

"We ford it, Southron."

James shook his head. Swirls of crosscurrents warned of a strong undertow, enough to suck a man into its brown depths. "We'll drown."

"If ye're afeard of getting yer skirt wet, stay and greet the buggers."

"Damned Scotsman," he muttered.

They continued downriver until the river narrowed and the swirling currents lessened.

"Best we'll get, lads. Prepare to swim," Johnstone shouted. He took the lead and plunged his horse into the river.

Cromwell's men drew closer. James cursed. Outnumbered and with wet muskets, he had no choice than to follow the moss-trooper.

James guided Sovereign into the river. He kept a firm hold on the reins and pressed his knees against the horse's flanks. The current was strong, and by the time Sovereign reached the middle, the waters had risen to his chest.

A sharp whinny pierced the air. One of the packhorses panicked and thrashed against the current, unsettling the horseman in front holding its lead. The man clutched his own horse's mane and fought to keep his seat. His shouts further unnerved the animal.

James urged Sovereign to the other side of the packhorse. "Easy, there," he said. Sensing Sovereign, the animal's wild-eyed terror eased enough for James to grab him by the bridle. Together they managed to get him safely to shore.

Sovereign's hooves sank into the mud as he climbed up the bank. He trembled from exhaustion and cold while James sagged with relief. They made it with the last of the fading light.

Across the river, the enemy Horse halted. Between the growing darkness and the rising waters, only a madman would have attempted it now. The Roundheads circled the shore, frustrated at losing their quarry, then turned around and headed back.

James released a ragged breath. They had eluded capture—for now.

*

They spent the next several days heading northwest. James continued to send scouts. Each day, fewer sightings were reported until James was certain they had steered clear of the English troops.

Twenty miles south of Hamilton, they stopped at an inn to get a meal and rest in a proper bed. It was late, and they barely made it through the gates before the landlord locked the doors. James tumbled into a straw-filled pallet. Whether from over-fatigue or the strangeness of the place, it took hours before sleep finally claimed him, and then he was already awake before the cock crowed.

As the hour was still early, James found the taproom empty and the fire still banked. The innkeeper appeared shortly, rubbing his eyes and scratching his chest.

"Aye, I'll send out cheese and bread," he muttered. He poured James a cup of ale before shuffling off to the kitchen.

James didn't notice the serving maid until she had crossed the room with a tray of earthenware tankards. Her hair was dark, nearly black, and she wore it loosely coiled, like Elizabeth. A dull ache tightened his chest. James crossed his arms and stared at the deep gouges in the table. He expected Elizabeth would be rising soon and attending any number of morning rituals he was not a part of.

A hand slapped the table, shattering his thoughts. Johnstone sat down across from him and swung one leg over the bench. "Up early, Southron." He caught the attention of the serving maid. "Bring us a bit o' porridge, lass, if ye has some, right."

"Aye, 'twill be ready by now."

"And my bread," James called out after her. "Oats are for horses," he muttered.

Johnstone grinned. "That's why ye English have the finest horses and we the finest men."

The maid returned quickly with their food. Up close, any similarity to Elizabeth evaporated. A smattering of freckles covered her cheeks, and her eyes were dark and widely set. As she placed the cheese down, she nearly upset James's ale. He waved away her apologies, and she withdrew to the kitchen.

"Came from the stables," Johnstone said.

"Aye, I was there earlier." James tore off a chunk of brown bread and tried to push thoughts of Warwick from his mind. "Was the ostler there? I couldn't find him."

Johnstone nodded and swallowed a spoonful of hot porridge. He blew on his spoon and tested it once more. He wiped his mouth with the back of his hand, but a few stray oats still clung to his beard. "Poor news. The town's on edge. Cromwell's man, Major General Lambert, has encamped near Peebles, just northeast of here. Close enough tae give the town burrs, but nae enough tae prick them."

"Numbers?"

"Three, maybe four thousand." Johnstone tossed the heel of the bread to a brindled hound that had slunk in.

"And Cromwell makes eight or ten thousand in the field," James muttered. "I wonder how many he has stationed around Edinburgh."

"Enough to run up and down Midlothian sacking fortresses while laying siege to Edinburgh Castle." Johnstone carved a thick slice of yellow cheese. "In all, twelve thousand, maybe fourteen. They had more, but the sickness reduced their numbers."

"What of the Scottish army?" James asked. When had he started worrying about those who had betrayed the late King?

"Which one?" Johnstone barked a short laugh that ended in a snort. "Central command likes to think they run Scotland from their position in Stirling, but south of the Firth of Forth, the Westland army has other ideas." Johnstone pulled on his beard and glanced over his shoulder before leaning in. "The ostler had a fair bit tae say, ken. Appears that Westland has broken with the King. In fact, they told central command to go fuck themselves."

"You jest?"

Johnstone shook his head. "That's Westland army."

Damned turncoats. James really hated it when Nathaniel was right. "They've thrown their lot in with Cromwell, then?"

"Nae, man," Johnstone said. "They told him tae shove it too."

James chewed on this information. "Where does that leave us?"

"Now we have two armies tae avoid," Johnstone said grimly.

James groaned and pushed his plate of crumbs away from him. "I would have liked to have given the horses another day's rest, but we can't stay here much longer. How much farther to Stirling?"

"Fifteen leagues," Johnstone said. "As long as we don't run into trouble, we can make it in three days."

How hard could it be dodging two armies in unfamiliar territory?

*

Elizabeth's hell became an isolated cell in the two-penny ward. Her quarters consisted of a rusted bucket for a chamber pot and tick-infested bedding. The walls were a constant source of dampness. A steady flow of water dribbled down the pitted stone.

Her only link to mankind was the two gaolers. The first, Clarence, was a stout man with thick sausage fingers. Everyone simply called him Cully. He spoke very little and ignored Elizabeth's overtures to gain news. The second gaoler, Flagg, a leathery man with sunken, pox-riddled cheeks, reeked of strong spirits. Elizabeth avoided all manner of speech with him, though that didn't stop his leering advances.

It had been Flagg's watch when they herded Elizabeth in.

"A cot will cost fourpence a night, bedding an extra pence. For a shilling, I can get you a dish of mutton twice a week. Of course," Flagg said, stretching, "I'm not above negotiating."

He turned Elizabeth's stomach, but she knew enough not to show fear. His type fed off weakness. "I don't care for mutton," she said and returned his hard stare without flinching.

Elizabeth had been in the gaol ten days when Flagg unlocked her cell and told her to get moving. "On your feet, ladybird."

"What—where are we going?"

"You'll see." He gripped her arm and led her down the corridor.

Flagg's sour stench nearly made Elizabeth gag. She glanced at the dagger at his belt. Sheathed and latched with a strap. No easy way to snatch it. His keys dangled at his belt. Those might be used as a weapon.

"Where are you taking me?"

"There's someone to see you." Flagg smirked.

"Is it my aunt?" Though they had accepted her aunt's coin for her keep, they wouldn't allow visitations. Maybe this had changed.

"Naught."

Elizabeth's heart sank. "Henry Grant, then?"

"Looking for a new bridegroom?" Flagg licked his lips and grinned. "Nothing stopping you from looking closer to home, ladybird."

Elizabeth steeled herself. "You wouldn't be my choice, gaoler."

Flagg twisted her arm and yanked her against him. An angry snarl twisted his mouth. Elizabeth bit back a cry. "You fancy Cully, now? The man's a fat slob and useless to you. Hasn't seen his toes in a decade."

Elizabeth gritted her teeth. "My visitor is waiting, Master Pockmarks."

Flagg scowled and shoved her forward. "Aye, that he is."

He led her upstairs to a better-kept section of the gaol and pulled her into a receiving chamber. "Here she is, sir."

"Gently, Sidney Flagg. You'll hurt our guest."

Elizabeth froze. That flat monotone had replayed itself in her head during her darkest moments. She drew herself to her full height and faced Hammond. The door closed behind them.

Hammond's hair had been freshly clipped, and instead of his russet uniform, he had donned a charcoal broadcloth coat. Beside him, a small repast was spread across a table. Yellow cheese and a crusty loaf of bread were laid out alongside a green bottle and a pair of goblets. A roasted fowl, its brown skin done to a crisp, rested on a platter surrounded by roasted leeks. Its aroma made Elizabeth painfully aware of her gnawing hunger, and her mouth watered.

Elizabeth tore her eyes away from the food. "What are you doing here?"

"I thought you would appreciate the company, particularly since you haven't any other visitors. My orders, in case you're wondering." Hammond smiled. "Take a seat."

"I'd rather stand."

"'Tis the Sabbath, mistress," he said. "The Lord's day of rest. Sit down."

Elizabeth's hair lifted on the back of her neck. She took the chair but moved it back another foot. Hammond's eyebrow lifted, but he reserved comment.

"You appear wan. I've brought you sustenance." Hammond walked over to the table and lifted a bottle. "Mead?" Without waiting for a reply, he poured a small draught into a goblet.

"No, thank you," Elizabeth said, laying a hand on her stomach. Even the thought of the cloying drink made her quiver. She couldn't be sick and have him guess that she carried James's child. "I don't favour the drink."

"You should reconsider, mistress," Hammond said, lifting his glass to take a sip. "The mead compliments the victuals quite well." He ripped a leg from the roasted bird and placed it upon a hunk of fresh bread. The juices stained the bread a nut brown, and the smell of fresh yeast mingled with warmed spices. Hammond sampled the bird but didn't offer her any. Elizabeth followed the dribble of pheasant grease that escaped the corner of his mouth. Her empty stomach rubbed against her spine.

"I've enquired at the inn for your lover. Odd that no one has heard from him," Hammond said as he chewed his dinner. "The innkeeper has his hands full these days and could spare me no more than a brief courtesy."

Elizabeth swallowed. "I haven't had any word of my aunt. I'm concerned about her health."

Hammond cut another hunk of bread and dabbed at the juices swimming in the platter. "This bread is first rate. Excellent texture." He took a sip of mead and smiled. "Perfect complement. Did you desire some bread, mistress?"

Elizabeth fought with herself. She wanted to snub the man and his bread, but her stomach protested. She had already thrown up the little food she had. Her pride might sustain her, but not the babe. "If it pleases you, Lieutenant."

"Mead?"

"Just the bread."

Hammond sighed and settled back in his seat. "Not one without the other."

"I'm not hungry, then."

"As you wish." Hammond helped himself to a slab of cheese. "Poor timing for Henry Grant, losing his ostler at such a time. There's a matter of unpaid ale quarterages. The landlord claims to have his affairs in order, but I have my doubts."

Elizabeth sucked in her breath. Hammond knew that James kept the inn's books. She fought to appear unaffected to give him no satisfaction. "You were saying about my aunt?"

"You've asked about your aunt, but not your errant lover. Why?"

"When James Hart returns to Warwick, I will know it. He will not suffer to see me here one moment longer. You will know it too, I daresay."

Hammond scowled. His controlled mask slipped a notch. "He's probably lying in a ditch somewhere, his throat cut by a brigand."

Elizabeth lowered her head so as not to show her fear. Hammond must not connect the thought of James with the highwayman.

"A feast for maggots and carrion," Hammond pressed on. "Like Prometheus chained to a boulder, sentenced to having his liver pecked by vultures until the end of days." He rested his elbows on the arms of the chair, his shoulders slightly hunched over, like the bird in the fables.

Elizabeth remained silent. Hammond's words struck at the heart of her fear. How often did she wonder where James was—if he was safe or wounded, or worse, lying dead? Had he even reached the King?

"A fitting penance for one with the arrogance to thumb his nose at God's laws." Hammond leaned forward and stabbed the pheasant, spearing a chunk of brown meat. "Since you do not want the food I've brought you, perhaps you'll prefer a lesson?" From the inside of his coat, he drew out a napkin and painstakingly wiped the grease from between his fingers and under each fingernail.

"Perhaps you have one on humility, Lieutenant? You should study it."

"I have thought to read from the book of Ruth. The lessons are an inspiration for all women to achieve her virtuousness." Hammond reached for his book, cradling it in his hands. He caressed its cover as though it were a lover, passing a hand down its spine before he splayed it open on his lap. Wetting his finger, he turned each page with care until he found the section he wanted. A promise warmed his pale blue eyes. Elizabeth wanted to retch.

"You bring me the tale of a widow?" She didn't doubt that there was a measure of wishful thinking on his part.

"Ruth left a wicked nation behind and discovered the Chosen Land."

"Would you have me lie at your feet as Ruth did to Boaz, her second husband?"

Hammond flushed. "Boaz was a godly man. She showed good sense."

"She had no choice," Elizabeth replied. "Did you happen to bring the story of Rahab? I like her better."

"A harlot? You want me to read you the story of a harlot?"

Elizabeth paused. A corner of her mind urged caution. *You go too far.* What if he linked the lesson of Rahab hiding fugitives in Jericho with the recusants that disappeared when they crossed into Warwickshire? She watched Hammond work through his outrage. For all his reading, he wouldn't understand the reference. In his mind, she was a harlot. Rebellion quashed good sense. She had been prodded and pushed, tormented and insulted. She had had enough. "Certainly. You can finish it off with the Magdalene."

"You disappoint me, mistress," Hammond said and snapped the book shut. His knuckles turned white, and a muscle beside his left eye twitched. He rose to his feet and walked behind her chair.

Elizabeth tried to turn, but his hands clamped down on her shoulders. His fingers dug into her; tiny shards of pain iced down her spine.

"You are behaving like a petulant child," Hammond whispered in her ear. "Is this any way to thank me for my interest?" His hands crept along her collarbone. Thick fingers, cold to the touch, encircled her neck. Elizabeth's breathing became shallow, and her heart fluttered. His thumbs stroked her throat before his fingers began to squeeze. She gasped for breath. Elizabeth's hands flew to break his hold, raking her nails against his hands, but instead of releasing her, he tightened his grip. She pushed her feet against the floor and tried to buck him off, but he had her pinned. Black spots danced before her eyes, and her strength began to fail. Just as she was about to pass out, he released her. The sudden inrush of breath choked her, and Elizabeth bent forward, sucking in a lungful of air. Tears flowed down her cheeks as she coughed.

"Careless of you, forgetting to breathe like that." Hammond slipped around to stand in front. "You know I'm here for you, don't you?" He bent down so his face was even with hers. "I will never leave you, Elizabeth. Never." The dread, the fear, pressed tight. "All others have forsaken you, but you have only me now." He held her chin so she could not look away. "Rejoice, for I am your guide to salvation."

Hammond straightened and returned to the table. He picked up the untouched goblet and once again offered it to her. "Mead? 'Tis just the thing to coat your sore throat."

*

The musket fire coming from the town of Hamilton ceased in the early hours before dawn. Snow and gunpowder coated the brisk wind. The

Scottish Westland army had attacked the town where Major General Lambert's English troops were recently quartered. Hidden in a wooded copse a few miles west of town, James's company waited for their scouts to return.

He wrapped his cloak tighter around his shoulders as he paced. The frozen ground crunched beneath his boots. In the aftermath of any skirmish, survivors fled for safer ground, and they couldn't afford to be dragged into this fight.

Roger raised the alert. "Captain, rider approaching."

Cocked hammers repeated in the forest glade.

A single horseman picked his way along the wooded trail. The trees cast long shadows under the grim light of dawn. As he drew nearer, James recognised his trumpeter, Davis.

"What happened?"

Davis halted before the gathered men. "Westland army won Hamilton." He whipped off his cap and wiped his brow with the back of his sleeve. "A hundred forty against Lambert's two thousand."

Murmurs of disbelief rippled through the men. Johnstone strode forward, a sceptical frown gathered on his forehead. "Ye jest."

"Nay. The vanguard caught the English by surprise. Lambert must have thought there were more of Ker's men. Not that I blame them. Who would have expected so few to attack the town against so many?"

Johnstone slapped his hand against his thigh. "Good lads," he said with a whoop. When James raised a brow, the Scotsman shrugged, his grin still firmly in place. "They're still ours, nae matter that their heads are addled."

"Where's Sheffield and Glencross?" James looked past Davis to the empty trail for his cornet and Johnstone's lieutenant.

"Near Hamilton, keeping watch. I came to bring the word. The Scots arrived with an extra fifteen hundred men. They showed signs of moving in to claim the prize. Sheffield didn't want to turn our backs on them."

Let them annihilate one another, James thought, as long as his men weren't caught up in it. "Did you find a route we could take to skirt around this mess?"

"Aye, there's a western road that should keep us out of their reach."

The boom of cannon fire thundered and shook the ground.

"That's not a victory salute," James said. A quick succession of musket shots chased the boom of answering cannon. "English wolves are biting back."

"Take us tae where ye left the lads."

Davis led the troop along the tree line, east towards Hamilton. As they neared the town, the thunder of cannon fire grew louder. The acrid reek of spent gunpowder carried in the wind, and a few of the younger horses, untrained in war, shied. Sovereign pressed on, unaffected. The old excitement coursed through James's veins.

They came in sight of Hamilton's rooftops and halted at the edge of the woods. Across the plains, English and Scots faced each other across Cadzow Burn, near the main gates of town. The waters were swollen, and the ground flooded and muddy. The Scots rushed across the stream, but the English had the advantage of higher ground from the east bank. The screams of men and horses rose above the clash of swords and musket fire. The grey of the Scottish cloaks mingled pell-mell against the russet coats of the English dragoons. As they watched, the Scots began to give ground.

James sat tense in his saddle. His and Johnstone's men watched in grim silence. They couldn't raise their swords to come to the aid of either side—not the English who had executed the King, nor the Westland army who had turned their backs on his heir.

Johnstone's mouth tightened. "This is unnatural. We can at least carry word tae Stirling." He looked around at the grasses and hillocks. "Where the bloody hell are Glencross and Sheffield?"

Davis scratched his head. "I don't know. I left them here. Sheffield mentioned wanting to get a better look at the town's northern defences."

"Christ's teeth," James said. "Let's find them so we can quit this place."

North of the town, they found the fighting sporadic, but the main arena blocked their path. The only way to get clear was to fight their way through two armies. And their men were nowhere in sight.

Ahead, along a flat stretch, a squadron of English Horse gave chase to half a dozen Scottish horsemen retreating from Hamilton. A shot rang out, and one of the Scottish troopers jerked forward. He slumped against his horse's neck and fell behind.

Two riders detached from the retreating party. One circled back to help the wounded Scotsman while the other headed straight for the English redcoats. The rider took aim and fired upon the advancing redcoats.

James recognised him immediately. "Sheffield."

Johnstone gave a curt nod to the other man. "And Glencross. Aye, we're in."

James called out to Roger, "Take a dozen men to their aid." He turned to his troop and raised his fist in the air. "The rest with me. We'll drive a wedge between our own and those Roundheads. Pistols ready—no quarter!" He pressed his knees into Sovereign's flanks and sent the black horse thundering down the slope.

They galloped across the fields, racing to cut off the English. Like a bowshot, James's and Roger's men split each to their quarry, their mounts fresh and eager.

James crouched over Sovereign, wind whipping in his face, heart pounding in his chest. He fixed his attention on the foremost English troopers, judging the shrinking distance in pounding hoofbeats. His success depended on intercepting the enemy at the precise moment, to cut across their path and break their charge with a round of musket fire. Reach the field too quickly and he'd only give the enemy time to pull back and form their lines. Too late and he'd be chasing their rear guard. James adjusted Sovereign's speed. A quick glance behind him showed his troopers riding in a tight line.

A hundred yards... fifty... twenty. Now!

James's men swept across field, and alarmed shouts erupted from the Roundheads. Stunned, a few managed to pull back, but most were powerless to divert their course. James levelled his pistol at the foremost dragoon. A barking of smoke and shot spit from his barrel. The man jerked backward and flew off his mount. James's men opened fire, and more of the English fell. A ricochet of gunfire and pounding hooves echoed on the field.

An English squadron wheeled around and assembled in a single file to return fire. A shot whistled past James's ear. He didn't break stride. With a blooded war cry, he and his men fell upon the first of the English Horse.

Drawn swords flashed, then the ring of steel biting steel. Horses scrambled to keep their footing in the melee. Sovereign ploughed forward as though wading through a field of barley. James's sword sliced through the arm of an opponent. The Roundhead released a blood-curdling scream before crumpling to the ground, and James swept past him. Another English trooper tried to block his way, and he charged, rising in the stirrups, his sword rising and falling while he slashed at the man's unprotected neck.

James whipped around for a second pass and saw Johnstone close by, face streaked with mud and splattered blood. The Scotsman's blade edged red as it rose and fell with deadly rhythm.

Half of the English bolted for the safety of Hamilton, leaving a stubborn handful to regroup and organise a stand.

James whistled and gathered his men aside to reload. Sweating and out of breath, a quick count showed all were still in the saddle. Another half minute and they were ready. "Second pass, men. Run the beggars to the ground!"

Johnstone pulled up beside James, his face flushed with excitement. With an angry snarl, he thumped his horse's flanks, shouted, "For the King!" and raced off with his shrieking moss-troopers close on his heels.

"The King!" James shouted and launched a second wave of attack.

A spate of gunfire erupted around them, and grey smoke obscured the field. They slammed into a wall of enemy troopers. Horses reared, and men screamed as swords sliced through meat and bone.

James swiped his glove across his face to clear the sweat from his vision. A flash of reflected light caught his attention. An English trooper raised his musket and prepared to fire at Johnstone's unprotected back. James aimed and fired, clipping the Roundhead in the throat. The man fell off his horse, his body crushed by those rushing past.

Johnstone whipped around and met James's gaze. As the Scotsman raised his hand in a salute, he stiffened. His eyes widened, and he shouted a warning.

James instinctively moved. He yanked Sovereign's reins but only managed a half turn before hearing the crack of a musket. James felt the blow in his side, a force as strong as a blacksmith's hammer. He jerked forward and fought to keep his balance. A searing pain spread like a hot burst. He ground his teeth and urged Sovereign forward to clear the field. His men closed ranks around him, forming a shield of buff coats and horseflesh.

"Are ye all right?" Johnstone asked when he finally reached him.

James grunted. "Aye."

Roger arrived with reinforcements, and the last of the English resistance shredded. "Grab what you can and let's get out of here."

James shook his head to clear the fog from his eyes. The voices faded to the distance. He lurched in the saddle before his vision dimmed.

Chapter Twenty-Two

When Elizabeth finished reading to Hammond, she lowered the tract to her lap and constructed a smile for him. He sat with his chin propped on his hand and watched her. Elizabeth knew how a bug felt under a glass, every flutter of its wings marked by the naturalist and every twitch of its antennae analysed.

Hammond cleared his throat and crossed one leg over the other. "As always, Elizabeth, you read well."

She repressed an involuntary shudder. His claim of her name was a personal, intimate gesture. She hated it. "Thank you, sir."

Hammond glanced at the Bible on the table before turning his attention to the tracts on his lap. Shuffling through the stack, he paused, read a little, and continued sorting them into an order of his choosing.

Elizabeth's campaign to lull Hammond had progressed during the course of his visits—a matter of survival. She meant to walk out of the gaol with her wits and health intact. At first, he had met her compliance with wariness and her interest in his texts with suspicion, but she courted him with skill. Carefully, she flattered his choice of readings. She paid extra attention to the passages that triggered a change in his demeanour, noting when he leaned closer, captivated. She modified her reading until he hung on every word. Secretly, she was amazed at her ability to manipulate him; a violinist coaxing a response from a wooden instrument. If she didn't loathe him as much as she did, she'd feel guilt over her deception.

I know how to handle Hammond. Had she not boasted this to James? A sudden lump lodged in her throat, and she forced it down. How naive she had been. She would never underestimate Hammond again.

Elizabeth's gaze drifted to the barred windows. A cold, grey light squeezed past the mullioned panes, casting squares upon the dusty floorboards. She hated her helplessness. Fear and despair coated the walls of her cell, and she was determined to rid herself of its taste. *Smile... appear modest. Blunt the edge of his vigilance.* She glanced up and met his unfathomable regard, and her breath caught in her throat. Had she miscalculated?

"Have you anything else you'd like to hear?"

Hammond began pacing, winding his way several times past the side table. He stopped before the fireplace and stared into the flames. Elizabeth wondered at his strange mood. His agitation increased her unease.

"I have brought something special, as a matter of fact," he said when he returned to his seat. "Your progress encourages me." He picked up the Bible and opened it to a section marked by a strip of red ribbon. Hammond turned the book so that its pages faced her. "Know you the book of Daniel?" The catch in his breath made him sound like a besotted lover whispering the name of his obsession.

"Aye," Elizabeth replied slowly as she tried to fathom his intent. "The lion's den."

"The least of its lessons." Hammond's brow furrowed.

"Of course," Elizabeth rushed to assure him. "I dare not mention the prophesies of Daniel."

The shadow fled Hammond. "Do you truly understand them?" His rising colour betrayed his excitement.

Elizabeth had never cared for any of those prophetic tracts, and her father had scorned them all. Thomas Seton had had little patience with those who had torn apart each word looking for a hidden meaning. "Dangerous work," he had often said. "Can't see the rocks for the sea foam." He had even less use for fanatics. Elizabeth knew better than to admit this to Hammond, so she picked her way along this strange shore with care. "Do any of us truly understand divine inspiration?"

Hammond beamed. "You speak well, Elizabeth. Truth commends you. Most men walk through this world cursed to darkness. The veil of ignorance has yet to be lifted from their eyes."

He slipped into the chair beside her and laid his hand on her arm. She forced herself not to flinch. "I was once a young man in Cambridge, studying mathematics, like an empty pitcher waiting to be filled. Then God sent me a dream." Hammond leaned in to close the narrow gap, and his voice dropped to a whisper. "I dreamt of a red lion holding a bloody horn in its maw. The beast suffered from grievous wounds and crashed to the ground. Beneath my feet, the earth shook, and the sound that filled

265

my ears was greater than the pounding of a thousand horses. Under the lion's left paw, a fissure spread, growing wider and tearing the earth asunder. I teetered on the edge, but instead of pitching into the chasm, a burst of hot wind buffeted me, and I tumbled back."

Hammond paused and dabbed the bead of sweat on his brow. "When I awoke, I lay in mortal fear upon my cot." He tipped his head back and closed his eyes as though searching inward. "Read to me Daniel 2."

A chill snaked down Elizabeth's spine.

"What are you waiting for?"

"Your vision overwhelmed me."

Hammond nodded. "Proceed."

Elizabeth mastered the urge to hurl the book at him and began to read. From the corner of her eye, she saw him mouthing the words under his breath, following her syllable for syllable. As she continued, Hammond became more animated. No longer content to mouth the words, his voice overpowered hers.

Elizabeth stopped reading, and Hammond continued in her place. "'A rock was cut out, but not by human hands. It struck the statue on its feet of iron and clay and smashed them.'" He looked up at her, his expression blazing. "Do you see it, Elizabeth? Know you its meaning?"

"I can't profess to understand." Elizabeth hid her alarm with a fluttering smile. That was not entirely true. The Rebellion had been a crucible for religious fanatics. They stoked the fires of honest fears, blown hotter by new interpretations of prophetic texts until they forged a new vision. The blade of their religion was sharpened on the grindstone of fear.

"Read, and it shall be made clear."

Reluctantly Elizabeth continued, each word a heavy weight upon her tongue. She reached the part where Daniel likened the parts of the statue to four great kingdoms, each metal representing a distinct land, the last being iron mixed with clay.

Hammond held up his hand and stopped her. "Do you see it now?"

"The divided kingdom is England," Elizabeth said. *When will it end?*

"Excellent! The Fourth Kingdom crumbled when Charles Stuart, that vile man of blood, yielded his corrupt head to the headman's axe. Oh, divided kingdom of iron and clay. You were doomed to grow weaker, as Daniel's dream predicted." Hammond's voice trembled with passion.

"The clay weakened the iron. All other kingdoms before were pure, one metal, but not the last. The strength of the iron was diluted by the baseness of the clay."

Hammond grasped Elizabeth's chin in a firm grip. The Bible tumbled from her lap and hit the floor with a dead thump. "Forget this base, corrupt world, Elizabeth. Another will come and prove stronger than any that came before." He brushed the column of her throat with his knuckle.

Elizabeth tensed beneath his rough touch. Her heart leapt in her throat, like a quivering hare before a fox.

Hammond's eyes were hooded. His hand still rested on her collarbone. "The Fifth Monarchy, shaped by God pure and unsullied, is upon us. The millennium is nigh, Elizabeth. King Jesus will sunder the clouds and lay claim to his earthly kingdom with the godly Elect at his side. The rule of the Saints has begun. Men like my lord Cromwell, God's own instrument." Hammond shivered and released her.

Elizabeth drew away, but the imprint of his grip still burned on her skin.

"I am one of the Elect." Hammond rose to his feet. "Repent, woman, repent all your sins, and you will stand under my protection. When King Jesus arrives, I shall present you to Him with honour." He looked at her with an intense longing. "I want you to stand with me, Elizabeth."

Elizabeth shrank into her chair. The noose of her flattery tightened around her throat. What did one say to a madman? "This has overwhelmed me. 'Tis beyond me, I'm afraid."

Hammond knelt before her. He reached up and tucked a lock into her dirty coif. She flinched. "I know, Elizabeth." His voice softened as he stroked her cheek. "Your sins are so great you worry there is no redemption for you." He gave her a tender smile, and her heart quailed. "Open your heart, Elizabeth. Prostrate yourself to the truth. I am here to help." Hammond picked up the fallen Bible and carefully brushed away the dirt from the cover. He held it out to her. "My gift to you."

Elizabeth stared at the volume. The air pressed in on her, stifling. Time. She needed time. Her hand shook as she accepted it.

*

Elizabeth remained curled on her pallet and stared at a stalk of mottled straw wavering under a draught. She had no will to move. Weariness had settled deep inside her, making it difficult to lift her head.

Everything was hopeless.

Hammond's game masticated her soul. Every moment became a skirmish with each square inch contested. She never knew what to expect.

Elizabeth fought against the shadows and searched for a memory of James's voice, a deep, husky timbre that never failed to stir her. But all that played in her head was the endless monotone of Hammond's drawl. She pressed her hands against her ears to banish the drone. Squeezing her eyes shut, she tried to frame an image of James, but rather than seeing her love's eyes crinkled with laughter, Hammond's pale, soulless glare haunted her.

I'll never be free of him.

Cully arrived with her evening tray, but Elizabeth had no will to stir. When the aroma of fresh bread reached her—a foreign, nearly forgotten smell—she lifted her head.

"A treat for you, Mistress Hart," Cully said. His words broke through Elizabeth's apathy. No one had acknowledged her right to that name. She searched the gaoler's coal-black eyes. In answer, he grinned and doffed his cap. A thatch of curls clustered around his round head. "I've brought you a sweet bun." He passed her the warm loaf wrapped in a towel. "Compliments of your aunt."

Elizabeth scrambled to her knees. "My aunt. Is she well? What news?"

"She bids me tell you to hold fast. Henry Grant has been petitioning Westminster for your release."

"Bless him. Bless them both." Though Henry would be battling uphill in an impossible mission, Elizabeth was deeply touched.

"I had better go before Flagg finds me here," Cully said. "He'll get his heat up, and it won't go well for either of us."

Elizabeth touched his arm. "Thank you, Clarence." She swallowed the lump in her throat.

Cully coloured and hastened to the door. Once more Elizabeth was alone, but she was no longer isolated.

The weariness sloughed off her shoulders. Exercising every ounce of self-control, she ate slowly, morsel by tasty morsel, careful to catch each fallen crumb. With every sweet piece, she took greater heart and laid a reassuring hand to her flat stomach.

As she feasted, she thought of Hammond. He would not win. She refused to allow him victory. One day, he would regret this little game of his.

*

James fought against losing consciousness again. He rode in the middle of the troop, buffered by his men as they raced to clear Hamilton. Every downbeat of Sovereign's hooves sent a jagged pain ripping through him. James felt every nuance in the road, from slope to rise, field to frozen earth. The burn he welcomed. As long as he remained aware, he would not slip into fatal oblivion. His life depended on staying in the saddle.

From the direction of Hamilton, the rolling of drums beat their war song above the retort of musket fire. Roger's voice carried from the front of the column. "Davis, take twenty horsemen and guard our rear. Load up with extra cartridges."

The metallic scent of blood mixed with the leather of his buff coat. Glancing down at his side, James saw a fist-sized circle of red staining through. He applied pressure on his makeshift dressing, and a surge of nausea made him dizzy. He sucked in his breath and clenched his jaw. Lurching in his saddle, he steadied himself by clutching Sovereign's mane.

Sheffield appeared alongside him. Even through the haze that clouded his vision, James saw the concern in the cornet's face. "All right, Captain?"

James worked his mouth. "Aye." When had his tongue become a wad of wool?

Johnstone rode on his other side. The Scotsman looked past James to Sheffield and nodded. "Aye, lad, he's still in the saddle. He'll be just fine. Won't ye, Southron?"

"'Twill take more than a Roundhead's musket to do the job," James said. A fresh spasm tore through him as they hit a rocky stretch.

A blast of trumpets sounded from the southeast, and the troop checked their pace. In the distance, a steady flow of English redcoats poured out of Hamilton, hundreds of red-crossed banners streaming in the chill wind. They fanned out, chasing after the broken remnants of the Westland army.

"Press on!" The order rippled down through the men, and they picked up their speed to avoid getting caught in the crossfire.

James pressed his thighs against Sovereign's flanks, but his legs had turned to jelly. *Stay alert.* He stuffed his gloves between his coat and dressing. The leather reins rubbed harshly in his bare hand.

James struggled to focus on the road. *Breathe deep. In and out.* An old cavalry drill drifted in his head, and he began to recite it under his breath, "March close. Keep tight ranks. Sword in hand. Receive enemy shot. Fire when close."

As the troop rode, scattered bands of fleeing Scots gave them wide berth. Eventually, Davis and the rear guard rejoined them.

"The Scots are returning to their kennels with the Roundheads in pursuit," Davis shouted. "We're in their path."

"Pick up the pace, lads," Johnstone shouted. "The Westland rascals will draw the English forces west and southwest after them. If we get past this mess and clear the Glasgow road, we may lose them all."

Five miles. Five miles and they would be safe. *Stay on the horse.*

A shout came from the back of the column. "Roundhead musketeers fast approaching from the east. Two squadrons, Lieutenant."

"Davis, rout the buggers," Roger cried out. "We need to purchase some distance."

Like a flock of starlings, Davis and fifteen troopers broke from the main company and veered to stave off this attack. Though the English outnumbered them, they didn't have the discipline of cavalry soldiers and broke formation.

Cheers erupted amongst the troop when Davis and his men returned. James managed a grim smile but had little strength for anything more.

"Two more miles, lads," Johnstone shouted. "Two more tae the Glasgow road."

The pounding of drums echoed in James's chest. Dots swam before his eyes, and he clutched Sovereign's mane. The reins hung slack in his hand. A sudden dip in the road jolted him out of his daze.

He couldn't keep up this pace. Any moment, he'd lose the rest of his strength and tumble to his death. The bracing wind slapped him in the face, and he welcomed its frozen sting. Breathing deeply of the cold air, James fought against unconsciousness.

What did it matter if he gave up, slipped into blessed oblivion? As though in answer, Elizabeth's face flashed in his brain.

Remember the drill.

"Ride close. Keep tight ranks. Sword in hand. Receive enemy shot. Fire when close." James timed the words with Sovereign's gait.

Another face filled his vision, a man with all angles and close-cropped grey hair. *Damnation, boy, what have you done?* His father shook him until his teeth chattered, then prodded him in the side with a switch.

James peered through a haze, expecting to see his father's house with its curl of smoke rising from the chimney. Instead, horseman after horseman passed him, and he wondered how he had managed the trick of riding backward while everyone else stood still. "Christ—"

A dull ringing filled his ears that sounded like Sheffield's voice. "Lieutenant!"

James hadn't been a lieutenant since before Hopton Heath. "I'm your captain," he muttered. Were they on their way to Oxford? A wave of dizziness washed over him, and he lurched in the saddle. He hung his head and gasped for breath.

"Lieutenant. Quick." Sheffield edged his horse closer to Sovereign and grabbed James.

Roger pulled up alongside them. "Rig something to keep him from falling."

"Damned if I'll let you truss me up like a boar on a spit," James ground out. "I'll ride like a man." A sour taste coated the inside of his parched mouth.

"Then you'll be carrion for vultures. I care not for your pride, James." Roger's voice sharpened. "Sheffield, find something to bind his legs to the girth and saddle. Cut up the leads from those horses. Quick with it."

Drowning in a sea of strange voices, James barely heard the muffled response. Why was he clutching Sovereign's mane? What happened to his reins? He lifted his head to tell them to go on and leave him behind.

"There's another English squadron coming this way."

The fog crowded James's brain, and he forgot the wound in his side. Strong hands locked his legs in place. A rope encircled his chest, and they pulled his feet one way and his body another.

They've rigged me up to a gibbet.

Darkness descended on him. Shouts followed the hissing of metal blades.

I will never see her again.

*

Elizabeth shivered when she entered the receiving chamber. Hammond stood at the cold hearth with his back to her. Blasts of wind rattled the windowpanes and whistled through the cracks. When he faced her, his expression remained inscrutable. Elizabeth forced a smile, but he didn't respond. Crossing her arms, she hugged her waist.

Hammond motioned to a pair of chairs. The side tables had been swept aside. "Make yourself comfortable." His tone was as icy as the crystallised frost on the windowpanes.

Elizabeth slid into one of the chairs. Rather than taking the other seat, Hammond gripped the back of the chair, drumming his fingertips on the top rail while he watched her with hooded eyes.

"I trust your health is well?" Elizabeth said.

"Well enough."

Elizabeth clasped her hands in her lap. "Have you brought anything you'd like me to read?" She didn't see the usual stack of books.

"Not today." He gave up his position behind the chair and took his seat. "I thought instead to discuss the book of Ezekiel. Know you it?" He propped his chin on his hand and gave her his undivided attention.

"Not well."

"I appreciate your honesty." His left brow twitched, and he tapped his finger against his cheek. "My sire honoured me with the prophet's name. As a child, I took great pleasure in hearing preachers teach from Ezekiel. I thought they spoke to me."

"A name is a powerful thing."

"Is that how you think of your own name, Elizabeth Hart?"

A chill ran down her spine. "You've never called me that."

Hammond's mouth tightened. "I don't believe in hiding behind veils. The Lord admonishes us to see with our own eyes. 'The morning is come unto thee,'" he quoted. "Ezekiel seven, verse eight."

Elizabeth shifted uncomfortably and attempted a modest smile. "The dawn of momentous times. You must find comfort in the fresh dew of enlightenment."

Hammond clasped his hands. "Indeed. 'The time is come, the day of trouble is near.'" His chair scraped against the bare floor when he stood up and began to pace. "Mischief, mistress, do you know it?"

"Mischief?" Elizabeth asked slowly, trying to grasp the turnings of his mind.

"I speak of villains who steal and waylay their way to damnation. 'They shall pollute my secret place: for the robbers shall enter into it, and defile it.'"

The hairs lifted on the back of Elizabeth's neck. "Robbers? I don't understand."

"Highwaymen," Hammond spat. "One in particular. The Highwayman of Moot Hill."

Elizabeth's mouth went dry. Taking a deep breath, she forced a light tone. "What news of the matter? Has the villain been caught, or has he robbed again?"

"Neither, mistress, a fact that I find most interesting."

"How so?"

Hammond smiled and reclaimed his seat. "With all of our attention devoted to locating your lover, a detail has surfaced about this highwayman."

Don't say it.

"You see, neither have been heard from—not Hart nor this highwayman."

Elizabeth struggled to keep her wits. "I would imagine that brigands lay low over the winter season, given the poor roads."

"You seem to know a great deal of the matter."

"'Tis only a guess."

"A good one, but I have another." Hammond drew forward, pale eyes blazing and voice like a whip. "Your lover is the highwayman."

"That's ridiculous. Where would you get such a notion?" Elizabeth forced a laugh, but her stomach roiled. She laid a protective hand over her belly.

"Ridiculous? Is it? Sir Richard's comment at your trial about the ill-fated carriage ride piqued my curiosity. I made some enquiries and to my surprise discovered your curious link to this highwayman. You were in Sir Richard's coach when that devil robbed you."

"Of course, 'tis common knowledge," Elizabeth replied evenly. "My introduction to Warwickshire did not come without controversy." She bowed her head and affected a saddened air. "'Blessed is the man who perseveres under trial because when he has stood the test, he will receive the victor's crown,' Elizabeth quoted. *James one, verse twelve.* When she glanced up through her lashes, she caught Hammond chewing his lip.

"Pray, Lieutenant, do not accuse James Hart of this heinous crime only because of my unfortunate association with the villain in question."

Hammond leaned back into his chair. One hand rested on his thigh while the other rubbed across his mouth. Elizabeth sensed his doubt.

"It wouldn't be the first time evil has misled the innocent." He chewed idly on his thumb without lifting his gaze from Elizabeth. "You deny any knowledge of this?"

"I do, sir, most heartily, for there is nothing to these suspicions of yours." She lifted her chin and matched his gaze. Though her soul be damned for her blatant deceit, she did not care. Hammond couldn't be allowed to continue down this path.

"You are wrong there. He is the highwayman, I will swear on it. You have been duped, Elizabeth. It distresses me to tell you this."

"James Hart is not a knave."

Hammond walked over to where Elizabeth sat and crouched before her chair. His anger had dissolved, and his glance became a caress. The smile he gave her trembled in relief. "He is, Elizabeth. As God has revealed His will, I know this to be the truth." He reached up to smooth her hair, then touched her cheek. Elizabeth shrank back. "Prove your resolve to the Truth, Elizabeth. Renounce this false idol. Renounce James Hart." He gazed upon her in earnestness and hope. "I will forgive you this transgression. You did not know the extent to which you sinned."

Elizabeth tried to smother her rising fear and panic. "You are wrong, sir. Listen to what you are saying. James Hart as the highwayman is as improbable as you being the villain. Please accept that you are mistaken, and we shall speak no more of it."

Hammond's grip tightened around the arm of the chair. "James Hart has abandoned you. He doesn't deserve your loyalty." He straightened and walked towards the empty hearth. "I will see justice done."

"You have no proof of the matter," Elizabeth said, her voice rising. *Sweet God, I have to convince him, or they will arrest him when he returns.* She jumped to her feet and rushed to Hammond. "No one in Warwick would ever speak against him. All know him for the good man that he is."

Elizabeth knew she had gone too far when Hammond's face darkened.

"Proof, madam, you want proof?" Hammond took a step towards her, and she backed away. "The highwayman is reputed to be an expert horseman without match, with one exception—James Hart. As an ostler, your lover has access to prime horseflesh at night when the inn's doors are shut, and he knows the countryside like no other, through running the post, if that is truly what he does."

"Lieutenant, that could be anyone," Elizabeth rushed on. "There are half a dozen in Warwick who can boast the same."

"How many are former Royalist soldiers with a strong rancour to the godly?"

"Sir, the war has divided us all." Elizabeth twisted the folds of her skirt in her hands. *Sweet heaven, stop this.* "Any number of men in Warwickshire fit that description."

"But what of Coventry?"

Elizabeth sucked in her breath. "Coventry?" Her back pressed against the wood of the mantel.

"Aye, Coventry." Hammond's eyes narrowed. "There was a man we arrested for treason against the Commonwealth. He would have stood trial and answered for his crimes, but this very highwayman sprung the prisoner from the Coventry gaol."

"Aye, I remember the house searches you conducted," Elizabeth said quickly. "You claimed the man's associates managed his escape." She steadied her breathing. "Are you suggesting that a peer has associated with brigands?"

A lengthy silence stretched.

"How did you know the man was a peer?"

Elizabeth felt the blood drain from her face. "You told me so when you searched Ellendale."

"I don't recall ever calling the man a peer. He is no peer of mine, traitor that he is." Hammond's mouth twisted in disgust. "You knew because your lover once worked for Sir Piers Rotherham."

"James spoke very little of his life in Coventry."

"That's very good, mistress." Hammond's voice lowered, and he tilted his head to get a better look at her. "Though you try to be controlled, you can't quite manage it. There, I see the tenseness around your blue eyes— so beautiful... so beguiling." Hammond slammed his fist into the mantel. The rotted wood cracked and splintered, and Elizabeth jumped. A muffled shriek escaped her as Hammond bore down on her, trembling with anger.

"How could you?" Hammond roared. "How could you lay with baseborn scum? How could you spread your legs without God's blessing and allow yourself to be damned? You knew him as a villain, and still you allowed him to claim you!" With a choked gurgle he turned away, but Elizabeth's reprieve was short-lived. Hammond whipped around and grabbed both her arms, squeezing so tight that he wrenched a cry of pain from her. "Do you hold yourself so basely, woman, do you? And yet you keep yourself aloof from men who deserve reverence. What black thread has been woven into your character?" His anguish warred with rage.

"I have never held myself cheaply," Elizabeth cried and pushed against him, but he did not release her. She tried to pry herself free, but he held fast. "Release me."

Hammond's face became a mask of open grief. "I had hoped you didn't know. I prayed that you were innocent of all this, a victim of his cunning ways. Betrayed but not sullied." His torment turned into rage. "You're past redemption, harlot."

"Do not call me harlot," Elizabeth snapped, pushed to the edge. "I have done nothing wrong and will not be forced to feel a shame that is not mine. What do you know of honour and justice? Hide behind your book and your pulpit. Preach deliverance and flatter yourself that you are one of God's chosen, but you and your brethren have usurped a crown for your ambitions. Blood stains your hands and will not be cleansed. Believe this is God's will if it will assuage your guilt, but I will not repent for a sinless crime."

Hammond grabbed her by the hair and yanked her to him, bringing her face inches from his own. "Shameless hussy," he said with a hiss. "'Now will I pour out my fury upon thee; and I will judge thee according to thy ways.'"

Elizabeth cried out. She clawed at his hand to pry off his fingers before he could rip a clump of hair from her scalp. The wildness in Hammond's eyes terrified her, a blazing rage that rendered him more animal than man. He's mad, she thought in panic. *He'll smash my head against the wall.* Powerless, all she could do was whimper at the excruciating pain. "Help me," she murmured under her breath. Tears blinded her vision, and she braced herself for the impact.

A new emotion stirred in the depths of his eyes. Hammond studied Elizabeth's face, his attention dwelling on her lips before his mouth crashed down upon hers. Elizabeth gasped, shocked. Hammond's hold on her tightened, and his tongue plundered her mouth. She squirmed and thrashed, trying to break free, but his hold on her tightened. The shock of his arousal made her want to retch. He reached up and kneaded her breast, his thumb rubbing against her nipple. Fresh rage burst in her brain.

Elizabeth bit down hard on his tongue. With a cry, he snatched away, leaving her with the metallic taste of blood in her mouth. She stepped out of reach and sucked in clean air.

Hammond wiped his mouth with the back of his hand. Breathing heavily, he stared without saying a word. The passion drained from him, and his face crumpled. Disgust and self-loathing replaced the lust. He backed away from her as though she were a serpent coiled to strike. When he turned his back on her, his shoulders rose and fell with each deep breath.

After a silent moment, he straightened his jacket. Clearing his throat, he turned around and once more affected an unruffled mien. The transformation was nearly as disquieting as his rage. "Do you know what the punishment is for highway robbery?"

Elizabeth knew.

"You've seen a man hang," he said. "I wonder how long your lover will take to suffocate. The record is twenty minutes. Imagine that, dangling on the end of a rope, legs jerking in empty air while the rope squeezes out your life's breath. 'Tis a short drop, and Hart is a tall man. He might yet beat that record. I will be sure to save you a spot in front of the gibbet so you can watch his face turn from purple to grey."

Every word drove through Elizabeth like a jagged blade. She lost the power of speech.

Hammond sneered. "Pity that highway robbery no longer carries punishment of quartering. They only reserve that privilege for high treason. But then, Sir Richard might make an exception, sorely vexed over this matter as he is. I would like nothing better than to see Hart's guts trampled on the ground while his head sits atop the West Gate. Let him gaze towards Moot Hill until the crows pick away his flesh."

Elizabeth's legs buckled.

"If you'll excuse me," Hammond said, "I have to post a warrant for James Hart's arrest."

*

James's skin alternated between hot and cold. The crackling of the campfire heightened his disorientation, and he waited for the dancing flames to consume him. His eyelids were as thin as parchment and as heavy as sand.

A shadow moved to his left. *Elizabeth.* He called out to her, expecting that she'd kneel beside him. Instead, he beheld only the cavorting flames. They had made love by a fire. She had consumed him with her passion as he buried himself inside her.

James heard a voice from the distance. "Drink this." He squinted, trying to figure out who stood over him. A flask pressed to his mouth. Water splashed over his lips and dribbled down his chin. He tried to turn away until the water hit his throat and reminded him of his raging thirst. He clutched the flask with the grip of a dying man and drank until he nearly retched.

"Too much."

More. His protest sounded like a moan, and his strength failed.

"Hold him down."

Someone grabbed his arms, and sharp talons dug into his flesh. A stick jammed across his mouth stifled his protests.

"Bite."

James perceived a tearing sound. Cool air rushed over hot skin. Liquid fire splashed on his side, and he bucked against it. He yelled and thrashed against his bonds. The talons tightened their hold on his arms and legs.

"Still now."

A stab of white pain burst in his flesh. He bit down and tasted wood and dirt. A lance probed into his flesh, burying its blade deep. Pus oozed down his side. Every jab sliced through him—a pound of carved meat, sliced and served on a platter. More firewater splashed over the wound, and he arched, nearly fainting from the pain. He tasted salt in the corners of his mouth.

"Did you get it?"

Someone wiped his brow.

"Aye."

"And the scrap of cloth?"

"All of it."

Someone removed the stick, and James coughed and spat out the splinters. A moistened cloth touched his lips, and he turned to it, sucking out every drop of moisture. He felt himself turned and lifted. Rough linen rubbed against his bare skin.

They were wrapping him in a death shroud.

Chapter Twenty-Three

James felt the rolling beneath him and heard the creaking of wood. The swaying nearly pulled him back into oblivion, but the drum pounding in the distance roused him from his stupor. An irregular clopping knocked around in his head, punctuated by the whinny of a horse. James pried open his sticky eyes to find a man in a russet coat staring down at him. Roundhead.

James sucked in his breath. Captured. A sick feeling washed over him. He tested his side and stifled a groan. "Where am I?" For the first time, he saw the high panels of a wagon.

To his annoyance, the man chuckled. "Faith, man, you're English, and not one of them bloody Scots." The Roundhead turned his head and called out behind him. "Did you hear that? This one's a Cavalier."

James heard someone grunt a response, but he couldn't see beyond the soldier who filled his vision. A blood-soaked bandage wrapped around the man's arm. James tried to sit up, but a lightning-sharp pain ripped through his side. He sucked in air between clenched teeth.

"Nasty wound you have there, mate. I'd lie back if I were you." The soldier sat back. "From the look of it, you'll not need a leech for the rest of your life."

"If he lives that long," a sullen voice muttered.

"Stop talking to the enemy, dolt," another grumbled.

The ground grew more rugged, and the wagon squeaked and rattled. James pressed his head back into the rolled horse blanket under his neck. His sight was limited to a cold, grey sky and the face of his captor.

No question about it, they were taking him to Edinburgh for trial. If he was lucky, he'd only get the gibbet. If he was not . . . James went cold just thinking of curved knives and hot braziers.

Where were the others? Escaped? Killed? Though the question burned on his tongue to ask, he swallowed it. The enemy wouldn't get any information from him.

The wagon lurched and jolted a gasp out of him. He clenched his teeth and rode out the white-hot spasm. If only he hadn't been shot, he'd have a chance to escape. But then he wouldn't have been caught.

"Where you from, Cavalier?"

James considered the question. They didn't need to know about Warwick. The thought of Elizabeth made his throat tighten. "Coventry." He had to find a way to escape. Information, he needed information, the only weapon left to him. "What company are you with?"

"The London bands." The soldier sighed. "Long way from home."

Aye. A few snowflakes fell, landing on his parched lips. "What day is it?" He searched his memory and remembered a blazing bonfire—*or was it a campfire?* The snow-heavy clouds gave nothing away.

The soldier scrunched his face, giving it some thought. "Tuesday. Aye, 'tis the third of December."

"What?" He had lost two days. James tried to remember the distance to Edinburgh and hoped he still had time. "When do we arrive in Edinburgh?"

"Edinburgh?" The soldier choked, then started to laugh. "Did you hear that?" he called over his shoulder. "Edinburgh! I should have such fortune. You've cheered me up, Cavalier."

The man's chuckles were cut off by a shout ahead. "Keep your distance, Roundhead. Leave that man." Another English voice, but one that James knew.

"Sheffield?" James struggled to sit up and forced down the pain. Panting, he managed to prop himself up on an elbow. When his head stopped spinning, he saw the cornet astride his bay charger.

"Joy to you this morning, Captain," Sheffield grinned. "The lieutenant will be pleased to hear you're awake."

"I thought—" James shook his head to adjust his thinking. He looked past the Roundhead and saw his mates, one with a bandaged leg and two others with their hands roped together. Peering over the sides of the wagon, James now saw several companies of Scottish blue bonnets, each trooper riding in formation behind their standard-bearers.

Johnstone rode up to the wagon. "About time ye've finally opened yer eyes, Southron. Ye English are naught but pampered bastards, aye. Any self-respecting Scotsman would have been up chopping wood by now."

James craned his neck to see the back of the wagon. "Where's Sovereign?"

"The man has his priorities, sure," Johnstone chuckled. "Don't worry, Southron. Yer horse is safe."

"What happened? Whose army is this?" James sank back on his pallet, the little strength he had depleted.

"Colonel Robert Montgomery's from central command," Johnstone replied. "Appears that the lads in Stirling didn't much care for the Westland army's cheek. Central command sent their man tae chastise them, nae expecting Cromwell would beat them tae it."

James grunted. "There's hope after all. What did I miss?"

"When Montgomery arrived, there wasn't much left for him tae do than beat back several English companies who turned their sights northward. You missed a nice little skirmish near Kilsyth—halfway between Hamilton and Stirling. Killed seven, left with these four." Johnstone nodded to the English soldiers in the back.

The wagon dipped and swayed as it followed a sharp turn and an incline. Underneath, James felt the wheels shudder then continue, going from dirt and loose shale to a smooth, hard-packed road. In the distance, a trumpet blared. When the road straightened, James glimpsed a stone castle rising from the sides of a cliff. A low bank of clouds hid its turrets.

Johnstone clicked his tongue, and his horse picked up speed. They passed through a gate, its vaulted arch dimming the weak light. The clip-clopping bounced off the cobbles and stone walls. When they emerged on the other side, Johnstone turned to James. "Welcome to Stirling."

*

The chirurgeon, Master Wiseman, was an unobtrusive man. From the time that James awoke in the sick ward, Wiseman spoke very little. "Lift your arm, Captain," or, "turn to your side," were the extent of his discourse. And yet the sickroom lads stumbled over themselves to do his bidding, needing little more than a nod and crook of his finger. James admired silent authority, but what he found most curious was that the man was English.

Wiseman tried to change the dressing, but the wound puckered and clung to the linen. James nearly jumped to the ceiling when the man stripped off the bandage. He clamped his mouth shut and nearly bit his tongue.

"The wound is clean, Captain," Wiseman said. "I'm pleased by its colour."

James didn't remember much of the past several days—each had pooled into the other. But now he was alert and temporarily free of whatever potions they had poured down his throat. Though the pain in his side throbbed like a battlefield drum, he preferred being conscious than otherwise.

"Hold still." The chirurgeon pressed his palm against James's shoulder to discourage any movement.

The rhythmic clipping of boots on the stone floor drew closer.

"I'm done here for now, my lord Secretary," Wiseman said over his shoulder. He released his pressure on James.

"We're in your debt, Master Chirurgeon." Yet another English voice.

James turned over and found someone he hadn't seen in five years. "Richard Fanshawe?" He hadn't seen Charles's personal secretary since Bristol.

"James Hart," he said, "dodging not one but two armies. I'm hardly shocked."

"May I continue to confound the King's enemies." James struggled to rise to a sitting position.

"Glad to see you survived, James. Don't get up." Richard settled on a stool beside the cot. He hadn't changed except for having thinner hair and carrying a stone less weight. His expression had lost none of the shrewdness that had stood him well against the political manoeuvring central to the royal court. "I've seen to the comfort of your men. Who provisioned them?"

"I did," and because he had no fear where Richard was concerned, he added, "courtesy of the Roundheads and a bit of highway robbery."

"How ironic." Richard smiled. "The King will be pleased."

"Had I been able to wait until the spring, you would have had more men," James said, studying the folds of his blanket. "I didn't realise you were in Stirling."

"I shouldn't have been," he said. "I was preparing to join the King in Perth when I heard that a Warwickshire troop had arrived and their commander near death. Quite a surprise to learn that it was you. I wrote His Majesty to explain my delay, and in response, he sent his personal chirurgeon to attend you."

That explained why the lads had fallen over themselves to suit the man. "I'm honoured." James searched his memory. "He called you my lord Secretary."

Richard smiled self-depreciatingly. "Secretary of State." He had always been a sober, reserved man, more concerned with a job well done than personal gain. "It came with a baronetcy," he added. "The King argued to Parliament that he could hardly have his chief minister serve without a fitting title. Still, my wife gushes her pleasure in each letter and takes great pride in signing her name, Lady Fanshawe."

The choice of words hadn't bypassed James. "Since when does His Majesty require justification for the gifts he bestows?"

Richard's mouth twitched. "Scotland is complicated."

For the first time, James noticed the fine lines etched across Richard's brow. From what he had heard over the years, the man's service to the crown had left him in constant upheaval. "How have you been?"

Richard sniffed. "It's been difficult, I admit. I relocated my family to Ireland for a time to manage the royal treasury. That is, until Cromwell decided to invade. We narrowly escaped. My wife has been forced to beg for funds, and the separation isn't good for either of us."

James stared into the distance. Separation was never good. "So the King is in Perth? I had hoped to present my sword to him." He paused, taking encouragement by the favour shown to him so far. "And offer my service in his Life Guard."

Richard Fanshawe, master of papers and former diplomat to foreign courts, didn't flutter a lash.

"Allow me to guess," James said. "It's complicated."

Richard sighed and crossed his legs. "What is your preference—bluntness or political nuance?"

"I'm not a perfumed courtier, Richard. I deal in plain speech."

"Very well. The King is in a difficult situation. Scottish Parliament must approve his companions and those named to his Life Guard. Unless you are a nobleman's son—nay, more specifically, the son of a well-heeled Scottish family—you don't have a chance to lick his boots. The Marquess of Argyll has *that* privilege."

"You're satisfied with this state of affairs?"

"Our King is winning concessions daily. The coronation is set for the first of January. At least they're no longer holding that over his head."

He frowned. "Though I speak openly, I count on your discretion." Richard rose, preparing to leave. "Wait until the coronation. Things may improve then."

Perhaps it had been the testiness of his wound or the physic they had doused him with, but James wasn't willing to accept a pat on the head and admonition to slink into the corner and lick his balls. "I'll serve the King in any capacity he requires," he said. "But I haven't led my men a hundred leagues from home to be a Scotsman's lackey. They deserve better than that. They were once the cream of Northampton's Horse and will bring honour to any commander." James's strength started to ebb. "If that quill of yours has any influence, Richard, I beg you to find us an English commander to serve."

"Ease your mind, Captain. We understand each other. You have a few more weeks of recovery." Richard paused at the door. "They have a saying here," he said. "Desires are a double-edged sword."

*

For the rest of his convalescence, James saw very little of Richard, and Charles not at all. He kept his disappointment to himself. As the Prince of Wales, Charles had very little time to himself; now, as the Scottish King, his time was consumed by attending Parliament. And yet James had secretly hoped that he'd spare him a few moments.

When James was finally cleared to ride, he and his men followed the court to Perth, where preparations were already underway for the King's coronation. When they entered the city, the excitement was palpable. Every draper in the city was cleared of every square inch of red velvet they possessed. The Kirk, in the meantime, spent the time devising a fitting penitence to prepare the King for the occasion. On the Thursday before the coronation, they decreed a public fast to pray for the sins of the King's family.

James imagined how that must have gone over with Charles. He needed no further proof that Charles had trapped himself in a corner. With his wound healing, and feeling altogether edgy and contrary, James decided against attending the services and instead invited his officers to his lodgings for their own pre-coronation celebration. The landlord wouldn't serve them anything stronger than small beer, but ever resourceful Davis came through for them and secured several bottles of aqua vitae—water of life, as they called it—from the landlord's daughter.

On the morning before the coronation, the last day of December, all of Perth emptied to cheer the King on his way to Scone. Townspeople had been there before dawn to claim a prime location. When a blacksmith's apprentice jumped on a barrel and shouted that the King was coming, a wave of people surged forward, jostling James and his men. A flare of pain ripped through James's knitting wound.

Following a long procession of noblemen and church leaders, Charles finally appeared riding a grey charger. The overgrown lad who had once been disguised as an apprentice to confound enemy patrols had matured into a man and was on his way to becoming a crowned monarch. Seeing his progress down the boulevard, it struck James how Charles differed from his father. The late King would have kept his gaze straight ahead, neither looking to the right nor left, but the son looked around with unfeigned interest, smiling and nodding as he passed.

Just as he reached James, Charles's gaze locked on him, and recognition lit across his face. His smile deepened, and five years melted away. Charles gave James a discreet wave before being swallowed up by his Life Guard. Long after the last man rode past, James remained looking after the procession.

The cold started to set in, and his healing side began to throb. He parted with the others and made his way back to his lodgings. When he passed the common room, the innkeeper tried to get his attention, but James was not in a mood to speak to the man—or anyone, for that matter. Pretending not to see him, he climbed the stairs to the second floor. He had just reached his quarters and was about to close the door when the innkeeper appeared, out of breath.

"Captain Hart," he wheezed, holding out an envelope. "A messenger came with this."

James accepted it and turned it over. A triple-stemmed thistle was pressed into the seal. "Thank you." He gave the man a coin for his troubles before closing the door behind him.

James cracked open the seal. A golden coin slipped out of the folded letter and landed at his feet. When he bent to retrieve it, he realised that the disk wasn't a coin. Stamped on one side, the King's profile depicted a crown and the collar of the Garter. On the reverse side, a royal lion *rampant guardant* held a three-stemmed thistle. The inscriptions confirmed that this was a coronation token.

James unfolded the letter and saw that it represented an invitation from Charles to attend his coronation.

*

Richard Fanshawe met James at the entrance to the Scone Palace.

"This way," he said, guiding him to the King's chambers. A bewildering crosscurrent of people darted through the halls as Richard navigated the twists and turns and multiple staircases. Charles's chamber doors were flung open, and a small army of servants and nobles were gathered inside.

High-ranking nobles circled closest to his orbit while a few unassuming people were shunted to the far corners. Charles was resplendent in richest crimson velvet with his black hair flowing over his shoulders. Every time he moved, the cloth's sheen rippled between red and burgundy. James was struck by how much had changed. He smiled to himself, remembering the rough apprentice clothes Charles had donned to slip out of Bristol unnoticed five years ago.

When they got closer, Charles looked up and noticed James. A smile spread across his face, and he called out to him, unmindful of the shocked glares from his nobles, "Captain Hart, well met."

"Your Majesty." James stopped before him and bowed. "May your reign be long and fruitful."

Charles touched him on the shoulder. "I am thankful you've come." James did not think he meant the coronation. He lowered his voice and added, "If I only had more with your resourcefulness and loyalty."

Before James could reply, one of his grooms brought the heavy ermine cloak and, stepping between them, proceeded to drape it across the King's shoulders. Another groom slipped in and fastened the royal Garter around Charles's neck.

Richard drew James away and navigated him to one of the far corners. James felt more at ease here, where plain linens replaced the showy velvets. The chirurgeon Wiseman stood beside a neat pair of women in crisp, white aprons.

"Captain Hart." The doctor nodded. "You've recovered well enough."

James touched his side. It still twinged when he tried to practise with a sword. "Aye, thanks to your skill."

A nobleman in deep blue satin edged with lace sidled up to Richard. Artfully curled blond hair framed a pampered face. "Fanshawe." He spoke to the secretary, though his eyes were latched on James. "We should have been in procession by now. These Scots can't keep a proper schedule."

"My lord Buckingham," Richard bowed. "May I present Captain James Hart of Warwickshire."

"My lord," James bowed. The Duke of Buckingham was one of the few English companions the Scots allowed Charles.

"Hart? I'm unfamiliar with that name. Where in Warwickshire?"

"Coventry, my lord," James said flatly. "The Harts have owned a modest freehold since old Queen Bess."

The duke's attention slid off James, and he turned once more to Richard. "Shame the ceremony couldn't have been held at Holyrood, like his sainted father's coronation."

"His Majesty is beckoning you, my lord," Richard said.

"Naturally." Without another word, Buckingham swept off to join Charles.

James shook his head. Like a cloying scent, the duke left a bad taste in his mouth. He better understood why the Scots allowed Charles this affectation. He could only show them in a better light. Still, the duke's thoughtless words bothered him. "We should not wish the King to emulate his father," he leaned in to murmur to Richard. "Let the coronation pave a new path."

Richard nodded. "To God's ears."

The King's nobles assumed their position, with a senior official on either side of Charles and four attendants holding his ermine train. The rest of the nobles aligned themselves behind Charles, leaving his household staff to follow at a discreet distance. James fell in beside Richard.

The procession headed down the long hallway towards the presence chamber, a grand room with a high, plastered ceiling. In the centre stood an ornate chair and over it a red canopy held in place by six attendants.

Charles took his seat and one by one received the Members of Parliament and leaders of the Council, who were all dressed in scarlet. After the last official paid his respects, a signal was made for the party to withdraw to the church. The highest-ranking nobles took up the royal regalia and in single file led the procession out of the palace. The six attendants holding the canopy arranged themselves around Charles so that as he walked, he was constantly covered by a crimson sky. As James watched, a cold shiver ran down his spine.

The procession headed across the grounds, along a sloping hill towards the stone church.

"They call this hillock Moot Hill," Richard said to James.

"What?" James asked, startled.

"Moot Hill," Richard repeated. "Ancient meeting place."

James smiled to himself at the coincidence—or irony, he couldn't decide which.

They passed through a lych-gate to enter the church. As there were so many people who had to pass through, James and Richard waited nearly twenty minutes to enter. James looked around at the large rectangular hall filled with clerics, nobles and officials. At the centre stood a platform with a throne chair and a pulpit off to one side. Charles had not yet ascended the throne and instead sat directly opposite the pulpit in a massive wooden chair. All the regalia were laid before the pulpit upon a table clothed in green velvet.

"This way," Richard said, leading him to a position in the western end of the church where the other members of the prince's household stood.

The energy was palpable in the church, and people did not bother to lower their voices. Friends greeted each other with rounds of self-congratulation, as though each one had a hand in this day.

The minister stepped up to the pulpit to start the coronation and began with a sermon. James braced himself for an invocation of hellfire and brimstone. Instead, the minister spoke with the soothing tones of a favoured grandfather, moderating his warnings and admonitions to fit the occasion.

When it was time, four noblemen went to each corner of the platform, announcing to the people at each quadrant, "Sirs, I do present unto you the King—Charles, the rightful and undoubted heir of the crown and dignity of the realm."

Charles ascended the platform and knelt before the minister. He held up his hand and swore the King's oath. When he reached the part, "I shall command and procure that justice and equity be kept to all creatures without exception," James drew himself to his full height. *Justice.* This was what this was about.

The officials helped Charles to his feet and, before the congregation, clothed him in royal robes of purple velvet, girded the royal sword around his waist and placed golden spurs on his feet. Lastly, a nobleman, the Marquess of Argyll, held aloft the crown of Scotland and placed it upon Charles's head.

The crowd shouted, "God save the King, Charles the Second."

Over and over, the crowd continued to chant, moving James by the strength of their fervour. At the age of twenty, Charles had done what his father could not—rally all the Scots to his cause; these fractious, passionate, fervent Scots. The price had been his oath to their covenant, and only the future would tell the true cost of that oath, but for the first time in over five years, James was filled with genuine hope. *First Scotland, next England.* He smiled openly.

"God save the King," voices thundered around him.

James lifted his own voice and said, "God save the King!"

*

James returned to Perth the morning after the coronation. He rode through the square, scattering the pigeons into a beating, frantic flight. A thin layer of snow coated the cobbles, and the frozen north wind snaked through the lanes. James drew his woollen cloak tighter around his shoulders and hunched against the cold.

Richard had given him a letter after the coronation, a summons from Major General Edward Massey, formerly of Parliament, currently the commander of the King's English regiment of Horse. Richard had promised James an English commander; he said nothing about the man being a former Roundhead. Sharper.

A clock chimed in the square. James pressed on. Though he didn't look forward to the meeting, he knew enough not to keep the man waiting.

Massey's lodgings were at the home of a Scottish merchant. James dismounted and handed Sovereign's reins to a groom. A maid opened the door and greeted him with a flattering smile until she heard his accent.

"The major general is expecting me," he told her.

"Aye, then, come in," she said and accepted his woollen cloak. "'Tis the first suite of rooms at the top of the stairs."

James nodded his thanks and climbed the stairs to the second floor. When he reached the suite, he gave a sharp rap.

"Enter."

Edward Massey sat behind a desk with his correspondence. A lace collar framed a long, narrow face, and a sallow complexion heightened dark smudges under his brown eyes. "Captain Hart? I'll be with you in a moment." After a few more scribbles, he sprinkled powder over the letter and sealed it with red wax.

Massey set aside his papers and stepped out from behind his desk. He crossed his arms and examined James. Strange to be staring at this man across a bare floor, James thought, when the walls of Gloucester once separated them. The man piqued his curiosity. This was the commander who had managed to hold that town against twenty-five thousand of the King's men. Even more telling, he had Sir Piers's respect.

"You're a long way from home, Captain," Massey finally said.

The man's tone annoyed James, as though implying that he had no business being here. If anything, he had more right to be in Perth than a former Parliamentary commander. "Aye, my lord, as are you."

"I understand that you served under Northampton."

"Aye, both the late Earl Spencer and his son. I led the Third Company of Horse."

"Northampton had a fine cavalry," Massey said, finally moving away from the desk. "He used Prince Rupert's tactics to good effect." His brow knit as he studied James. "I've heard that you're an ostler? I can hardly credit it."

"A temporary arrangement," he said. "You should know that I clerked for Sir Piers Rotherham before the war."

"You know Piers?" Massey exclaimed, taking on a new interest. "How is he, well?"

"Well enough," James said, recalling the letter he received from Sir Piers when the man arrived safely in Lancashire. Of his health, Piers said naught.

"An honourable man, a fine leader. And yet you did not follow him in the war? You chose a different path."

"I followed my conscience, my lord." And as the devil rode his shoulder he added, "Respectfully, I could say the same for you. You did not follow your master to the field, either."

Massey's eyes narrowed, and his moustache quivered. "I too followed my conscience, Captain, as I do now. I don't offer you an explanation. Indeed, 'tis not your right to receive one. My argument died with the late

King." He paused. "We are up against a new regime, and I for one will not tolerate Cromwell as *de facto* king. There is only one King, and 'tis him I serve."

"I seek nothing more than to serve His Majesty," James said.

"Then you must serve under my command."

"His Majesty is surrounded by those who once raised arms against his family," James said.

"We're all loyal to him, Captain."

James had a hard time keeping his ire in check. How easily did loyalty turn in this world where oaths were just words and actions meaningless? Since arriving in Scotland, he had heard Scottish lords who had won notoriety for their exploits against the late King speak from both sides of their mouth and win favours. Yet honest men who had not faltered in their support for the crown were relegated to subservient positions.

James had considered his course from the moment he received Massey's summons. If he and his men had to serve a former Roundhead, he'd secure the best position he could for them in the regiment. They wouldn't serve without distinction.

"That I'm here and you know of my record speaks to the recommendation you would have received from Sir Fanshawe. I will serve you, my lord. My men will be yours. They have been tested in war and were the cream of Northampton's former cavalry. I only ask that you name us to the first company."

"And you as first Captain?"

"If it pleases you."

Massey didn't answer. He stood and mulled, giving nothing away of his thoughts. "You're not gentry, nor is your father. Your men are saddlers and farriers."

"And were you not a London apprentice, my lord?"

A ghost of a smile played across Massey's face before he returned to his desk. "His Majesty speaks very highly of you." He pulled out a crisp piece of paper and began to write.

"Your commission, Captain Hart." He handed it to James. "You will take command of the First Company of Horse under my regiment. I accept your sword on behalf of the King."

*

The baby quickened the day Elizabeth gained her release from the gaol. The sensation of a butterfly testing its wings soon intensified to a consistent fluttering. She followed Cully down the stark corridor, past the stairs she would normally take on days that Hammond visited.

"Are you sure I am to be released?" Elizabeth asked again. She feared that this would be another, crueller game of Hammond's.

"Aye, mistress, there's no mistake."

"But it's a month early."

"I'm sure of it," Cully said. "Sir Richard wrote the order himself, and the lieutenant was not best pleased. That alone should convince you."

When they reached the outer hall, Elizabeth slowed down. At the clerk's desk, a man with sleek black hair stood with his back to her. The gentleman glanced over his shoulder.

"Nathaniel Lewis?" Elizabeth said under her breath.

The lawyer resumed his conversation with the clerk without the least sign of recognition.

"You know Sir Richard's man?" Cully asked.

"What?" A sick feeling washed over Elizabeth. When did that happen?

"Best come along," Cully said, urging her forward. "The exit's just ahead—out you go before Hammond has anything more to say about it."

When Elizabeth reached the threshold, she froze. She stared at the iron-studded door, wondering if this was the moment when the promise snarled into a nightmare. She imagined Hammond on the other side, taunting her for supposing she could ever get away.

Cully opened the door. "Go on. Henry Grant is waiting to take you home."

Elizabeth squinted against the hard grey light. An icy wind blew, carrying with it the scent of snow. James's babe fluttered again. She descended the stairs in a daze.

"Mistress Hart!" Henry crossed Gaol Hall Lane and hurried to her. A few people gawked, for few prisoners left on their own. Elizabeth clutched her filthy cloak tighter.

Henry met her at the foot of the stairs. His breath was visible in the chill air. "Is all well with you, lass?" His tone had a quality normally reserved for the skittish and fragile. "Clarence promised to look out for you. Keep you safe."

Elizabeth smothered the compulsion to look back at the silent building. "Aye, he did."

Henry nodded, relief flooding his face, but not enough to wash away the dog-eyed guilt. "Let's get you home, lass. We'll get you sorted out there." He took her elbow and guided her to the inn's wagon. Elizabeth settled on the rough perch and huddled under the folds of her cloak.

As they pulled away, Elizabeth's attention drew to a smoulder of red in the shadow of a laneway. *Hammond.* He filled that narrow space with the force of his brooding fury. Her stomach twisted, and she began to tremble. How long would she have to endure him?

Henry craned his head to see what drew her attention. His jaw tightened, and he slapped the shire's reins to pick up their pace. "He'll not be troubling you. I'll look after it."

They drove through Warwick in silence. A light dusting of snow coated the rooftops and sills. Elizabeth noticed the placards posted on the buildings. Now the reward was for James Hart, Highwayman of Moot Hill.

"Have you heard from him?" Her voice was small, barely a whisper.

Henry shook his head. "Don't worry. The lad's a canny one. I've seen him get through more puddings than a Twelfth Night supper." They continued past the inn. "This is the man who hoodwinked a bailiff who tried to serve me with a warrant and bested the Roundheads after others had thrown down their weapons. Aye, I know his worth."

A small knot of people turned to stare as they rolled past. Elizabeth drew her hood over her head. "He can never return."

There was a pause before Henry answered. "I suspect not."

They passed through the East Gate and headed towards Ellendale in an awkward silence. Elizabeth was reminded of her first journey to Ellendale. But instead of Daniel's sheepish looks, Henry's reticence spoke of another emotion.

"It's not your fault," Elizabeth said.

Henry's jaw tightened. "James trusted me to see to your welfare. I failed you both."

"I was released early. A near impossible feat."

Henry coloured. "You shouldn't have even been there."

"How is it Sir Richard signed my early release?" Elizabeth asked. It made no sense. She had not forgotten how furious he had been with Isabel. "Did my aunt soften him?"

"Don't think she's made amends with him," Henry said. "The only thing that would have moved that one was if Westminster had applied more pressure to release you than any influence Hammond had over him."

The wagon wheels bit into the gravel drive when they turned into the Ellendale lane. Elizabeth saw the house looming before her. She should have felt something. Instead, she was again a stranger.

Isabel waited for them by the gate. Henry slowed the shire, and the wagon pulled up before her. Wrapped in a woollen shawl, her aunt looked small, with a quality like translucent porcelain.

Elizabeth couldn't move. Her throat closed over a painful lump. She didn't know what to say. For two months, she had whispered to the damp cell walls everything that she had wanted her aunt to know. Now nothing came out.

Isabel held out her age-spotted hand to Elizabeth, and it shook slightly. "Welcome home, dear."

The next moments were a blur. Elizabeth couldn't say how she found herself gathered in her aunt's embrace, enveloped by the scent of warm honey. She sagged and clutched her aunt tightly. The layer of ice cracked, and she couldn't stop crying.

Chapter Twenty-Four

It took Elizabeth several weeks to get the sour taste of gaol out of her pores, and still more to sleep through the night without waking in a cold panic. Isabel allowed her to stay with her in her chambers until Elizabeth finally decided she no longer needed to be coddled. She had to consider being strong for the growing babe.

Hoping to restore herself to some semblance of normality, Elizabeth threw herself into helping Jennet. Together they overturned the spring-rich soils and expanded the kitchen garden. Elizabeth was determined to spend as much time outdoors as she could. The enclosure of walls, even the dark wainscoting that hugged Ellendale's parlour, increased her anxiety, though she did not want to burden her aunt with the admission.

Since the work consumed her, she did not at first notice the changes at Ellendale. A nagging feeling of disquiet had taken root, and it was only when she tried to unearth its source did she find the signs of unwanted change. Where once they would have a weekly stream of callers, now no one came.

When she mentioned this to Jennet, the maid attempted a smile. "'Tis better this way, truly. Your aunt says that the work tires her. She's not missing the continuous requests."

Elizabeth found it painful to walk into the stillroom and see the sterile surfaces, uncluttered by herbs and roots, and the mortar gathering dust. It was as though some vital essence had slipped away.

Hammond had done this. He had poisoned Warwick against them. He had made reclaiming her life impossible. Elizabeth avoided going into town, either for market or church; it didn't matter to her.

"Let them fear for my immortal soul," she said wryly to her aunt when asked about attending service. "They already do."

Eventually, everyone would learn of her condition, if they didn't already know, but she couldn't bear to feed the fires of controversy. Not now. Not yet. She needed time to harden herself to the whispers and raised eyebrows. The unfair sentence had made a bastard of her child, and she couldn't wash away the bitterness she felt towards the architect.

Hammond's shadow cast enough reach to still threaten her at Ellendale. Though he never called on them, heavier patrols were posted in the area, and a troop of garrison dragoons routinely rode up to the door with ridiculous requests to water their horses. The more brazen dragoons archly admitted that they were there compliments of Hammond.

The strain of their presence flayed Elizabeth's nerves. She kept to her chambers when they were about, watching from her window as they poked about the barn and scattered their chickens with a burst of ribald laughter. There were even times, particularly near dusk, that she looked out the parlour window and saw a brooding russet horseman at the top of the lane, an angry beacon in the fading light.

One Sunday in late spring, Elizabeth had grown weary and could do little more than mending. A drumming rain had fallen for three days, and a throbbing pain persisted in the small of her back. She didn't realise they had a caller until the door knocker echoed in the hall. Jennet hurried to get the front door, and Elizabeth eased out of her chair, immediately wary.

Hammond's cold drawl brought a rush of revulsion and loathing that weakened Elizabeth's knees.

"I insist on speaking to Mistress Stanborowe on a matter of urgency." Heavy boots drew closer and Hammond burst into the parlour despite Jennet trying to stop him. When he saw Elizabeth, his eyes dropped to her rounded belly, and he stared, stunned.

Elizabeth wrapped her shawl around her and rested her hand on her stomach. "What do you want?" She found herself shaking.

Hammond's eyes narrowed, and an ugly flush stained his neck. His eyes dipped again to her middle, and his expression hardened. "Harlot."

Elizabeth raised her chin. "You've already called me that. I suggest you find another tune."

Hammond's nostrils flared. "Where's your aunt?"

Jennet had run off to get Isabel and now returned with her. "What can I do for you, Lieutenant?" Isabel said in an icy tone.

"Your attendance at church is deplorable, madam," he said. "Your household has not prayed at service these past months."

Isabel snorted in disbelief. "Sir Richard must not have sufficient work for you if this is how you occupy your time."

"Answer the question, madam."

"What question, Lieutenant?" Isabel said with the dignity of a queen. "Regarding the matter of your madness? I admit, I'm thoroughly baffled."

Hammond scowled. "Do not trifle with me." When he took a step forward, Elizabeth hurried to stand by her aunt. "Warwick is my concern, and I will not suffer papists."

"Papists?" Elizabeth asked. "You think we're papists? Wherever would you get such nonsense? Just because we don't attend *church*? My aunt has been ill, and I am indisposed. There is nothing illicit about our decision to pray at home."

"If you care for the Sabbath as you profess, why have you broken it to accuse us?" Isabel asked with a slight arch of her brow.

Hammond's mouth pressed into a thin white line. "Papists use incense in their ungodly practises."

"You've come to sniff that out. Fancy yourself a bloodhound, do you?" Elizabeth said. "And do you detect any? I should think not."

Hammond ignored her as he toured the parlour. Occasionally, he tapped on a section of wainscoting. It made a dull sound.

"What are you doing?" Elizabeth asked.

He didn't answer but continued his progress, rapping every five feet or so. Always the same sound. After he travelled the length of the wall, he turned to Elizabeth and Isabel. "If you insist on not attending service and being malignants, you will be fined for each Sunday you miss."

"Very well." Isabel said, tight-lipped. She strode to the china cabinet and opened a side drawer. From it, she withdrew several coins. Handing the currency to Hammond, she said, "This should cover us to the fall. Now leave my home, or I *will* address this with Sir Richard."

Hammond looked as though he would argue the point, but then he bowed. "Good day, madam." His gaze flicked one last time to Elizabeth before he strode out of the house.

When the front door slammed shut, Elizabeth clamped her hand over her mouth and started to tremble. "I'll never be free of him. He will hound me to the end of my days."

Jennet came into the parlour. "Can you speak to Sir Richard about this fiend's behaviour?"

Isabel didn't reply. She sank into her armchair and stared at the chequerboard floor.

"Thank heavens we didn't have any visitors from the Knot," Elizabeth said.

Isabel lifted her gaze, and the realization hit Elizabeth. They were useless as a safe house. They had been for some time, and she had been too preoccupied to realise it. She shut her eyes and shook her head, trying to deny what she knew to be true. All of her aunt's warnings, spoken so long ago and received with such resounding deafness on her part, all came back to roost. There would no longer be a Knot, at least not for Ellendale. The one thing that her aunt guarded so carefully was gone because of her.

Elizabeth knelt at her aunt's feet. She didn't know what to say. "I'm so sorry. You warned me, but I couldn't..."

Isabel smiled wistfully and touched Elizabeth's hair. She bent over and kissed her on the forehead. "I know. We've done good work so far. There are other ways we can fight this battle."

A lump formed in Elizabeth's throat, and she blinked back the tears. She laid her head on her aunt's lap. Her aunt stroked her forehead and Elizabeth closed her eyes. As though from a distance, she heard her aunt say, "Dark as the woods, my maiden faire..."

*

The ripening wheat stalks ruffled under the summer wind. For months, the King's forces had been entrenched from south of Sterling to along the Firth of Forth, a watery bulwark that protected the Scottish north from Cromwell's army encamped to the south near Edinburgh. Whenever James had a chance to go on a new foray against the enemy, he seized the opportunity as a hungry man searching for his next meal. But none of their attempts to push the enemy back had succeeded, and lately the King had shifted his strategy to gathering intelligence.

James rode abreast of Roger with Sheffield and Davis flanking either side of them, returning from their latest adventure. Each man wore a New Model Army russet coat.

Before they reached the first outpost, they dismounted to change. Their sentries knew to fire upon the colour of their coats, and James didn't relish being shot a second time. The uniforms had been part of a shipment destined for Cromwell's men, recently intercepted. Others had seized the crates of muskets and shot, rightly excited over the prize, while James looked upon the red infantry uniforms as an even better catch. The other troop leader, Geoffrey Morsten, had thought to burn them in effigy. Fool.

"This wool itches," Davis said as he yanked his off. "I wager the Roundheads fashion these for maximum discomfort."

"Yours has been a nest for a family of rats. I didn't want to alarm you," Sheffield said with a grin. He carefully tucked his away in his saddlebag.

"Don't forget to pull out our colours, Davis," James said impatiently. Sweat dribbled down his shoulder blades. He would be glad to get back into his normal gear, and Sovereign needed a good brushing. Before leaving camp, James had rubbed the horse down with chaff to dull his sleek coat. Even his saddle blanket had been chosen for its moth-eaten appearance, to better blend in with Cromwell's half-starved, worn troops.

The reconnaissance had worked better than James had hoped, fortunate since Morsten had nearly swayed Massey against the enterprise. In the beginning, Morsten promised to be a reasonable companion, but lately the man set James's teeth on edge. Grand designs poured out of his mouth, yet he had all manner of resistance to James's proposals. The self-entitled son of a baronet, Morsten had ingratiated himself with the Duke of Buckingham, no doubt to gain better access to the King. Even though he held the same rank as James, he was forever dropping hints that his commission to the King's Life Guard was eminent.

"I can infiltrate Cromwell's camp," James had announced during a council of war. Cromwell had been more quiet than usual, and Massey was determined to discover what he was up to.

"How?" Morsten had demanded.

It had been on the tip of James's tongue to mention the coats, but Morsten's condescending tone checked him.

"It'll cost you to find out. I'll wager a day and a night in Cromwell's camp against ale for my troop."

Morsten had chewed on his lower lip. He couldn't refuse without losing face. "Loser buys ale. Bring back a prize as proof."

James looked forward to reaching the King's camp and collecting.

They slowed their pace as they approached the first outpost. When the sentries recognised Massey's colours, they lowered their muskets and waved them through. They rode into the Torwood to the sound of cheers and banging drums. Before they reached the centre grounds, a crowd had swarmed them, including many of Morsten's troopers

The very devil appeared as James dismounted. He wore his finest coat, and his boots had been buffed to a gloss. "Don't try to peddle some glib tale of how you snuck into the enemy camp, Hart. I won't believe it."

James grinned while he loosened Sovereign's girth. From his saddlebag, he pulled out a green banner with a red cross on the upper fly and tossed it to him. "Ale, bought and paid for."

"Bastard." Morsten stared at the flag as though it were a trick. "You simply rode into the enemy camp?"

James thought about it. "Aye."

"With a handwritten invitation, no less."

"Aye, the finest invitation." From his saddlebag, James pulled out his red coat and showed it to Morsten. "You will recognise it as part of the captured stash, though I believe you were in favour of burning them?"

Morsten gave a tight smile. "We can't all have your foresight, Hart, or your timing. Massey has called a council meeting. He'll be eager to hear your report."

"When?"

"Top of the hour."

"Just enough time," James said and gave the reins to a lackey. "Give Sovereign an extra ration of oats and a good scrubbing." With a tip of his hat to Morsten, he headed straight for his tent, russet coat tucked under his arm. The moment he ducked inside, he tossed the uniform into the corner.

Sitting down on the edge of the cot, he stared at the ground. The afternoon sun hit the side of the tent and cast a mustard glow at his feet. From outside, the sounds of laughter continued. Davis's voice carried across—he was already placing wagers for the evening's entertainment.

James couldn't blame his men for the high spirits. He'd been just as bored with the past months of drills and patrols. From the time his troop had joined Massey's regiment, they had hurried to remain still. They had seen little action, only random strike-forces to harass the enemy.

Now they were entrenched on the edge of the Torwood forest, a fortified position overlooking east and west. Redoubts had been built on the hillside, and a long trench ran along the eastern footing. With the River Carron directly in their path and swampy ground to the west, they could hold the north against Cromwell for some time.

The thought filled him with melancholy. He needed something to happen, anything to break this stalemate.

From his breast pocket, James withdrew the linen satchel Elizabeth had given him before he left. He pressed it against his lips.

What day is it? Saturday. Market day. He pictured Elizabeth moving through the stalls with her wicker basket, stopping by the bookseller's to see what chapbook he had for her. James imagined that she'd glance up at the inn's loft and smile. If he were still there, she'd be climbing the stairs to join him. The pressure across his chest tightened.

"Captain? Colonel Massey—" a voice called to him from outside his tent.

James sighed. "Coming."

*

James climbed the hilltop to Torwood Castle. He still had a few minutes before the council, but better early than late. A wise man never kept Massey waiting. During the months he had served the former Roundhead, James found his commander to be a man of keen intelligence. When faced with a challenge, Massey would lean back in his chair, weighing each course until he made up his mind. But if tested, his cold rage flayed any man's pride. James felt a grudging respect for him.

Instead of a true fortress, the castle was a large grey-stoned manor given to the King's commanders for their use. Inside, a row of rush-lights lined the hallway, and James followed the corridor to its end. He halted when he reached Massey's door and found the royal honour guard flanked on either side. When had the King arrived?

One of the sentries rapped on the door and paused to hear a response. "They're waiting for you."

James strode into a crowded room. The King was settled in Massey's armchair with two of his commanders, General Leslie and Lieutenant General Middleton, flanking either side of him. Along the wall stood the Scotch Contingent, as James had begun to think of them en masse. Sons and nephews of grand families, normally on opposing sides of longstanding feuds, now fawned over the one overriding factor—power. Morsten had managed to occupy the orbit between the Duke of Buckingham and Lord Wilmot, the King's friend.

James bowed to the King, who was simply dressed in the buff coat of a cavalryman. "Your Majesty." Then he saluted Massey, "My lord." James gave the Scotch Contingent a brief nod. The tension was thick in the air.

"And Hart has returned," Massey said sharply. "Kind of you to join us, Captain. I hope we haven't inconvenienced you? Council started a half hour ago."

James's eyes darted to Morsten. The man didn't flinch, nor did his smile fade. *Craven bastard.* "My apologies, my lord. I misheard the time."

Massey sniffed. "'Tis the King's forgiveness you should beg."

"No need," Charles said. "I already know the captain's worth."

Morsten's smile stiffened on his face.

"Massey has just been apprising us of your daring adventures, Captain Hart," Charles said. "I understand that you've recently been a guest of our dear friend Oliver Cromwell."

"Aye, Your Majesty, though he wasn't aware of it."

"Let's not trouble him, then. The man has enough to worry about as it is." He leaned back, drumming his fingers on the chair's arm. "Regarding your latest caper, what can you tell me about the devil's operation?"

"I reconnoitred his position at Linlithgow. Cromwell has seven regiments of Horse and Foot there. I counted only three thirteen-pound cannons."

"Seven of each?" General Leslie asked.

"Nay, together."

"Where is he hiding the others, I wonder?" Massey frowned.

"Anything more?" Charles asked.

"If it pleases Your Majesty, I did hear strange talk about boats."

"Ships?"

"Nay, my liege, they mentioned boats."

Charles propped his chin in his hand and didn't speak, though the others erupted in a ripple of conjectures.

"What devilry! He can't seize the Fife with a handful of boats," General Middleton scoffed. "Besides, we'd have ample warning of their approach."

James had quickly learned that maintaining their hold on the Fife was the key to securing Scotland. Johnstone had been keen to explain it to him as though he were a small child, "As long as the Firth of Forth separates us, we control the north, and they flounder in the south, God rot their soul."

"What do you think, Captain?" the King interrupted the discussion.

"It may be nothing more than a rumour spread thin."

"Do you believe that?"

James thought about it. They were mired here and would likely remain so until they were all old and rheumatic. But some unease gnawed at him. Until now, he had chalked it up to a combination of inactivity and futile patrols. "I sense there is something afoot. Far-fetched rumours often have a foundation in truth."

Charles scratched his cheek. "Captain, are you still a master at the game of Irish?"

All eyes were on James. He could hear the mental tallying of the Scotch Contingent and Morsten most of all.

"Aye, Your Majesty. I'm still unbeatable."

Charles smiled. "A master once told me that a patient holding game wins every time." The King turned to his commanders. "Extra vigilance is required. Increase the patrols. We must not be caught with our shirttails dangling. If there is nothing more…"

"Ah, Your Majesty," the Duke of Buckingham came forward. "One more pressing piece of business that you were keen to consider."

Charles looked past Buckingham to Morsten, who did his best imitation of a preening peacock. The man gave an elaborate bow, extending a finely turned leg.

"Of course, you were recommending this gentleman for my Life Guard?"

"Your Majesty." Buckingham stepped into the centre of the floor. His dove-grey coat was the finest weave, and the scalloped lace that formed his collar was worthy of a king's ransom. "The quality of your attendants should be the marvel of the civilised world, as celebrated as any of King Arthur's knights. The brightest flock to your august presence, vying for the opportunity to shine in your glory." Buckingham continued on, his narrative weaving a golden thread.

Morsten smiled openly, and all James could think of was that in the next few moments, the bugger would receive his cherished commission. *A pox on him.*

Buckingham paused, and Charles took advantage of the break to lift his hand and interrupt him. "Geoffrey Morsten?"

"Your Majesty." Morsten lowered his head.

"I'm aware of your family's wealth and influence. The Morsten estates are in the shadow of Buckingham's holdings."

"We're honoured that my lord Buckingham has taken an interest in our welfare."

Charles leaned forward in the chair. "You are currently serving in Massey's regiment?"

"Aye, Majesty," Morsten said.

This is it, James thought sourly.

Charles turned in his chair and looked at Massey. "Edward, one of your commanders wants to leave your command. What think you of that?"

"I defer the matter to Your Majesty," Massey said. "Captain Morsten is a capable soldier."

Charles nodded, all trace of humour gone. "I place a high value on loyalty. Captain Morsten, you would do more for my cause remaining with your commander."

Morsten's expectant smile faded.

"And Captain Hart?"

James looked up, startled. "Your Majesty?"

"Choose your best riders and step up the patrols. I plan to beat Cromwell at this game."

*

Another contraction ripped through Elizabeth, leaving her gasping for breath. She had been in labour since daybreak yesterday, and a new dawn was peering through the cracks in the shutters. She clutched the sheets in fistfuls and clenched her teeth to ride out the pain. The pain coursed over her, and she prayed for the retreating ebb. Just as the last one faded, another contraction charged through her.

The pain lessened and retreated like a spring tide. Elizabeth collapsed against the bolster, drenched in sweat and gasping for breath.

"Here, child," Isabel's voice reached her. A soaked cloth dribbled cool water in her parched mouth. Elizabeth opened her mouth, greedy for more.

"Do you see the baby's head?" Elizabeth's voice sounded as cracked as her lips. Jennet wiped the sweat from her brow, and now she felt cold despite the blazing fire in the hearth.

"Not yet."

She should, Elizabeth thought. Her eyes pried open, sticky through her tears. Isabel and Jennet were hazy in her sight, and she had to blink several times to get them into focus. The first signs of fear curled around her heart when she saw Isabel's shuttered expression. *Oh God.* Elizabeth knew that look.

"Has the baby turned?"

Isabel squeezed her hand. "Aye, dear—just relax."

Elizabeth turned her head and squeezed her eyes shut. They were not telling her something. She wanted James. Dear God, he should be close at hand, pacing outside in the hallway, only a mere shout away. What if...?

Elizabeth tensed. Another wave began to build. *Not again.* A keening moan escaped her lips. She felt herself torn apart, and she couldn't keep control over the pain. How much more could she endure?

When the last contraction lessened, she lay motionless and barely registered what her aunt was doing. Jennet gave her a sip of something bitter and smoothed the wet tendrils from her brow.

"The baby hasn't dropped," Isabel said in a low tone to Jennet. "The baby is labouring too. Help me get her to her feet. Elizabeth, love, you need to walk."

Each woman took Elizabeth by the arm, and together they managed to get her up. Another contraction knifed through Elizabeth. She bit her lip and tasted blood. Waves of agony flooded her, but still no desire to push. They walked, only stopping when another contraction came. Still the baby hadn't dropped. Elizabeth didn't need to assess her aunt's grim face to know that this wasn't going well.

The shuttered room was sweltering and thick with the cloying scent of lily oil. Elizabeth couldn't stand it. Breathing was difficult, and the heat was leeching the strength from her. She couldn't go on. A horrible fear seized her by the throat, and she started crying, dry, racking sobs followed by trailing tears.

"I can't lose the baby," she cried, holding on to the bedpost. "I can't... it's the only thing I have left. Oh my God, I'm going to lose the child."

Her legs weakened, and had it not been for the support, she would have crumpled to the ground.

Isabel's stern voice cut through her delirium. "Elizabeth. Listen. Look at me." She forced Elizabeth to look into her eyes. "You won't lose the baby, but you have to breathe. Focus. Clear your mind. Can you do that? Breathe."

"I can't—"

"You will. You must."

Elizabeth shook her head weakly. "I have no strength."

Isabel gripped her by the shoulders. "I'll be your strength."

Elizabeth latched on to the steel in her aunt's eyes and nodded. She had to do this. Breathe. She filled her lungs and released slowly. Just breathe.

They continued pacing, one hour, then two. Each time a contraction started, Elizabeth focused on the contact with her aunt. Finally, she felt the pressure to push.

"Good girl," Isabel said, helping her to bed.

Elizabeth focused on everything she had. She cast aside doubt and worry and pushed past pain and fear. Her aunt's voice filled her head, urging her on. A keening moan hissed through her gritted teeth. One final push. Then... *release*.

The first cries of the baby reduced Elizabeth to a puddle of relieved laughter and tears.

"A boy," Isabel said, holding up the child. "A healthy boy," she added, laughing at his strengthening wail.

"A son," Elizabeth breathed. James's son. She opened her arms to receive him, and Isabel settled him in her arms. Elizabeth's fear and pain were replaced by awe. Black curls were matted on his round head, and beneath the lashes a hint of grey softened his blue eyes. *James's eyes.* Even his little mouth and chin reminded her of him. Their son. A perfect blending of both.

Elizabeth traced the downy curve of his cheek with a light touch, and his mouth puckered. Suddenly, he stretched and startled. His little fingers splayed in the air, and for a moment a frown creased his brow. Then he settled once again, his hand curling around her finger. *Soft, I have you.*

Elizabeth tucked her son's fist into his blanket. People would try to cast slurs against him. Let them try. He would not learn compliance at her hand.

"I shall name you Thomas, after my father," she whispered. "Thomas Hart."

Chapter Twenty-Five

The next few months flew by for Elizabeth. Her world had been tied to the cycle of Thomas's needs, and she had only just realised that in a blink, summer had aged.

It was nearing the end of July, and Lammas approached. Normally, this was a time to look forward to the ripening harvest, and Elizabeth wondered if the rest of the year would reap hope or sorrow. She couldn't take another year like the last and resolved that the purge of a bonfire was in order. Hammond had posted an edict against traditional Lammas bonfires, denouncing them as pagan rites, but he could hardly arrest her if she lit it a fortnight early.

It didn't take Elizabeth long to assemble a reasonable frame. She tossed a last handful of twigs to the growing structure of wood and dried straw. She dusted the grit off her hands and circled the pile, judging the integrity of its design.

The sun had dropped beyond the willow trees, and the first evening star blazed above the horizon. She tilted her head and lost herself in the endless cup of pearl, gold and azure of the deepening twilight. Elizabeth revelled in the energy around her and extended her fingertips to touch it all.

Isabel made her way across the yard, carrying a flickering lantern. She picked her way, using her cane for support.

"Thomas is fast asleep, dear little man," she said when she joined Elizabeth. "I've asked Jennet to mind him for us."

"Thank you," Elizabeth said. What would she have done in these past few months without these two golden women? They not only kept the gossipmongers away but also gave her and Thomas a safe home. "The bonfire is ready to be lit."

"Lammas blessings," Isabel said.

"Wisdom and strength," Elizabeth said, picking up a willow branch.

"From the fire to God's ears." Isabel leaned on her cane and tilted her head to the sky. "Have you an offering, Niece?"

"Aye." Elizabeth drew from her apron a three-inch square of red muslin, snipped from the cloth that had joined her and James's hands so many moons ago. Carefully, she tucked it between the crisscross of twigs and branches.

Isabel brushed away the tangled strands from Elizabeth's cheek. "You are the youngest daughter of a youngest daughter, true for three generations. May the willow's strength be yours."

Elizabeth felt a surge of love for her aunt, and she squeezed her hand. Taking the light from Isabel, she lit the end of a twig and started the bonfire.

Together they watched as the orange flames spread through the pile of wood and straw. Fragrant smoke curled around the logs while a shower of sparks shot to the sky. The red muslin twisted and curled until it became a black cinder. As the fire gained life by consuming the old, a dull roar filled the growing darkness.

Come back to me.

As she watched, Elizabeth remembered her first Midsummer's Eve after the war. A wild and lonely night, the wind had stoked the blaze hotter than any blacksmith's bellows. For the first time, she and her mother had built a bonfire in the privacy of their garden. It had seemed furtive to Elizabeth—all wrong. As she had helped her mother place faggots of wood into a triangular frame, she imagined others at the beach joined in communal laughter and song. She and her mother had always been different, but until then, Elizabeth had managed to pretend otherwise.

Elizabeth slipped her arms around her aunt's waist. They stood in silence and listened to the crackle and hiss of the flames.

"I remember the bonfires in Weymouth," Isabel said. "We lit them along the beaches. They were so bright that they could have been seen across the Channel." The flames illuminated the smile fuelled by her memories. "I can see your mother dancing round the flames like a wee sprite. Our father had passed away a few years earlier, and many tried to shame my mother into applying a firmer hand to her daughters."

"What did she tell them?"

"'It is who we are,'" she said. "Then she called them scolds and sent them on their way."

310

Isabel cupped Elizabeth's face and leaned in to give her a kiss on her forehead. Sudden tears blurred Elizabeth's vision, and she squeezed her eyes shut. Stray tears spilled through her lashes and wet her cheeks.

"Be true to yourself and those you love," Isabel told her. "The rest does not matter."

*

Elizabeth awoke in the morning, blinking at the growing light outside her window. She glanced at Thomas's cot nestled beside her bed and smiled. Still asleep. She had time to draw some water and get fresh linens.

She pushed aside the quilt and didn't bother wrapping herself in a shawl. Already the day promised to be another unusually hot one. Carefully, she opened the door so as not to awaken Thomas and slipped into the corridor.

Jennet appeared at the top of the stairs, bringing a tray for her aunt. "Good morning, mistress. I've left the kettle on the hook. The water is already hot."

"Thank you, Jennet."

Jennet stopped at Isabel's door and knocked.

Elizabeth walked down the corridor and heard Jennet knock again, this time more insistently. Something about the sound made her stop and turn around. Despite the warmth, a shiver passed over her skin.

"Let me try." Elizabeth received no answer. She turned the handle and opened the door while Jennet peered over her shoulder. The bed curtains were drawn, revealing Isabel in sleep.

Jennet entered with her tray and placed it on the dresser. "She must be very tired, the poor lamb. That bonfire burned late into the night."

Elizabeth didn't reply. A coldness lifted the hairs on the back of her nape. She approached the bed haltingly. Isabel's hands, as pale as stone, were folded on the coverlet. Elizabeth reached out to touch her. The coldness of Isabel's skin pierced Elizabeth to her core. A cry choked in her throat, and she began to shake. Her knees weakened, and she crumpled to the floor.

*

A month of patrols had blurred together. James lay in his cot, restless. The air was thick and stifling, as though the clouds had dug themselves into the sullen hills. He left the flap of his tent open to catch a stray breeze, but none could be teased in. A thunder of hooves diverted his attention. One of the scouting parties was returning. James rose from his cot and emerged from the tent.

Roger pulled up, his mount lathered. Davis rode past and headed straight for the castle.

"What news?"

Roger swung down and allowed his horse to be led away. He tried to catch his breath. "Cromwell has crossed the Firth of Forth. Two thousand on the shores of Inverkeithing."

Christ's teeth. "Does the King know?"

Roger bent over as though to ease a stitch in his side and nodded. "Aye, we came from Stirling."

Securing that shore was key to holding the north. Grimly, James spun on his heels and headed straight for the castle. By the time he reached the track rising to the hilltop, Roger had caught up to him. They marched past the sentries and straight through to Massey's quarters. The door was ajar.

The major general's voice rose sharp and brisk. "Fetch my officers."

A soldier rushed out of the room and halted when he saw James and Roger. He pulled his cap down, tried to explain, and then realised it wasn't needed. "I'll get the others."

James pushed the door open and found Massey standing in front of his desk, holding a missive. Davis stood before him, begrimed.

Massey lifted his head. "Hart. Cantrell, you've already filled in your commander?"

"Aye, my lord."

Massey didn't respond but continued pacing, as though he begrudged every second. In less than ten minutes, Morsten and the other officers had scrambled in.

"Hart's scouts have returned from Stirling with word of an English invasion," Massey said. "At Inverkeithing Bay."

"My lord, you mean across from Inverkeithing Bay?" Morsten said.

"You heard me correctly," Massey said. "Sometime during the night, the enemy crossed the estuary and are now digging entrenchments."

The hairs on the back of James's neck lifted. "How did they make it across?"

Massey's expression was grim. "At the narrowest part of the strait, at Queensferry."

It suddenly made sense to James—the whispered talk in the enemy camp. "He's outflanked us with boats."

"Aye, Captain, a flotilla of flat-bottomed boats. I thought you would understand."

"An act of madness," Morsten said. "Surely, they know how vulnerable they are landing a party there, pressed between the high ground and the Firth of Forth."

Massey glanced down at the paper in his hand. "Precisely why General Leslie is dispatching two thousand to dislodge them before they dig in further."

Many visibly relaxed when they heard. Men started talking at once.

"Where's the rest?" James lifted his voice.

"There's no rest, Hart," Morsten sneered. He had barely been civil since the meeting with the King. "Either Cromwell is mad or he's testing us. This is surely a test."

"No one throws two thousand strong on a game of chance," James said. "Tell that to the devil."

Massey raised his hand and stilled their argument. "Hart is right. Cromwell's genius is in taking calculated risks when all others pause. 'Tis a desperate ploy, I agree, but I never like my odds when Oliver is the one throwing the dice. I've been on the short end of that before." Massey folded the missive carefully before tucking it in his doublet. "Our orders: within the hour we break camp and march north."

"To Inverkeithing?"

"Nay, we fall back to Stirling. Somewhere out there, the rest of Cromwell's soldiers are on the move. Damned if I let that man outflank us on two fronts."

During the next hour, everyone scrambled to break camp, pulling down tents, yanking up stakes, and extinguishing the cooking fires. James was tightening the straps securing the folded canvas to his backpack when Johnstone rode up with his men, flying Montgomery's colours.

"Running away so soon?" James asked.

"Eat shit, Southron," Johnstone said with a grin. "Montgomery is sending four companies of moss-troopers tae Inverkeithing tae give the English a thrashing."

"I wish you joy of it, then." James tried to smother the envy that sprang up. He didn't want to run and hide, or worse, hunker down in a siege. Better to feel the rush of blood when charging against a real enemy instead of this gradual wearing down through inconsequential posturing. "Good hunting."

"Good hiding," the Scotsman said, chuckling. With that, he slapped his horse and cantered off to join his men.

"Lucky bastard."

James swung atop Sovereign and gathered his men for the march five miles north. His duty was here, preparing to defend Stirling against an attack, not charging off in pursuit of Roundheads. *Repeat that five times.* By the time they had turned their back on the Torwood, James had managed to reconcile himself to his fate.

*

For once, James wished he hadn't been right. There was a certain comfort in ignorance, and Morsten wallowed in it. The arrogant son of a bitch was able to sleep and eat during the hours of wait and doubt until the moment when even he could no longer cling to delusion. Then the gnawing in James's gut proved sound. They had finally learnt the whereabouts of Cromwell's troops.

As the early morning sun burned off the mist, Cromwell's army materialised, marching towards the Royalist position at King's Park at the base of Stirling Castle. Red-crossed banners floated in the light breeze, ghostlike. James stared at the host in growing disbelief; for a moment, he wondered if he saw an apparition. Then the trumpets rang, and the pounding of drums shattered the stillness.

"Defensive position, men," Massey's order went down through his troops.

"Saddle up, First Company," James bellowed.

Orders rippled down the ranks. Breastplates were secured, pot helmets adjusted and weapons primed. In no time, they were in formation, a line of grim men forming a barrier between the usurper Cromwell and their King.

Naught but a rolling hill separated both armies. James scanned their own force, swollen with reinforcements sent down from Stirling. Though they outnumbered Cromwell, the bastard was desperate enough to attack.

Cromwell drew up his army and halted. James peered along his line with a careful eye, waiting for the signal to charge. Silence. He sat in the saddle and watched the Roundhead army.

"I see no sign of movement," Roger said.

"None at all." James rubbed his gloved hand across his stubbled beard. Cromwell had drawn up his troops in formation, with cavalry collected behind the infantry. Still no sign of an impending charge.

"Is he waiting for reinforcements?" Roger asked. "Is there another bloody way to get us from the rear? I wish I knew this country as well as Warwickshire."

James scoured his memory for the layout around Stirling. How many times this past summer had he ridden from there to Perth and through the shires along the Fife? "Only through the north shore. If we can't hold on to Inverkeithing, they'll take Stirling." James turned to Davis. "Run to your mates in the major general's staff and find out if they've any word."

The hours stretched, and still no sign of attack. By midday, the Roundheads fired a cannon, a single test shot landing far short of the Royalist position. Nothing more.

"What game is he playing?" James muttered. *Attack, damn it.* This could end it. Their King against the mad bishop. One battle to settle it all, exactly where it should have been settled, on the battlefield and not in the back rooms of Whitehall or on a scaffold. One last roll of the dice. Winner wins the stakes.

What are they waiting for?

No answer came—only more confusion. As the sun began to set, the English pulled back into the hills.

James watched in stunned disbelief. "Was that a dream?" He kept thinking they had missed something significant, a sickening feeling.

By the next morning, they received their answer. Inverkeithing had fallen.

*

The King's army scrambled to regroup. Inverkeithing had been a stunning loss. The English had ferried two thousand across the narrowest crossing of the Firth of Forth, and by the time the King's generals had realised the threat, Cromwell's men had started digging entrenchments. More enemy troops flowed across, swelling the English ranks to nearly five thousand. For reasons that James, or any of Massey's captains, could not fathom, the Scottish commanders willingly gave up the advantage of high ground in a misbegotten attempt to push the enemy back. The English seized upon the error and destroyed the Scottish ranks. Three quarters of the King's army at Inverkeithing were killed or captured. Johnstone and his moss-troopers were one of the few companies to escape the bloody rout.

With Inverkeithing lost, the way was open for Cromwell to overcome northern Scotland, and the King's options were either to retreat to the Highlands or be squeezed west. After ten days of frenzied council meetings, Charles made his decision. No retreat—they'd strike for England.

The Scots were appalled. They had been through an English invasion before and didn't relish the prospect. But James, with grim exultation, readied his men for the march. No more darting in and out to harass the enemy—no more wear-down tactics. Time to seize the bit and finally take the offensive. They were going home.

The King's army of fourteen thousand strong covered a hundred miles in six days through the Scottish lowlands. The hot, dry weather held, and the passage south remained unchallenged. They took full advantage of both, spending gruelling hours in the saddle.

"Mind your horses," James repeated to his men. At this pace, if they weren't careful, their mounts would collapse from exhaustion, and they'd be walking back to England.

Massey ordered James to select his finest riders to form the vanguard. There was no question. James was personally leading this one, and he was the first to reach the border.

Pausing on a ridge, James considered north and south. Behind him, the King's army spread out like a moving herd, royal pennants flapping in the breeze. The blue of the Scots' bonnets mingled with the montero hats of the troopers. But an even more glorious sight lay before him to the south. *England.*

While Cromwell's troops were chasing ghosts north of the Firth of Forth, the Royalists would be halfway to London. They may only have fourteen thousand, but once in England more would flock to the King's standard.

The road ahead wound through the valley and gave way to green and gold fields. The air smelled of sun-baked grass and rich soil. High up against a pale blue sky, a hawk circled. James heard the drums throbbing in the distance. A sweet breeze blew across the hills, laced with a hint of salt and peat smoke. If he were that hawk, he would be soaring above this summer wind, riding its waves to Warwick.

James couldn't wait to see Elizabeth. Their route would take them straight through Warwick. The thought stirred a deep ache. In his mind, he heard her laughter and imagined her arms flung around him, her body pressed against his. He could nearly taste her on his lips. A short leave, that's all he'd need. By God, he'd manage it.

Roger and Davis pulled up on either side of him. Stephen, cool and unruffled, followed close.

"What day is it?" James asked Stephen.

"The fifth of August, Captain. Why do you ask?"

James looked across the pass, and an exultant fury seized him. "This is the day we return to England. This is when we reclaim our country from the usurpers."

Chapter Twenty-Six

It should have been pouring the day of Isabel's funeral. To Elizabeth, the sunshine felt like a betrayal, a mocking reminder that the world moved forward while some things did not.

"The Lord calls us home." The vicar's words drifted across the knot of mourners. "To each his time."

But it didn't make the parting easier, Elizabeth thought. Not when she had lost a second mother.

She held Thomas in her arms, Jennet and Henry on either side of her. Sir Richard had come to pay his respects and stood with the other mourners. Isabel's daughter still hadn't arrived from Worcester, but they had delayed the funeral for as long as they could. Selfishly, Elizabeth was relieved—she didn't have to relinquish her aunt and share her grief with a stranger.

Elizabeth and Jennet had seen to Isabel. They had bathed and anointed her with rosemary and lavender, then wrapped her in fine linens. They sat vigil so Isabel would not be alone. And when Henry arrived with Samuel and Daniel to carry her to church, Elizabeth said her private farewell. Bending over her aunt, she'd kissed her cold cheek. "One for you," she whispered, then kissed the other. Her words had choked in her throat. "And one for my mother when you see her."

I will miss you, Isabel. Elizabeth's lip trembled. She squeezed her burning eyes shut and pressed her cheek against the top of her son's head.

"Isabel Stanborowe was a godly woman," the vicar intoned as he listed off her virtues.

Elizabeth lifted her head. Isabel would have taken exception to being called godly. *Call her instead a spiritual woman.* Isabel's god was not the same severe god these Puritans feared and worshipped. A wistful smile tugged her lips.

"Brothers, sisters, it is time."

As Henry, Samuel and Daniel lowered Isabel's shrouded body into the grave, a company of dragoons arrived with Hammond at their head. They halted beyond the church stile and made no attempt to join the mourners.

Elizabeth tightened her hold on Thomas. If she ever doubted the depths of Hammond's rancour for her, she no longer did. He intended no comfort, and his presence was lye on an open wound.

People filed past Elizabeth to throw a handful of soil into the grave. She only saw the wall of dragoons that waited behind Hammond. His attention did not waver.

When it was Elizabeth's turn to sprinkle an offering, Hammond abandoned his vigil by the stile and strode into the churchyard.

Henry stepped between Hammond and Elizabeth, but it was Sir Richard who asked, "What is the meaning of this, Lieutenant? This is a private service."

"Paying my respects." Turning to the vicar, Hammond said, "Is this not permitted?"

The vicar grew visibly uncomfortable. A thin sheen of sweat beaded his forehead. "On behalf of the family, I thank you, Lieutenant," he said with an uncertain smile. "You're, ah, perhaps you might want to return with us to Ellendale for biscuits and cider."

"He is not welcome," Elizabeth said.

A hush fell among the crowd.

"Are you the new mistress of Ellendale?" Hammond asked. "I didn't think so. Refusing guests... tsk... your aunt would be horrified if she knew how poorly you served her memory."

"Do not presume to know my aunt's mind."

"Perhaps that is why she died so suddenly," Hammond said. "Malignancy is a fatal infestation." His eyes dipped to the baby in her arms, and his expression hardened.

Elizabeth shielded Thomas with his blanket. "Then leave and save your mortal soul."

Hammond's cold smile did not reach his eyes. "As it happens, my duties call me elsewhere. I'm raising Warwickshire's militia." His glance raked over the assembled mourners and settled on Sir Richard. "Have you not heard? The Scottish King has invaded England with a band of devils." Shocked gasps rippled through the crowd, the loudest from Sir Richard. "They are headed straight for Warwick," Hammond continued, "but fear not, we will rout that baggage. The Lord will not fail our cause."

Elizabeth's heart fluttered. *James! He's coming!*

"But that isn't the worst," Hammond raised his voice. "It's come to our attention that a Warwickshire contingent accompanies the Scottish King, led by that villain James Hart."

Elizabeth clutched the baby tighter to her chest. Thomas began to mewl.

"This is who fights with the heretic Charles Stuart—highwaymen and villains. Since Ellendale is connected to traitorous activities, I will be keeping a close watch on the estate." His attention centred on Elizabeth. "You have been warned."

*

The King's army was as determined to force the bridge at Warrington as Parliament was to defend that pass into Lancashire.

James rose in the saddle and slashed his opponent with his sword. The steel bit deep, half severing the Roundhead's arm. Without breaking stride, he pushed against an enemy wall of Horse and Foot. His troop pooled together in a tight mass, driving a wedge through the Roundhead Horse.

After an hour and a half of fighting in close quarters, James's muscles ached, and his sword arm began to tell. Sweat streamed down his face. All around him, the sound of dying and wounded men rose against the ringing clang of steel.

A loud bellow rose above the din, and Morsten's troopers surged forward to shore up their left flank. The enemy fell back towards the stone bridge. "Retreat!" The call rippled through the enemy ranks.

"Give chase," James shouted and dug his heels in Sovereign's flanks.

Roger rode to James's right, his sword coated in blood. "To the bridge!"

As one body, they pressed their advantage, the enemy slipping farther and farther back across the bridge. A trumpet blew, and the last of the resistance shredded. Retreat! The enemy doubled back in earnest. A last roar of artillery spat through the smoky air. A desperate attempt by the Roundheads to destroy the bridge only netted chunks of stone and crumbling mortar, but the bridge held.

James surveyed the site of the skirmish. The last of the resistance dissolved—fifteen regiments of Horse disbursed. He whipped off his helmet and savoured the cooling wind. His damp hair lay flat against his skull. The smell of gunpowder clung to his buff coat.

He tipped his head back and roared his triumph. "Victory!" Their first skirmish, and they had driven the enemy back. Now Lancashire lay ahead with the promise of badly needed support from the county Royalists. Massey vowed to deliver them to the King.

James's men brandished their swords with lusty cries. Roger caught James's attention and held his fist in the air. James grinned and returned the gesture. He dismounted and stretched his stiff muscles.

A volley of cheers erupted, and James lifted his head. Charles appeared on the field, weaving through the men on his grey charger. There was pride and exultation in his glance. Men pressed closer, laughing in easy camaraderie. *Here is a king that men can follow*, James thought. If given the chance.

Nearly two weeks since crossing the border, passing one village after another, they received no support. Instead of the townspeople rushing to welcome them, they shut their gates and hid behind their doors. Charles's success depended on gaining recruits.

Roger strode up to James with a pamphlet clutched in his gloved fists. "Here," he said and passed it to him.

As James read, his anger flared. Issued by Parliament, the pamphlet warned of the Scots riding down from the borders, raping and burning. "Where did you find this?"

"Found it on one of the fallen Roundheads."

"Damned lies," James said. Charles had warned that any man found pillaging would be shot. To his men, James added that he'd do the honours himself. "A pox on them."

"Explains why we have no recruits."

"I'll show it to Massey—he'll want to bring it to the King," James said. "It'll be sure to light a fire under the major general when he speaks with the Lancashire Presbyterians."

"I hope so," Roger said. "Not sure how long we can keep this pace. Cromwell can't be far behind."

"Agreed." James wiped the blood from his sword and searched the field for Massey. They would no doubt find somewhere to camp, then he had business to attend.

Sir Piers was staying in Warrington, in the home of his close relative, Sir Anthony Birchall. James looked forward to paying his respects and bringing him news of their victory first-hand.

*

James stood over the grave. A handmade cross marked the slight mound. Grass had begun to take root, and soon nothing would have marked the place. The Birchall servants had directed him here after they assured him that Sir Piers had died without pain or regret.

James bowed his head. A hard lump lodged in his throat. He gazed across the small Warrington churchyard towards the west and watched the sun disappear behind a row of elder trees. In his hand, he held the letter Piers had left for him.

A smile had been on James's lips when he called on the Birchalls and asked to see his old master. The servant's expression had dropped, and he broke the news of Piers's death. James felt as though he had been punched in the gut.

It was odd, James thought as he stood before the burial mound, to look at words written by one whose life was measured in days. When he pressed the seal, did Piers know how little time remained to him? Based on the contents, James suspected he did.

He took a deep breath and unfolded the paper again. It was all there. Though it had not been Piers's secret, or his to speak, in death all rules were broken. James closed his eyes and struggled to comprehend what was plainly written. His father, Edward Hart, had not reneged on his word to support Parliament out of cowardice. Instead, Edward Hart had decided that facing his only child across a battlefield was not worth the price of honour.

James had no defence against this revelation. He stood there, stunned. Why hadn't his father told him? All these years, Edward Hart had allowed everyone to call him a coward—worse, he had accepted James's condemnation without flinching. All the slurs James had cast at his father's feet made his mind reel. He needed time to think.

Taking a step back, James slipped the letter inside his shirt. Bowing to the cross, he left the burial mound.

*

The pounding on the front door startled Elizabeth. Without waiting for Jennet, she rushed down the hallway. The urgent thumping continued unchecked. Just as she laid her hand on the handle, a force slammed against the wood. The portal flew open, and Elizabeth stumbled back, hitting her head against the wall. Pain exploded, and for a moment she fought against the spots dancing before her eyes. A company of dragoons rushed past her into the manor.

She shook her head to clear her wits. "What is this?" she called out, but they ignored her.

Jennet's voice rose from somewhere down the hallway. "Get out of that parlour! What is the meaning—" A crash sounded, and Jennet shrieked, "What are you doing? The cabinet!"

Elizabeth raced to the parlour. The dragoons were ransacking the room. Two soldiers were hauling Isabel's old china cabinet away from the wall. The remaining dishes flew off the shelves and smashed into pieces. Others threw aside the mantel painting and yanked down the window curtains.

"What are you doing?" Elizabeth yelled, but they shoved her aside. One dragoon pulled down the mirror, shocking her into action. "Get away from that." Elizabeth grabbed the edge of the mirror just as the dragoon released his hold. It pitched forward and shattered at her feet.

The dragoons were tapping on every panel, searching for hidden rooms. But Hammond already knew there was nothing.

"Dragoons!" Hammond strode into the room and planted himself in the centre. Slung across his coat was a bandolier, and a carbine was tucked in his belt. "Found anything?"

"Not yet, Lieutenant."

In the next instant, a splintering crash rippled through the manor. *The stillroom!* Elizabeth pushed past Hammond and rounded the corner to her haven. Ripped from the walls, the bookcases toppled, their frames twisted and fractured across the worktable. Shattered glass jars littered the floor while puffs of herbal dust floated in the air. Bunches of dried rosemary swung on their hooks as though dancing on a gibbet. Even the mortar, crafted of inch-thick stone, lay on the ground split in two.

Elizabeth stood at the door, stunned. Everything she had worked for lay broken at her feet. *All of it.* A strangled cry was wrenched from her, and she lunged forward, but Jennet pulled her back.

"Nay—your bare feet." Jagged glass shards were strewn on the floor.

Elizabeth slumped against Jennet. She covered her mouth and stifled a sob. *Everything. Gone. Swept away.* She stared at the room in horror. It was like the broken body of a dear soul.

From the kitchen, her baby's cries cut through Elizabeth's despair. *Thomas.* She raced back to the kitchen and found Thomas alone in his cradle, his little legs drawn to his chest. He drew big gulps of air between his screams as fat tears streamed down his red cheeks. Cuddling him to her breast, she covered his ears against the sound of destruction. She cringed every time more glass shattered.

Above their heads, the sound of thundering feet ran across the upstairs rooms. A loud thump shook the rafters. Startled, Thomas started to cry again. "Hush, my love," she said, rocking him in her arms.

A movement from the corner of Elizabeth's eye caught her attention, and she lifted her head. Hammond sauntered in and headed for her. She tightened her grip on Thomas and backed away.

"Show me the little brat."

"Stay away." Elizabeth was prepared to tear his eyes out if he touched her son.

Her fury must have shown on her face, for Hammond halted his progress. "The bitch defends her pup."

"Aye, I promise you that," she said with a hiss.

"You promised much before," Hammond said.

"That was your arrogance and desire."

Hammond's brow darkened. "Is that Salome's defence?"

"As you wish," Elizabeth said.

Hammond took another step forward, his gaze fastened on Thomas. For a moment, he didn't guard his expression, and raw loathing twisted on his face. *Oh my God.* Elizabeth had seen that look before. Desperation and terror gripped her. *Not my son. Not Thomas.* Holding her baby tight, she retreated as far as she could until the edge of the hearth brought her up short. Seizing the poker, she brandished it like a sword.

"Threatening an officer of the Commonwealth?"

Undeterred, Elizabeth tightened her grip. "If you try to harm my son, I swear I'll gut you." A surge of rage coursed through her veins. She would do it, damn the consequences. Neither moved. Each assessed the other's next move.

A soldier rushed in, breathless. "Lieutenant!"

"Not now."

"But I have word from the garrison. It's urgent."

Hammond tore his gaze away from Elizabeth. "What is it?"

"Worcester has capitulated to the Scottish King."

"What?" Hammond snatched the missive from the man's grip.

James is in Worcester! Elizabeth's heart hammered in her chest. *Less than forty miles.*

Hammond's scowl deepened as he read. "Round up the men. We ride posthaste." He crumpled the paper. A sneer disfigured his face. "Livingston!"

"Aye, Lieutenant?" Another dragoon approached.

"Prepare to take this woman to Warwick gaol. She's violated the terms of her release." Hammond turned to Elizabeth. "I'll deal with you when I return."

Chapter Twenty-Seven

Elizabeth couldn't return to the gaol. It would kill her—or Hammond would. And Thomas—*oh my God, Thomas*! What would happen to her son? Who would protect him from Hammond's wrath? She felt nauseous. Help. She needed help, and there was no one.

Hammond had left behind two dragoons to take her to Warwick—one had gone to the barn to prepare the horses while the other stood in the kitchen arguing with Jennet.

They will not take me. She had to protect Thomas.

Elizabeth seized the warming pan from the hearth. She crept up behind the soldier and swung it with all her strength. *Whack.*

The dragoon's body flew forward, and his forehead smacked hard against the floor.

"Sweet Christ," Jennet gasped.

"Come on," Elizabeth threw the pan down. Her palm felt numb from the vibrations of the handle. "We must leave. There's no time to lose."

"Is he dead?" Jennet stared with naked horror at the prostrate dragoon and refused to budge.

Elizabeth didn't care. Scooping Thomas from his cradle, she wrapped him in a quilt. She grabbed her cloak and paused when she saw her aunt's silver brooch on the table. Without another thought, she snatched it.

"*Jennet*! With me," Elizabeth ground out. Still, the maid would not move. They didn't have time—any moment, the other dragoon would return from the barn. "You can't stay here. Hammond will have his revenge when he doesn't find me."

The bang of the front door startled Jennet into her senses. She grabbed her cloak and dashed after Elizabeth into the night.

When they reached the end of the courtyard, they heard a shout. They dove behind the hedgerows just as the dragoon skidded to a halt in the open doorway.

"Blast you—I know you're out there!" He ran into the courtyard and stopped twenty feet away from the hedges. He whirled around to look for them.

The moon hid behind a bank of scudding clouds, threatening at any moment to pierce through. Thomas stirred in Elizabeth's arms, and Elizabeth bent over him. *Quiet, dearest.*

"Give it up. You won't get far." He swore, then bolted down the garden path.

Jennet peered over the hedgerows. "He's heading for the barn."

"The river—quick, before he returns," Elizabeth whispered. She could barely speak with her heart in her mouth. He wouldn't think to search for them there.

The women dashed across the field as fast as they could. The stand of willows beckoned ahead. If they could reach their shelter, they stood a chance. In the distance, they heard the neighing of a horse. A pinprick of light bobbed up and down.

"He's brought a lantern," Elizabeth gasped.

The women reached the willows and plunged into the heart of their darkness. They tore past the swaying branches, stumbling on roots and a ground that suddenly dipped. The slope plunged downward to the river. Elizabeth scrambled down the bank to the gurgling water. The soldier's flame snuffed out behind them.

Halfway down, Elizabeth stumbled. Her feet seemed to fly under the power of loose soil and exposed roots, and she pitched forward. Instinctively, she tucked in, cradling her son to her chest as she rolled and slid down the bank. Her hips and knees took the brunt of it. She shot her hand out to brace her fall, and a stab of pain jarred her wrist. Rocks dug into her skin, and she bit back a cry. When the world stopped careening, Elizabeth rolled to a sitting position at the bottom of the bank. Her skirt was torn, and her knees were enflamed. A trickle of blood snaked down her leg. Elizabeth looked at Thomas, touching his arms and legs. His eyes were wide and startled, but he seemed unhurt.

"Are you all right?" Jennet rushed to help her to her feet.

"Aye." Elizabeth's legs wobbled like jelly. She tested her throbbing wrist—only a sprain.

Thomas started whimpering, and from the way he scrunched his face, Elizabeth knew he'd be roaring soon. "Soft, love," she said. Tears of desperation slipped down her cheeks. "Mama can't save you if you cry like that." She rocked him in her arms and crooned in his ear. *Quiet.*

The muffled drumming of hoofbeats along a spongy turf warned them. They crouched low and shrank under the overhang of the bank. The horse slowed as he drew near. Elizabeth held her breath, praying Thomas would remain quiet.

The animal nickered, and with a click of reins, the horseman continued on.

Elizabeth exhaled. "What now?" She hadn't thought beyond escaping the dragoon.

"We should head for Samuel," Jennet said. "He can get word to Henry Grant."

Elizabeth's mind whirled. She opened her mouth to agree but stopped. Once Hammond discovered that she had escaped his men, the Chequer would be the first place he'd search. In the meantime, if the soldier had any brains, he'd head over to the Ledbrook cottage now. "Neither is safe. They'll find us sure enough."

"But where—"

"We'll follow the river, but in the opposite direction," she said. "There must be some shelter." But she couldn't travel any distance holding Thomas, not with a sprained wrist. "Help me secure him." Elizabeth unwrapped Thomas's quilt, and Jennet helped her tie the ends around her neck to make a sling.

"As tight as an anchor knot."

Elizabeth made a final adjustment. "Let's keep going."

The women followed the river northward, canting their ears for the sign of pursuit. The moon still hid behind the bank of clouds, both a blessing and a curse. Though it shielded them from unfriendly eyes, it made it difficult to know where they were going.

For over an hour, they followed the river. The night grew cooler, and strange sounds startled them: the flapping of wings and the hoot of an owl. Stones dug into Elizabeth's bare feet, and her wrist throbbed. Jennet steadied her as much as she could.

When the river veered eastward, Elizabeth halted to ease the stitch in her side. "Where are we?"

Jennet looked around, squinting. "Coventry is to the north. Too bad Bideford is closed to us. Our need is as great as the Giffards now."

"Coventry?" A mad thought came to Elizabeth. "James's father lives near Coventry."

"Edward Hart has shut his door to his son," Jennet said. "Why would he help us?"

"What choice do we have?" Elizabeth said in desperation. She knew it was an insane thought, but it was their only hope. "But I don't know where he lives."

"Stoneleigh? I know it," Jennet said.

"You do? How?"

"I grew up near there—everyone knows the Harts," Jennet said. "Aye, it's between Whitley and Coventry. We need to turn north."

They found a steep trail leading away from the river. At the top stretched a silent meadow, its boundaries broken by hedgerows and shielded to the west by a jutting hill. Ahead lay the main road, a dark winding slash, its western end swallowed by a thin stand of trees.

As they approached the road, Elizabeth heard a sound. "Wait—is that thunder?" Then she realised. Horses—hundreds of them. "Quick—hide!"

They whirled around and dashed back towards the copse half a field away. "There!" An isolated clump of saplings was their only chance.

They scrambled behind the trees and crouched together in the damp grass. If they kept still, maybe the party would think them shrubs or rocks in the darkness. Provided the moon did not show herself.

A wave of horsemen thundered down the road, churning dirt in their wake. Thousands of Cromwell's Ironsides headed for Warwick, banners streaming in the dark.

Choking on the dust, Elizabeth pressed her sleeve against her nose. Jennet huddled closer. Elizabeth wasn't sure how long they crouched, muscles cramped in a frozen position, until the last horsemen rode past. The rumbling finally faded.

"I can't believe it," Elizabeth said, rising. She looked around in a daze.

"Let's not wait for more to come," Jennet said, brushing the dirt and grass from her skirt.

"How much farther do you think?" Elizabeth's shoulders slumped. What if they had skirted too far to the east and missed Stoneleigh?

"Another half hour."

They continued on until they reached a narrow river that cut through their way.

"We have to ford it," Elizabeth said. They couldn't risk backtracking to the main road, nor did they have time. The night was aging rapidly.

Clutching the baby to her chest, Elizabeth waded in, gritting her teeth against the shock of the cold water. No different from padding along a Weymouth shore, except this water proved unfriendly and tried to suck her down. She tentatively tested each rock with her bare feet, careful to avoid any stones that wobbled. In the centre, the water rose as high as her hip, and her skirts were as heavy as leaden weights. One false step and they'd be drowned.

Elizabeth closed her ears to Jennet's muffled cries of fear and focused on reaching the opposite bank. She walked against the strengthening current and held Thomas as high as she could so he wouldn't get wet. Just as she thought she could not take another step, the water began to recede to the level of her knees, and before she realised it, she was standing safe on the other side. Jennet soon joined her, looking as harried as she felt.

Elizabeth had no energy for speech. They had been walking for nearly three hours. Surely, they were close.

"Whitley is that way." Jennet motioned to the east. "Stoneleigh must be close."

Elizabeth trudged behind Jennet. Nagging second thoughts roosted with each step. What would they do if James's father wouldn't shelter them? Fugitives on his threshold, bringing God knows what mischief on his head—what made her think he'd help? *This was a mistake.* Samuel or Henry would have known how to hide them.

They came to a stacked stone wall and followed its parameter until they came to a farmhouse. As they drew closer, they saw that the front roof had been destroyed. Charred beams jutted like jagged bones. Elizabeth shivered.

The scent of wood smoke coming from the back gave them hope that the place was not deserted, and they pressed on. A small light shone between the shutters, and a curl of smoke rose from the sturdy chimney.

From nowhere, a shadow bounded towards them. Elizabeth shrieked and stumbled back, wrapping her arms around Thomas to shield him. Furious barking erupted. A hound circled them, barking incessantly.

Elizabeth and Jennet drew together, every last trace of resistance leached out of them. They had no defence against it if it tried to rip open their throats.

A whistle pierced the dark, followed by a sharp command. "Sena!" Someone approached with a lantern. The light swung in the distance, illuminating homespun breeches and boots. The man raised his lantern and peered at them. Brown eyes set in a lined face widened in surprise.

"Who are you?" Though he didn't look like James, there was a quality in his voice that Elizabeth recognised.

"Edward... Edward Hart?"

"My identity isn't in question, woman," he said with a wry twist. "I repeat, who are you?"

"I'm Elizabeth Hart. Your daughter-in-law."

The lantern nearly slipped from his grasp. "Devil take me."

*

The sound of thunder roused James in the early hours of dawn. For a moment, he couldn't remember where he was. He stared blankly at daub walls and the grey light that filtered through the window. The second rumble cleared the fog from his head. They were still in quarters at the village of Hanley Castle at Upton upon Severn, immediately south of Worcester. Massey's regiment had been sent to guard the southern crossing. Then it hit him. This wasn't thunder—he heard musket fire.

James leapt up and yanked on his breeches. Outside his room, he heard men running down the hallway, underscoring cries of, "Enemy at the river."

He stuffed his doglock pistols in his belt, grabbed his carbine and sword and rushed out of the room. Morsten crashed into him.

"What the devil?" Morsten said, stuffing his shirttails into his breeches. "Weren't your men on sentry duty? How did this happen?"

"Out of my way, Morsten." *How indeed?* His anger strengthened with each step.

He rushed to the stables, where the boys were scrambling to get the horses ready. With no time to wait, James saddled Sovereign himself and set out.

The town's streets were clogged with Royalist soldiers. James followed the sounds of gunfire to the old stone church on the banks of the River Severn. Across the river, a troop of enemy horse gathered. They rode back and forth, looking for a place to ford the swollen river. A long, narrow plank lay across the crumbled sections of the bridge, barely wide enough for a man to cross on foot.

How the hell did they manage that?

James swung down from Sovereign and hefted his carbine. Crouched low against the church, the pikemen thrust their spears into the shattered windows, and the enemy returned fire. Another unit tried to force their way inside, but they couldn't make it past the steps for the barrage of musket shot from inside.

"How many?" He strode up to Roger, who had a musket trained on a window.

"About eighteen."

An enemy soldier stuck his head up, and Roger fired. The man ducked, narrowly missing the shot. Grimly, Roger tapped more powder into his musket pan. "A patrol discovered them crossing the churchyard. Now they're besieged inside." He rammed the shot, cocked the hammer, aimed and fired.

James assessed the field. Massey hadn't arrived, which left him in charge. "No time for a game of poking the hornet's nest," he shouted. "The buggers can hold the church all day if we let them." Meanwhile, enemy dragoons were on the other side of the river looking for a way across. At least the waters were high. "We need to end this now. Set fire to the church! Someone get torches—as many as you can find. Keep throwing them through the windows. Smoke them out!"

Men gathered up any kindling they could find— faggots, rushes, anything to burn. One by one, they dashed across the churchyard with their flaming torches, dodging musket fire to get close enough to throw them inside.

"Keep their attention focused here," James shouted to the musketeers. He loaded his carbine and waited for his quarry. A head lifted in the window. *Aim. Fire.* The man arched backward, shot in the temple. James reloaded.

By the time Massey arrived on the field, the church had taken flame. "How in Christ's blood did the enemy get past us? What happened to the sentries?"

"Deserted their posts for the inn, more like," Morsten said.

"By God, we were sent to hold this bridge, not a bloody tavern!" Massey raged.

"I take full responsibility," James said. No use pretending otherwise.

Massey glared at James, his mouth disappearing in a tight line. "We will speak of this later, Hart."

A shout of alarm sounded from the river. The enemy cavalry had managed to ford downriver and were now on this side of the river.

Impossible! James stared at the water, amazed that they hadn't drowned, but a hundred troopers were charging towards them.

"Fall back!" Massey shouted.

"First Company, with me." James ran across the field to Sovereign. A last shot from the church missed his foot, sending a clod of dirt flying.

Gone their normal order. Disoriented at having to face an unexpected threat, the men scrambled to regroup.

"Close ranks—forward!" Massey roared as he dropped his hand and slapped his bay's flanks.

James raced after his commander. They had to drive the enemy back towards the river, or Upton would fall. If that happened, the bulk of the King's army at Worcester would be left with its throat exposed.

Rushing towards the enemy dragoons, James crouched over Sovereign. He saw his path between two enemy troopers. He fired his carbine, hitting one of them in the chest. James discharged his pistol and shot another in the shoulder. Drawing his blade from its sheath, he swung and ploughed his way through the melee. More shots sliced through the air. From the edge of his vision, James saw men fall, their bodies trampled by enemy horse.

The Roundhead advance began to stall. Massey's men pushed the enemy back towards the river, but even more were streaming across. The enemy now held the bank.

A trumpet sounded from the village across the river. More enemy troopers rode towards the river to join the battle.

Outnumbered. *Christ's teeth.* James checked his charge.

"Fall back to camp." Massey's order rippled through the ranks. "Retreat!"

As Massey's regiment fell back, they fought to protect their rear. A shot whistled past. Massey jerked in the saddle and clutched his thigh.

Another shot, and he lurched. His horse stumbled, and Massey threw himself clear before the beast crashed to the ground.

James spurred Sovereign and wedged himself between the enemy and Massey. He drew his last pistol and fired. "Guard our backs!" he yelled at the men closest to him. James dismounted and rushed to Massey's side. "Can you stand?"

Massey struggled to his feet. His breeches were soaked in blood. James ducked his head under Massey's shoulder and half walked, half dragged him back to Sovereign. Any moment, the enemy dragoons would break past the crumbling wall of his men.

They finally reached Sovereign. A trooper grabbed the reins and helped James haul Massey over the horse. James then swung up behind him.

The last of the Royalist resistance failed.

"Retreat! Retreat to Worcester!"

*

"I've staunched his blood," the chirurgeon, Wiseman, said.

James had managed to make it back to Worcester bearing Massey and news of the loss of Upton. The Commandery, a daub-and-wattle manor home situated right outside the city gates, had been converted to Royalist headquarters and a chirurgery.

"Fortunate for him that a major vein wasn't pierced, though his leg is worse than I care for." Wiseman cleaned his hands in a bowl of water. "The man needs rest."

"He doesn't have that luxury," James said, rubbing his forehead. "The enemy will be upon us soon enough." His gut twisted. This was his failing, his fault.

"Captain, I've heard that often enough, but it no longer factors into my assessment."

James sank on a stool. He watched in silence as Wiseman ground something in a pestle. The action reminded him of Elizabeth, and he saw her face in his mind. The tightness in his chest became unbearable.

A servant entered the room. "Captain, His Majesty wants to see you."

"Now?"

"Aye, in the library."

James rose to his feet. "Show me the way." He owed the final accounting.

The servant led him up the stairs to a spacious room running along the back of the manor. Charles stood alone before a bank of windows, staring at the Fort Royal batteries. When he heard James enter, he turned around. The servant closed the door behind them.

"Captain Hart, we owe you our thanks for saving our dear friend Massey."

The formality boded ill. James stared at the floorboards of knotted wood. "I deserve your displeasure, Your Majesty, not your praise. Upton should never have fallen on my watch."

"Interesting." Charles looked at him keenly. "I've heard nothing this past hour except blame and finger-pointing. You're the first one who hasn't ducked."

"I'm prepared to resign my commission." The words were chalk in James's mouth.

"I understand we were outnumbered."

"Aye, four regiments to one."

"Little worse than what we're facing here in Worcester." The King glanced back at the battery and traced the edge of the windowpane with his knuckle. "But that isn't tonight's business." He left the window and stopped before James. "I'm taking back your captain's commission."

Waves of shame washed over James, and he nearly missed his next words.

"And granting you the commission of major, to reward you for your bravery in saving Massey. For your honesty and loyalty, you shall have that position in my Life Guard."

James's jaw nearly dropped. Were his ears ringing? Everything he had worked for, offered now. How ironic that it had come to him this way. "You honour me, my liege."

Charles laughed bitterly. "With Cromwell converging on us from the north and south, I haven't done you any favours, James. I should instead promote anyone who bears me a grudge and force him to forfeit his life to protect mine. But I do care more for my life than poetic justice. Guard me well."

*

The drums started beating before dawn.

James grabbed his gear and rushed out of the Cross Keys Inn, where he'd been quartered for the past two days with the rest of the King's Life

Guard. The attending grooms had Sovereign ready for him. Within minutes, James joined his new unit at Sidbury Gate beside the Commandery. The King was already there, riding his grey charger and wearing the buff coat of his troopers. The blue cross of St. George encircled his neck, the only mark of his status.

A Scottish force guarded the river crossings south of the city at Powick, the site of the first battle nine years ago. Johnstone's moss-troopers had been carrying reports between Montgomery and the King of the enemy's advance. The latest: across the river waited Cromwell himself. Combined with the army amassed to the east at Red Hill and Perry Wood, a total of thirty thousand were aligned against the King's fourteen thousand. They expected their attack at dawn.

James surveyed the host gathered to the east. Deep in his marrow, he knew—this battle would be the last.

By mid-morning, cannon fire belched from the south. Grey puffs of smoke became visible over the rise of the hills. The Scots General Leslie rode out with a reserve force of three thousand cavalry to align themselves north of the city. James readied Sovereign, anticipating the signal to move, but the remainder of the King's forces held their position.

Over the next couple of hours, James adjusted his helmet and checked the priming of his weapons countless times. Enough cartridges—sword honed to a hair-split edge. He stared at the enemy host gathered to the east. They stood between him and Warwick... *Elizabeth and home.* He pictured her at the riverbank, standing under the dappled shade of the willow. Her eyes, so blue, rivalled the summer sky. In a corner of his mind, he remembered her laughter above the flow of the dimpled stream. A deep warmth spread inside.

"Riders from the south," a cry went out.

James tucked away the images and prepared to greet the flesh-and-bone trooper riding his way. "What's happening, man?" he called out to him.

The trooper checked his lathered horse. "The Scots line holds—barely. Fighting hard to keep the devil from crossing the Severn." The trooper continued through the gates to the cathedral where the King waited.

"God brace them," James muttered. The guns had not abated. With each distant boom, his body tensed until he felt like a coil set to spring. One more notch and he'd snap.

Runners continued to bring word from Powick. "Cromwell's Ironsides have crossed the juncture. The Scots are falling back."

The King returned to the gates with his generals, and the order ran up and down the ranks. "Prepare for battle!"

This was it, James thought, with a mixture of relief and anticipation. He took his place in the King's Life Guard, and as they rode through the army, he passed his old regiment, now led by Morsten. Though they had made him acting commander while Massey recuperated, he barely looked at James, wearing the King's colours. James turned his attention to his old troop, where Roger had been promoted to captain.

"Step to the mark, Captain Cantrell," James called out.

"We scorn quarter, Major Hart." Roger held up his fist in the air. The rest of the troop unsheathed their swords and followed his example.

James returned the gesture. "From base rogues and rebels!" The old Earl of Northampton would have been proud of them.

From their batteries at Fort Royal, a volley of artillery spat. Across the fields at Perry Wood, an answer of cannon rumbled like thunder.

"Open order march!"

Ranks of musketeers started forward, flintlocks riding on their shoulders. The pikemen followed at a steady jog, their weapons bobbing like mastheads. Cavalry flanked either side.

The King led the advance. Once on the field, he veered towards the enemy fortification at Red Hill while another force headed towards Perry Wood. Banners snapped in the breeze, following the King's triple lion standard of gold and red. James kept pace with the trooper on either side of him. A trumpet sounded. The unit increased their speed.

As they neared, James assessed the enemy strength. This was a different force than the one he had last faced with Northampton. That army had been gritty, worn down by years of constant battle, brittle and ready to snap. This army of Cromwell's was different, as though he had purged the loose element from the ranks and boiled the remainder down to a concentrated stew.

"First ranks, present." The cry went down the line. A spat of fire discharged.

Another trumpet blared. Charge! James kicked his heels, and they raced for the enemy lines. Three hundred feet. James raised his carbine. His body tensed. One hundred. *Aim... fire.*

A solid wall of flame and smoke erupted as both sides opened fire. Several troopers fell from their mounts, but the rest didn't break stride. A second round of carbine fire thundered from the King's men, thinning out the enemy ranks. Thrashing horses crashed to the ground. Piercing screams filled the air.

James wheeled to the rear and fell back to reload. The next rank of Horse rushed past to engage the enemy. The air was thick with musket smoke.

"Close ranks forward!"

James circled to take a second pass. His heart pounded furiously. Advancing on the enemy musketeers, he discharged his carbine then pulled out his pistol. An enemy horseman spurred towards him. *Crack*! The Roundhead tumbled from his horse and was trampled underfoot. James jammed the spent pistol in his holster and unsheathed his sword.

Rising in the saddle, James pressed his advantage. His sword rose and fell as a scythe against grass. The enemy musketeers fell back, retreating behind their Pike. Even the enemy Horse lost ground against the King's onslaught. A surge of excitement washed through James, and he bellowed his triumph. Against all odds, they were pushing the Roundheads back. The sword in his hand grew lighter as he cut a swath forward.

A volley of shots cracked overhead, and the Life Guard formed a shield around the King. An enemy trooper broke through their defences and charged straight for Charles.

James raced to intercept. He fired with his reserve pistol but only grazed the man's shoulder. James wheeled around to take another pass, but Charles beat him to it. The Roundhead jerked back and fell from the saddle.

"You're welcome, Major," Charles called out, his face smeared with soot.

James grinned and saluted him.

Panicked shouts broke out, followed by a hasty trumpet blare. A rider raced to Charles. "The Scottish lines are broken," he cried. "Cromwell has recrossed the Severn. He's racing this way."

A surge of reinforcements swept from the south, flying Cromwell's banner. They swarmed like ants pouring out of a hill, a flow of red coats, pikes and horses. Any advantage the King's troops had gained now slipped from their grasp. The enemy infantry, seeing reinforcements, took fresh courage and shored up their weakened flank. The King fought to keep the ground they had recently purchased.

"Hold the line!"

James spurred Sovereign and charged at the red wall of men threatening the King. A shot whizzed past his head. Crouched low, he drove forward, slamming into body and bone. The space began to shrink, and more and more enemy pressed in on him. He whirled Sovereign around, looking for a break. A gap opened, and he darted for it.

"Fall to! With me, men!" Charles shouted.

James shook his head to clear his ringing ears. "With the King!" he heard someone shout, then realised it was he. They were being pressed on three sides. James looked around, desperately praying for a miracle, or at the very least expecting to see General Leslie's reserve troops flying to their aid. Nothing. *Where the hell are Leslie's men?*

Throwing his strength in with the others, James regrouped to form a buffer between the King and the enemy as they fought their way back to town.

"On my count," James yelled. "One, two, now!" And they rushed against the Roundheads. When he wheeled around to take another pass, he saw that Charles was nearly at Sidbury Gate.

The rest of the engagement became a rout. Men on both sides fought to reach the town. James kept a tight hold of the reins, manoeuvring Sovereign through the field of fleeing men and broken bodies.

An overturned cart cut off the King's escape. Precious seconds remained. Sensing blood, the enemy closed in. Charles launched himself from his horse and clambered over the cart to reach the town.

Needing to buy him time, James charged the melee. A pikeman swung his spear, but James grabbed the upper shaft and drove the man backward, squashing him between Sovereign and another horse. He yanked the weapon from his grasp and turned to the gates in time to see Charles escape into Worcester.

James was trapped—stranded on the other side of the barricade with no time to reload. Cut off.

This is it. This is where I die. Elizabeth... I'm sorry.

A coldness seized him, a detachment he hadn't thought possible.

So be it. I scorn quarter.

James faced the enemy hordes. "Damn your black hearts to hell!"

Hunching forward, he hefted the spear in his right hand and levelled it against the rushing Foot. With a loud battle cry, he drove Sovereign straight into the thick of the fray.

Chapter Twenty-Eight

Elizabeth hurried across the yard to the Stoneleigh barn, dashing through puddles. Gusts of wind lifted her woollen skirt, and a slanting rain spat in her face. She desperately needed to be alone.

After a few attempts to lift the stubborn latch—hitting and throwing her weight against the door—she stumbled inside and slammed the door behind her. Sagging against the wood, Elizabeth sucked in a deep lungful of air, trying to dislodge the hard knot in her chest.

Had it been only a week since the fall of Worcester? Seven days of waiting for word of James. A lifetime, if measured in fear. Thousands captured. Thousands dead.

She tipped her head against the door and shut her eyes. *Where are you?*

Every moment since hearing of Worcester, Elizabeth tried to keep busy, to shut out Jennet's pitying looks and pretend not to notice how Edward's voice dropped when she entered the room. It was not enough that he now had this to contend with.

Elizabeth had to do something, so she feverishly worked on a knotted wreath to hang on the gate. "James may not know I'm here," she explained to Edward when he nailed it in place for her. "He may not make it back to Warwick—" She paused, swallowing the lump in her throat. "He would do well to avoid Warwick. If he sees the wreath, he'll know it's safe to return."

A foolish, impossible sentiment. Even she knew that.

But Elizabeth couldn't pretend any longer. Thread by thread, she was unravelling. The uncertainty festered like an uncauterised wound. Not even little Thomas could provide her comfort, for every time she looked at his soft face, he reminded her of his missing father. She sank into the straw, drawing her knees to her chest. *God, I can't breathe.*

The sudden flutter of roosting doves startled her. Agitated wings beat above the rafters until they settled on another perch. The milch cow gave a lowing sound, and a horse nickered in one of the stalls.

Elizabeth's ear's pricked. It didn't sound like one of theirs.

She rose to her feet and stared towards the darkened stalls at the far end of the barn. There, again—this time an impatient snort. The plough horse should have been bedded down.

A voice whispered in the corner of her brain—*Fetch Edward.* But a streak of defiance and recklessness seized her. Careful not to make a noise, she sidled to the farm tools hanging on the wall and grabbed a pitchfork.

She crept towards the stalls. A scuffle drew her to the first one. With heart pounding, she raised the tines and braced herself. "Show yourself. I know you're there." Nothing. "'Tis no use—you'll not get past me."

She tensed at the sound of shuffling straw. A man's head appeared over the gate, followed by two others. Elizabeth gripped the pitchfork tighter.

"We mean you no harm," the first man said, holding empty hands in the air. His buff coat was stained, littered with chaff and twigs. The others were just as filthy and looked to have lain in bogs and ditches. Cautiously, he opened the gate.

Elizabeth pointed the prongs at them. Though they looked exhausted and worn, she didn't lower her guard. "Who are you? What are you doing in our barn?"

"Fugitives begging shelter, mistress. Captain Roger Cantrell, at your service, and my men, Trumpeter Davis and Cornet Sheffield."

Elizabeth's mind whirled. She lowered the pitchfork to the ground and now used it to support herself. "You were at Worcester?" Her mouth became chalk.

"Aye. Parliament soldiers are beating the roads for us," Cantrell said. "The knot was posted at the front gate—we heard that shelter would be given to those who follow it."

A coldness drenched her skin. "Where did you hear this?"

"Our former captain spoke of it once," the cornet said.

Elizabeth's heart hammered in her throat. "Your captain? Who—pray, speak his name."

The men looked at each other before Cantrell answered, "James Hart."

A wave of nausea swept through Elizabeth. She swayed slightly and croaked a whisper, "*Where is he?* Where is my husband?"

Startled, the three men looked at each other and avoided her gaze.

"What's happened to him?" She took a faltering step. *Dear God, I can't hear the words, no, I cannot.* "Tell me."

A long pause while the men looked at each other again, then Cantrell's face darkened. "We don't know. He was with the King during the battle. The fighting was hottest there. I'm sorry. If you haven't heard from him by now... I'm afraid he might—it could be that.."

Dear God, he's dead. The pitchfork clattered to the ground.

*

Elizabeth scored the gatepost with the tip of her dagger, one inch long. Twenty gouges in all. Each notch signified a day—another one since Worcester.

You will return. No one saw you fall.

As Elizabeth knelt in the mud, the steady drizzle soaked her shoulders and back. The cold seeped into her knees. She traced her finger over that first mark, dug with a fierceness as though its depth could somehow steer James home. Any day, he'd turn up in Warwick, and Henry would send him to Coventry.

Come back. She touched her forehead to the post and closed her eyes. *Oh, my love.* Her hand went limp, dropping into her lap. *I miss you.* The musty scent of sodden wood filled her senses. Rotted. Decomposing.

A crunch of footsteps sounded behind her.

"'Tis cold, lass," Edward said, hunched against the splattering wind. "Come inside where it's dry. You'll catch the ague out here."

Elizabeth hadn't been warm since hearing of Worcester. She turned her attention to the post. "I have work to do." This latest mark was faint, not worthy of being called a score. *The knife twists and drives deeper with every breath I take.* She leaned into her blade and pressed harder.

"What will you do when you run out of post?"

Elizabeth continued to scrape the wood. "Start another."

Edward's hand wrapped around her wrist. His face was grey, as though all blood had been leached out of him, and his brown eyes mirrored her pain. "He isn't coming home."

Elizabeth yanked her hand away. She squeezed her eyes shut, riding out a wave of fresh anguish. Surely, she would know if James was truly gone. Deep down within the marrow of her bones, she'd know. Then she'd feel grief instead of a horrible, gaping hole.

Edward laid a firm hand on her shoulder. "You know I'm right."

"You're not!" She pushed his hand away and scrambled to her feet. *Don't do this to me.* "He's coming back, I tell you!" Tears started to course down her cheeks, and she swayed. The dagger fell from her fingers and landed with a splash in the pool at her feet.

"Twenty days, lass," Edward said. "We would have heard if he had been taken prisoner. The gaoler is always the first to be paid."

A shiver snaked down her body, and she shook her head. The ringing in her ears became unbearable. "You don't know your son—he's the most capable man I know. If he vows to scale Warwick Castle, ask when, not how. He told me he'll return—I have to believe that." Her voice caught in her throat.

"Elizabeth, listen to me—"

"Nay!" She backed away. The pain in her chest nearly ripped her apart. "God can't be so cruel to take him from me before he knows he has a son." She was now openly crying. "Because if He has, they have truly won. Those Puritans have foisted their stern, unrelenting God on us, and no matter what we do in this life, it won't matter. We are damned, just as they have predicted." The rain intensified, and rivulets streamed down her face. "Though you gave up on him, *I will not.*"

"I *never* gave up on my boy." Edward's voice thickened with anger. "For his sake, I did not go to war and was branded a coward for it. Generations of Harts have been true to their conscience, but I allowed my good name to be corrupted. I threw away *everything* not to give up on my boy." He lifted Elizabeth's jaw and forced her to meet his gaze. "And you can't give up on yours. You must look to Thomas. You can't walk about like a wraith, paying him the mind of a stranger. For his sake, you must accept the truth. James is dead."

Elizabeth shook her head and covered her ears. "Don't say that."

Edward gripped her shoulders, his expression bleak. "He *is* dead."

She snatched away and buried her face in her hands. Twenty days, and each one a rock adding to the weight already crushing her. Edward's words echoed in her brain. She didn't want to believe it... but she knew. If he could, he would have returned.

He's really gone. Elizabeth's legs cut out from under her, and she sank to the muddy ground. *Oh my God! I can't.* "You have my heart in your keeping," he had told her. *But what of mine?*

She curled into a tight ball as a keening wail shuddered through her.

*

Elizabeth had no will to lift her head. Her sky consisted of a patchwork quilt and her earth a straw-stuffed mattress. At times, like the turning of seasons, the door opened and soft footsteps pattered close. Always a long pause, then the rattle of crockery settling upon a wooden stool.

"Mistress," Jennet whispered and then with more insistence, "you haven't eaten anything. Mistress, it's been days—you need to rise. We've had to give the babe cow's milk."

Elizabeth curled up as tight as a frond and prayed they'd leave her alone. This was her winter. A long pause, then the door shut until the next turn of the clock.

Elizabeth turned her head into the bolster. The linen was damp beneath her cheek.

What do you dream, love? James's voice drifted to her. In the nether space between sleep and awake, he existed. She reached out and brushed his mouth with her fingertips, and he kissed each tip back. *I dream of skimming storm-tossed waves. I dream of you.* He smiled but didn't laugh. He never laughed at her or made her feel foolish for dreaming beyond herself. *What do you dream,* she returned the question? This time his expression became searching, as a child who feared ridicule. *An impossible dream.* His voice was now dusty and cracked—fading.

Elizabeth sensed his withdrawal. *Don't leave me.* She thrashed about the sheets, drenched with sweat. With a strangled cry, she bolted up. Night. The room's only light came from the dying fire.

She collapsed and stared at stark, whitewashed walls. *I should never have let you go.* Was that why God hadn't seen fit to return him to her in death? Somewhere, his body lay unblessed and unprepared by loving hands.

Slowly, she drew the quilt over her head once more.

The door opened. Instead of Jennet's careful footsteps, rough boots tramped across the floor. A pause, but instead of the rattle of dishes, she heard a creaking of something laid on the floor near her bed. The boots retreated.

A whimper, a cooing of a dove seeped through her haze. Then a babbling, like water tumbling over moss. Elizabeth peered out from under her cover and saw the top of a wicker cot. When she lifted her head, she saw Thomas's dark curls. His little feet kicked against the walls of his cot. *When had he outgrown that?* When had she stopped noticing? The blanket slipped off his shoulders, and chubby arms flailed around, delighted at being freed.

She had allowed the fire to die down, and there was a dampness in the air. *He will catch his death.*

Where was Jennet? She should be attending him.

Get up.

Elizabeth burrowed deeper into the quilt. *They'll not leave him here alone.*

The wind whistled through the crack in the window and carried the scent of rain. Thomas was going to freeze.

Elizabeth lifted her shoulders from the bed and pushed the quilt aside. Her feet touched the cold floorboards, and her toes curled in protest. When she tried to stand, her legs trembled, and she clutched the bedpost.

Goose bumps lifted on Elizabeth's arms. The baby started whimpering. He had managed to kick off his blankets, leaving only a thin linen gown for warmth.

The cot was too far. She didn't have any strength to reach him.

"Jennet?" This time louder. "Edward?" Damn them, did they wish to see Thomas die too?

Elizabeth tried a step and nearly pitched forward. The pull to return to the bed was overwhelming. Her knees dropped, and she hovered between slinking back and staying on her feet.

Coward.

Thomas started crying with more energy. His feet were red as they stiffened from under his gown. The door remained shut. No help.

"I'm coming, dearest," she said and took another tenuous step. Biting her lip, she concentrated on putting one foot in front of the other.

Elizabeth reached Thomas, and when she bent to lift him from his cot, the sudden movement made her head spin. She waited until the wave passed before taking him in her arms.

Poor mite. His bare arms were chilled. The moment she hugged him closer to her chest, Thomas stopped his crying and smiled up at her. It pierced her heart, and fresh tears welled in her eyes. She hadn't thought she had any left.

Elizabeth slipped back into bed with Thomas tucked in beside her. Watery grey eyes studied her face, and a smile tugged at the corners of his bow mouth. He lifted his arms and touched her cheeks with his searching hands. A lump formed in her throat. He smelled of sunshine and life.

Elizabeth turned her face into his dark curls.

I will face this. I am not a coward. Neither his father nor his grandfathers were cowards. Her son would not learn this from her.

"Know that I love you well," she whispered and touched her lips to his forehead.

Chapter Twenty-Nine

James should have been dead. When surrounded and harried by an enemy tasting victory, a sane man would have thrown down his weapons and resolved for capture. Charging at the enemy at close quarters had been an act of madness, but it had saved his life. In the brief few seconds before he reached them, the enemy realised they feared more for their hides than he for his.

As though the dogs of hell snapped on his heels, James had barrelled through them. With the enemy determined to reach the King through the gates, the resistance against James had fallen apart. He'd cleared the melee and continued racing north along the city walls until he reached St. Martin's gate. There, he'd found Charles, re-emerging from the city, riding with a company of fleeing lords.

Within a few hours on the northern road, two hundred desperate men had slowly whittled down to sixty. James watched them slip away, one by one.

All was lost—James had tossed the dice, and they came up short. He wanted to throw his head back and howl. He couldn't immediately return to Elizabeth, or he'd put her in danger. He needed time—time for the hounds to lose his scent.

They continued riding north, the only way not blocked by Cromwell's army.

After several hours in the saddle, James fought through grinding exhaustion. The horsemen rode slowly, their weariness marked by slumped shoulders. With only a couple of short breaks, it was a miracle that their mounts hadn't collapsed. Charles alone looked as if he could press on to Scotland, riding with a fierce alertness.

The night grew crisp at predawn. They were now in Staffordshire. James became more on edge, unsettled by the absence of Roundhead pursuit. Several miles back, a Staffordshire officer, Major Giffard, had taken the lead and promised to take them to a place where they could safely rest. His name captured James's attention—same as the family he and Elizabeth had once helped.

The officer led them off the main road and struck for a forest tract. James urged Sovereign past the others until he rode abreast of the man.

"Are we far, Major Giffard?"

"Five more miles."

James studied the sky. They needed to reach their destination before the sky lightened or risk being seen.

In another mile, the road split in two. Giffard pulled up and considered both directions with a troubled expression.

"What's wrong?" Charles asked.

"We won't make it to Boscobel before dawn. 'Tis the hunting lodge of my late cousin, as safe as any place can be found." Giffard chewed his lip. "We might make it to their manor house at White Ladies. The family is away, but they've left their servants there as caretakers."

"Servants?" James asked. "It won't be possible to hide the King from them."

"The Penderells are as loyal as children. They have always kept the family's secrets."

"Your recommendation will suffice, Giffard," Charles said. "Lead on."

They pressed through the forest, trying to outrun the dawn. The sky lightened, sharply defining every tree and root. When they finally broke through the woods, they found themselves in a meadow. The early morning mist rose from the ground like a ghostly wraith. A manor house stood beside the crumbling ruins of an old priory. The last call of a nightjar broke the grim silence.

Everyone dismounted. James loosened his sword and kept his hand on the pommel. He was about to insist they remove the King until they could be sure of their welcome. Then he spied a knotted wreath hanging on a post.

*

James managed a couple of hours of rest, curled before the hearth with only his cloak as bedding. Hearing raised voices, he paused at the door and listened to a heated argument about which road the King should follow.

By the time they made a decision, he thought, Cromwell would be knocking on the door. He wondered whether he should join them or leave them to their debates. What decided the matter was when he heard

Giffard say, "General Leslie and his men have been sighted near Tong Castle—three thousand horse. We must to them."

James's outrage flared. He strode into the room, startling the score of men gathered around the King. "Forgive me, sire, but where was Leslie and his reserves at Worcester?" James glanced around at the gentlemen, lords and senior officers. His question did not sit well with them, but he didn't give a damn. "Where were they when we were being driven back by the usurper and our men were being slaughtered? Three thousand men could have won the day for us."

"Indeed, Major," Charles said, "the men who deserted me when they were in good order will never stand to me when they've been beaten."

"We must join them, Your Majesty, 'tis our only hope," Buckingham insisted. "With such a force, no one would oppose our way back to Scotland."

"What if I were to head to London instead?" Charles asked.

Giffard blanched. "Surely, sire, you won't consider going into the hornet's nest!"

"They would never anticipate that," Charles said, thrumming his fingers on the arm of his chair. "I could dress up like a washerwoman and parade before them with a basket of laundry on my head. No one would look at me twice."

Shocked gasps rippled through the room. James studied the ground, amused. *They are a thick lot.*

"And you, James," Charles said. "What's your counsel?"

"I don't think you should dress up as a washerwoman."

Giffard cleared his throat. "Our best chance for escape lies with Leslie's forces. I beg you, sire, we should join them posthaste before they move from the area."

"I'd rather be hanged than return to Scotland," Charles said, rising. "The damned Covenanters used me most servilely, setting me as a puppet. Renounce my father, denounce my mother, repent my sins— that's all I heard from those harpies. I've had enough of them. Where have they landed me now?" He paused a moment and looked around the room. "I'll not chain any man to me. I release you from your oaths. Go with my blessing."

*

350

James went for a long walk to consider his plans. A light drizzle of rain shrouded the trees in mist, and he lowered the brim of his hat. He startled a black raven that took flight and settled on a higher branch. For the next two hours, he wandered through the woods, unmindful of where he was going.

For eight years, he had bled for the crown and harried the Roundheads. For Charles's sake, he had aligned himself with another country and left behind the woman he loved. He was now released from his oath, and the rush of relief surprised him. Only one oath now bound him, a silken ribbon entwined around his heart. He had to find a way to return to Elizabeth.

And then what? They could travel to Wales, where they would make a fresh start. James could take up his former trade, clerk for a man who would not care that he was a Royalist, or once more hire himself out to a stable, where his politics were his own business. Whatever he had to do, he would ensure that his wife was not cursed to be a wandering fugitive. They would build a new home together.

James smiled. He had been caught in the past long enough.

Backtracking through the woods, he headed to the stables. Inside, a young boy forked hay into the stalls. "Lad," he said to him, "saddle my horse—aye, the Frisian. I'll be leaving shortly."

James rushed back to the farmhouse to gather his things and take his leave of Charles. He found him in the parlour alone with the White Ladies caretaker, John Penderell. They both seemed surprised to see him.

"James, you're still here—you've not left with the others," Charles said.

Something in his tone halted James. A hint of relief, a darker vein of desperation. "What do you mean?" James asked. "Where did they go?"

John Penderell snorted, and Charles answered evenly. "They've gone after Leslie."

James stared, stunned. "I don't understand." Some of those lords were tied to Charles through blood. How could they have just left him? "Even Buckingham?"

Charles smiled wryly. "Especially Buckingham."

James cursed and started pacing. Useless buggers.

"It's better this way, James. Enough men have lost their lives for me," he said in a self-mocking way. "I'll head for London—there are a few men who I could trust to find me a ship to the Continent."

James rubbed the back of his neck. Charles wouldn't last more than a day on his own, much less cover the hundred and forty miles to get to London. A fool would recognise him in a thrice, turn him over to Cromwell, who would ensure he met the same fate as his father. Christ and damnation.

Before James could respond, John's brother George rushed into the parlour. "Sire, grave news," he gasped. "Leslie's men were just captured at Tong Castle by a regiment of dragoons—including the men who departed this morning."

James's gut twisted. "How far away is Tong?"

"Less than three miles."

James watched helplessly as his plans to return to Elizabeth crumbled to ash. *Devil take me.* He knew he couldn't leave Charles to certain capture. What would she even think of him if he abandoned Charles now?

Pushing aside all thoughts of Warwick, James focused on what needed to be done. "We have to leave now, but not to London. The might of Cromwell's army lies between Staffordshire and London. We'd never make it."

"We?"

"I am your only chance for survival," James said grimly. "I wish that it were otherwise, but if you have a care for your life, you'll follow my lead."

"What do you have in mind?"

"We'll make our way to Wales and find you a ship bound for France. No different than Cornwall. We'll take the back roads just like the last time. We'll cut your hair and disguise you as a servant. With some measure of luck, it might serve."

"A highwayman's luck?"

James nodded. "The devil's own. Let's get going."

*

James and Charles quickly discovered that Wales was sealed off to them. Parliament had posted a thousand-pound reward for the King's capture, and dragoons were stationed at every ferry crossing. They had no choice than to return to White Ladies under the cover of darkness.

"A *thousand* pounds?" James exclaimed when John Penderell told him. They had no chance. Not only would they be dodging Cromwell's soldiers, but every enterprising cove looking to line his pockets for two lifetimes. He stared at the Penderells gathered at the table near the fire, eating their plain pottage. John offered James a bowl and a place on the bench beside him.

They couldn't stay and endanger these people, even though they were part of the Knot. Companies of dragoons scoured the area, rooting out more Scottish refugees—only a matter of time before they searched both Giffard holdings, White Ladies and the nearby hunting lodge, Boscobel House. Even with the thick copse stretched between the two houses, there were only so many trees they could hide in.

When the night settled in, James approached John Penderell. "If we were searching for a knotted wreath, where would you take us?"

"Moseley Old Hall in Wolverhampton," the servant said. "I'll make arrangements."

The next evening, John and one of his brothers brought James and Charles to Moseley. Charles had taken James's advice and switched his royal clothes for a coarse shirt, breeches and a cap. And with his hair shorn, Charles looked years younger.

As they neared the gardens of Moseley, the moonlight illuminated the pattern of the hedge maze—a knot garden. *How Elizabeth would have admired that*. Pain flared in his chest.

John led them through the orchard to the back entrance. He rapped softly on the iron-studded portal and waited. When it opened, yellow light flooded the doorstep. A man stood there, staring owl-like. The light from the candle shone on his high forehead.

"God save you, Sir Whitgreave," John said and removed his cap.

"And you, John." He looked past him to James and Charles, his attention lingering on the latter. "Welcome to Moseley. Thomas Whitgreave at your service." Twice he looked as though he wanted to bow but stopped himself in time. "Enter quickly, where unfriendly eyes will not mark you."

They stepped into a small vestibule at the base of a staircase, and Whitgreave shut the door behind them. "Being the Sabbath, my servants have retired early. None will disturb us."

Halfway up the stairs, a man waited. A plain cross hung around his neck.

Noticing James's attention, Whitgreave said, "Aye, we practise the true faith. We've had sufficient experience hiding fugitives." A wry smile twisted when he turned to Charles. "When you come into your own, I trust this won't be held against me."

"Faith, it will not be forgotten, but held against you? Never," Charles said. Before he followed his new host up the stairs, Charles laid his hand on John Penderell's shoulder. "Thank you for everything you've done for me. When I come into my own, you and yours will be rewarded for your loyalty."

John reddened and nodded, suddenly tongue-tied.

James offered his hand to John. "I too am in your debt, more than I'll ever be able to repay."

"No debt between men of the Knot," John said, gripping his hand. "Consider it a payment in full for what the Giffards owe you for one of their own. God save you."

For a moment, James hesitated, thinking to ask if John could deliver a letter to Elizabeth for him. Too risky. He'd find another opportunity.

*

James stood by the window of the guest room, restlessness gnawing at him. Whitgreave sat with him, keeping watch while Charles slept in the canopied bed. Behind them, a small fire crackled in the hearth and illuminated the wainscoting panel that hid the priest hole. Plates with biscuit crumbs and glasses with the last of the sack were left on a table. A backgammon board had been pushed aside.

James hated this wait. Maybe at night, he thought, he'd slip out to the stables and go for a ride on Sovereign. They could explore the trails leading to their next safe house, Bentley Hall. *Fool if you believe that will settle matters.* James tapped his knuckle against the windowsill. Warwick may as well have been half a world away—Elizabeth was cut off from him. He really didn't give a damn about the trails.

Sit tight, he reminded himself. No need to fuel the servants' curiosity more than they had.

Whitgreave had assured Charles that he'd keep their identity a secret from his staff, but with all the Royalist fugitives in the area, it wouldn't be hard to guess that the new houseguests had come from Worcester. James hoped that this was the extent of their suspicion. With the priest hole built into the room and a priest in residence, the servants were accustomed to turning a blind eye to the family's outlawed practises. Still, they couldn't rely on it, given the posted reward. Fortune had a way of testing loyalties with a finer edge than religion.

"We should hear from Colonel Lane of Bentley shortly," Whitgreave broke the silence.

James nodded. *After Bentley, where next?* Ultimately, they needed to reach Bristol to find a ship bound for the Continent before Cromwell closed the ports.

"You hate sitting still, don't you, Major?"

James broke from his thoughts. "It's a personal failing of mine." Crossing his arms across his chest, he faced their host. Over the past two days, he'd had a chance to observe Whitgreave. The way he folded his hands, carefully smoothed a book before he laid it down or adjusted the bottle of sack on the table all bespoke of a minute attention to detail. And yet, according to a comment made by John Penderell, Whitgreave worked his fields like a tenant. "You have not always been a farmer."

"Nay," Whitgreave said. "My training is in the law, but I no longer practise."

"Change of heart?"

Whitgreave sighed and crossed his legs. "Hardly. Farming keeps the estate running and my household fed. But I enjoy the quietness between harvest and planting when I can return to my books for a time. Only then I find myself going through farming guides instead of treatises."

"Why did you leave it?"

Whitgreave worried a loose thread on his breeches. "I'd have to forswear my religion to continue practicing. 'Twas the faith of my father and his before him. I owed them not to revoke that for which they fought. Not for my gain, at least. An unfortunate choice, but there you have it."

James looked down at the floor.

From behind them in the room, Charles cleared his throat. "I'm learning a great deal on this journey, Whitgreave. Come here and we'll talk further."

James turned his attention to the window, where his reflection cast against the glass. A man who had discarded every blessing stared back.

A movement through the trees caught his attention—a ribbon of russet cantering towards Moseley.

"Dragoons!" James hissed and slammed his back against the wall.

Whitgreave rushed to the window in time to see them turn down the lane. He paled and slipped behind the curtains. "Faith, there's an entire company of them—and a priest-catcher."

James swore. *Clever bastards.* They were facing a thorough search.

"Will they find the priest hole?" Charles asked, leaping for the secret compartment.

"Pray they do not." Whitgreave seized a candle and helped Charles spring the latch. The wainscoting swung open on well-oiled hinges.

James cast an eye into the hidden compartment built beneath the floorboards. Rough bedding had been placed in there just in case. Barely enough for two grown men, but better than the alternative. Charles scrambled down into the compartment. Just as James lowered himself into the hole, a hard knock sounded on the door,

"One moment," Whitgreave called over his shoulder. He handed James the candle before shutting them in.

James crouched in the tight space and pressed his ear to the opening. Though the sounds were muffled, he could easily make out the voices. Whitgreave raised his voice for their benefit.

"What is it?"

"My lord, dragoons demand an audience," the maid's voice wavered.

"Have they said what they want?"

"Sir, they have questions about your probation. They claim you were at Worcester."

"But I wasn't," Whitgreave said sharply. "Did you not tell them so?"

"Aye, but they are not convinced."

After a pause, he said, "I'll come and sort out this matter."

"Shall I close up here?"

James pictured the girl staring at the hidden room.

"Tidy up quick, but leave the door open. They shouldn't think that we have anything to hide."

Clever man. James heard their footsteps lead out of the room, followed by silence.

"An excuse for them to search the house?" Charles whispered.

"Aye, my guess, too. If they find this hole, they'll not go empty-handed." James drew his pistols, and by the light of the wavering candle primed them.

"What are you doing?"

"I'll get two shots, but no more." James handed Charles his cloak. "If they come, cover yourself and lie flat. In the confusion, they may think I'm the only quarry in the hole."

James held his breath, straining to hear every sound. A half hour stretched into an hour, then two. James's legs began to cramp. *What are they waiting for?* If he had been chomping on the bit before, he crawled out of his skin now. He glanced over his shoulder to Charles, who shrugged a question. James shook his head. *Nothing.*

The candle flame started dipping and darting. James heard running footsteps, then felt a hiss of air. He motioned to Charles to hide under the cloak and snuffed out the light.

The darkness swallowed them. James prepared to spring. The footsteps stopped at the panel. James aimed for the centre of the door and drew back both hammers. The latch snapped, and the compartment opened to reveal Whitgreave. His eyes widened when he saw the pistols levelled against him.

Exhaling, James lowered his weapons. "What happened?"

Whitgreave looked dishevelled, and there was a tear in his sleeve. "They left." When Whitgreave offered his hand to help them out, James noticed how it trembled. "Dear God, I don't want to go through that again."

"They're gone?" Charles asked. "Are you sure?"

"Aye, sire."

"Did they leave anyone behind, perhaps in the stables?" James asked.

"Nay, though the priest-catcher spent some time questioning my stableman. The dear fellow claimed all horses belonged to me."

"What happened?" James asked again.

"They claimed I fought with the King at Worcester and very nearly searched the house for fugitives. I urged them to enquire with my neighbours. Thank God they vouched for me."

"A miracle," Charles said.

"We can't press our luck. They may return," James said, adjusting the weapons at his belt. "We leave as soon as it gets dark."

Chapter Thirty

Day seven.

At the last safe house, Bentley Hall, James and Charles gained an entourage and a travel pass to Bristol courtesy of their host, Colonel Lane. Over ninety miles lay between them and a fast ship.

Initially, the travel pass was meant for Colonel Lane's sister, Jane, her escort, Harry Lascelles, and her servants. The lady had long ago made plans to visit a close friend who was expecting her first child. It was a stroke of luck that James and Charles could join the party under the travel pass. Colonel Lane entrusted Jane and Lascelles with the truth of Charles's identity. James had expressed concern over too many people knowing the secret, but Colonel Lane vouched for them. When his other sister, Withy, and her husband, John Petre, unexpectedly showed up, intending to join their travel party until Stratford, Colonel Lane drew the line for confidences. He simply introduced Charles as William Jackson, the son of his tenant farmer.

James exchanged his buff coat for livery emblazoned with the Lane family crest while Charles was placed in charge of Jane's horse. Charles had adopted the mien of a commoner surprisingly well, even down to the flavour of his speech. James had caught him practicing his phrasing when he thought no one was within earshot.

The moment the party crossed into Warwickshire, James experienced a tightness in his chest. Fifteen short miles to Warwick, but his road did not lie there. Three hours of brisk riding and he could be home. He gripped his reins and kept to the agreed route, south through Stratford. The pain did not ease.

The farther south they rode, the more dragoons they passed along the highway. James's skin crawled whenever their party drew attention, but with effort, he maintained an unruffled mien. The presence of the women blunted the dragoons' suspicions, and they were allowed to continue without challenge.

Town after town, the news grew increasingly grim. Cromwell had deployed his troops in a full-scale manhunt to find the King. Even the townspeople spoke of nothing other than the thousand-pound reward.

Charles claimed to be flattered by the sum, giving James leave to turn him in if he was short of funds.

"I'm waiting for them to raise the stakes," James had retorted when they were alone. "A thousand is hardly worth the bother. Now at two thousand, watch your back, Stuart."

"That's William Jackson to you." Charles grinned. "How much for a Royalist officer?"

"A short drop at the scaffold."

"I have you there."

He did at that.

When they neared Stratford, an overwhelming sadness tugged at James. Without immediately realising it, he slowed his pace. Keeping Sovereign on the main road became unbearable when he saw half a dozen routes to Warwick. *Only twelve miles from Elizabeth.*

They reached the village of Wootton Wawen, where the road took a sudden turn through the parish. When they came in sight of the town, James reined Sovereign in sharply. A barricade—formed by a full regiment of dragoons.

Christ's teeth.

Charles drew his horse alongside James and pushed his cap off his forehead. Jane craned her head over his shoulder while Lascelles and Petre pulled up on either side. "What do you think?" he asked James. "Turn back?"

"Of course we must, sirrah," Petre's voice rose, and he started backing up his horse. "I will not go past those soldiers."

James lifted his brow in surprise. Petre was a soft-spoken man content to let his wife decide on the thickness of his meat. This was no time to assert an opinion. "We must go forward," James said. "For certain, the red shanks have marked us already. They'll wonder if we were to show our backs and may even send a trooper to question us."

Charles's expression was grim. "We brazen it out, then." He glanced over his shoulder at Jane, who rode pillion behind him. "With your permission, mistress."

Jane chewed her bottom lip but gave a small nod and a nervous smile. "My safety is in your keeping, William Jackson."

"I refuse," Petre said. "I will not place myself within reach of their rough handling. Never again. My wife and I will turn back. God save you."

James scowled. He could hardly drag the fellow along with them. Hopefully, the man's retreat wouldn't tell against them. "Lascelles? Which road will you take?" James stared hard, silently willing him to choose in their favour. They couldn't afford another defection.

Lascelles looked at Jane and the retreating Petres. Grimly, he nodded. "Lead on."

All in or not at all. James adjusted his hat to sit at a jaunty angle and held the reins in his left hand while his right rested casually on this thigh. With the others following close behind, he started down the last half mile to the village. He kept Sovereign at a smart trot, not too fast so the dragoons would note his rush, yet not too slow that they would wonder at his hesitation. Just the right touch, like skipping stones in a stream. His stomach flipped as he remembered Elizabeth at the riverbank. *Focus...*

Ahead, the dragoons spotted their party and fanned out to block the road. The muscles between James's shoulder blades tensed. *Relax, or they will smell fear.*

He rode up to the leader and brought Sovereign to a halt. "God save you, Captain," he said, tipping his hat.

"And you, good sir," the soldier replied, his chest puffing out. "'Tis only cornet."

Of course. James smiled. "Cornet, then, well met." He kept his attention on the sentry instead of the other dragoons gathered near.

"Where are you headed?" he asked, taking note of their numbers.

"We are for Bristol. My lady is expected in the home of her close friends, the Nortons. We have papers if you care to see them," James said.

"Normally, I wouldn't insist, but with cavalier fugitives still at large...,"

James forced himself to relax while the cornet examined the pass. The soldier lifted his eyes from the paper and glanced at the party, his lips moving as though he were counting. The man frowned and consulted the pass again. *Did they have the right numbers?* Colonel Lane had assured

James that everything was in order. Fool that he hadn't checked. A cold film coated his brow.

"What news of the road ahead?" James asked lightly.

"Rather quiet when we passed."

"With so many soldiers, I shouldn't wonder." James chuckled. "The Scots haven't invaded again, have they? I've assured the lady's brother that no harm shall befall her."

"That scurvy lot?" The man handed the papers back to James. "Nay, don't you think on it. Running with their tail tucked between their legs, more like. We're still picking up a few here and there."

"I wish you well in your search," James said. "By your leave, we shall press on."

"Carry on, then." The cornet patted Sovereign's flank and tipped his hat at James. Nodding to the soldiers, the way opened up.

The hairs on the back of James's neck lifted as they passed wave after wave of russet red. By sheer grit, he maintained their leisurely pace and refrained from glancing back. They entered the village and found three more companies of soldiers. He braced himself for a whistle and a shout of discovery, but none came.

Fifty yards away, the road curled around a church. As they neared the building, a man descending the steps caught James's attention. Though his head was lowered, James recognised him immediately. *Hammond.* James lowered the brim of his hat and averted his head. He couldn't believe it.

James's eyes darted to the road ahead. Penned in. Two companies already mounted. They'd seal the road quicker than his party could charge past. James loosened his pistol from its holster. Hammond reached the last step just as their group passed directly in front. One shout and Charles's life would be forfeit. James looped Sovereign's reins around the saddle's pommel and gripped the butt of his pistol. *One shout and the bugger gets a shot between the eyes.*

Hammond paused and patted down the side of his coat. *Any moment, he'll look up.* James tensed, bracing himself for action. Hammond frowned and withdrew a pamphlet from the inside of his coat. With his attention drawn to the paper, he flipped through the pages while James and the most wanted man in England rode past.

James turned his head slightly as they cleared the lieutenant's position. Hammond continued on his way, oblivious.

There was indeed salvation in one of Hammond's tracts.

*

Day forty.

The cold wind carried a blunt edge, uncompromising like the giant stone circle it whistled through. The locals called it Stonehenge. James had never seen anything like it. Massive sandstone blocks punctuated a grassy field where nary a pebble could be found. The strange sentinels were as foreign in this landscape as a Warwickshire man in Salisbury. *Elizabeth would have liked to see these.*

James sat on the flat rock in the centre of the stone circle. Six days of waiting while local Royalists, men trusted with the secret, searched for a ship. So many starts and stops. Nothing had been found for them in Bristol, but at Bridport, they came close. Arrangements had been made only to have the captain fail to show. A replacement was no sooner found when the vessel was commandeered by Parliament to carry troops across to Jersey to break the Royalist resistance there. Had fortune finally deserted them?

James looked around the stone circle. Their present host, the mistress of Heale House, told him that time didn't have the same meaning here. He hoped it was true, though he feared it was not.

Charles occupied himself by measuring the distance between the giant rocks. Upon their return to Heale each evening, and long after the servants were abed, Charles worked on his calculations. His was a furious pursuit of occupation, arising from the same frustration that James struggled against.

James felt crushed by a growing lethargy he couldn't shake. His sleep had been full of dreams, none of which offered comfort. Elizabeth would have blamed the influence of these stones had she been here. She would have placed her hand on the pitted and worn surface and turned to him with a smile. "Do you sense it?" she would have asked, her head slanted to one side. He could almost feel her warmth. A sharp band squeezed his chest.

James reclined on the flat stone and gazed up at the cool autumn sky. Already the thirteenth of the month. When had October happened? Just yesterday, it seemed, he had charged a wall of Parliament soldiers outside Sidbury Gate. When had forty days disappeared?

Charles returned from his exercise and sat beside James. "I'm not sure how long we can go on like this."

Normally, James would have tried to reassure him, but this time he didn't have it in him. "Aye, time is running out."

Charles wrapped himself in his cloak. "They say ancient Kings are buried here. There are ghosts within this circle."

Ghosts. Spirits or regrets? "You needn't fear them. They will respect your claim to this place."

Charles thought for a moment and nodded. "My father did not deserve his fate." With a broken stick, he traced a pattern on the pitted stone. "He was a good man, no matter his faults."

James sat up and drew one knee to his chest. *No matter his faults.* He still had the letter Sir Piers had written before his death. Aye, his father had faults too, but more courage than James had realised. "How did you hear of his death?"

Charles ran his hand through his shortened black hair. "They must have drawn lots as to who would tell me. The chaplain, poor bastard, lost." He dug his stick into a fissure in the rock. "He stood before me, stammering and fumbling for words. Then he mastered himself and began again, only this time he started by calling me 'Your Majesty.' He didn't need to continue." He looked through the stone sentinels across the lonely plain. "A week before my father's execution, I sent a blank letter to Cromwell and another to Parliament."

"Blank?"

"Aye, save for one thing written at the bottom."

"What was that?"

"My signature."

A chill crept down James's spine. Charles would have given everything away for the sake of his father. James's father had thrown away his honour and pride, all for him. What had James done for those he loved? What had he given Elizabeth except an uncertain fate?

Charles walked away, straight-backed. *A signature on a page.* James should have been angered that this man, whose legacy they'd spent eight years fighting for, would have so easily relinquished it. But as James watched, he knew him to be the greater man.

*

The *Surprise*, a seaworthy barque, was moored upriver from the small fishing village of Shoreham. Her master, Captain Tattersell, was reputed to know every landing on both sides of the Channel, legal or otherwise, and he guaranteed discretion.

An hour before dawn, James and Charles slipped through the shuttered village with Lord Wilmot bringing up the rear. They had found one of the King's gentlemen in Brighton just before their meeting with Tattersell. There, bold as day, an undisguised Wilmot rode through the bustling streets of Brighton, not even attempting subterfuge. Charles had been thrilled to find his old companion and friend. James wasn't entirely cheered. Normally, James would have admired such brazenness, but he suspected that it had less to do with a calculated knowledge of human nature and more with overwhelming hubris.

The three men left the village and turned on the shore road with its marshy smell of river and mud. They startled a pair of oystercatchers. The black-and-white birds flapped their wings and, with a cry, beat across the river. The road dwindled down to a rough trail, allowing for only single file. In another half mile, they came to a dead tree.

"We're here," James said in a low voice. He looked around as he dismounted. Deep shadows clung to the river. The only sound was the lapping of the water against the bank. He loosened Sovereign's girth and stroked the horse's neck. A good steed, the best he had ever owned. Tattersell had arranged to send a boy to collect the horses after they sailed. For a silver half crown, the captain promised to deliver a letter to Elizabeth.

James had the letter tucked in his saddlebag. It started with *I will return* and ended with *I love you*. When, he couldn't say. The last six weeks had proven that he could not easily ride into Warwick and take Elizabeth away with him. He'd return when it was safe—perhaps spring or by the summer. For now, he could do nothing except bring her heartache and danger. She was safe at Ellendale. He'd have to take comfort in that.

Charles tied his mount to one of the gnarly branches on the tree. He constantly looked over his shoulder at the road behind them. "What if the captain doesn't come?"

"Of course he'll come. The purse was generous," Wilmot said. "If he's a base scoundrel, we'll simply find another ship."

James rubbed his stubbled beard. "He'll be here if I read the man aright. He doesn't look the type to change his mind with a shift in wind." At first light, the captain had promised.

James didn't want to admit that the captain's recognition of Charles had unsettled him. In six weeks, Tattersell had been the only one to see past the rough clothes. A thousand pounds was more than ten times the price of their inflated passage. James loosened his sword in his scabbard just in case. His doglock pistols were already primed.

As the sky began to lighten, the shape of a prow lifted from the darkness. Wilmot nudged Charles. "Look."

"Thank God."

The wind picked up. James strained to hear beyond the slapping of water and the creaking of a mast. "Riders." He cocked his pistols and positioned himself in front of Charles. Wilmot unsheathed his sword, the courtier suddenly replaced by a capable swordsman.

Five riders approached with Tattersell in the lead, all sailors by the look of them. When the party arrived, the captain swung down from his mount. A rough-hewn man with a healthy girth, Tattersell reminded James of Henry.

"Well met, lads," he said, shaking James's hand. His manner didn't change when he turned to Charles. "Are you set?"

"Aye, I'm at your disposal."

Tattersell grinned. From the inside of his coat, he withdrew a red scrap of linen and waved it at the barque. He waited a moment, then repeated the signal. Across the river, a sailor appeared at the rail and lifted his arm in the air. Following a sharp whistle, the sound no different than water birds calling out to one another, more men came into view. Together they lowered the longboat into the river. A pair of sailors descended a ladder and climbed into the craft.

James watched as they pulled on the oars, heard the creaking of the oarlocks and the splashing of the water. Odd, this detached calm as he waited to leave. Away from Elizabeth.

The longboat drew closer. James saw the sleek line of its prow. The sailors bent over, hauling in unison, their oars rising and dipping. Elizabeth's father had been a shipwright, probably made hundreds of crafts like this one. James stared at the water. The rising dawn was reflected on its surface.

The longboat reached the shore, and Tattersell waded into the river to pull it in. "All aboard," he called over his shoulder. Charles followed after him and took hold of the gunwale. Before he hauled himself over, he glanced at James standing on the riverbank. "France awaits, my friend. Time to embark."

But James couldn't move. Every nerve screamed against it.

"James, come on!"

He couldn't do it. James couldn't leave without Elizabeth. He had once told her that he didn't give a damn how many dragoons were stationed between them. Time to prove it.

"I'm staying."

"What?" Charles stepped away from the gunwale.

"Sire, what are you doing?" Wilmot called out, standing up in the longboat. "Get into the boat."

Tattersell struggled to keep the craft from drifting. "We have to leave now, or we'll lose the tide."

Charles ignored them both and waded out of the water. "James, have you gone mad? There's the boat. It'll take us to France, and the bloody redcoats won't get us. You do remember they're chasing us?"

James shook his head. He was a damned fool, but for the first time in a very long time, he knew his path. "My road lies to Warwick, back to my wife. I won't leave her behind. I gave her my word."

Charles gripped James by the arm. "You rather like the idea of wearing a rope collar? A traitor's knot?"

"I might as well be dead if I leave her," James said.

Charles swore. "You'll come back, man. In the spring or summer. The Roundheads will move on to other matters, and you can slip back."

"I will *not* leave her," James said. "If I go now, I can never return."

"What good will you be to her if they capture you?" Charles pressed. "If they discover how you've helped me, Cromwell will display your severed head at Whitehall. Come with us and spare her the horror of your death."

"I'll risk it," James said. Death was not certain, but there was no life without her.

"After all you've done for me, I won't leave you to that butcher."

James smiled and placed his arm on Charles's shoulder. "Then let's make sure he never finds out. Wilmot will see you the rest of the way."

"Are you sure of this?"

"Never more sure of anything in my life." He'd be half a man without her.

"I'll never forget this."

"You should," James said. "An association with a highwayman is a crime. You're reviled as it is."

Charles finally smiled. "Our secret, then." He drew James into a hearty embrace. "If there is anything I can do for you, I will. Godspeed, friend."

"May God save and protect you."

After a last clasp of James's shoulder, Charles returned to the longboat and pushed away.

James watched as the *Surprise* set sail and knew a swelling hope. Time to head home.

Chapter Thirty-One

Elizabeth rubbed her forehead to ease the dull throbbing. She hoped to have finished her mending before the light failed, but Thomas had distracted her. From his cot, the child kept pulling the hound, Sena, by the ears, and for a reward received an enthusiastic wash by a sticky pink tongue. This was the third time she had to nudge them apart.

She lowered her sewing to her lap and closed her eyes. *So tired.* Each moment was a trial, and every night she tumbled into bed grateful for the hours of darkness. *When will it get better?*

Elizabeth put aside the smock. She glanced over at the hearth where Jennet stirred the contents of an iron cauldron. The cooking fire warmed the room, and puffs of grey steam curled above the pot. The earthy aroma of stewed rabbit and thyme filled the air, yet it failed to whet Elizabeth's appetite.

She should help her. The men would be returning from the barn soon. Roger, Davis and Sheffield had stayed on as Edward thought it safer until the patrols eased up. Beyond that, they had no plans except that they couldn't return to their old lives.

The old life. Elizabeth fought against the melancholy. She couldn't afford to dwell on the past.

Edward came inside and pulled up a stool across from Elizabeth. Sena rose and took her place beside him, and he absently scratched behind the hound's ears.

"Lieutenant Hammond is making enquiries," he said. "He's searching the shire for you."

Elizabeth rubbed her arms, suddenly cold. "'Tis well that I'm not in Warwick, then."

Edward sniffed. "He's posted a reward of five pounds for news of your whereabouts."

Startled, Elizabeth looked up. Her mouth curled bitterly. "I should be offended. He offered ten for James." Though it hurt to say his name, she clutched at it like a prized possession.

"Sooner or later, lass, they'll turn their sights to Coventry," Edward said. "We're not so isolated that you can remain hidden for much longer. I fear for you and the boy."

Elizabeth nodded. She had been thinking about this for several days and knew their time neared an end. "I should return to Weymouth. It would be safer for us there." People would believe the worst of her when she returned with a fatherless child. Then there was the matter of how she would support herself. Old Nick could be counted on to drop off a fish or two—an extra bit of catch, he'd say, to save her the embarrassment of charity. She'd even break her grandmother's rule and sell her tinctures to feed her son.

"I should make preparations to leave before the winter sets in," she said dully. "I'll send word to Weymouth."

"You won't be going alone, lass," Edward said. He held out his finger to his grandson and smiled when the boy brought it to his mouth. "I'll be coming with you."

Elizabeth blinked, not believing she heard him right. "What do you mean?"

Edward braced his hands on his knees. "I have nothing left here, but I mean to do right by my boy."

Elizabeth's eyes misted, and she wiped away a single tear that escaped her. "I can't ask you to give up your home for us. Not your land."

"And why not?" Edward said. "I have no tenants, no hired hands. No one else counting on me. You and the child are the only family I have." His mouth tightened. "I've never had a daughter, and I mean to be a proper grandfather to your boy."

Family. Elizabeth swallowed the lump in her throat, unable to speak.

"Weymouth will be a fresh start for us both," Edward said. "While I live, none will question the child's name, nor will either of you starve."

Elizabeth couldn't speak. She reached across and squeezed Edward's hand.

*

Edward arranged for a private carriage to take them south at week's end before the worst of the autumn rains washed out the roads. Elizabeth protested over the expense, but he wouldn't hear of his grandson being at the mercy of the elements. In that, she was glad. The late autumn dampness settled deep into the bones, and she didn't want to risk Thomas's health.

In the gravel lane, a messenger now waited to take her letters to Weymouth. She had made an effort to write Kate, wasting three sheets of precious paper before settling on a simple request: Could she let the old cottage from them? Galling yet necessary. And because Elizabeth couldn't be certain of Kate's response—or rather her husband's mood—a second letter had been written to Old Nick.

Elizabeth stared across the harvested fields. At the thought of leaving, a melancholy settled over her shoulders like a heavy cloak. Too much of her remained here. A vital piece of her.

Sheffield had joined Edward and the rider, and the three men were engaged in a discussion of the roads. Tomorrow, James's men would be setting out for Wales. Elizabeth had maintained a guarded distance from them. Part of her hungered to know about James's time in Scotland—anything, however trivial—but she knew that enquiries would only erode the sandbank that separated her from despair. Ultimately, a question of why hung over these three men. *Why had they escaped and not my James?* She hated herself for the thought.

Elizabeth drew her shawl tighter across her shoulders.

A crunch of footsteps made her turn her head. Roger Cantrell stopped beside her, content to wait by the gate instead of joining the others.

Normally, Elizabeth would have made an excuse and taken her leave, but this time she stayed. "Tell me what you knew of my husband."

Roger proceeded to tell her of James's command and how he had earned the regard of his King and the dedication of his men. "He carried your token with him always," Roger said. "It had become grey from the grit of the road, but he never put it aside."

Elizabeth lowered her head. She remembered how James had kissed the satchel when she pressed it in his hand before he left. The memory was another stab to her heart.

The messenger lifted his hand in farewell and rode down the lane. Edward and Sheffield started back to the house.

"Work to do, lass, best get on with it," Edward said with a wink as he passed.

"Come inside, mistress," Jennet said.

"In a moment." Elizabeth didn't want to return to the house. Something rooted her at the gate. Perhaps it was the curl of wood smoke in the damp air or the rustling of the fallen leaves scattering across the gravel pathway.

Sena padded to her side and, settling on her haunches, stared in the direction of the road. Elizabeth rested her hand atop her head. The hound's unrelenting attention to the empty road sent a chill down Elizabeth's spine.

*

James halted Sovereign and looked around the wooded tract that led to Moot Hill. Only the hardiest of gold and orange leaves still clung to the trees. In places, the rains had smudged the trail, but the road held fast, undaunted. A shriek from a sparrow hawk cut through the stillness of the forest. A full year had passed since he had left. Nothing seemed changed.

Clicking the reins, James pressed on to his old campsite to water and take a brief rest. Though he could reach Ellendale in a couple of hours, he dared not go farther until darkness had settled. Dusk couldn't come too soon.

Over the past week, James had ridden late in the night, slipping into barns for a few hours' rest and vacating them before the cock crowed. Time enough to consider his decision. *You're a fool.* And yet his uplifted heart made him not care. Fool to think he could stay away from Elizabeth. No more running. He meant to prove that he had as much courage returning from war as his father had by not leaving. James had been in tight quarters before. He'd steer their way clear of this. If not Wales, then perhaps Cornwall.

James reached his old campsite. The clearing was mostly as he had left it except the charred logs were scattered past the firestones. The brook was cold and clean, and bending to take a drink, he welcomed its bite. It had been a long journey.

The wind whistled through the hollow. James tightened his cloak, but the cold still penetrated. A small, contained fire would not be seen from the road a mile away. After gathering dry kindling, he bent over the char cloth with his flint and steel. A spark ignited and spread through the wool. Before long, flames were licking over the kindling, sizzling and crackling, spreading their warmth.

James held out his hands over the small flame, and his mind began to drift. *Tonight.* He'd be with her soon, he thought impatiently. James closed his eyes, thinking of Elizabeth's warmth and her passion. In a few hours, he would lose himself in her again. He released a ragged breath. No choice but to wait until moonrise.

James looked up to gauge the hour, then frowned when he saw the rising billow of smoke as the wood burned off the damp. *Christ's teeth.* Where was his head?

He shifted, about to bank the fire, when he heard a twig snap. The back of his nape prickled. He slipped his hand into his boot and grasped the hilt of the blade. Another sound—the rustle of leaves. With one fluid motion, he leapt to his feet, dagger drawn.

Hammond stepped into the clearing as one might enter a fair. "Welcome home, highwayman." He motioned to a half dozen dragoons, who emerged from the cover of trees.

James tensed. "You missed me, Roundhead. I'm touched." He gauged the distance between him and Sovereign. "If it's the reward you're after, you should have left your friends behind. Now you'll have to share."

Hammond shook his head and scraped the heel of his boot against a rock. "Every cur returns to its kennel. I was counting on that. And to think, I nearly rode past this time," he said. "I trust you enjoyed your long sojourn in Scotland, treasonous dog."

James readjusted his bearings. He hated being unbalanced. Time to return the favour. "I answer to Major Hart. Promoted by His Majesty, Charles Stuart, rightful King of England, Scotland and Ireland." He took satisfaction in seeing Hammond's upper lip quiver. "You should have warned me you were planning to call." He edged back. Ten paces to reach Sovereign. "I would have had a selection of dusty tracts awaiting your pleasure."

"Thoughtful," Hammond said with a sneer. "But you're best saving them for your wife. She has more need of them."

"Elizabeth?" James stopped. His gut twisted. "What do you mean?"

Hammond gloated. "I have tried to show her the light, but she insists on wallowing in the darkness of your blighted branches. Your harlot is resistant to salvation."

James balled his fists. "Call her that again and I'll rip out your tongue. She's above you in every way."

373

"The courts would disagree."

"Courts? What baseness this?"

"Justice served and a fornicator duly punished."

"She's my wife, Roundhead." An icy chill coursed down James's spine.

"A fornicator's marriage, no more," Hammond snapped.

A sick feeling seeped into him. "What have you done to her?"

"Locked her up in the gaol." Hammond sneered his triumph. "I am the Lord's instrument and wield the sword of vengeance against the ungodly."

With a snarl of rage, James lunged for Hammond.

Two dragoons leapt in his way and slammed into him. They knocked the dagger out of his grasp. James drove his knee into a groin, and the man howled and dropped. Before James could push past him, the other hauled him back and drew his knife. James shifted his weight and prepared to drive his shoulder into the man's side but froze when he heard the click of a fully cocked musket.

Hammond's carbine was levelled against him. "Soft, highwayman. I have no problem ridding Elizabeth of you."

A cold fury gripped James. "She's not yours to call by name." The dragoons twisted his arms behind his back, and he clenched his teeth to keep from crying out.

"And who has the greater right to her, heretic?" Hammond spat. "I, who fought for her soul and lost, or you, who corrupted her body and left?"

James's nostrils flared. "Where is she?"

Hammond motioned to his dragoons. "Tie the traitor up. He can walk behind his horse all the way to Warwick. Let him think on his sins as he trudges in horse shit."

"What have you done to her?"

The dragoons grabbed James roughly. They tied his hands behind his back and looped another rope around his neck, which they strapped to Sovereign. James pulled against his bonds. "Bastard! Tell me where she is!"

Hammond looked down at James from his sorrel mare. He chewed on his bottom lip before he answered. "Gone," he finally said. "Wherever she is, may she rot in a dank hole with your bastard son."

The guards marched James into the gaol cell while Hammond smirked at the door.

"Welcome to your new lodgings, highwayman," Hammond crowed as they untied his hand. "You should feel right at home here in the dank bosom of this rat-hole. These accommodations were good enough for your whore."

James lunged for Hammond, but two of the dragoons intercepted him before he could reach the Roundhead's throat. Another dragoon yanked on the rope that was still tied around James's throat, choking him. They wrestled James to the ground, and though he tried to throw them off, they still managed to slap a pair of irons around his ankles.

"Widow's alms," Hammond said referring to the shackles. "Portentous."

"Bastard," James spat as he struggled to his feet. "Base coward." Once more he tried to reach Hammond. He overstepped his chains, lost his balance and hit the ground. The sound of Hammond's laughter drove daggers through him. James pushed himself up, spitting dirt from his mouth.

One of the dragoons drew his knife and pressed the blade against James's throat. James refused to flinch and glared at the man. With a chuckle, the dragoon sliced off the rope around his neck and gathered the cords.

"You thought we'd leave you something to use against us?" Hammond sneered. "Think again."

The door clanged shut behind them, the protest of rust sliding against rust. Bellowing his rage, James slammed against the door, earning himself a bruised shoulder and a derisive laugh from the gaoler on the other side.

James paced the length of his cell like a caged animal. His shackles rattled with every step. Ten paces by ten. A floor of mouldy straw and a pallet not worthy of the name. A stinking chamber pot in the corner. For a light, he had half a tallow candle.

The realization hit him like a fist to the gut. The bastards had imprisoned his wife—here in this pit. He leaned against the damp wall and sank to his haunches. *Bastards. What had they done to her?* The memory of clothes scattered in the baggage train at Naseby burned in his mind. The terrified eyes of Lillian, sole survivor of the massacre, blurred until she became Elizabeth, cowering under a blackthorn tree. James tipped his head back against the wall and howled his pain. Tears streaked down his cheeks.

James buried his head in his hands. This was all because of him. He had left the woman he loved at the mercy of depraved bastards even when he knew they couldn't be trusted. With their son...

A son. He had a son. But where were they? The coldness of the wall seeped into his bones.

What have I done?

Chapter Thirty-Two

Elizabeth carried the last of the linens in her basket, folded and ready to be packed in the trunk. The wicker rode on her hip as she left the washhouse, and Sena followed a step behind. She was about to turn towards the farmhouse when a horse and wagon in the distance caught her attention.

She wandered over to the gate. The wagon clattered down the lane, pulled by a sturdy shire. Henry?

Elizabeth couldn't move. Her limbs were leaden. She clutched the basket tighter, and the hound brushed against her. Except for sending Henry word of her whereabouts, she had not seen the landlord. He vowed to stay away so as not to alert Hammond of her whereabouts unless there was an emergency.

The wagon rolled to a halt. Henry's shoulders slumped forward. He climbed slowly down from his perch.

Elizabeth started shaking. "It's James?"

"Mistress—"

"Pray, did they give him a Christian burial?" Her voice cracked. *Or did they throw him in a hole with the others*?

Henry crossed the distance between them. "He's not dead."

Elizabeth dropped the basket, spilling the linens into the mud. Her knees buckled, and she gripped the gate for support. At her side, the hound started howling. "He's alive?" *James is alive*? Henry's expression still had not changed. No smiles, no relief—his manner still spoke of grief. "Where is he?"

"Warwick gaol."

Hammond. She swayed, and Henry steadied her. The hound ran around in circles, barking madly.

"He's not been harmed," Henry said, gripping her arms. "They're keeping him a close prisoner."

"When?"

"Yesterday, at Moot Hill. On his way home."

Oh my God. He was returning to me. He was coming home. Her head started swimming.

Edward came running from the barn. "What's happened?"

Elizabeth tried to steady herself. The ringing in her ears drowned Henry's words to Edward.

"My boy." Edward rubbed a hand across his brow. The grief he had been holding back finally cracked, and his hand trembled. "My boy."

Henry's face darkened. "He's being held with charges of high treason and highway robbery."

"High treason?" Elizabeth shut her eyes and leaned against the post. *He'll be hanged, drawn and quartered.* The nightmare closed in. Hammond would not rest until he had posted James's severed head atop the East Gate. She wanted to retch.

"He could plead his innocence and throw himself on the county," Edward said. "Or plead the right of clergy and read any passage they put before him." Edward turned away, his expression taut. "Others have saved themselves with such a defence."

"The lad won't be let off that easily," Henry said. "They are congratulating themselves in Warwick even now."

The darkness smothered Elizabeth once again. *There's no hope. Where there is Hammond, there is no hope. Vengeance is mine, saith the Lord.* "Hammond will never be satisfied until James's blood is spilled."

"I will not give up on my boy," Edward said fiercely.

Elizabeth needed space, a wounded creature needing to lick its wounds. She wanted to pound on the stone wall and scream to the wind. She stumbled a few paces away from Edward and Henry—two good-hearted men who were at a frantic loss as to what to do. How could she lose him twice? It would tear the last of her apart.

I will not give up on him. Not again.

Overhead, a grey harrier circled, its large speckled wings outstretched as it glided over the fallow fields. In a blink, the bird swooped, skimming the top of the brown grasses before darting in to snatch a field mouse. With a triumphant shriek, it soared to the sky, prey clutched in its talons.

A fierce fury seized Elizabeth.

Hammond must not win. He was a malignant tumour that needed lancing before it corrupted healthy flesh. He would not take James from her. Hammond would not ruin Thomas's life before he was even out of his cot—he would not rob her very soul. It fell to her to draw out his poison.

Hammond will not win. She'd destroy him first.

*

The upper hallway of Coventry's Fox and Hound was deserted. Elizabeth insisted that Edward wait for her in the common room. At first, he balked, but when she remained steadfast, he capitulated to avoid a public argument. Her cold resolve had deepened since hearing of James's capture. There was only one course of action, and she would not fail.

Elizabeth knocked on one of the guest rooms. She didn't wait long before she heard footsteps crossing to the door. The portal opened, revealing Nathaniel Lewis, partially clothed in a silk velvet dressing gown. He drew back, surprised. Elizabeth smiled to herself. *This has started in my favour.*

"I ordered a bath. You aren't the chambermaid."

"Kind of you to notice, Master Lewis," Elizabeth said. "The inn's kitchens are busy. It may take some time." Not waiting for an invitation, she walked past him into the room. "You have enough time to request a handful of dried comfrey for your bath." She pointed to the slight rash on his neck. "'Twill soothe the redness."

Nathaniel closed the door and tightened the belt around his waist. By the time he faced her, he had assumed his unruffled composure. "You are a healer, I recall. Is it your custom to frequent inns providing unsolicited advice?"

"Only for barristers who have the ear of a certain justice of the peace."

Nathaniel's expression remained unfathomable. "I have heard about that matter."

That matter. Elizabeth was once again in Weymouth market, passing women who whispered behind their hands. *Shame about that matter.* "Put a name to it, Master Lewis. I prefer plain speech. My husband is in the gaol facing charges of high treason and highway robbery."

"And?"

"We need an advocate."

"Your understatement is charming." Nathaniel walked to the hearth. "Why come to me? Why not petition Sir Richard directly, though I warn you this will be a notch in his cap when he delivers your husband to the assize courts. A famous highwayman, now traitor to the Commonwealth.

The chapbook printers are rubbing their hands in glee," Nathaniel said. "And then there's our Lieutenant Hammond, who is keen to redeem himself from that Coventry debacle with Sir Piers. He bears a strong rancour against your husband and will want his satisfaction."

"I'm confused. Is it your suggestion that I appeal to Sir Richard?"

"Most women in your position would."

"I'm no fool," Elizabeth said. "Justice is an arbitrary concept."

Nathaniel smiled. "Now you have my interest."

"You are a man with connections at Westminster, are you not?" She waited for his acknowledgment, but he remained noncommittal. "Perhaps you can encourage the circuit judge to be merciful. James fought at Worcester with other Royalists. Let him share the same fate as the other captured prisoners." *At least he'll be alive.*

"The Tower is an unhealthy place, and the colonies, to where they will eventually be shipped, even less so," Nathaniel said. "Cromwell isn't offering mercy, I can assure you." He approached the sideboard and tipped a draught of golden wine into a cup. "A glass of sack?" He offered it to her, but she shook her head. "Then there's the matter of the rumours floating about London."

"Rumours?"

"Cromwell seems to have misplaced a king."

"I spare no sympathy for him," Elizabeth said. "But I fail to see the connection to my husband."

Nathaniel took a sip of the amber liquid and watched her over the rim. "Your husband is now a major, appointed to the King's Life Guard. Had you heard?"

"I have," she said softly, her hard-earned detachment easing.

"Charles Stuart has only recently arrived in France. Rumours have closely linked the disappearance and reappearance of both men, particularly since your husband has been revealed as a highwayman. Who better to hide a King than a master of passing unnoticed?"

"Coincidence."

"Rumours are founded on less," Nathaniel said. "The word circulating London is that a highwayman had a hand in the King's escape. An odd story, but you see how coincidence becomes proof when the pieces link together."

Elizabeth wished she could still believe that they couldn't convict from only hearsay and coincidence. "What now?"

"Parliament will want to question him in London. I expect they are now arranging a secure cell at Newgate," Nathaniel said. "Prepare yourself, madam, the trial and execution will not be bearable."

Elizabeth latched on to her resolve. James would do nothing less for her. "Then we must save him."

"You are no longer suggesting the role of mediator."

"Correct."

Nathaniel's expression did not change. "This is where you remind me of Sir Piers Rotherham's gaol escape."

"I wouldn't insult you in that manner, sir."

"And coin? You won't insult me by offering that, I take it?"

"Absolutely not, nor could I." She smiled when puzzlement flickered across his face. "Can you not do anything for the sake of it being right and just?"

"I am not a charity, madam." Nathaniel placed the empty glass down on the sideboard.

"And yet you have involved yourself in our affairs before," Elizabeth said. She went very still, watching Nathaniel readjust his masked expression.

"I thought you weren't going to speak of Sir Piers."

"I'm not," she said. "I was let out of the gaol a few weeks early. Do you know why?"

Nathaniel poured himself another draught of sack. "Tell me."

"Sir Richard received a letter from Chief Justice Blackmore of Westminster expressing his concerns over Sir Richard's application of the new fornication statute."

"Did the gaoler tell you this?"

"Henry filled in the gaps."

Nathaniel smiled. "The chief justice stays current with all the judicial reviews."

"I'm amazed that his interest extends to Warwickshire."

"Sometimes one must test the planks to be sure of the soundness in the floor."

"Now that you've tested the floorboards, put that knowledge to our service," Elizabeth said. "If the rumours of my husband's service to the crown are true, His Majesty will look upon your help as a personal favour."

Nathaniel considered Elizabeth. A ghost of a smile tugged the corners of his mouth, and she suspected he had made up his mind some time ago. "When shall we begin?"

*

The door creaked open, and the gaoler peeked inside with bloodshot eyes. Seeing James a safe distance in the corner, he relaxed and stepped inside. "A visitor for you."

James rose from his pallet, both fear and hope warring in his breast. *Elizabeth?* Instead, his father appeared. He went very still. Christ's teeth. He didn't need this.

"Hello, boy."

"Father."

Edward turned to the waiting gaoler. "A moment alone with my son."

The man shook his head. Lank, greasy hair hung over his stained coat. "That wasn't our deal. Get you in, we agreed—nothing more. Hammond will toss a fit on my head if he hears I've let anyone in, but he'll string up my guts if I've left you alone."

"Indeed." Edward offered his hand to the startled man. "I insist on being on good terms."

The gaoler glanced down. When Edward stepped away, James saw the man's fist close around a coin.

"Ten minutes, then." The gaoler's sunken, pock-ridden cheeks twitched. "Less if I hear anyone coming."

Edward gave a curt nod and waited for the door to close. The heavy iron clanged shut, and a bolt slid into place. The grate in the door slid open an inch. Edward turned his head slightly before facing his son. "You're displeased to see me."

"Surprised." James contemplated his father, searching for clues to his mood. There was something different about Edward's manner—like a wolf testing its boundaries. "I can imagine your disappointment finding me here—or maybe not. How did you know?"

"How does an old hand at Irish know when the board's been set? You still play?" Edward rubbed his finger down the side of his nose.

James frowned at his father's signal to play along. He glanced at the grate. "Aye. I've become unbeatable."

"You haven't played me," Edward said. "You'd be well to mind that."

James considered his father. They hadn't had a civil conversation in nine years, yet here they were posturing about backgammon. "If the gaoler can spare us a board, then we'd prove the matter."

Edward smiled. "You were always in a rush to strike and never understood the value of a well-positioned anchor. Playing the same old running game has always been your downfall." He drew closer. "I always anticipated that in you, boy. Unless you've learned it by now, you'll never get ahead in the count. To win, you need patience and trust that with one solid roll of the dice, your opponent is one step closer to defeat."

What game are you playing, old man? "You'd be surprised by how my understanding has grown."

Edward grunted. "Is that so? Too bad you didn't prove it when you came to see me last." He paused and held his gaze. "You would have found me reasonable."

James tensed. He hadn't forgotten either the day or the reason for his visit. His father's brow rose slightly. *Could it be?* James glanced again at the door, heart racing. "You've never been reasonable."

"Hard to be when a man can't walk across his threshold without tripping across his son's troubles."

James exhaled slowly. Blood pounded through his temples. *Sweet heaven, he has them.* The relief nearly weakened his limbs. "I didn't mean for you to be so burdened."

"Really? You didn't mean for this to happen?" Edward's brow darkened in the first true sign of anger. The controlled facade finally slipped. "Not good enough, boy. A real man thinks before he acts."

Though his father didn't lay a hand on him, James nevertheless felt the sting. "I did," he hissed. "I left my *affairs* in the best order I could. I would never have done anything less, no matter what you think." It was on the tip of his tongue to blame his father—*if only you hadn't been so hard when I came to you, Elizabeth would have been safe.* He hunched his shoulders and turned away. If only he hadn't left. Raw anguish roiled in his gut. "Never mind. The tune doesn't change even all these years."

"Why should it?" Edward lifted his finger and tapped James square on the chest. "You had it in you to raise your lot—to earn a better living than mucking stables, but you never hunkered down to work for it, sweat and blood. What did you think, that glory was owed to you for the cleverness of your glib tongue? Life is a mad, hard scramble to scale a dung pile, and naught but a sliver of fortune separates a man from disaster." Edward's gaze hardened. "You're set to hang—they'll quarter you if they can. How has this played out?"

"At least I haven't reneged on my oaths," James flared. The moment he said it, he wished he could take it back. *Calm down.* He exhaled slowly and stepped away. *The fault is mine.* Lashing out at his father would not ease the guilt ravaging him. James braced his hand against the wall and picked at a piece of moss growing in the cracks of the stone. "Sorry. I know better."

"Do you?"

"Aye." James straightened and faced his father. "I do. Sir Piers wrote to me about why you refused the muster—that you didn't want to face me across the battlefield. Is that true, or did he romanticise the reason for your refusal?"

Edward's jaw twitched. "Aye, he had the right of it. But it wasn't his to tell."

"And when would you have told me, if ever?" James asked. "Why did you let me believe you were a coward?" His voice dropped. "Did my regard mean so little to you?"

Edward turned away, and for a moment James saw a tired, worn man. "When does a father need to explain himself to his son?"

A long pause hung between them. Their eyes locked. "He doesn't. Not when his son has come to understand the truth of what is important." *Even if it's too late.* And for James, an unspoken hope. He measured his words carefully so that they did not fit through the narrow space in the grate to reach the ears of the gaoler. "A son must trust that his interests are protected and kept close to his father's breast." *Please keep them safe.* He wanted to ask how she was, what his son was like. James blinked away the sudden tears.

Edward nodded. "They are—rest easy on that score."

The bar sliding against the rusty lock signalled the end of their time. "Shame to break this apart, but your time is up, old man."

Edward turned around and faced him. "I've heard things about you—how you're quick to mistreat those under your care."

The gaoler's eyes darted to James, and as quickly, he looked away. "Never mind that rap. I do my job."

James stared at the man with new eyes. He glanced around the cell, remembering who had previously occupied it.

"A warning. Any slight against a Hart will not go unpunished," Edward said with particular emphasis. "See that my boy is taken care of and there's an extra coach wheel for you. May your greed overcome your base nature. Do I make myself clear?"

"Aye," the gaoler said.

Edward met James's gaze.

James nodded. *Perfectly clear.*

*

James kept to the shadows. The cell door creaked open. A drawn dagger appeared in the gaoler's hand. The man's eyes darted around until they settled on James in the corner.

"There you be," he muttered. Annoyance laced every word. "Here's your vittles." He dropped the tray on the floor.

"Stale heel of bread and a bit of mouldy cheese." James did not move so as not to chase the man away. It took every ounce of willpower not to strangle the cur. "You have me on half rations. I ate better in the field."

The gaoler smirked and rubbed his pockmarked chin. "Your father didn't leave much for your keep. 'Taint my fault."

James smiled grimly. *Liar.* He shifted his stance, and the shackles rattled. The gaoler started. "What's your name?"

"What does it matter?"

"A man should always know who holds the keys to his prison."

The man shrugged. "Sid Flagg."

James nodded. "How do I get a dish of mutton, Flagg?"

"'Taint hard to find if you have the coin, which you don't." The gaoler scratched his lean chest. "Hard to source out your mates for a quid when we have strict orders to keep you in close confinement. Hammond ain't allowing visitors."

"These orders must be eating into your profits. Can't be healthy for your purse, friend."

Flagg's chin lifted, and his expression became speculative. "I admit, I'm short a few coppers."

"Hammond has always held himself too high."

"He's had a thing for your mistress, too," Flagg chortled but choked back his laughter when he caught James's expression.

"I'm keeping tally, never fear."

Flagg paled. His complexion took a yellow cast under the purple pockmarks. "I better go."

"But you haven't heard my offer." James moved into the light. "Forget the mutton. Gaol meat is like chalk on the tongue, tough and sinewy." He had Flagg's undivided attention. "You can make more on my exit that you ever will on my stay."

Flagg frowned. His eyes darted to the closed door. He licked his lips and shifted his weight from one foot to another. "You can't afford it."

James smiled. "Did they not tell you? I'm a highwayman. I have gold."

"Gold?"

"Aye."

Flagg licked his lips. "Hard for you to lay claim to it in the gaol."

"I have a friend who can. Given the right word, he can be your friend too."

Flagg grinned, showing a sparse row of teeth. "I'll need ten unites."

Greedy bastard. "I don't have ten," James said. He mentally calculated the coin he had entrusted to Henry before he left. How much was left? "I'll give you five."

"Five isn't worth my neck." Flagg chewed on his lower lip, but he didn't turn away.

"That's all I have." James considered the man's bloodshot eyes and bulbous nose. "But I'll throw in some bottles of your favourite brew to sweeten the pot."

Flag grinned. "Deal."

"Tell Henry Grant at the Chequer our terms. He'll make it known to my friend. Your purse will be healthier by tomorrow night."

Flagg chuckled as he unlatched the door. "Aye, tomorrow." The door clanged behind him and echoed dully in the chamber.

James's expression hardened. *All is fish that comes to net.*

*

Elizabeth watched Edward reacquaint himself with his son through the personal things James left behind at the Chequer. Her father-in-law wandered around the loft, first picking up a book, then lifting the lid of a box.

A hard lump formed in Elizabeth's throat. She hadn't been in this room since James left. Standing before the shuttered window, she thought of their last night. She remembered strong arms encircling her and lips brushing against her cheek. Elizabeth pushed aside her melancholy. She didn't have the luxury of dwelling in the past. The future depended on keeping her wits. "How did he look?" she asked Edward again.

"Well enough."

"Do you think he understood?"

"He knows you're with me," Edward replied.

"Knowing he's close and I can't see him—"

"Sit tight, else Flagg will have another Hart to mind."

Elizabeth shuddered. "You needn't remind me."

"You were right about the gaoler," Edward said. "He's in agreement."

Elizabeth glanced over at her sleeping son, tucked safely in the middle of the bed. His little arms flung wide, startling himself. He opened his mouth to cry but found his thumb instead. A trick, newly mastered, since coming to Warwick.

"Not a good habit," Edward muttered. The firelight showed the softness in his expression when he gazed down at his grandson.

Jennet rose from her chair beside the bed, her hands planted on her hips. "Let the lamb be. Habit today, passing memory tomorrow."

A single rap sounded on the door, followed by three shorter ones. Elizabeth hurried to admit Henry. In his arms, he carried a wooden crate. Nathaniel Lewis followed behind.

"Excuse me, mistress." Henry crossed the floor and deposited the crate on the table. Bottles clinked as they settled.

Nathaniel strolled inside as though he were in Whitehall's Banquet House instead of the inn's loft quarters. "Mistress Hart," he said with a bow. A froth of lace gleamed against his suit of charcoal broadcloth.

"We don't really need to give the man twelve bottles of bragget do we?" Henry peered inside the crate and pulled out one of the green bottles.

Nathaniel joined Henry at the table. "Why wouldn't we?"

Henry slid the bottle back into the crate. "A waste, really."

Nathaniel lifted a brow. "'Tis not the time to be a miser, Henry. An astute man will ask, 'Why six bottles or seven and not a full case?' These are questions that fester in the curious mind and lead to more questions—worse, answers. Nay, good Henry, we need a full case or none at all."

"Wouldn't a small keg of ale work just as well?"

"No, it would not," Elizabeth said flatly.

Henry looked contrite. "Aye, fair game."

Elizabeth nodded and crossed her arms. "Any news, Master Lewis?"

Nathaniel selected a seat by the fire and straightened the cuffs of his sleeves. "Sir Richard received the summons to prepare the prisoner for transfer to London on All Hallow's Eve."

Day after tomorrow. A sick feeling roosted in Elizabeth's stomach. "So soon? That doesn't leave us much time."

"Everything should be ready."

"*Should* is a horrible word, barrister," Elizabeth began to pace, taut like a drawn bow. "Full of missed possibilities and gaps unclosed."

"Everything *will* be ready."

Edward pulled up a stool. "Tell us what happened, what they discussed. Spare nothing."

Nathaniel smiled. "I must say, I passed an entertaining evening at Sir Richard's."

"You have a strange sense of what is entertaining," Edward said.

"You remind me of your son. He is fond of calling me pond scum though."

Edward lifted a brow. "I've taught my boy to know his mind. I'm not entirely convinced of you."

Elizabeth gave Edward a pleading glance. "Go on, Master Lewis."

The barrister nodded. "We were at dinner—a lengthy, tedious affair, but one that I bore with grace." He leaned back in the chair, his hands folded in a steeple. "Our Lieutenant Hammond arrived in a froth, demanding to see Sir Richard about the dispatches from London. He went off his head."

"Indeed? Whatever could he object to?" Edward scratched his head.

Nathaniel toyed with his ring. "Our ambitious lieutenant considered the orders a slight to his dignity."

Henry scoffed. "What isn't?"

Nathaniel smiled. "Hammond came close to chewing on the floorboards. He demanded that Sir Richard send back a stern rejection, letting Westminster know that Warwickshire could manage their own affairs."

"So they won't send James to London after all?" Elizabeth drew closer.

"I didn't say that." Nathaniel raised a finger. "Sir Richard refused to break with Westminster, and certainly not for Hammond."

Elizabeth walked away, her heart racing. "So this is it. This is all the time we have."

"Correct."

Elizabeth tugged at her fingers. She felt sick and suddenly wanted to be alone. Taking a deep breath, she turned to the men who now stared at her. "Next step?"

Nathaniel rose from his chair and walked to the table. He drew a blue velvet pouch from his coat and untied the ribbon drawstring. He tapped the contents of the purse until he selected a single gold coin, untarnished and gleaming in the firelight. Satisfied, he dropped it back inside and pulled the strings tight.

"You have your wish, Henry Grant. I've changed my mind." Drawing a single bottle from the crate, he dropped the pouch in its place and handed the bottle to Henry. "This will be one puzzle that a curious mind won't linger overmuch on."

Chapter Thirty-Three

James lay on his pallet, one arm crooked over his face and his mind racing. He hated being powerless while others determined his fate.

Flagg had come to him at the end of his last shift with news that Parliament was sending an escort of dragoons to fetch him on the morrow for Newgate gaol. The sand had nearly run through the glass.

"You get no gold if I'm turned over to the dragoons," he'd told the gaoler.

"Aye, not an idiot."

"Have you made contact with my friend?"

"Aye, and an oily prig he was. He made good on your word, though not before balking at the price."

James's brow had lifted. *What was Henry playing at?* "When will I be blessed by the fruit of your labours?"

"If I get my boon today, then at dawn when the other gaoler's shift starts. Better they blame Cully than me. There'll be plenty of knocked heads over this one, and mine won't be one of them."

Caw-handed by-blow. It had taken a great deal of willpower not to seize the man by the throat.

Meanwhile, the wait was unbearable. James felt stretched out, worn in the middle, as though he were a thrice-scraped piece of leather. He had to guess the passing of time between the steady drips of water and the changing light through the grate—his only company thoughts of revenge.

This wouldn't be over until James served Hammond a taste of his own. Pistols? Over too soon. Swords? He'd enjoy carving up the Roundhead. *I'll let him pick.* The coward would be sure to choose swords, anticipating James's skill with pistols. So be it. He'd carve out his liver.

The handle rattled, and the outside bolt slid across the bar. "About bloody time, Flagg," he muttered.

Before James could rise, a pair of dragoons stormed into the cell. They hauled him to his feet and dragged him to the centre of the room. Hammond appeared at the door, tapping a switch against his thigh.

James tried to throw off the dragoons, but he couldn't get purchase with his shackled ankles. They pushed him down onto a stool.

"Enjoying your stay, Captain Hart?"

"'Tis Major now," James said, relishing Hammond's annoyance. "That disturbs your sense of order, doesn't it?"

Hammond's lip curled. "You're naught but an ostler, no matter how many commissions you claim. An ostler who thinks to rise above his station."

"What do you want, Hammond?"

"Your audacity surprises even me. Most would plead for consideration, but not you. You lay here as though you've all the time in the world, which you don't."

"A lesson in cheek, is that why you're here? Well met." James pretended to relax. "Alas, I won't have time for your instruction. Flagg tells me I'm to be moved to London."

"Indeed?" Hammond's tone held a hard edge. He adjusted the line of his coat and straightened his shoulders. "We should ask him." Turning to the day gaoler behind him, Hammond said, "Cully, see if your friend can spare us a few moments."

The man stepped into the hall and motioned to someone. "He's ready for you."

Another pair of guards entered the cell, half dragging Flagg. The man hung limp as a haunch of meat, face bloody and eyes half-closed. James froze. *Damn me.*

"You have it all wrong, Lieutenant," Flagg blubbered. He spewed out a mouthful of blood and broken teeth. "I did nothing, I promised nothing. I wasn't going to let him out—I swear. No harm in taking a bit of coin for his keep. That's all—a tuppence for his meat."

Hammond bent closer and shook his head. "Sidney Flagg, did you really think I wouldn't find out?" He lifted Flagg's chin with the tip of his switch. "Cully has sworn that he overheard you negotiating with this heretic. He's even led us to the purse you hid... two gold unites and three half crowns of silver. Is this the going rate for a gaoler?"

James frowned. *What happened to the rest?*

Flagg snarled at Cully. "Lying bastard! I got nothing—you planted that purse."

"Take him," Hammond said. "Lock him up with the murderer."

"Nay! Stop!" They ignored Flagg's pleas as they hauled him down the hall.

When the cries faded, Hammond turned to James. "I'm disappointed in you, Hart. I expected you to have devised a more creative means of escape than Flagg."

James struggled to mask his frustration. "I work with what I have, blunt tools included." He didn't waste a thought on the gaoler—if he had understood his father's veiled references, Elizabeth had been at his mercy. The bastard had this and more coming. *But couldn't he have received his comeuppance after he got me out of this piss-hole? I'd have served him a lesson by my own hand.*

"Your wit is lacking." Hammond grinned, flush with the thrill of besting him. "You already bribed one gaoler."

"Did I?"

Hammond scowled. "You know you did—Caleb in Coventry. He was in your pocket with that Rotherham affair."

"Indeed?" James maintained a stony expression. "No need to blame Caleb for your incompetence. He has a family to feed and won't thank you for these attempts to salve your manhood."

Hammond drew his arm back and slashed James across the face with his switch. James jerked back. A line of fire snaked down his cheek. With a snarl, James sprang from his stool, but the guards seized him and slammed him down.

"Never underestimate me," Hammond spat in contempt. "My blindness has been lifted, and the devil can no longer deceive. The beast sends false aid to my enemies while the Lord bestows upon me the tools for their destruction."

"Here I thought this was simply a gaol break," James said derisively, straining at his captors. "Imagine my chagrin."

"Your arrogance will be your downfall." Hammond stepped away and rolled his shoulders. "You would do well to confess to your crimes now. 'Twould go better for you in London."

James narrowed his eyes, noting Hammond's agitated pacing. Hammond hadn't liked Whitehall's interference with Piers either. James smiled to himself. A canny man did not need to wield a blade to cut deep. "What did you want to know?"

"Did you help the Scottish King escape Worcester?"

To admit to it would seal the charges of high treason and place a lesser charge beyond his grasp. He almost snorted. Rope and knives or just rope. No matter. They'd lay the worst at his door, but at least he could have the satisfaction of baiting Hammond. "Call him Charles Stuart, rightful King of the three kingdoms, and I will freely admit it."

Hammond drew back, a mixture of surprise and disbelief. "Where is he now?"

Tread carefully. James couldn't be sure if the King had made it to France yet. "I last saw him on a ship bound for the Hague. There by now, I'd imagine."

"To his sister, the Princess of Orange."

"Indeed."

"Who else was involved?"

James thought of all the men and women who had helped them during the past six weeks—servants and middling families who had risked their lives. "My lord Wilmot, close friend of the King."

"That fop?" Scorn laced Hammond's laughter. "You expect me to believe that a man who can't lace his own boots without a lackey helped Charles Stuart evade capture?"

James nearly laughed. "Call it divine providence, then. A sign that the Good Lord favours the King's life."

Hammond ignored the jab. But he looked as though he were mulling James's story. "And how did you manage it?"

"We headed for London, where the crowds would hide us. From there, Wilmot found a ship to spirit him and His Majesty away."

"The name of the ship?"

"I don't recall," James said. "My lord made the necessary arrangements."

"Again, Wilmot."

"The very same."

Hammond tapped his switch against his thigh. "And just how did you get Charles Stuart aboard without being sighted?"

James smiled. "We dressed him as a washerwoman and piled a basket of laundry atop his head."

"Through the streets of London? And no one looked twice?"

"Forsooth, had he made a more fetching maid, perhaps someone would have," James said.

Hammond struck him with a backhanded slap. James recoiled from the blow, and his head snapped to the right. "Shall we start again?"

"Certainly," James said, testing his jaw.

"How did Charles Stuart escape? It wasn't with the help of Lord Wilmot."

"Not at all," James said. "'Twas with the help of my lord, the Duke of Buckingham."

"The duke?" Hammond leaned in closer, his pale eyes gleaming. "Now that is more credible."

"Aye, the duke and the King disguised themselves as local gentry with a pair of goshawks on their wrists," James said. "Had they been stopped, they would have laid claim to hawking in the countryside."

Slam. James's head jerked back, and he flew off the stool. Sharp needles exploded in his head. He rolled over and muttered, "This is getting tedious." As he got to his knees, he spat on Hammond's polished boots. In the next instant, Hammond kicked him in the ribs, sending him sprawling in the straw. Before James could defend himself, Hammond drove his boot again and again into his stomach. Fire ripped through James's gut, and he curled into a ball. The air flew out of him, and he bit down, willing himself not to cry out.

"Lieutenant," one of the dragoons called out. "Lieutenant!"

One final kick to the face. James groaned. He fought down the nausea and the pain. "Perhaps I'll tell the Whitehall man what really happened," he said, spitting out a stream of blood. He chuckled at the strangled fury that crossed Hammond's face. "No doubt, the man who carries this tale to London will find himself covered in glory." He struggled to rise, one arm holding his stomach and the other braced against the floor to keep him from pitching forward. "But you, whoreson, will not profit *a farthing* from my tale. Devil take you."

Hammond grabbed James by the hair and yanked. "Laugh, base heretic, but you'll regret it soon enough. I'll not rest until I find your whore and make her repent. My name will be the last she speaks as she begs forgiveness," he spat and shoved him away.

Rage exploded inside his head. Roaring, James sprang at Hammond, driving his shoulder into the man's stomach and tackling him hard. Hammond hit the ground with a loud grunt, and his head snapped back. Before he could roll aside, James twisted and pinned the Roundhead to the ground, one hand gripping his throat. Black fury broke over James, and he rained blow after blow upon Hammond's face. He felt the crunch of his nose giving away to spurts of blood. Hammond yelled and tried to throw him off, but James's fury gave him extra strength. Every hit meant one more payment against the debt Hammond owed him. *Damn him to hell.* He'd personally deliver the bastard with his fist clamped around his throat.

Frantic shouts erupted, and James found himself hauled off Hammond and dragged a few feet away. He thrashed against the dragoons, but their hold tightened.

"If you harm either my wife or son, I will hunt you down, in this life or the next." James directed his venom through each word. "Pray for a merciful God, for the devil will not save you."

Hammond struggled to his feet, livid. Dishevelled and panting, he advanced on James. "You've sealed their fate, scum traitor." The blood flowed down his nose and trickled down the cleft of his chin.

James lunged forward, but the dragoons yanked him back. "Whoreson!"

Hammond's hand shot out, grabbed James by the throat, and began to squeeze. James struggled against his captors, but they had his arms pinned. Spots danced before his eyes. Just as his vision began to fade, Hammond released him. James sucked in great gulps of air and coughed and sputtered.

"I will find them," Hammond said, his tone cold and cutting.

James lifted his head and glared his hatred. "A pox on you." *They are beyond your reach.*

Hammond raised his fist. James braced himself, but the lieutenant paused. His anger was replaced by a dawning of understanding. "You know where they are." His gaze bore through James. "You do. But how can that be? You haven't been allowed visitors—" Hammond turned his head slightly as though considering the door. "There was one. Flagg confessed while he blubbered about everything else." His pale eyes widened. "Ah, the prodigal son. She's with your father."

The bottom of James's stomach dropped.

Hammond leaned in. A triumphant joy mingled with a fierce resolve. "The noose is around your neck, highwayman. While you rot in Newgate, I will capture Elizabeth. She will be tried as an accomplice to your crimes and hanged. Your bastard will be thrown into a workhouse, emptying chamber pots full of piss and dung from the time he can walk," Hammond hissed. "Think on that when you climb the scaffold and smell the hot coals of the brazier preparing to roast your entrails."

The guards shoved James back. The shackles tripped him, and he pitched to the ground. He scrambled to get to his feet.

Before the door closed behind him, Hammond paused and faced James with a cold smile. "I'll give your regards to Elizabeth."

The bar slid across the iron groove, a dull clang echoing in the cell. Rage rose like bile in James's throat, and he exploded with a feral roar. Again and again he threw himself at the door, pounding his fists and howling his fury.

*

The rising sun stained the sky blood red. In the shadow of a building, Elizabeth and Edward watched the entrance to the gaol. Being so close, she felt its pull and raw desperation. Though the width of the street separated her from the building, her nostrils flared with the remembered reek of its cells. She adjusted her hood and pressed the woollen cloth to her nose.

As the sky grew lighter, she felt brittle, ready to snap. Would this work? Elizabeth scanned the street. Soon the mercer would begin his morning route, and the town would stir. They had to be gone by then.

"They're late," Edward said, his breath visible in the icy air. The cold light of morning cast his features in granite. "Timing is everything."

"The hour is not yet past," Elizabeth said to reassure herself; but he was right. Their success depended on a finely balanced pin.

"I like it not. You shouldn't be here," Edward said. "You were best to wait with Thomas."

"Jennet will keep him safe." Elizabeth's breath caught in her throat. "If all goes ill, this may be the last I see of his father."

Edward looked at her as though he would argue, but then nodded. His hand squeezed her shoulder.

The hollow sound of trotting horses echoed down the street. A prison wagon with an escort of two horsemen pulled up before the gaol, their russet coats vivid in the grey light. Edward drew Elizabeth back to the lee of the building. She watched, her heart fluttering in her chest.

No quarter.

Dawn. James paced the cell, his movements constrained by the shackles around his ankles. No way to send word to his father, to warn him that Hammond had discovered where Elizabeth was. The fear nearly crippled him. Where the hell was Henry? And his father—no further attempts to send or receive a message. James didn't give a damn for himself—he'd hang twice if it ensured Elizabeth and his son's safety. But he was useless to them this way. Powerless and without leverage.

Any moment, the dragoons would arrive to take him to London. He had to escape. There had to be a way. Door hinges were solid; window too small even for a child. No blade, no rope. *Nothing*! His rage surged, and James slammed his fist against the portal. A mocking echo was his only answer.

James hung his head. *Elizabeth*. His fear for her unmanned him. *My God, what will happen to her*? He had failed her again.

The lock rattled. One last chance. James rushed to the hinge side and pressed against the wall.

Cully, stepped inside. "Time to go—"

James lunged for the gaoler and grabbed him in a stranglehold. When Cully struggled to break free, James tightened his grip. "Aye, you have that right."

The click of a primed pistol echoed in the chamber. James stiffened. He whipped around and used the gaoler as a shield. Three dragoons stood in the doorway, the foremost holding a carbine. Roger, Davis and Sheffield. All three in New Model Army russet coats.

James's mouth dropped.

"Prisoner, release that man," Roger barked and motioned to James with his musket. Davis and Sheffield drew their swords. From behind them, a clerk peered around them, his ledgers clutched against his chest.

James and Roger exchanged a long look. James eased his hold on the gaoler, and Cully coughed and sputtered. "You can't blame me for trying," he said with a frown. Where was Hammond?

Roger didn't lower his carbine. "I will thank you to cooperate and come without trouble." He motioned to Cully. "Gaoler, strike off those shackles. My man will secure his hands."

While the gaoler took a mallet to the pin and unlatched the irons, Sheffield grabbed James's hands and began to bind them together. As he worked, the cornet managed a curt nod. James knew Sheffield's talent with a knot. He could make it appear sound, but it would take only seconds to unbind his hands.

"Search him for weapons," Roger ordered.

The clerk appeared agitated. "Gaoler, was he not searched?"

"I know my business," Cully said with a sour sniff.

"There's been a foiled escape," Roger told the clerk. "We need to be sure the last gaoler didn't pass him any weapons. Davis, see to it."

"Aye, Captain." With his back to Cully, Davis patted down James's breeches. He cast a glance to the side and, when assured no one paid him any attention, transferred a short blade from his coat sleeve into James's boot. Straightening, he gave him a quick wink.

"Clear?"

"Aye, Captain. "

Turning to the clerk, Roger asked, "Your papers are in order?" Both Sheffield and Davis moved in closer.

The clerk bobbed his head. "Aye, the seals are in order. But Lieutenant Hammond—"

"What of him?" Roger asked.

"He has given orders not to release the prisoner without his approval," the clerk stammered. "We can send a boy—"

"I don't have time for that nonsense," Roger snapped. "Westminster has called a hearing in three days. Shall I send you to London to explain our delay to Chief Justice Blackmore?"

"Nay."

"Good. London awaits." With Roger in the lead and Davis and the clerk taking the rear, James left his cell flanked by Stephen and the gaoler.

They descended quickly to the main hall. Two dragoons looked up from their post. James hesitated, but Cully gripped James's arm tighter. He bent closer and said in a low voice, "Look straight ahead and keep walking."

James's mind stumbled. Resisting the urge to look at the gaoler, he continued on as instructed. When they passed through the outer doors, Cully leaned in. "Your wife sends her blessings."

In the street outside, James spied a prison wagon hitched to a pair of horses: a chestnut and a fine black with a chalky-white blaze on his forehead.

*

Elizabeth started when she saw James emerge from the gaol. She covered her mouth, and her eyes feasted. Though he looked unkempt—hair longer, beard unclipped—the sight of him made her heart race. *Dear God.* Her vision misted over.

James walked down the steps with Roger, Davis and Sheffield. Just as planned, in plain sight. Everyone had thought her idea mad—except Davis, who had tipped his hat to her, and Nathaniel, who smiled and got to work initiating the gaol transfer.

Nearly there. Elizabeth grabbed Edward's hand and squeezed it. The older man gave her a wink.

James nearly reached the wagon. A few more steps and he'd be inside. A few more minutes and the wagon would pull away and leave Warwick. No reason to look for him, not until London made enquiries. By then, it would be too late.

The rattle of horse's hooves echoed down the street. A rider rounded the corner and rushed up to the gaol. Hammond!

"Nooo—" The bottom dropped from Elizabeth's stomach.

"Christ's teeth—what's he doing here?" Edward said.

"Where's Nathaniel?" Elizabeth said with rising horror. The barrister had promised he'd deal with the man.

Across the street, Hammond jumped down from his horse and charged towards Roger and James. Davis stepped to block him, but Hammond shoved him aside. Elizabeth watched, frozen in a horrific nightmare.

"I knew it—I knew enough not to trust that crafty lawyer," Edward muttered. "Damn, I can't hear what they're saying. He's betrayed us. I'm sure of it."

Roger placed himself between James and Hammond before holding up a clutch of dispatches. Roger shoved the seal under Hammond's nose—that undisputed seal that Nathaniel had sworn would work. Hammond slapped the papers aside and tried to seize James.

Sheffield and Davis closed in from behind and began to draw their swords, but the arrival of the other dragoons from inside the gaol made them pause. The cornet and trumpeter exchanged glances and stepped away.

Oh God. Everything was unravelling. The tide had turned, and Elizabeth was powerless to stop it from sweeping James out. The rising panic nearly drowned her. They had to get him out now—there wouldn't be another chance. What evil genius rode on Hammond's shoulder where James was concerned?

"I'm going in," Edward told her. "If all goes ill, hie yourself away before the bastard can nab you." He grabbed Elizabeth's arm and made her face him. "Clear?"

"What will you do?"

Edward clenched his jaw. "In the game of Irish, you sometimes need to distract your opponent with an open draught. Hammond hasn't arrested Roger yet, so he must not suspect. All we need is one moment—long enough for Roger to get him in that wagon. After that, Hammond must concede that James has passed from his authority."

Elizabeth stared at Hammond. *It won't work. Not like that.* She grabbed Edward's arm. "I'm the draught we need."

"Impossible—"

"We don't have time to argue this," she said. "Any moment, Hammond will sense treachery. I'm the *only* one who can distract him. I can make this moment count."

Edward swore under his breath, and for a moment his expression was stubborn and unyielding, but then he nodded. "I'll be close."

Elizabeth stepped away from the shadow of the building. No turning back. Her whole focus centred on reaching James. Thirty feet separated them. She had to get between him and Hammond. Elizabeth was equally consumed by her love for one and her hatred for the other. One moment... that's all she needed. She darted across the street.

James lifted his head. Elizabeth finally saw his bruises and cuts, and her heart lurched. Their eyes locked. In a second, his expression changed from surprise to fear.

"No! Stay away," James yelled. He started towards her, but Roger and Sheffield pulled him back. "Release me." He tried to push them off, but they both dug in and started hauling him back to the wagon. "Get her away from here," James screamed. "For the love of God, get her away!"

Hammond whirled around. His face bore the scars of a dirty fight—swollen eye, purple nose and split lip. Surprise turned into exaltation. He lunged forward and seized her.

"I knew it," he said. "You couldn't stay away from him. Like a bitch in heat."

"Take your hands off me." Elizabeth tried to pry herself away. She twisted to see James's progress; he tried to throw off both Roger and Stephen, but together they had him nearly into the wagon. None of the dragoons interfered with Roger. All eyes fastened on her and Hammond.

Make this count.

Elizabeth slammed her boot into his shin, then slapped his cheek with her free hand. Tiny needles of pain fanned out from her palm. "Bastard," she spat. "Release me. You'll not stand between me and my husband."

Hammond pulled her roughly to him. His hand gripped her jaw, squeezing until she thought he would crush her. His pale eyes blazed. "The closest you'll get to that traitor is the straw he warmed and the chamber pot he pissed in. You are mine now."

"I hate you," she said through gritted teeth.

"Hate? You know nothing of its true depth." His face betrayed a mixture of anger and self-loathing. "My hate has no bounds, daughter of Delilah."

"*I curse you, Ezekiel Hammond,*" Elizabeth spat each word. "May your soul rot in hell." Hammond blanched but didn't release her.

"Let go of her, bastard," James screamed, pushing past Roger and losing precious ground from the wagon. "I'll *kill* you."

Hammond ignored James's shouts, his entire attention riveted on Elizabeth. "I am a corruptible man, and you, my sickness," he hissed, his breath hot against her ear. "You have already cursed my soul with your dark witch's locks and ensnared me like the serpent of Eden."

Elizabeth's stomach lurched. Once more she was back in the gaol, threatened and controlled, crushed beneath this man's rigid boot. His scent was the stench of her prison. Desperation seized her.

She tried to drive her knee into his groin, but Hammond shifted his stance. She heaved against him and managed to free her arm. Her hand flew to his face. Directing every ounce of rage into the only weapon she had, she sank her nails deep into his skin. From brow to cheek, she raked the left side of his face, tearing through his already bruised skin. Hot, sticky blood coated her hand.

Hammond howled and recoiled. Elizabeth stumbled, her skirts twisting around her legs as she pitched to the ground. Immediately, she scrambled backward to get away from him. When he lunged at her, Edward blocked his way, dagger drawn and stance ready.

"You'll not touch her."

"Step aside, old man," Hammond said. Twin bloody furrows snaked down his cheek. He looked wildly around. "Dragoons—seize this woman."

Elizabeth rose, her attention focused on the prison wagon. Roger and Sheffield hadn't wasted the time she had given them. Struggling against James, they had managed to get him into the wagon. For one brief second, when the world was rushing around them in chaos, their eyes met.

The dragoons closed in. Elizabeth didn't care. Roger slammed the prison wagon door shut on James while Sheffield clambered up to the perch. White knuckled, James's hands grabbed the iron bars. His desperate shouts rang out.

A hand clamped around her arm. "I have her, Lieutenant."

Davis drew Elizabeth away from Hammond.

"Take her inside and throw her into a cell," Hammond yelled, beside himself with rage. "You will burn for this, witch."

The prison wagon began to pull away. She had done it—separated James from Hammond. The rest did not matter.

From down the street, the sound of hooves clattered and rumbled. They grew louder, and a company of dragoons galloped around the corner with an outraged Sir Richard in their lead. The dragoons cut in front of the prison wagon, and Sheffield was forced to rein in the team. Elizabeth's stomach dropped. She yanked up her hood to cover her face and stepped behind Edward and Davis.

"Where is he?" Sir Richard hollered as he reined in his horse. "Where is that rank traitor?" He swung down from his horse and looked around. "There!" Sir Richard pointed a finger at Hammond. "Arrest that man."

Hammond stared, dumbfounded. He looked around at the dragoons swarming him. "What is the meaning of this, my lord?"

Sir Richard strode up to Hammond, holding a dispatch. "This came for me an hour ago! Know you what it is?"

Hammond shook his head, puzzled.

"Word of a viper in my midst."

"My lord?"

"The esteemed Chief Justice Blackmore warned of a plot to give succour to the Scottish King—right under my nose."

"Plot?"

"Aye, plate, men, weapons, everything." Sir Richard leaned closer. "You know of what I speak."

Hammond flushed, his expression showing both horror and outrage. "You accuse me? Why would I help the Antichrist?"

Sir Richard held up a velvet purse and undid the ribbon drawstring. Grimly, he poured out a stream of coins right at Hammond's feet. "Ten gold unites."

"I've never seen that. I don't know—" Hammond drew back, his eyes wide.

Sir Richard almost gloated when he showed Hammond the coin tucked in his palm. Untarnished, it gleamed fiercely in the sunlight. "But what of this?"

Hammond bent forward to get a closer look and paled.

"I found this tongue token with the gold," Sir Richard said. "Stamped *CS*. Charles Stuart."

"This is a jest," Hammond's voice choked as the noose tightened around his neck. "Where did you find that?"

"In your quarters, tucked in a case of mead," Richard said. "You grasping, self-serving bastard."

A grim smile spread across Elizabeth's lips. *Vengeance is mine, saith the Lord.*

Sir Richard snapped his fingers, and the dragoons grabbed Hammond. "Secure him."

"'Tis not mine! I've never touched that," Hammond sputtered. "A bag of gold, that means nothing. And the case of mead—" He frowned and snapped his head up. "Where is she? Where is that *bitch*? It's all her doing."

Elizabeth stood still, peering through the thin gap between Edward and Davis. Any moment, he would spy her and call the justice down upon her head.

"Silence him," Sir Richard said. "I've had more than enough of him. Remove him from my presence."

Hammond tried to push off the dragoons, but the double click of a carbine halted him. Roger stood, feet braced apart, with Hammond in his sights.

"My thanks, Captain," Sir Richard said. With a nod to the dragoons, he said, "Carry on."

The dragoons seized Hammond and hauled him up the stairs to the gaol. "You will regret this! Colonel Harrison will hear of this! You will be removed from your seat." He continued struggling. "Harrison has the ear of Cromwell—you will fall to your knees and beg my forgiveness."

Edward took Elizabeth by the arm and drew her aside. Roger motioned for Davis to follow.

"One moment, Captain," Sir Richard called out and halted Roger.

"Aye, my lord?"

Elizabeth half turned and lowered her head. Edward and Davis pressed in close.

"I would appreciate it if you could pass a message to my dear friend Chief Justice Blackmore."

Roger hesitated for a moment. "It would be my pleasure."

"Thank him for the timely warning," Sir Richard said. "We are indebted to his vigilance."

"I most certainly will, my lord." Roger gave a short bow. "I beg your pardon, but we must be on our way. London awaits."

"Godspeed, Captain." Sir Richard lifted his hand and motioned to the dragoons blocking the prison wagon's road. As he turned away, he caught Elizabeth's eye. She braced herself for his shout of alarm. Instead, Sir Richard gave her an imperceptible nod before he followed the dragoons into the gaol.

"And godspeed to you, sir," Roger said and strode to the wagon. He slapped the wooden panel, and Sheffield started the team once again.

Elizabeth watched as it rolled down the street. *Safe. My God, he's safe.*

She no longer resisted when Edward hurried her away.

Chapter Thirty-Four

The prison wagon sped down the highway.

"Damn it, Roger, stop!" James pounded on the wooden panel that separated him from the driver. "My wife! Elizabeth! Christ's teeth, halt!" *Is she safe—had she gotten away?* His voice had become hoarse from shouting, but the wagon continued without slowing. He yanked on the board with all his strength, but it held fast. With a last curse, he slammed the panel.

She had to have gotten away. He sank down on the bench and bent over his knees.

The wagon turned off the main road, swaying and bumping down a rough tract. Through the slats of the window, James saw them pass under arching branches. The wagon continued for another quarter hour before a shrill whistle sounded. The team turned in a semicircle and slowed to a halt. In a moment, the padlock jiggled, and the door swung open, revealing Sheffield.

"I wish you joy of your freedom, Major," the cornet said. Behind him stood Roger and Davis, grinning in their russet coats.

James didn't know whether he wanted to embrace or shake them. He jumped out of the wagon and tried to push past them. "I don't know how you pulled this off, much less avoided capture after Worcester—and I owe you all my life," he said. "But I'm going back for my wife."

"That won't be necessary."

James froze. That voice—with its unmistakable soft lilt. The most beautiful sound he had ever heard.

Elizabeth stepped around the wagon. Her eyes were bluer than even he remembered. "After what we went through to steal you from the gaol," she said, "you're not returning to Warwick."

James reached out his hand to touch her, half-afraid that she was a spirit and he lost in a dream. Elizabeth met him halfway. In a heartbeat, James pulled her into his arms and held her fiercely. He squeezed his eyes shut, awash in emotion. Elizabeth burrowed her face into his shoulder and clung to him tightly.

"I thought I lost you," Elizabeth's voice was muffled in his chest. "Twice."

James loosened his hold and cupped her face. "Are you all right?" He found his voice. "Did they hurt you?"

She shook her head, and her smile strengthened despite the tears that clung to her lashes. "I'm made of sterner stuff, sir." The laugh caught in her throat. "I am from Dorset after all."

Relief flooded him, and James chuckled. Their foreheads touched, and he closed his eyes. He traced his thumb along the line of her jaw. "My love." James bent to claim a kiss. His mouth slanted over her parted lips, and she tasted of honey. He twined his fingers in her hair, stirring the scent of lavender. Elizabeth leaned into him, breasts crushed against his chest while her arms encircled his neck. The intensity of their kiss increased.

"James," she murmured against his mouth. "No dream, this?"

"Nay, love, the nightmare is over."

Elizabeth began to laugh and cry all at once, and her hold tightened around his neck. His lips found hers again.

A pointed cough interrupted them. James lifted his head to see his father approaching, holding the reins of two horses. After pressing a last kiss on Elizabeth's forehead and squeezing her waist, James faced his father. An awkward silence hung between them.

"I'm ready to concede the point." James glanced at the ground before looking up. "You are unbeatable at Irish."

Edward lifted his chin. The corners of his mouth betrayed a ghost of a smile. He handed the reins to Davis. "Keep your point. Your wife's better at it than either of us." Edward laid his hand on his son's shoulder and drew him into a fierce hug. "My boy."

James tightened his embrace and buried his head in his father's shoulder. Nine years melted away. "I'm sorry." When he straightened, he coughed to dislodge the lump in his throat.

His father squeezed James's shoulder. "I am proud of you. Always have been, even when I wanted to choke you."

James chuckled and opened his mouth to retort when the sound of horses clattering in the distance made him freeze. He pulled Elizabeth behind him.

"Carriage approaching," Roger called out. He tossed James a pistol before priming his own. Davis and Stephen followed suit, everyone's attention focused on the road. Through the trees, a black conveyance appeared, rattling down the road.

The carriage rolled to a stop, and before the driver could jump down and open the door, Nathaniel alighted unassisted.

"Barrister?" James rubbed his stubbled beard, puzzled. The others eased back, relieved.

"Highwayman. Congratulations on your release."

James frowned. He turned to his father, who shook his head as though pained. "You worked with him?"

"Aye, I know him for an oily bastard," Edward said, "but handy with quill and ink."

Nathaniel smiled. "Chief Justice Blackmore would swear the orders for your transfer were made by his own hand."

James remembered the clutch of documents that Roger had bandied about. "I'm surprised you took such a risk."

"I don't take risks," Nathaniel said. "There were at least three people between me and those dispatches, all ignorant of the other. It never fails to amaze me how otherwise intelligent men can be undiscerning when presented with fine parchment."

"God help us all if you ever took to highway robbery."

"You have your pistols, and I, my quill—both to the same effect." Nathaniel smiled. "But I warn you, there is one in our midst who is more cunning than either of us and has managed to steal the greatest prize." He gave Elizabeth an elegant bow. "Mistress Hart, our man Hammond has been ruined."

"Good," she said. "But you gave us quite the turn, Master Lewis, setting Sir Richard on us in that fashion. I thought the game up. You were to have arranged for Hammond's arrest earlier."

"My departing present to you, mistress. I thought you might want to see our godly lieutenant taken away in chains."

"I would have preferred to carve him up," James muttered. "Since you're in a charitable mood, bring him back so I can have my satisfaction."

Edward knocked James on the arm and shook his head. "You'll live with it."

James's anger dissipated as he gazed at Elizabeth. They had both been through enough. "Aye. I will."

Elizabeth craned her head to look past Nathaniel's shoulder. "Aye, mistress," the barrister said, "I have improvised even further. You will thank me for it."

James watched Elizabeth cross to the carriage. When she was out of earshot, he turned to Nathaniel. "I saw the gold pinned on Hammond. 'Twas a goodly amount. Where did you get it?"

"What an odd question," Nathaniel said, scratching this cheek. "I would have expected a 'Thank you, Master Lewis, how could we have managed without you, Master Lewis?' not 'How much did it cost me, pond scum?'"

James narrowed his eyes. "I'm grateful for your assistance; now whose coffers did you rob?" He stepped closer and said in a low undertone, "None of mine can afford your price."

Nathaniel smiled. "Rest easy, highwayman. I consider it an investment. I've already written to His Majesty to aprise him of the matter. I'm sure he'll be quite pleased with the resolution."

James shook his head. "You really are self-serving pond scum."

"Now don't be hasty." Nathaniel motioned James to follow him to the carriage.

When they reached the coach, James caught a glimpse of Elizabeth inside—*when had she entered*? With a quick smile, she descended the steps carrying a bundle in her arms. Jennet followed close behind.

"Is that—?" James saw the tuft of dark curls and a button nose. His gut tightened. He knew exactly who this was.

Elizabeth brought him their son. "I present Thomas Hart." There were tears in her eyes.

A son.

"Hello, boy." James took the babe from Elizabeth. The baby stared up at him as though memorising his face. A handsome lad. *A son.* James swallowed the lump lodged in his throat. A surge of love swept through him for both the child and Elizabeth. He'd gladly spend a lifetime protecting them both. He curled his arm around her waist and drew her to his side, brushing a kiss across her temple. "He's a sturdy lad," he said thickly.

The weight of their predicament pressed down on him. He glanced across at Roger and the lads. They had unhitched Sovereign and the other horse from their traces and were saddling them.

"We'll be fugitives, love. It can't be helped, but I'll see us clear of this. We should make for Wales. The crossings will be passable by now."

Elizabeth shook her head. "I've made other plans."

*

The screech of wheeling gulls welcomed the fugitives to the old Seton home. The wind was from the west, laced with sea spray and the tang of peat smoke. Mist shrouded the winter hills and the view of the bay, but Elizabeth heard the moan and crash of the sea in the distance. She was home, for a brief few days at least.

Old Nick had agreed to take them across the Channel to the Continent—not to France with the new blockades, but to The Hague, where an uneasy peace still existed.

Elizabeth hung back at the gate with her sleeping son in her arms. She watched as Jennet, Edward and all of James's men filled the walkway. It had been years since the old doorstep had overflowed with people, stirring memories of simpler times when family friends would arrive at the cottage, eager to share the passing of another day. She wanted to savour this moment as her new family mingled with memories of the old.

James paused at the threshold and looked around for her, having realised that she hadn't followed. He descended the steps and joined her by the gate. "Anything wrong?"

Elizabeth closed her eyes and listened to the flood of laughter and voices that drifted from the cottage. She smiled. "Nay, nothing. Everything is exactly as it should be." She slipped her hand in his and led him inside.

*

The day for their departure dawned cold and grey. In less than a couple of hours, they'd be snug in Old Nick's barque, sailing to a new life. While Elizabeth readied Thomas, she listened to the others as they made their preparations. Fingers of rose spread in the horizon, fanning against the darkness and lightening the sky. James's voice was distinct to her ears. She smiled down at their son. An excited stirring at the base of her belly made her eager to start their journey and build the life they would share. They wouldn't have to look constantly over their shoulder and fear discovery.

Elizabeth reached for Isabel's brooch. She traced her finger along the silver ridges, following the forwards and reversals as it turned upon itself. *What was will be.* She pierced the pin through her blue cloak and adjusted its position. Smiling, she picked up Thomas and left the room.

Downstairs, she found the main floor a mad scramble of activity.

"Morning, mistress," Sheffield greeted her as he hurried past with a bundle of rope in his arms.

In the kitchen, Jennet was bent over a basket packed with linens and thick woollens, clucking to herself. "It's bound to get cold. Davis—fetch me those blankets, there's a good lad."

Elizabeth kept out of their way. She savoured a bittersweet melancholy as she stared at the pallet in the corner where she had last cared for her mother. She pictured Mary sitting up and patting the spot beside her, a familiar invitation to curl into her embrace. She fought the tears that misted her eyes. If a soul impressed their mark in a corner of the world, Mary Seton's lingered here. In years ahead, where would Elizabeth impress her own bit of soul?

Elizabeth wandered to the window with Thomas riding on her hip and craned her head to stare at the lane. The rising sun topped the cedars, and as she watched, a pair of cobs jogged down the lane pulling a wagon. Behind them sat Old Nick, puffing on a pipe set between his teeth, but this time he was not alone. Her sister, Kate, sat on the perch beside him.

Elizabeth met them outside at the gate. Kate took great care in descending the wagon. When she finally lifted her head, she folded her hands primly in front. Elizabeth was rooted to the spot. Old Nick broke the awkward silence.

"Where's your man, lass?" he asked Elizabeth. "I have to discuss the matter of the horses he intends to transport. There, I see him now." He paused to tickle Thomas under the chin and received a reward of a dimpled smile. Before he moved on, he glanced between Kate and Elizabeth. "I suspect you have a few things to jab about. Best hurry. We've a tide to catch." Old Nick winked and headed for the barn.

Elizabeth searched for a clue to her sister's temperament. "How are you, Kate?"

"Well enough. You have a husband and child now." Kate's gaze lingered on Thomas.

"I'm glad you came. I can't say when we may return." She braced herself for Kate's censure, but her sister nodded.

"I've brought you something," Kate said. A flush spread along her cheeks. From a pouch at her belt, she withdrew a small clay jar and handed it to Elizabeth.

Thomas's hand darted out to grab the jar, and Elizabeth moved it out of his reach. "What is it?"

"Here, let me help you." Kate removed the lid and tipped the jar to reveal a buttery salve. The scent of roses filled the space between them.

Elizabeth tested the cream between her thumb and forefingers, admiring the silkiness of its texture. "It's wonderful. Where did you—?"

"I made it myself."

Elizabeth lifted her eyes. "Truly, Kate?" Her reserve dissolved, and she beamed. "Oh, I'm so very glad!" Thomas poked his finger in the cream, and Elizabeth laughed, wiping it off before he could put it in his mouth. "First rate—as good as anything that Mother made."

Kate flushed. "I just wanted you to know—what you said about being raised with a greater sense of worth. You were right," she said. "I haven't forgotten myself. I wanted you to know."

Elizabeth swallowed the lump in her throat. Until now, she hadn't realised how important it was for her to hear that and how much she missed the sister she had before the war. Elizabeth took Kate's hand and received an answering squeeze. "Thank you."

Kate blinked furiously. "You have to go." She glanced over her shoulder to James, who hovered near. "Your husband awaits."

Elizabeth smiled. "My life awaits."

*

James stood with Elizabeth at the rail and watched the prow slice through the current. Overhead, the sails snapped in the stiff breeze. The *Ithaca* sailed into the bay and headed southeast. A pair of seagulls soared, riding the crest of air above the masts.

Roger, Davis and Sheffield gathered farther down. His father stood in companionable silence near Old Nick as the captain guided his ship out of the channel.

James tightened his arms around Elizabeth as she leaned into him. She fit his embrace as though she were moulded for him. He rested his chin on the top of her head and inhaled the tangy sea breeze that scented her hair. They would build a new life, no matter the challenges.

He held up a shiny gold coin for Elizabeth to see.

"What is that?"

"A coronation token," James said, turning it over as it reflected the sun. "I kept it hidden in my boot when I got captured. Flagg never found it. This is worth more than any of the gold that I promised him."

"What will you do with it?"

"Present it to the King's sister, the Princess of Orange, when we arrive in The Hague." He pressed it in her hand. "God willing, this will secure our future."

"I'd like a little cottage with a view of the sea."

James kissed the top of her head. "As my love wishes. Hopefully, this will help us secure a modest tract of land," he said, sharing his thoughts. "With decent grassland and good water, we can build a modest stable of horses."

"A modest stable?" Elizabeth tipped her head to look up at him. "You'd be satisfied with that?" Her glance was half-teasing and breathlessly expectant.

James grinned. "Only if they are the best horseflesh for leagues." His arms tightened around her. "Let the devil keep the rest."

A seagull alighted on the rail and settled its wings. It was a large creature, staring ahead with a contentment not found in its species. With a sharp cry, it spread its wings and flew into the air. Soaring higher, it wheeled and turned, revelling in the freedom of the wind and the blue expanse of water.

James focused on a new horizon, but this time, he was not alone.

Historical notes

The historical novelist has a challenging task, to respect both the historical record and the precepts of storytelling while balancing both. I'm a firm believer that history has a far better imagination than any novelist; it's not hard to find inspiration in the historical record. But at times, the novelist must rule on the side of fiction.

The escape of Charles II following the loss at Worcester in 1651 is one of the best-documented dramas of the 17th century. Letters and contemporary accounts, written during the Restoration, corroborated the details of this famous escape. For the sake of the story, I've only featured the key dramatic events and did not include everyone connected to the escape. Those familiar with the history will know that Lord Wilmot accompanied Charles's, though for the most part they only rode together during the latter part of the adventure. Prior to that, he was generally considered to be scouting ahead.

Though the later historical accounts never mentioned Charles travelling with a highwayman, it was the subject of speculation in the weeks and months following Worcester. Rumours had spread through London that a famous highwayman, Captain Hind, had helped the King escape the battle. In fact Parliament was so convinced that this was true, when they managed to capture Hind two months later, they spent the next year trying to prove it. They eventually found him guilty of High Treason for having fought at Worcester and had him hanged, drawn and quartered.

A tantalizing corroboration for this rumour appears in a letter written by the Venetian Ambassador to the Doge of Venice in November 1651 when Charles finally arrived in Paris. The ambassador wrote, "After the battle, [the King] escaped with a gentleman and a soldier, who had spent most of his days in highway robbery and had a great experience of hidden paths." Whether truth or rumour, this was too precious a nugget for a historical fiction writer to ignore.

The Crabchurch Conspiracy is one of those gems of local history. I discovered this thrilling chapter of English Civil War history through the writings of Dorset historian, Mark Vine. The story stood out for me because townspeople (tanners, fishermen and merchants) tried to win back the twin ports of Melcombe and Weymouth for the king, fighting against a resolute Parliamentary garrison equally determined to hold the town. The heroism extended to both sides and ended with a Royalist defeat. If you are interested in learning more, I highly recommend Mark Vine's, *The Crabchurch Conspiracy* or his blog by the same name.

The Knot is purely my invention, but it is inspired by the history of the age. During this time, anti-Catholic sentiment was only eclipsed by the witchcraft hysteria. Since the Reformation, Catholics were persecuted, levied with heavy fines, barred from public service, and forced to worship in secret. Charles was able to travel from one safe house to another thanks to the existing network within this community. It is not inconceivable that such an underground organization may have existed, even if informally. As long as there have been people persecuted for their religion or heritage, there have been courageous souls who have sheltered them. I dedicate this to my paternal grandmother who, like many Greeks, sheltered Jewish fugitives during WWII at great risk to themselves.

To learn more about the 17th century and the English Civil War, or to hear about future releases, visit me at cryssabazos.com and sign up for my newsletter.

Thank you for reading *Traitor's Knot*. Kindly spread the word.

Cryssa Bazos

Printed in Great Britain
by Amazon